Deb

FEIGNING LOVE FOR ONE MAN, THALIA LONGED FOR ANOTHER . . .

Ian grabbed her roughly into his arms, his insides melting as her breast crushed against his chest. "I'll return you to your husband." He wove his fingers through her hair and drew her lips close. "But I have something to give you first. When you are in your husband's arms, think of this!"

His mouth seized hers in a hard, long kiss, his tongue probing her lips apart. Then he released her and silently looked down at her, his eyes charged with dark emotion.

Stunned anew by the passion that had just been exchanged between them, Thalia stepped away from Ian, touching her lips with her fingertips. She was so overc___ ___ ith rapture that she felt lightheaded ___

Yet sh___ ___lf these wondrous

Other Leisure Books by Cassie Edwards:

WHEN PASSION CALLS
EDEN'S PROMISE
ISLAND RAPTURE
SECRETS OF MY HEART

CASSIE EDWARDS

Roses After Rain

LEISURE BOOKS   NEW YORK CITY

DEDICATION

For Alicia Condon, a special, multi-talented editor who, in so many ways, shows that she cares about her authors!

—Cassie

A LEISURE BOOK®

October 1990

Published by

Dorchester Publishing Co., Inc.
276 Fifth Avenue
New York, NY 10001

Printed in the United States of America.

POEM

You loved me for a little,
Who could not love me long;
You gave me wings of gladness
And lent my spirit song.

You loved me for an hour
But only with your eyes;
Your lips I could not capture
By storm or by surprise.

Your mouth that I remember
With rush of sudden pain
As one remembers starlight
Or roses after rain . . .

Out of a world of laughter
Suddenly I am sad . . .
Day and night it haunts me,
The kiss I never had.

—SYDNEY KING RUSSELL

CHAPTER ONE

ADELAIDE, AUSTRALIA—1864

THE HARD AUSTRALIAN SUN BOUNCED BACK FROM the fine white beaches as a ship inched its way into Adelaide Harbor. Thalia Drake, orphaned at seventeen, now eighteen, clung to the ship's rail, her heart pounding as she took her first close look at Australia.

Disappointment assailed her, for from this vantage point the town of Adelaide, her destination since she left England, was not all that impressive. Past the moored ships, squat and leaning warehouses lined the shore to the left of the wharves. Straight ahead, unpainted stores straggled down the warren of streets that crept to the west at varying angles, packed with wagons and carts and jostling men on horseback.

Thalia's spirits lifted when she looked past the town to a lush valley dotted with wildflowers,

9

where flocks of sheep moved across the land like clouds. Farther still, a magnificent forest of gum trees that stood hundreds of feet high was visible in front of jagged red-and-yellow cliffs in the far distance, great treeless plains of shimmering gray grass lying in their shadows.

And beyond that, if one was not prepared to enter, men had been known to shrivel up and die in the arid bushland known as the scrub, Thalia had been told. But beyond the scrub lay the gold fields.

The men on the ship had spoken excitedly of gold lying around everywhere on the ground and in the gullies of the rough country around Mount Alexander. Men had come from all corners of the earth—adventurers and speculators who had rushed to Australia's fields, the gold giving them cause to dream.

As the ship sidled up to the wharf, Thalia looked down into the Torrens River. Australia's south coast had been washed clean by a pure, cold sea where seals basked, sperm whales cruised, and fairy penguins perched on ancient rocks worn smooth by waves. But the river that had brought the ship eight miles from the sea was not as clean, or as attractive. Thalia's gaze locked on a black line of rats running along a rope that reached from the pier to a moored ship.

A movement in the water just below where she stood drew her quick attention away from the morbid sight of the rats. Both intrigued and afraid, she watched a shark's fin moving in threatening circles at the ship's bow. She had heard gossip aboard the ship that sharks came this close to shore for Adelaide's debris that was dumped into the river. She had heard the tale of a man who had taken a spill into Adelaide Harbor and, in one bite, a shark had bitten him in half.

Thalia cringed as the shark moved closer to the ship, its round, gray eyes seeming to seek her out from all the others at the ship's rail. She shuddered, estimating that the shark was at least twenty feet long, its jaw open wide, displaying what were surely a hundred sharp teeth!

Her attention was drawn away from the shark to the creak of the chains as the anchor was being lowered into the water. She was tired and hungry, but her pulse raced and her eyes looked anxiously forward; she had never before been so eager to set her feet on land. It had been a long and grueling trip. She had traveled more than fifteen thousand miles for eight months and a day, having left her beloved ten-year-old sister, Viada, behind with her Uncle Jeremy until Thalia could send for her.

A sudden panic rose within Thalia as she realized that she was not the only one anxious to depart this filthy, miserable sea vessel. Attempting to leave the ship, pushing and shoving one another, people were pressing in on her from all directions. Thalia clung to the small valise that contained her meager belongings, her side paining her as she was pushed harder and harder into the ship's railing.

"Please!" she cried, fearing that she might be trampled to death. She tried to push the people away from her. "Oh, Lord, stop! Get away from me!"

Something drew her eyes back to the water, and

a cold numbness spread through her. She knew now what her true fear should be. With everyone in such a frenzy all around her, she could be knocked overboard, a quick meal for the shark! Her eyes followed the movement of the shark's fin that was now circling in a lazy figure eight, as though awaiting a mis-step by someone among this maddening throng of people.

Her heart pounding, her knees weak, Thalia looked desperately back at the people who continued to push and shove at her. They were pressing her more painfully against the rail, their eyes wild in their intense desire to flee the dreaded ship.

A keen sadness overwhelmed Thalia; she understood why these people were so eager to leave this ship of horrors. Although Australia had the reputation of being a far-off trash heap to dump cargoes of convicts from Britain's overcrowded prisons, it was also a place of hope—of dreams. Settlers were arriving daily from England, grabbing the bush country that was there, waiting to be taken.

In common with most of the other ship's passengers, Thalia's passage had been paid by the ship's owner, the ship companies going so far as to send agents out on the streets of England to get people to emigrate, paying a commission on each passenger they brought in. The greedy ship owners were making a handsome profit from carrying emigrants, placing them in their ships like sheep, and feeding them next to nothing.

These past months on the sea there had been a constant scramble of people trying to get enough to eat and fresh water to drink. Many of the infants and elderly had died from malnourishment and had been tossed overboard. Some lay half dead in the hold even now, food for the rats.

Thalia felt lucky to have survived the terrible voyage and now hoped to get employment as a dairymaid or servant—perhaps even be lucky enough to find a husband. Though bone-weary and thinner because of the lack of proper nourishment these past months, perhaps she was still attractive enough to draw attention to herself in Adelaide. She had always been petite, yet in the past few years she had silently witnessed her bustline developing into the sort that drew men's second glances. Most called her pretty for her auburn hair worn long to her waist and her slightly slanted blue eyes fringed with thick, long lashes.

Yes, she was lucky to have survived the voyage with only the loss of a few pounds; perhaps she could latch onto a husband and her woes would soon be over. She could send for her beloved sister, and all would be right in the world again for the first time since her parents' untimely death on the dark streets of London, at the hands of a robber who had then stabbed them to death.

Suddenly a man slammed into Thalia. She gasped when the crowd pressed harder against her, unknowingly lifting her from her feet and causing her to lose her grip on her valise and the ship's rail. She screamed and grabbed at those who were paying her no heed. It was like grabbing for air, for just as her fingers touched someone, they would be shoved away from her.

And then the inevitable happened. She felt herself toppling over the side of the ship, the gray water meeting her head-on as she plummeted into it.

The impact momentarily stunned her. She lay limply in the depths of the river for a moment, then stirred back to consciousness as her lungs began to ache for air. Fighting a light-headedness that continued to try to claim her, Thalia made desperate strokes that soon bobbed her to the surface of the water.

Choking and coughing, she treaded water, her heart beating wildly. The shore! She must reach the river bank! In her mind's eye she could still see the shark. What if it was still close by? It could swallow her whole with just one bite! She was afraid to look around to see if the shark was still there. She had to concentrate solely on swimming to shore! Thank the precious Lord that her father had taken the time to teach her how to swim when she was a child!

Though weak and so frightened she was almost sick to her stomach, and fretting over having lost her personal belongings in the fall, Thalia found the strength to begin swimming toward shore. She was aware of many eyes on her as people watched her from the wharves, yet no one attempted to help her. Surely they had heard the same rumors as she about how swift death came to anyone foolish enough to share the Torrens River with man-eating sharks.

And why would anyone risk his life to save someone like her? She was just one of the countless defenseless women fleeing England every day to try to find a fresh start in life for themselves in this land of promise.

Shrieks and screams and people yelling at Thalia caused her to stop swimming. With an arched eyebrow, she looked up questioningly at the crowd, then grew numb when she recognized stark fear in their eyes and saw how they were gesturing toward something in the water behind her.

The word *shark* came from the crowd as though someone had hit Thalia in the face with a blunt instrument, and she knew that she did not have to turn around to see that the greedy, crafty fish was there in the water close behind her.

Stiffening and closing her eyes, Thalia awaited the feel of the shark's teeth clamping down on her.

But when she felt nothing and everyone grew silent, Thalia turned slowly in the water and looked behind her. A cold, stark fear grabbed at her insides. The shark was so close she could almost reach out and touch it; yet strangely enough, it did not move in for the kill.

But it did move closer, its eyes challenging Thalia, as though purposely playing a game with her. She had to wonder if it did this with all of its prey. Just how long would the game last before it opened its mouth and made a meal out of her?

One minute? Two?

Or perhaps sooner!

A pole floated past Thalia. She grabbed it. She glanced down at it and then looked at the shark again. Since no one else was daring enough to come to her rescue, she had to try everything within her power to save herself.

Her hands trembling, she raised the pole and started thrashing the water with it close beside the shark, hoping that would scare it away.

To her dismay, the shark opened its wide jaws and bit the pole in half!

Undaunted by this first unsuccessful attempt to save herself, Thalia took the remainder of the pole and rammed the side of the shark's head with it, but again to no avail. It just continued its game of "when shall I eat this frightened maiden?" as it swam on past her, its eyes watching her, ever watching. . . .

Feeling death very near, as though it were breathing down her neck, Thalia knew that she could not have much more time. Surely she could not tread water much longer!

Panic rising inside her, she searched frantically through her mind for what she had read about sharks while attending school in England.

Suddenly, her eyes brightened with an idea. She recalled reading that sharks would suffocate unless they kept moving. If only . . .

Courage almost failing her, for surely the shark was tiring of playing with her, Thalia waited for it to make another pass. When it did, she tried to jam the broken end of the pole inside its mouth.

The shark determinedly chomped down on the pole—and ate it.

Thalia bit her lower lip with frustration and tears began streaming down her cheeks when the fin began circling her again. It was now obvious that the shark was purposely tormenting her before moving in for the kill, just as a cat plays with a mouse after catching it.

A resonant voice broke through the silence from somewhere behind Thalia on shore. "Miss!" the voice shouted. A man waved at her, trying to draw her attention. "Luv, stay calm! I'll do what I can!"

Continuing to tread water, but growing weaker by the minute, Thalia turned her head slowly to one side to see this stranger, who from all of the many observers had been the only one to offer her assistance. He must have just arrived and seen the dilemma she was in.

Her gaze found the man who was not on the wharves, but on the road that ran alongside the river. Even though she was in immediate danger from the shark, Thalia could not help but, in a fleeting moment, notice the stranger's total handsomeness. He had hauntingly dark and compelling eyes. Deeply tanned, his features seemed sculpted beneath a slight growth of light-colored whiskers. Sandy red hair reached to massive shoulders that filled out a fringed kangaroo-hide shirt.

Her attention was drawn to king-sized Colt revolvers that hung at each hip, then to a lovely black stallion pawing nervously at the dirt street behind him. A dark-skinned Aborigine, attired in only a brief loincloth, sat astride a snow-white horse reined in beside the black stallion.

Thalia's eyes locked on the handsome stranger again as he turned to his horse and whipped his carbine out of its saddle boot and cocked it. He turned around and faced Thalia again.

"Just . . . stay . . . put," he shouted. "It'll be over soon."

After leveling his short-barreled, lightweight rifle, Ian Lavery took half a breath and cocked it. When the shark took a wide swing away from the girl in the river, Ian put four shots into the base of its fin. Blood bubbled up to the surface as the shark sank from sight.

After thrusting his carbine back into its saddle boot, Ian dove into the water. He swam to the girl and grabbed her. Holding her with one of his strong arms, he swam her to shore, where he carried her to safety on the river bank.

As he placed her feet to the ground, their eyes met and held.

"Are you all right, ma'am?" Ian asked, his dark eyes imploring her.

"Yes, I'm fine," she said, coughing and sputtering. Then she ceased to make a sound at all. Her heart was racing, and the pit of her stomach was strangely weak, affected more by the stranger's handsomeness than the fright she had just experienced in the river. Never had she seen such beautifully sculpted features or deep, dark eyes!

"I'm glad to hear it," he said, weaving his fingers through his tangled hair. "There for a while I wasn't sure."

"Nor was I," Thalia said, smoothing her own hair back from her face with her hands. "If not for you . . ."

As the stranger's lips lifted into a slow smile, Thalia was catapulted into a world of sensuality she had never experienced before, causing her to forget what she was saying to him. The sensual feelings quivering through her could only be the sort that a woman experienced when she became infatuated with a man!

This, and her total gratefulness, caused Thalia to do something quite out of character for her. She drifted into the man's arms and hugged him and kissed him with a passion she could not hold back. Her knees almost buckled beneath her when he returned the kiss, jolting her back to reality.

Embarrassed and afraid of her feelings, Thalia stepped away from him. She very soon discovered that she was not the only one embarrassed by her over-exuberant way of showing her gratitude. The man who was the recipient of her kiss was blushing.

Thalia was even more in awe of him now. How she wished that somehow he could be the man to ask for her hand in marriage, or at least seek her out for his dairymaid or servant. Any man who had the ability to blush was a man of gentleness—a man of heart!

Thalia studied his attire again and his slight growth of whiskers. Surely he was a prospector just in from the gold fields and could not even lay claim to owning a home. Surely he was a vagabond, definitely not in need of a woman who would stifle his freedom. . . .

Her chin held high, forgetting her wet and clinging clothes and her tangled, dripping hair, Thalia thrust her hand out to him. "Sir, I want to thank you kindly for rescuing me," she said, her voice faint from thrills that shook her anew when he reached his hand to hers and their flesh touched. "Seems you were the only one who cared if I lived or died."

"Mighty glad to oblige," he said, gripping her hand firmly but with a slightly puzzled frown, as if his own reaction to their encounter was as strange to him as to her.

Thalia glanced around her at the gawking men

on the pier and then down at her clinging attire. She gasped and her cheeks flamed with color, knowing that those men who had been too cowardly to rescue her were now only interested in what they could define through her clinging dress.

She cleared her throat nervously and firmed her chin again as she looked up at her rescuer. "The other men are cowards," she said. "Lowdown cowards!"

A sudden activity a few feet out in the water drew Thalia's attention, causing her to drop her handshake and step quickly behind Ian. She peeked meekly around his massive body and watched the sharks that were approaching the bloody remains of the one that had been shot. From everywhere fins were slicing through the water. She watched and listened as the sharks killed each other off, tearing each other to bits, having gone into a frenzy over the blood.

Ian frowned as he watched the sharks, then turned and placed a hand to Thalia's elbow to lead her away from the gruesome sight.

Thalia was pale, and she was finding it hard to breathe. "If not for you, I would be a part of the slaughter in the water," she said, her voice trembling. She looked quickly up at him. "How can I ever repay you?"

"You can start off by telling me your name," he said, his eyes twinkling down at her.

"Thalia," she said, flinching when she heard more thrashing sounds in the water behind her. More sharks had joined the kill. If not for Ian, it could have been her in the water being fought over!

"Thalia Drake," she quickly added.

She looked at the dreaded ship from which she had so awkwardly departed and nodded toward it. "I just arrived from England," she said, smiling sheepishly up at Ian. "Of course, I had not planned to make such a splash upon my arrival on Australia's shores."

"You don't say," he said, chuckling low. "I thought that perhaps you entered all ports the same way—if you are the sort who enjoys challenges, that is."

Thalia was glad that she could see the humor in his words, and she laughed along with him, realizing just how she must have looked while the shark had been toying with her. She was proud that she had not gone berserk with fear, screaming and flailing her arms, which could have caused the shark to attack without dilly-dallying around as it had. It had to prove that she was not like so many women who screamed and ran at the mere sight of a tiny garden spider!

"Ma'am, Ian's my name," he said. "Ian Lavery."

Ian's eyes showed his approval as he searched Thalia's lovely facial features, and then lower, where the nipples of her breasts were defined beneath her wet and clinging cotton dress. If ever a woman could cause him to give up his wandering ways, this was the one! She was not only beautiful, there was a genuine, innocent quality about her that was scarce in women these days.

"That's a nice name," Thalia said, melting inside when their eyes met and held again. "Are you originally from England?"

"No," Ian said, drawing her next to his horse as they continued to talk. "America. To be exact—

Seattle, a prospering young city in the territory of Washington." He was not in the mood to talk about himself. Rarely did he. Too many disapproved of how he chose to live, so he tried hard never to get into any discussions about it.

He peered intently at the ship Thalia had arrived on. "Surely you are wanting to search for your parents in the crowd," he said, one wedge of eyebrow lifting as he looked down at her. "They will want to know that you are all right."

"I did not travel with my parents," Thalia said solemnly, watching to see his reaction when she told him that she was orphaned. If only he would lay claim to her! If only it had been their destiny to meet! Oh, she could make him happy. She would never disappoint him if he took her and made her his own! "My parents are dead. I made the journey from England by myself." She swallowed hard. "It was a most trying, fretful voyage. I hope I shall never be forced to get on any ship again for any reason."

Ian felt blood rush to his cheeks, understanding now that Thalia was among the women who ventured to Australia in search of employment—or better yet, a husband. She was looking up at him with trust in her eyes, as though she expected him to take her under his wing!

He was tempted.

Oh, God, he was tempted!

Yet, he had no time for women. Perhaps in a few years . . . But, God, not now. He was enjoying his life too much.

A large-boned, middle-aged, and fleshy woman with gray hair protruding from beneath the edges

22

of a straw hat rushed to Thalia's side. She drew Thalia into her embrace and hugged her. "Thank goodness you are all right," she exclaimed in a silken purr. "When I saw you tumble overboard, my heart plumb froze." She glanced at Ian over Thalia's shoulder. "If not for Ian . . ."

Thalia slipped from the woman's embrace and smoothed her hands nervously down the front of her dress. "Who . . . are you?" she asked guardedly, yet having found a woman's embrace and caring voice very welcome in this land that thus far was more of a challenge than she had ever anticipated.

First the shark, then Ian . . .

The woman took Thalia's hands and squeezed them affectionately. "I'm Daisy Odum," she said, smiling warmly at Thalia. "Most call me a 'philanthropist.' You see, I pride myself in giving a helping hand to those women arriving from England who are half-starved and too weak to fend for themselves. I run Odum House. It's a half-way house where the women can find bunks to sleep on, and hot soup on my stove for the taking. I bed and feed the women who arrive from England until they find gainful employment—or a man to marry."

Daisy's eyes ran over Thalia, seeing her wet and clinging attire. Then she looked around her, having not yet seen anyone coming to claim her. She glanced at Ian again, knowing that his only claim on this waif had been an act of chivalry. Everyone who knew Ian understood that his lust was not so much for women, but for being foot-loose and fancy free.

It would take quite a woman to change Ian's ways.

Daisy focused her attention on Thalia again. "Young lady, can I be of service to you?" she asked softly. "Have you arrived on Australia's shores unescorted by family or husband? If so, dry clothes and food await you at Odum House."

Thalia was at a loss for words, in total awe of this woman whose generosity went beyond anything Thalia had ever known before. Why, this Daisy Odum was an angel of mercy!

Thalia suddenly saw hope in her future. Surely between Daisy's and Ian's concern, things would be made right again in her life!

"Ma'am, I accept your kind offer of help," Thalia said. "I am alone in my venture to Australia." She looked at Ian again, her eyes wavering. "So very much alone."

Daisy, still clutching one of Thalia's hands, started walking her away from Ian. "Well, my child, you are no longer alone," she said. "Daisy Odum will see that you are taken care of." She cast Ian a look over her shoulder. "Perhaps a man will seek your hand in marriage. No man could resist the likes of you—you are like a breath of fresh air in this town of Adelaide."

Blushing, Thalia followed Daisy's gaze and she found it quite determinedly on Ian Lavery. Ian's dark and brooding eyes, and the way he stood so jauntily, with a hip cocked, disturbed Thalia from her head to her toes, causing a strange melting sensation to warm her insides. She had to turn her eyes away for fear that he would read the message deep within their depths, crying out to him to claim her, to take her with him and make her life a paradise within the muscled strength of his arms!

"As I was saying," Daisy continued, explaining further what she did for the waifs who were dumped on Australia's shores. Thalia's eyes turned back to her, yet her heart was left adrift. . . .

"I was once a homeless woman on a ship from England myself," Daisy said. "I was one of the lucky ones. I was taken in by a fine man and married almost as soon as I reached Australia."

"Oh, how nice," Thalia said, encouraged to hear that it could happen the way she had dreamed.

"My Henry soon after struck it rich in the gold fields," Daisy continued, her tone flecked with sadness.

"My goodness," Thalia said, turning to stare at Daisy. "Truly?" She wondered about the shine of tears in Daisy's eyes. Why should Daisy shed tears? Her life had been so blessed. Oh, but if her own could be! Since her parents' deaths, her life had been nothing but plagued with sadness.

Daisy smoothed the tears from her eyes with her pudgy fingers and lifted her chin courageously. "My Henry was murdered before he and I had a chance to enjoy our newly found riches," she confided, her voice breaking a bit.

Thalia gasped. "I'm so sorry," she said. "So very, very sorry."

"Yes," Daisy said in a monotone. "My Henry was gone from me so quickly, leaving me desperately alone again. But I always try to find something positive out of sadnesses, and recalling the desperation that I had felt on the long and terrible sea voyage from England to Australia, and the conditions under which I traveled, I decided to put my sudden wealth to good use. I began assisting worn-out and penniless women as they arrived on these distant shores with no one to care for them. I could not shut my eyes to the misery of those unfortunates.''

Thalia looked at Daisy incredulously. "Never have I met such a—a charitable person," she murmured.

"I do not do this for praise," Daisy said, smiling at Thalia. "Perhaps you might say I do not do it unselfishly. You see, I am no longer alone either, Thalia."

Thalia returned the smile.

Ian rested a hand on one of his holstered Colt revolvers, watching the gentle sway of Thalia's perfectly rounded hips and the bounce of her hair that the Australia sun had quickly dried. It was damn hard not to go after her. Damn hard! There was more than lust for her body that he felt. It was something new to him, a feeling that had never been involved with wanting a woman before. This time he wanted the woman to protect, to cherish, to wake up to each morning so that he could look into those beautiful blue eyes that would be speaking silently to him of a sort of love that would be everlasting, not just for one night.

Shaking his head, not wanting to let such thoughts encompass him, for a woman was the last thing he wanted at this moment in his life, Ian turned and grabbed his horse's reins. With his Aborigine companion following beside him on his white horse, he led his steed across a rut-filled dirt road, his eye on Joe's Pub. He would down a few drinks and head back into the scrub, the outback.

That was where he found the sort of excitement that any hot-blooded man would give his right arm to share with him. He was the best at what he did! The damn best! And it had not taken a woman to build the sort of reputation that he could boast about!

Yet he could not help taking another look at Thalia as he wrapped his horse's reins around a hitching rail.

Standing in the shadows of a warehouse down by the wharves, Paul Hathaway, a well-dressed, distinguished-looking man with square, steel-rimmed spectacles perched on his nose, had closely watched Thalia's rescue and had seen the instant attraction between the young lady and Ian Lavery, a man Paul Hathaway always had to be on the watch for over his shoulder. Paul smiled slowly, fingering his narrow mustache.

Kenneth Ozier, a young stockman with shoulder-length golden hair and a thin physique, was standing beside Paul. He was also watching Thalia, until he shifted his gaze to the other women who were still debarking the ship that had just pulled into port after its long voyage from England. He leaned close to Paul. "How about it, mate?" he asked. He shifted his boots nervously on the dirt road, his fringed buckskin attire hanging loosely from his undeveloped muscles. "'Ave you seen a rabbit among those new arrivals that gives you an itch in your groin? 'ave you seen any among them that'll make life a wee bit more interesting at the ranch?"

Kenneth nudged Paul with an elbow, his youthful blue eyes dancing with excitement. "There's several lookers among the lot."

Paul nodded, giving Thalia the once over again as she walked alongside Daisy Odum. His eyes followed the gentle, seductive sway of her hips. "I'm planning to take another woman to the ranch today, and I know exactly who she'll be." He straightened his ascot, pushed his spectacles more securely onto the bridge of his nose and cleared his throat. "And I had better make haste before some other woman-hungry gent lays claim to her."

"How long do you think this one'll be around?" Kenneth said in a lazy drawl. "Lisa Bono lasted only one month."

Paul turned quickly and faced Kenneth. With fire in his eyes, he grabbed the young man by the throat and squeezed his fingers into his flesh. "Sonnie, you'd best learn when it's smart to mind your own affairs," he threatened between gritted teeth. "If you know what's good for you, you'll never mention Lisa's name to me or anyone else again." He peered icily into Kenneth's wide, frightened eyes. "Do you understand, mate?"

Paling, Kenneth nodded. Paul dropped his hand away from him. With a look of utter distaste and contempt for his cowhand, Paul wiped his hand on his breeches. "I hired you for many reasons," he said, "and you know what they are. I should never have to spell them out to you."

Kenneth anxiously nodded again. "Aye, mate," he said, gulping hard. "I understand. I understand."

Paul smiled slowly. "I knew that you would," he

said, a nervous twitch tugging at his left cheek. "I knew that you would."

Terrified, yet full of admiration for the power that Paul possessed over so many men and women, Kenneth watched his boss walk briskly away. Someday, he hoped, he would be just like him.

CHAPTER TWO

CHILLED TO THE BONE FROM HER WET CLOTHES AND dip in the river, and well aware that nothing was left to the imagination beneath her clinging attire, Thalia was glad to have the opportunity to go with Daisy, although she feared that once she lost sight of Ian, she might never see him again.

She cast him a sad look over her shoulder while Daisy further explained her establishment to her, then quickly noticed that several other women from the ship were being ushered along behind her by other caring women who were more than likely employed by Daisy Odum. Surely Thalia and the others were in the hands of an angel. Thalia felt quite protected at that moment.

Her attention was drawn to a long, squat building that stood among the other warehouses lining the busy thoroughfare. Out back, where there was hardly enough room for one person to walk, the drop off into the river was so close, clothes whipped in the breeze on a clothesline. A young woman who appeared to be Thalia's age was pinning clothes to the line. She had a strange sort of hump on her back, and her body twisted grotesquely each time she reached down to pull more wet clothes from a huge wicker basket.

"I see you've got a glimpse of Ava," Daisy said, giving Thalia a wistful glance. "She's been with me the longest. She draws stares from everyone but not the sort that is pleasant. No one wants her around, for most think her appearance distasteful." She tsk-tsk'd. "What a shame, for Ava is such a dear!"

A keen sense of pity swept through Thalia, recalling a woman on board the ship from England. She had been tormented so mercilessly that she had been driven to take her own life by jumping into the sea. The recollection made Thalia's eyes mist with tears.

"There are many injustices in the world," she finally responded. She looked quickly away from Ava, not wanting Daisy to think that she was staring. "I was not aware of them until the death of my parents. Since then I have seen and experienced much that will surely cause me to have nightmares until the day I find peace in death."

Daisy placed an arm around Thalia's waist. "Now, luv, I don't want to hear no more talk from you about death," she said, whisking Thalia from the street toward the door of Odum House. "You've a whole lifetime ahead of you to find the sort of happiness that you wish for. Perhaps I can make it happen for you. Unlike poor Ava, you've a pretty face and a perfect back. The men who come here lookin' over those who have arrived today from England will end up fightin' for you. Why, I imagine that you won't even have an opportunity to sleep one night in Odum House. You'll be swept away by a man as quickly as I show you off."

Before Thalia was ushered completely into Odum House, she looked once more for Ian. Her mouth and heart dropped, for he was nowhere in sight. He had most surely forgotten her as soon as his eyes left her.

But she would never, never forget him!

"Now, Luv, let's get you a bath and into dry, clean clothes," Daisy said, taking Thalia through a room of intense feminine activity.

In a quick look, Thalia saw various women sorting through piles of clothes as others looked on. There were odds and ends of chairs and tables around the room where other women were eating and chatting. In a far corner a woman younger than Thalia was standing with her face cushioned in her hands, sobbing loudly, while an elderly woman was standing over her, speaking to her in comforting tones.

That room was left behind and Thalia was led down a long, narrow corridor where doors were closed on each side. She could hear women's voices in the rooms behind the doors. Again she became aware of someone crying. It was so lonesome a sound that it tore at Thalia's heart, recalling her own reasons for being in Adelaide.

Suddenly her loneliness welled up inside her and she emitted a sob that she could not control.

Daisy turned to Thalia, her jaw tight but her eyes deep with compassion. She took Thalia into a room where a tub of water was most prominent.

"Luv, you take a long, slow bath," Daisy said, her voice a comforting, silken purr. She unfastened Thalia's dress and drew it over her head. "I'll be bringin' in a pretty dress for you to wear and then you can get your stomach warmed with soup."

She helped Thalia out of the rest of her wet clothes, down to her shoes. "Perhaps after that I can show you off to some of the gents," she said, smiling reassurance at Thalia. "There should be several arrivin' soon. Many just wait and watch for the ships to arrive with you homeless girls. I'm sure you'll be one of the lucky ones to be chosen today."

Thalia self-consciously folded her arms across her breasts. She turned and looked down at the water in the tub, thinking about the hope and promise in Daisy's voice. Oh, if she could only be right—that Thalia could be either gainfully employed by this evening, or have a man show interest in marrying her.

Thalia could not shake thoughts of Ian from her mind.

If only he . . .

Daisy helped Thalia into the tub and handed her a bar of soap and a washcloth. "Now doesn't that feel better?" she asked softly, lifting Thalia's hair from her shoulders as she sank lower into the comforting warmth of the bathwater.

The water up to her chin, Thalia closed her eyes

and sighed. "I doubt if anything ever felt as good," she said, lying, recalling how wonderfully delicious it had felt to be in Ian's arms, tasting his kiss on her lips. Nothing could ever compare to that.

She would remember that forever!

"Well, we'll see what you think of my fresh turtle soup and Sydney rock oysters," Daisy said, laughing as she opened the door to leave. "Come downstairs as soon as you are dressed. I'll have a place set at the table just for you."

Thalia opened her eyes and smiled at Daisy, touched anew by her continuing kindnesses. "Thank you for everything," she murmured. "If not for you, I'm not sure what would have become of me. I had not expected such a—such a crude city as Adelaide. In my dreams I had conjured up images of much, much more." She lowered her eyes. "I don't know why. Surely life is the same everywhere as it was in England. I suppose someone spread tales of Australia that were quite false."

Daisy went back to Thalia. She placed a caring hand on her shoulder, causing Thalia's gaze to move up. Their eyes met and held. "Luv, what you've seen today is not how it is in all of Australia," she said. "After you've recovered from the excitement of your arrival and some lucky man has you at his side, you will see that the tales were not entirely false and that much of this country clean takes the breath away. Do not despair. You'll soon see what I'm talkin' 'bout. Not all that far from Adelaide, paradise begins. Birds of all sizes, shapes and colors roost in trees. Black swans, as well as white, swim in the ponds and lakes." She sighed as she rolled her eyes back in pleasant memory. "Ah, there is so much, luv. So very, very much that will gladden your heart!"

Being transported along in Daisy's lovely vision, Thalia bolted with alarm when a loud knock on the door jerked her back to reality.

Daisy cleared her throat and straightened her hair with nervous fingers, then went to the door and opened it. Ava, her shoulders heavy from the hunch in her back, stood there. She held a dress over her arm, which Daisy laid over a chair near Thalia's tub. But Ava still waited at the door, apparently with something on her mind.

"Yes? Well? What is it?" Daisy asked softly.

"M'um, there's a gent in the sitting room come to speak with you about . . ." she hesitated and craned her neck to look past Daisy at Thalia, then pointed at her. "He came about her—the young woman who fell in the harbor and almost got swallowed whole by the shark."

Thalia heard Ava and her stomach did a strange sort of mushy flip-flop, hoping that the man Ava spoke of was Ian!

Who else could it be? Only he had shown concern for her when she was shoved overboard. Surely he had come for her after having had time to think about it! Perhaps he would give up panning for gold long enough to get her settled in somewhere.

Perhaps he would even marry her first. . . .

"Who is the man?" Daisy inquired, taking Ava by the elbow to usher her farther out in the corridor where Thalia couldn't hear them.

Ava ducked her head, then looked slowly up at Daisy. "You ain't goin' to like it, m'um," she said, tight-lipped.

"Now how do you know that unless you give me the man's name?" Daisy said, irritation setting in. Then her spine stiffened. Who but Paul Hathaway frequented Odum House for women more than any other Adelaide gent? Too often as far as she was concerned. She had grown not to trust him.

"It's—" Ava began, but Daisy interrupted her.

"Paul Hathaway," Daisy said dryly. "Am I right, luv?"

Ava nodded, smiling crookedly. "Aye, it's Paul Hathaway all right, m'um," she said, smiling crookedly. She sidled close to Daisy. "Do I send the bloody bloke away?" she whispered harshly. "He makes me skin crawl, he does!"

"It's the tales you've heard about the man that make you dislike him," Daisy said. "You know there ain't nothin' wrong with his appearance. He's a man of class, that one."

Ava glanced into the room where Thalia was supposed to be bathing, seeing that she was, instead, hurriedly donning the dress Ava had brought. "But this girl seems so special, m'um," she said, frowning. "Are you sure you want to let Paul Hathaway take her away with him?" She inched closer to Daisy and spoke into her face. "M'um, you know that more than one girl has disappeared from the Hathaway sheep station."

Daisy nodded. "Yes, I know and I shall question Mr. Hathaway about that further before I give my consent for Thalia to go with him," she said, patting Ava softly on the cheek.

Ava smiled sheepishly. She began twisting the tail of her apron around her fingers. "Want me to get her?" she asked, gazing at Thalia as she slipped into her shoes, her eyes anxious. "She's through with her bath."

"Yes, and instead of taking her where we usually feed our girls, take her to the kitchen and give her a bowl of soup and anything else her sweet heart desires," Daisy said, walking away. "I must have plenty of time to speak with Paul Hathaway before Thalia meets him."

"Aye," Ava said, shuffling her feet as she walked into the room where Thalia stood waiting in a freshly ironed, high-necked, yellow cotton dress, the cuffs of the long sleeves trimmed in neatly gathered white eyelet lace. Ava envied Thalia her loveliness, especially her flawlessly straight back.

Yet she was not bitter toward Thalia for her appealing womanly features. She was used to her lot in life and accepted friendship wherever and whenever she could get it, hating no one.

Ava reached a hand out to Thalia. "Come along with me, miss," she encouraged her, relieved when Thalia did not stare with disgust at her twisted, ugly back. "We've got to get some food in you. You need to get back some of that strength you lost fighting off that dreadful shark!"

Thalia looked past Ava, disappointed that Daisy had gone ahead without her. "But I thought a man came for me," she said, her voice lilting. "I am anxious to see who."

Ava gave off a groan of sorts and took one of Thalia's hands. "Do not be so eager to leave Odum House," she said, taking Thalia from the room and down the long, empty corridor toward the smells brewing in the kitchen. "I'd choose livin' here any day over livin' with—"

Ava cut off her words and glanced at Thalia, having almost gone against one of the strictest rules that Daisy Odum set down for all of the women under her employ. Never were they to discuss the men clients with any of the women who waited at Odum House to be chosen. Today was no exception. It could cost Ava her job.

And she had nowhere else to go.

Thalia looked quickly over at Ava. "You were saying?" she asked. "You'd choose living here over living with whom?"

Ava took Thalia on into the kitchen, ignoring her question. She gestured toward an unpainted table where onions and potatoes were stacked high and fresh potato peelings lay beside a soiled knife. "This table'll do," she said, smoothing the potato peelings aside. She scooted a chair over to the table. "Sit yourself down while I dip you some soup."

Thalia eased down onto the chair, lurching when one chair leg that was shorter than the others banged hard against the floor, tilting the chair awkwardly forward. She steadied the chair and looked around the room. It was drab in every way. There were no curtains at the tall, dirty windows at the far end of the kitchen. The floor was made of wooden planks with wide cracks between them which revealed the ground not that far beneath it. A large, pot-bellied wood-burning stove stood only a few feet from Thalia, glowing orange from the fire burning so intensely within it.

Thalia began to perspire from the heat.

Several huge pots sat on the stove from which came wondrous, mouth-watering aromas. Thalia watched Ava eagerly now as she sank a wooden ladle in one of these pots and began dipping soup out into a bowl. For now, Thalia would not think about who had asked to see her, almost positive that it could not be Ian Lavery. Ava's reaction to her question was not the sort that a handsome man would cause.

No. It was not Ian.

But who . . . ?

Smoothing some loose tendrils of hair back up into the bun atop her head, Daisy walked slowly around Paul Hathaway, looking him over carefully. She had dealt with him many times before.

"Mr. Hathaway, explain to me again the disappearances of the other women you've taken from Odum House to your sheep station for employment," she said, stopping to challenge him with a set stare. "Too many have disappeared without ever having been heard from again. How do you explain that?"

Paul cleared his throat nervously. He rocked back and forth from his heels to his toes, his hands clasped tightly behind him. "Like I've said countless times before," he began, his voice scratchy. "It's the Aborigines. They are surely responsible for the missing women, yet no proof has been found. You know there's many Aborigine women stolen from their camps by white-skinned, women-hungry bushrangers. The dark-skinned people retaliate in kind by stealing white women."

"Yes, I see how that could be possible," Daisy said, stroking her chin contemplatingly. "Yet, I don't know. My reputation lies at stake here, Mr. Hathaway. If many more women disappear, whom I have entrusted to my clients' care, I shall lose all credibility and Odum House would be threatened."

Paul placed gentle hands on Daisy's shoulders and looked down at her with a slow, easy smile. "Trust me, Daisy," he said soothingly. "Let me have this one more chance. And to prove to you just how serious I am about wanting to make things right, I will even marry Thalia instead of just taking her to my sheep station to be my servant. I would dare anyone to try and abduct a woman I have made my wife!"

This man had never before promised anything even akin to a marriage proposal for her girls, so Daisy stepped back away from him, surprise in her eyes.

Yet he did sound sincere enough.

Looking him slowly up and down again, Daisy reassessed the situation. Oh, but didn't he always display such gracious manners and wear such handsome clothes? Though plump, his facial features bland, he wore a mustache well and his dark hair was combed to perfection to his shirt collar. His square, steel-rimmed spectacles added to his sophistication, proving to Daisy that he was an educated man.

All of these qualities made him appear to be the most sincere and trustworthy man in the world. Daisy could not help but give him another chance with one of her girls.

"I will let Thalia go with you, but I demand that you sign a contract this time stating that you will not only treat Thalia fairly, but you will also make provisions so that she is protected from those who might have cause to steal her away," Daisy said, her words slow and calculated. "The contract will also state that I will be allowed to come to your sheep station to check up on Thalia from time to time."

Daisy thrust out her chin stubbornly. "Only by these terms shall I let that sweet thing go with you, Mr. Hathaway," she said flatly.

Paul shuffled his feet nervously. He scooted his eyeglasses farther back on the bridge of his nose, glad that the frames of his glasses hid the twitch in his left cheek that anger always caused. He did not like having to bargain with anyone, especially this woman who was a threat to his privacy. Coming to his sheep station for an inspection, indeed!

Yet, he knew that he had no choice. Not if he wanted Thalia. And he did.

For many reasons.

"I don't like contracts of any sort and most times I refuse to have anything to do with them," Paul grumbled. "But if it's necessary to take Thalia with me, give me the damn contract and make haste. I need to be on my way. I've taken too much time in Adelaide as it is."

Daisy went to her desk and removed a slip of paper, then a quill which she dipped into ink. "Over here," she said, motioning with a nod of her head. "Just place your name on the bottom line, date it, and Thalia will be yours."

"It'll be my pleasure, ma'am," Paul said, chuckling beneath his breath as he took the quill in hand

and scrawled his name on the contract.

When he heard footsteps enter the room, he lay the quill aside and turned slowly around. His heart skipped a beat and he had to force desire from his mind when he saw just how incredibly beautiful Thalia was now that she was no longer drenched with water from the river and was dressed in a neat cotton dress trimmed with gathered lace. Her auburn hair flowed like rivers of satin across her shoulders and down her back. Her face, radiantly innocent, was the face of an angel! How could he not want anything but to treat her well? How?

"Thalia, I'd like you to meet Paul Hathaway," Daisy said, giving Thalia a gentle shove closer to Paul. "He's come to take you with him to his sheep station. Luv, he offers you his hand in marriage."

Hesitant, Thalia took another step closer to Paul, feeling anything but pleased with the announcement of her upcoming marriage to a stranger, a man who was not at all pleasing in her eye! She knew that she should be thrilled to be singled out so quickly from the many girls who had arrived in Adelaide today. But she could not help feeling disappointed that it was this man making the offer, not Ian Lavery.

But in truth, she had no choice but to accept. Ian had not made any offers to claim her and he had seemed the restless sort—the type of man who would probably never own a house to take a woman to. He more than likely spent most of his time digging for gold, hoping to one day strike it rich.

And he was also the type who never would.

And Thalia also had her sister's welfare to consider. Always when thinking of her own future, she tried to include her sister. Thalia had left Viada behind in hopes of bringing her to Australia later, after Thalia had become established.

She hoped she could include her sister in this bargain today.

Her thoughts were catapulted back to the day of the sad farewell in England. Viada, nine, vulnerable and sweet, had clung desperately to Thalia.

"Please take me with you, Thalia," Viada cried. "We have never been apart. Why must we be now?"

Thalia hugged her sister tightly, not sure if she would ever get the opportunity again. "It is best that you stay with Uncle Jeremy until I send for you," she said, choking back a sob. "Once I find employment in Australia I will send for you, Viada. You know that I will."

Viada crept from Thalia's arms and looked woefully up at her. "But, Thalia, what if you don't find employment there?" she sobbed. "We shall be parted forever. We've never been apart. Never!"

Thalia touched her sister's cheek gently. She gazed at her, seeing a mirroring of her own self at age nine—the braided auburn hair, the trusting blue eyes. "Australia is the land of promise," she murmured. "I shall find employment, Viada! I shall!"

She took Viada into her arms once again. "Viada, we never shall be apart again once I send for you," she said softly. "Trust me, Viada. Trust me. . . ."

Thalia had carried her promise to her sister with

her all the way to Australia. She clung to it as though Viada were there now, looking trustingly up at her. . . .

"Sir? Daisy? I appreciate the kind offer," Thalia said, looking from one to the other. "It is not only myself that I am speaking for when I am asked to respond to this kind offer of marriage."

Daisy quirked an eyebrow. "My dear, whatever are you talking about?" she asked. "You said that you arrived from England alone."

"I did, ma'am," Thalia said, swallowing hard. "My sister stayed behind in England, but I had hoped not for long. She is living with our Uncle Jeremy. She should be with me, her sister. My plans were to find employment and then send for her." She looked Paul straight in the eye. "If you take me, you also take my sister."

She was taken aback by how her declaration had caused Paul's mustache to quiver on his lip as he slowly smiled down at her. Suddenly he looked so sinister! So—so evil! And there was Ava's reaction to the man! She had refused to be totally open to Thalia about him. Why? Was there something that Thalia should know about him? What could it be?

Yet Daisy had agreed to let Thalia go with him—even to marry him. Surely he was all right! Thalia was surely only imagining things. Since her parents' deaths, she had learned not to trust so easily, yet sometimes she felt she was becoming too fearful for her own good.

"A sister?" Paul said, twisting the end of his mustache between his thumb and forefinger. His eyes lit up. "I see no problem with that. My dear Thalia, if you will marry me I will see to your sister's arrival in Australia quite soon."

Thalia smiled weakly, yet knew that she could not ask for more than that. A fleeting memory of Ian Lavery troubled her deep in her soul, but she knew that she must brush thoughts of him from her mind.

She was going to marry Paul Hathaway.

Daisy grabbed Thalia and hugged her. "I'll come and see how things are for you quite soon," she promised. "Be happy, luv."

Thalia slipped her arms around Daisy's thick middle and returned the hug. "I shall try," she whispered, looking at Paul over Daisy's shoulder, an uneasiness building in her when she saw that his friendly smile had been replaced with a cold frown as he checked his pocket watch for the time.

"It's time to go," Paul said, thrusting his watch back inside his vest pocket. He reached a hand for Thalia and took her by the elbow. "Come along, Thalia. We've a good piece to travel."

Thalia gave Daisy a final smile over her shoulder as she was whisked away, then left Odum House and was led to a wagon guarded by several men. She looked at them, feeling uncomfortable in their presence. She gave Paul a questioning glance.

Paul helped her up into the wagon. "Those men are my stockmen. They serve as personal body-guards against attacks from bush rangers and Aborigines when I travel into the city," he explained, going around to the driver's side and climbing aboard. He sat down beside Thalia and reached for the horse's reins. "My sheep station is a two-hour drive from Adelaide. My place sits beside the Murray River. If you cross the Murray, you will enter the scrub. Some call the scrub the outback. Some call it the bush.''

Thalia shuddered. She had heard about the scrub, the bush rangers, and the Aborigines. She was glad that she would be protected from them all, just as Ian Lavery had protected her from the shark.

Out of the corner of Thalia's eyes, she searched for Ian. Her heart lurched when she saw him enter a pub, his back to her. Her gaze moved to the Aborigine who was still on his horse reined in beside Ian's outside the pub. She wondered in which capacity of friendship the native was to Ian. It seemed strange to see a black and white man as riding companions.

She then looked at Odum House. Daisy had gone inside, but Ava was standing just inside the door, peering sadly out at Thalia. Thalia lifted a hand and waved good-bye, smiling when Ava returned the wave.

Then as the wagon wheels began rolling along the rutted, dirt streets toward the edge of the city, Thalia listened to Paul explaining about his sheep station. When he had come to Australia from England, he had picked out a sheep and cattle property for himself on the Murray River and had squatted there. Since then, along with many hired men, he had cleaned, fenced, and tended his herd of cattle and flock of hardy, heavy-fleeced Merino sheep.

"I came to Australia with eight hundred sheep and five hundred cattle, and in eight years my stock has been reduced by half," Paul said with a coldness in his voice. "The Aborigines have been the cause. Their reasoning is that if the white man can kill the kangaroos that belong to them, they can also kill the white man's stock. Until recently they speared my cattle and sheep at their pleasure." He gave Thalia a triumphant stare. "But of late, none have dared to venture close to my place."

Paul grew quiet and turned his eyes back to the road. Thalia could see a quiet, seething hatred in the depths of his eyes.

She was again fearful of him, this man who would soon be her husband.

CHAPTER THREE

IAN SAUNTERED INTO THE PUB, A PLACE OF HEAVY-hanging smoke and noise, where the air was rancid with the smell of spilled beer and whiskey. Working his way toward the bar around tables where overnight poker games still droned on, he smiled at one or another cardplayer and nodded his head in a silent hello. He leaned low so that his head would miss what was left of a chandelier hanging in the center of the room. He glanced sideways up at it. The patrons liked to use it for target practice, and bits and pieces of it had been shot away; the ceiling above it was riddled with bullet holes.

Ian stepped past the player piano that was filling the room with a clatter of music mixed with shouts for more whiskey. He stepped up to the bar and slapped a friend good-naturedly on the back.

"G'day, Ridge," he said heartily. "How's it goin', mate?"

Ridge Wagner lowered the glass of whiskey from his mouth and wiped his lips dry with the back of his hand as he turned to Ian. "Same as always," he said, laughing gruffly. "And you?"

Ian sat down on a stool beside Ridge and motioned with his hand to the publican. "Bring me what my friend is drinking," he shouted over the noise. "On second thought, bring me a mug of beer, instead." He slipped several coins from his pocket and scooted them across the slippery bar.

"Well? 'ow's it goin', Ian?" Ridge persisted, tipping his glass to his lips to take a large swallow of whiskey. "Been out in the scrub for a spell, I hear."

"Yeah, for quite a spell," Ian said, his eyes showing amusement as he looked Ridge up and down. "And you? Seems nothing has changed. You're still wandering, aren't you?"

Ridge chuckled as he set his empty glass down on the counter. "Another of the same, publican!" he said, searching in his pockets for the two shillings it cost for the whiskey. He slapped the coins on the counter, then nodded as he met Ian's questioning stare, trying to keep his eyes steady so that Ian would not catch him in the lie he was ready to tell. "Aye, I'm doin' the same as I was the last time you saw me. It's what I want, mate. No use trying to fit me into what you think a man should do with his life."

Ridge looked away, hiding his uneasiness from Ian's searching eyes. "Now take what you do," he said blandly. "I don't need that sort of excitement. I prefer the easy life. You live longer that way."

Ian nodded a thank-you to the host as a mug of beer was placed before him on the counter. He took a swallow, eyeing Ridge quietly, feeling that something was amiss in his behavior today, an uneasiness of sorts. Ridge's raven-black hair hung long past his shoulders and his green eyes were strange, piercing slits in the narrow face bronzed golden by the sun. He wore loose-fitted kangaroo-hide jacket and trousers, and boots that reached up to his knees. Ridge was a *swaggie*, a man who was always on the move. He had no home. He was a footloose wanderer, a tramp.

A woman's laughter drew Ian's thoughts from Ridge, transporting him back to his precious moments with Thalia Drake. He gulped down another swallow of beer, trying to blot her from his mind, but it was all to no avail, for she was a part of him now, perhaps a part he could never shake.

And what of her?

What sort of life had he abandoned her to?

It ate away at his gut to realize that she could end up working for, or even marrying, some unscrupulous scoundrel. Australia, especially Adelaide, was full of such rogues who had their pockets filled with enough gold to pay for innocent women, to do with as they saw fit!

He set the mug down and drummed his fingers nervously on the counter, fighting the urge to leave the pub and go claim her for his own.

But he did not want to be saddled with a woman!

Sometime in the future, yes, but damn it, not now!

"Ian?" Ridge said, breaking through Ian's troubled thoughts. He looked at Ian cautiously. "What do you think of the continuing raids on the Aborigines? There's gossip that the women that are being carried off are being sold in the illegal slave trade. Most say it's the escaped convicts who are abducting them. The bastards. Some of those being sold as slaves are just girls of ten and eleven years old. I've heard tales of them being dragged screaming from their camps as their male protectors' heads are bashed in with the butts of muskets. Your friend Hawke—has he spoken of any sort of trouble in his village?"

"Hawke?" Ian said, fidgeting with his mug of beer, scooting it back and forth on the wet counter. "I don't guess you heard."

"Heard what?" Ridge asked, belching as he wiped his mouth dry again with the back of his hand.

"Hawke's wife was abducted and murdered and now Honora, his daughter, is missing," Ian said in a low, troubled voice.

Ridge paled. "Honora is missing?" he gasped. "Why, that's godawful, Ian." His jaw tight, he ordered another whiskey.

"I feel like I'm to blame," Ian said.

"Why would you?" Ridge asked, slapping more coins on the counter. "You've been a godsend to Hawke and his people. You've done more for the Aborigines than anyone else I've ever heard of. You're their advocate. No one else has bothered to speak up for them the same as you."

"Perhaps that's true. Yet, had I not hired Hawke to be my tracker he would have been with his people and his wife and daughter would have never been abducted," Ian said glumly, staring down into his beer. "But being in the business I am, a good tracker is of the utmost importance. That Hawke can follow tracks left by a man's shadow and can hear him breathe two miles away. Because of him, I've earned quite a reputation as a bounty hunter. I always bring in my man."

"Ian, Hawke's more than just a tracker to you and you know it," Ridge said, placing an affectionate arm around Ian's powerful shoulders. "He's a friend. He's your sidekick. Your companion."

"That's true," Ian said, glancing over at Ridge. "But no matter what you say to try and make me feel better about things, I know that my friendship with him caused him to lose a wife and daughter."

Ridge frowned into his whiskey. "You know how I feel about Honora," he said, his voice drawn. "I should've married her long ago. I could've made everything right for her." He ran his long, lean fingers frustratingly through his black shock of hair. "But, damn it, I'm no different than you. I didn't want the responsibilities of a wife then. I don't now. What the hell am I to do, Ian? What?"

"Just keep hoping that Honora is still alive," Ian said. "Hope that you'll get another chance to marry her some day." He glared at Ridge. "And, by God, Ridge, marry her then. It's about time you take on responsibility for something other than your own selfish hide."

Ridge gave him a wavering, hurt look, then gulped down another shot of whiskey.

Thalia came quickly to Ian's mind, his speech to Ridge seeming to apply as much to himself as to his *swaggie* friend. He had to forget her. Damn it, he had to. Just because he had saved her from a shark did not mean that he was destined to be her protector forever!

He fought his feelings, forcing himself to focus his thoughts on Hawke, drifting to the day that he had first met his dark-skinned Aborigine friend. . . .

It had been one of those hellish hot days in the scrub when it felt as though the sun was frying your brains. Up just ahead through the trees Ian had heard the sound that accompanied the savagery of dingo dogs in the midst of an attack, and then the screams of a man in pain. On his black stallion, Ian had gone to Hawke's rescue, his carbine drawn and firing. The dingoes that had not been shot right off had scattered, yelping.

He still bore the scars of that attack, but Hawke's loyalty to Ian since had been unwavering. He had become Ian's constant companion.

But Hawke's wife had been found just recently in a shallow grave, mutilated; his daughter, Honora, had been abducted. . . .

"Damn those who are responsible," Ian growled. "If it's not one thing causing the Aborigines grief and terror, it's another. The season of the swan's egg is approaching. You know how important that is to them. They are afraid to start on their march to the sea for the celebration of the gathering of the eggs. They fear being attacked by the bushrangers or whoever the hell is causing them problems these days."

"Mate, the Aborigines had the right to call the white explorers 'white ghosts' when the explorers first came to Australia's shores," Ridge said, knowing firsthand what the Australian natives had been through. In his earlier wandering days, when he had been a true *swaggie*, he had seen it all—so much that even Ian was not aware of.

"The white men became a quick spark of mystery, suspicion, and fear to them," Ridge continued, frowning darkly.

Ian lifted his refilled mug of beer toward Ridge. "Drink up, mate, and let us speak of other things," he said.

Ridge clinked his glass against Ian's and forced a laugh, Honora's lovely, trusting face swimming before his eyes, remembrances of stolen kisses and embraces bittersweet and painful. "Aye—like talking about you," he said. "A bounty hunter, a man who stamps out the insects of evil. How do you like that description, mate?"

Ian's eyes twinkled. He looked over the rim of his glass as he watched Ridge raise his glass to his lips, drinking the whiskey as though it were only a glass of tea.

He set the mug down again and excused himself when he emitted a soft belch, then pushed the mug away from himself, knowing that he had had enough.

"I just returned from Adelaide Prison, where I dropped off one of the orneriest men I've yet to encounter in Australia," Ian said, in his mind's eye recalling how he had cornered the cuss and lassoed him as though he were an animal—but he was worse than that. The man had slain at least twenty innocent people while traveling the back roads of Australia. "It took me a few weeks, but damn it, I finally got the bastard."

He glanced at Ridge. "I spent a lot of time in the scrub this time," he said irritably. "Those damn bushrangers always escape in the scrub. Like most hunted animals, they feel safer in a pack. But this time, this bloody bloke rode alone, so it took me longer to find him. He was worth two thousand pounds to the Government. I earned that two thousand pounds, Ridge—every last shilling of it."

"I imagine so," Ridge said, nodding. He squirmed uneasily on his stool, knowing that when Ian hunted down a man, he always got him. Even an old friend—should he be given cause? "What do you think of the daily attacks on the supply and wagon trains? Every third or fourth wagon is raided. No one's life is spared. People are killed—some mutilated."

"Yeah, I know," Ian grumbled. "And you know who is getting blamed, don't you? The Aborigines. The Aborigines! Now would you tell me how anyone could come to that conclusion? Except for Hawke, who has conformed only because of me, most Aborigines travel by foot, having some sort of hocus-pocus superstition about riding on horses. So how in the hell could they attack the wagon trains and succeed? The Overlanders travel in covered wagons. Most are in prairie schooners. Damn, those are huge, high drays, hauled by teams of up to a dozen bullocks. The Aborigines would have no luck in hell raiding something that massive. Why, chances are they'd be trampled to death by the young bulls pulling the prairie schooners."

"I understand what you're sayin'," Ridge said uneasily, tipping his glass to his lips again.

"The Government has kept me too busy hunting and bringing in the escaped convicts to be able to join the army to help guard the wagon trains," Ian said, glowering. "Since I suspect the attacks are for the most part the work of escaped convicts who have joined bushranger gangs, it is important to find and take in the escaped convicts before they have a chance to join the gangs."

"Aye, I would think so," Ridge agreed, his voice fading into something solemn and distant.

Ian placed his arm around Ridge's shoulder again. "Mate, I can see that I'm giving you cause to think," he said, laughing. "One day I hope to convert you into a full-fledged bounty hunter. You'll leave your *swaggie* days behind and be a better man for it."

An elbow bumped against Ian as someone sat down on the stool to his left.

"Sorry, mate," a youthful voice said, drawing Ian's quick attention.

Ian turned and smiled roguishly at the young lad. "Are you sure you're in the right establishment, son?" he taunted as he looked Kenneth Ozier slowly up and down. "Why, I bet your mama's still wiping your nose for you, isn't she?"

Used to such teasing and realizing that he looked much younger than his twenty years, Kenneth ignored Ian. He placed a coin on the counter and scooted it toward the publican. "A whiskey," he said flatly.

"Sonnie, are you sure you don't want to order milk instead?" Ian further taunted, meaning no harm. He was ready for a light moment or two after his weeks in the scrub. Perhaps it could also help erase thoughts of Thalia from his mind. "Why, you're nothing more than a kid just letting loose from his mama's apron strings."

Kenneth's eyes narrowed and his spine stiffened. He looked at Ian, glaring as he recognized him. Ian Lavery's reputation preceded him. "Mate, I think your mama taught you the wrong sort of manners," he drawled angrily. "Now let me have my drink in peace, or else—"

Ian's eyes were twinkling. "Or else what?" he prodded, laughing beneath his breath. "Or else you might challenge me to a duel?"

Ridge placed a hand on Ian's shoulder. "Don't you think that's enough?" he whispered. He looked past Ian at Kenneth, locking eyes with him. "Let him be, Ian. There ain't no need in startin' trouble."

Ian's smile faded. He looked from Ridge to Kenneth, then back at Ridge. "Do you know this boy?" he asked, seeing something in Ridge's expression that gave him cause to suspect a kinship of some sort between the young man and his good friend. But what?

"Aye, I know him," Ridge said, his eyes still locked with Kenneth's. "In passing."

Ian looked back at Kenneth, stunned at how quickly the young man downed his whiskey and left.

Ian started to question Ridge again but was drawn to other thoughts when a soft voice behind him made his heart jump. He turned with a jerk and found himself staring down upon a face that was gaudily painted, yet not so much that it hid a trace of innocence still alight in the violet eyes. Ian looked the young woman up and down as she very boldly offered herself to him with a seductive smile and wandering hands that stopped at the juncture of his thighs. His face flooded with color as she squeezed his private parts through his buckskin breeches, causing a flame to ignite within him where she now so skillfully stroked.

"Afternoon, luv," Beatrice said in a lilting purr. "Ain't seen you for a while, Ian. 'ave you been crook? Or 'ave you been in the scrub chasin' down scruffy old duffs?"

Ian did not want Beatrice to know that her fingers were arousing him, did not wish to be led to her bed like the last time he had arrived in Adelaide after a long spell in the scrub. His thoughts were too full of Thalia and how innocent and sweet she still was.

His gut twisted as he stared down at Beatrice, knowing that at one time she was as innocent as Thalia—and look how she had changed! Coming to Australia had done this to her. She made her living whoring, giving herself to any man who had enough coins to pay for her service. She had turned into one of the highest paid whores in Adelaide.

"Well, luv?" Beatrice asked, inching closer to Ian so that he could see the great gift of breasts that she was offering. Her dress, covered with red sequins, was so low-cut that her nipples were almost fully exposed.

Beatrice cocked one of her legs up on Ian's, revealing that she wore no undergarments beneath the short, skimpy dress. Her black hose were held up by a tempting black garter belt.

Reaching a hand to Ian's hair, she wove her fingers through its reddish-golden threads. "Ian, ain't you goin' to pay for a poke?" she asked, curving her lower lip into a seductive pout. "It's been a long time. I've missed you. Ain't you missed me just a wee little bit? Ain't you gonna take me to your fancy place for a poke like last time? I'd make it worth your while."

Ian was acutely aware of how Beatrice was continuing to affect him. It had been a long time since he had found release in a woman's arms.

Yet he could not keep his mind from drifting to Thalia and her sweet, innocent loveliness. As Beatrice had been—and still was—Thalia was vulnerable in every way to everything evil in Australia. Although he had never wanted a woman to get in his way, to complicate his life, he could not stand the thought of letting Thalia slip away from him and into the clutches of another man who could use and abuse her!

Nor could he let her turn into another Beatrice. . . .

"Sounds invitin' to me, Ian," Ridge said. He laughed boisterously and winked at Ian. "Now how can you say no to this pretty little thing?"

Ian looked from Beatrice to Ridge. He placed his hands on Beatrice's upper arms and bodily moved her over to stand in front of Ridge. "She's yours, mate," he said, chuckling as he rushed from the pub.

Once outside, he quickly mounted his horse and glanced at Hawke, who had dutifully waited for his return. "Hawke, it seems I'm being sidetracked again," he said. "I've got to go to Odum House and get myself a woman. Don't ask me what I'm going to do with her, 'cause I don't even know myself."

Ian didn't give Hawke time to respond. He rode to Odum House and dismounted, taking the front steps two at a time. Inside, his eyes searched the busy room for Daisy. When he spied her, he went to her and took her aside. "I've come for Thalia Drake," he said, eyeing Daisy warily. "Take me to her."

"Ian, she ain't here," Daisy said, staring up at him. "Why didn't you come sooner if you wanted her? She's of good stock. You knew she'd go fast."

Ian's head was swimming. A strange sort of emptiness was assailing him. "Who, Daisy?" he said thickly. "Who came for her?"

"Paul Hathaway," Daisy said, her voice drawn, knowing that as astute as Ian was, he had heard the same gossip about Paul that had caused Daisy to be hesitant about letting Thalia go with him.

Ian's insides grew cold. He had suspected for some time that Paul Hathaway was the leader of a bushranger gang, yet he had been unable to prove that he was anything but a rancher and a kind, God-fearing man. Having kept busy enough capturing convicts, Ian had never taken the time to actually pursue Paul's guilt.

Now he felt like a fool for having made such a blunder.

"How long have they been gone?" Ian asked anxiously. "I'm going after her."

Daisy's eyes wavered. She clasped her hands nervously behind her. "That won't do you any good," she said.

"Why the hell not?" Ian asked.

"Because, by now, Thalia is probably Mrs. Paul Hathaway," Daisy said, wincing when the news reaching Ian's ears caused him to pale and his jaw to go slack.

"What are you saying. . . . ? he gasped.

"That Paul Hathaway's intention was to marry Thalia," Daisy said softly. "There ain't no preacher in the scrub, so I'm sure they got married right here in Adelaide before headin' out for Paul's ranch."

Ian raked his fingers frustratingly through his hair. "No," he said, so low that Daisy could not hear. Cursing himself for having delayed too long in the pub, and for having been too cowardly to go and speak up for Thalia earlier, he turned and rushed toward the door.

"Ian, I'm sorry!" Daisy shrieked from behind him. "Truly I am. If I had known—"

Ian did not give himself a chance to hear the rest of Daisy's apology. He went outside and quickly mounted his horse. Although Thalia could be Mrs. Hathaway by now, that was not going to stop Ian. He was going to rescue her from the life that could soon be forced upon her. If Paul Hathaway was the leader of a bushranger gang, that meant only one thing—he was a heartless bastard. Such a man would be anything but gentle with a wife.

"Hawke, let's ride!" Ian shouted, slapping his reins against the sides of his stallion. "I've a woman to save!"

Hawke's horse sprang along beside Ian's as they rode through town. "What you mean?" he asked, having learned the art of English well enough from Ian. "You did not get woman from Odum House?"

Ian quickly explained to Hawke what he had discovered while talking to Daisy. "Hawke, we can't let Thalia stay with Paul Hathaway," he said firmly. "By God, we're going to go to Hathaway's ranch and abduct her!"

Hawke's dark eyes were shadowed by thick, dark lashes. "Best leave her from your life," he said gruffly. "Women bring sadness in man's life. My heart heavy still for my wife and daughter."

Ian cast him a troubled glance.

Adelaide was now many miles behind, and Thalia tried to forget what she may have gotten herself into by focusing on the beauty of this new country. Myriad flowering bushes and trees delighted her senses with brilliant colors, a parade of splendid shapes, a collage of waxy, fuzzy, and prickly surfaces. The buckboard wagon in which she was traveling was now following a trail through steep ridges of alpine ash and peppermint trees. Towering mottled-bark eucalyptus grew along the banks of the warm, slow-moving river not far from the trail. Platypus, a strange beast with a soft bill shaped like that of a duck and fur like a beaver's, could be seen moving through the brush toward the river. A koala bear, a furry little animal with black, button-like eyes, was clinging to a eucalyptus tree, feasting on its glossy leaves.

"God's country, isn't it?" Paul said, drawing Thalia from her reverie. He gave her a guarded smile. "I'm sure you are finding Australia much lovelier than England and its drab, blustery weather. Here you can find sunshine almost every day.

And with the sunshine come exotic flowers and birds."

"Yes, sir, I have just begun to notice," Thalia said, smiling weakly at him.

"Sir?" Paul said, quirking an eyebrow. "You address me as sir? Call me Paul, Thalia. Call me Paul."

A quick panic seized Thalia when she suddenly realized that she and Paul Hathaway had left Adelaide without first exchanging wedding vows. Surely no minister could be found away from the city to perform the marriage. This aroused her suspicions of Paul Hathaway anew.

"Paul, when will we be married?" she blurted out, stiffening when he gave her an icy stare.

"Married?" he said, his voice now cold and uncaring. "My dear, I have never had any intention at all of marrying you."

Thalia's insides became gripped with a clammy fear. She turned her eyes away from Paul and stared straight ahead, seeing nothing and fearing everything.

CHAPTER FOUR

TIRED AND CONFUSED, THALIA SLUMPED DOWN IN A chair in her assigned bedroom. She looked glumly around the room, for the moment having privacy, yet not knowing what to expect in the hours and days to come. For the most part, the journey from Adelaide had been made in silence, especially after Paul had revealed to her that he had never intended to marry her.

"What sort of game is he playing with me?" she whispered to herself, shuddering at the thought of being so easily taken in by the roguish man.

Yet Daisy Odum had believed in him also and she did not seem the sort to hand out innocent women to scheming, evil men.

"What do I do?" Thalia whispered. She was glad that Paul had at least let her go to her room when she arrived at his ranch, asking him for a moment of rest before proceeding with whatever he had planned for her. "Oh, what do I do?"

Her gaze moved slowly around the room, feeling some comfort in her surroundings. The decor was pleasing to the eye, yet it made her miss terribly her bedroom in England. Pangs of loneliness shot through her. She had always shared a bedroom with her sister, Viada, at least until their parents had died. Then their world had been torn apart. They had been ordered by the court to live with their Uncle Jeremy, who was so poor he rarely had enough coins to put food on the table. And Thalia's and her sister's meager inheritances had been too little to last.

"Nothing has been the same since mama's and papa's deaths, nor shall it ever be," Thalia whispered, rising from the chair. "What does the future hold for us, Viada? Which of us will survive? Which of us shall be blessed with children?" She doubled a fist at her side. "Probably neither!"

She began moving around the room, touching the smooth finish of the oak furniture. The four-poster bed was beautifully carved and spread with a lovely maroon velvet comforter; fluffed pillows were propped against the headboard. A candle flared its golden light around the room as it burned its way down in a brass candleholder on a nightstand beside the bed. A huge chest sat at the foot of the bed, with brass strips running from the back to the front, a large key protruding boldly from the latch and keyhole.

A window was open at the far end of the room,

and gauzy sheer curtains billowed gently in the evening breeze. French doors led out to a balcony overlooking the ranch and the view of the Murray River and scrub not all that far from the house. A courtyard and pasture was all that had to be crossed to reach freedom. . . .

Thalia spun around with a start when the bedroom door squeaked open behind her. She stiffened, expecting to see Paul enter the room. Instead, a beautiful Aborigine woman, perhaps Thalia's same age, entered, carrying a basin of water.

"For you to cleanse yourself," the woman said meekly, in English. She carried the basin to the nightstand beside the bed and set it there.

Anxious to get answers about Paul from this woman, Thalia went and stood beside her. "My name is Thalia Drake," she said softly, startled by how the woman seemed suddenly so frightened at being spoken to. Her hands trembled as she took a washcloth and soap from a drawer in the nightstand, gingerly placing them beside the basin of water.

Then, seemingly afraid to move, she inched around and stared cautiously at Thalia, her eyes wide, her breathing shallow.

Wondering about this, for she had not given the woman any reason to be afraid of her, Thalia looked at her carefully. She was dressed neatly in a cotton dress, a white collar hugging her thin, dark neck, and her brown hair hung in one long braid down her narrow back. She bore the distinct features of the Aborigine. Her eyebrows were feathered across a prominent bony ridge, her lips were thick, and her nose was flat and broad. There was something innocent and exotically beautiful about her.

Then Thalia sucked in her breath with a loud gasp. Upon closer scrutiny, she could see deep scars crisscrossing the flesh of the woman's arms where the sleeves of her dress stopped mid-point between her shoulders and elbows. She started to reach out to touch them but the woman jerked away from her and cowered, as though expecting to be hit.

"I'm not going to hurt you," Thalia was quick to explain. "I saw the scars. How did you get them?"

"Honora must leave your room," the woman said, inching toward the door. "Honora not talk to you. Get in trouble!"

Thalia was taken aback by what the woman said, the fear no less in her eyes as she reached the door. Her escape was fast. "My Lord," Thalia whispered, placing a quivering hand to her throat. "She seems to be frightened of everything."

Swallowing hard, fear building in her heart for herself, Thalia rushed to the door and closed it. She leaned against it, her heart pounding, wondering about the young woman's scars. Surely they had been inflicted by Paul Hathaway!

But why? The woman seemed so sweet and willing to please.

At least Thalia had made one discovery. She knew the woman's name—Honora.

Heavy footsteps approaching in the hallway made Thalia scurry away from the door. There was no lock to protect her; she was at the mercy of whoever chose to come into the room. Perhaps one day soon she would feel the sting of a whip on her flesh also! Like Honora, Thalia would be scarred for life.

She watched the door guardedly, then sighed with relief when the footsteps passed on by her room, at least for the moment giving her a reprieve.

Restless, waiting with a fearful heart for Paul to come and claim her body, since he in a sense owned her, Thalia went to the basin and splashed water on her face, then dabbed it dry with the towel. She turned and eyed the French doors. Perhaps a breath of fresh air might calm her nerves.

Silhouetted by the candlelight behind her, Thalia opened the doors and stepped out onto a balcony that overlooked Paul's spread of land. The moonlight flooded sheep and cattle and the Murray River in the distance, and bunkhouses and a stately barn nearby. Paul's vast domain was surrounded by a rail fence in an effort to keep the sheep and cattle in, the kangaroos and Aborigines out.

Thalia turned and stared up at the belltower that she had marveled at upon her approach to the ranch earlier in the evening. It loomed upward into the darkness, as though some sort of sentinel, as if the house in which Paul made his residence was an old Spanish mission. . . .

"Thalia?"

Thalia jumped with alarm, not having heard Paul enter the room or step up behind her on the balcony. She turned with a start and felt her insides tighten as his lips curved into a sardonic smile, his mustache quivering.

"I've brought you something," he said, offering her a glass of milk. "It's warm goat's milk. It will relax you so that you can sleep better."

Thalia inched her hand out slowly toward him and took the glass. "Thank you," she murmured, yet not relishing the thought of drinking the unappetizing liquid. Slipping past Paul back into the room, Thalia placed the glass of milk on the nightstand beside the bed.

"I've brought you something else," Paul said, following her into the room. He stepped up to her and took her left hand, while with his right hand he fished inside his front breeches pocket for something. "Ah, here it is."

Thalia's eyes widened as he brought out a beautiful golden wedding band from his pocket and slipped it on her finger. "A ring?" she gasped, studying the ring. "A wedding band?"

Paul nodded as he dropped his hands to his sides. "Do not get the wrong impression," he said blandly. "Though it is a wedding band, I still do not wish to make you my wife. I shy away from such legally binding documents that are required when a man takes a wife."

Thalia toyed with the ring, turning it nervously in circles on her finger. "Then why must I wear the ring?" she dared to ask. "I don't understand. What are you not telling me?"

Paul clasped his hands behind him and rocked back and forth from his heels to his toes. "I guess I do owe you an explanation," he said. "My dear, the ring is just for show. I want you to pretend to be my wife because Daisy Odum preferred this arrangement over any other. When Daisy comes to check on you, it is best that you pretend to be married to me, or Daisy will take you back to Odum House, and more than likely, the next man who chooses you will not have the funds that I have to send for your sister. For your sister's sake, you must cooperate fully."

The threat that Thalia was already feeling in the presence of this man was two-fold now. He was a man of deceit—a man not ever to be trusted. And now even Viada was being included in his schemes!

This arrangement, this ultimatum of sorts, sent waves of fear through her and her thoughts went to Ian. If only she could somehow find her way to him and ask if he would take her away from this danger in her and her sister's lives!

Yet Ian looked poorer than a church mouse and probably did not even own a home to take Viada to if he even came up with the money to send for her!

No. Thalia must see this thing through with Paul. She truly had no other choice. Though she hated to admit it, he seemed the only person who gave a tinker's dam about her or her sister.

If only the caring were genuine! If only she could learn to trust and care for him!

But in her mind's eye she was recalling the terrible scars on Honora's arms.

Was Paul truly responsible for them?

She brushed such thoughts from her mind. She must concern herself with her own welfare.

Thalia gazed at Paul guardedly. "This wedding band," she said, holding her hand out so that the candlelight reflected in the gold. "You say I am not to be your wife. But you did not say whether or not the ring gives you all claims that a wedding band usually gives a husband. Will you frequent my bed? Am I to expect nightly visits from you?"

Paul shifted his feet nervously. He cleared his throat. "No," he said, his voice drawn. "I am not interested in you, sexually. To help my standing in the community, I want you as a companion so that I will appear to be happily married."

Paul took a step closer to her and looked directly down into her face. "I have many slaves who perform various duties for me," he said. "I will depend on you to see that things are kept organized neatly in my house, something that no Aborigine woman has knowledge of since they are born into ignorance in the scrub."

His eyes gleamed when he thought of another reason for having chosen Thalia—because of Ian Lavery and Ian's show of interest in Thalia at the quay. Paul hated the man with a vengeance. Ian was the reason so many escaped convicts had been recaptured, keeping them from joining Paul's bushranger gang. And Paul had to be on the lookout for Ian every minute that Paul was in the scrub. Until bounty hunter Ian Lavery had come to Australia, Paul and his gang had been free to roam the scrub and everywhere else they damn well pleased on their nightly affairs. Now they always had to keep an eye on their backs.

Just for spite and damnation, Paul would keep Thalia for himself. This was one woman Ian Lavery would not take to his bed. Let him just cry in his beer over her at Joe's Pub!

A great surge of relief swept through Thalia.

71

Although Paul had told her that he would not be approaching her sexually, she could not help but be puzzled by it, but, preferring to leave well enough alone, she did not dare inquire into his reasons.

"Paul, just how proper is it to be using the Aborigines as slaves?" she asked, without thinking of the implications of such a question. It seemed an innocent-enough inquiry to her—or so she thought until she saw the dark scowl that turned Paul's face into something quite close to grotesque!

Paul placed his hands firmly on her shoulders. "No one must ever know about the Aborigines being used here in my house," he growled. "When Daisy Odum or anyone else from the city comes to call, the natives are all locked away, out of sight." He spoke now between clenched teeth. "Do . . . you . . . understand?"

Thalia nodded anxiously, her fears of Paul building. She was beginning to think that Viada might be better off in England after all. Thalia could not help but conclude that she herself would even be better off at Odum House!

"Sir, I do not wish to stay here with you," she blurted out, paling when she saw the rage that lit his eyes. But she could not keep her thoughts quiet. Something deeply within her told her that she must flee.

Now! For if she did not now, she never would!

"I don't like it here," she said icily, stubbornly firming her chin. "This arrangement displeases me immensely."

Paul grabbed her painfully by the wrist and

leaned down into her face. "I don't want to hear any more such talk from you," he said, his voice filled with venom. "Others have said the same and have run away. They didn't live long enough to regret it." He smiled smugly. "And must I remind you that you have a sister's welfare to consider?"

Fighting back tears, Thalia stared up at him. "My sister's welfare is what concerns me the most," she said, hating it when her voice broke. "I don't want Viada to be a part of this place. I don't want her here! I want her left in England. She is young and impressionable. She is sweet. She is dear to me!"

Paul unclasped his fingers from her wrist. He laughed sardonically. "And so she is, is she?" he mocked. "Just remember, then, that all I have to do is say the word and your sister will be sought and killed or placed on a ship bound for Australia. You have no choice but to cooperate, Thalia. Totally!"

Thalia became numb with fright. Now she understood too well that she had to go along with Paul Hathaway. Too much was at stake for her not to. "Please don't harm my sister or place her on a ship to Australia," she begged, hating to be forced to humble herself to this evil man. "If you promise these things to me, then I will cooperate."

Snickering, Paul picked up the glass of goat's milk and stood over Thalia. "If I can help it, I don't make promises to anyone," he said. "Just you remember that whatever happens to your sister is all up to you now."

He forced the glass of milk into her hand. "Drink the goat's milk," he ordered flatly and turned and began walking away.

Thalia stared blankly down at the milk, then at

Paul as he swung around to face her again.

"And another thing," he said matter-of-factly. He nodded toward the huge chest at the foot of the bed. "Feel free to choose any garment you desire from the chest. There is everything there from thin nightly apparel to dresses of all styles and material. Surely among them you can find something in which to be comfortable."

At that, he bowed mockingly, then left.

Thalia choked out a sob of relief, so glad was she to finally be alone. She cried softly, worrying not only about herself and her sister, but also about other innocent women who might be brought to Hathaway Ranch. Perhaps worse would be done to them should she find a way to escape. She understood too well why the others had fled—to escape Paul Hathaway's tyranny!

Thinking that perhaps the milk might soothe her nerves after all and make her sleep better, Thalia placed the glass to her lips. But she had swallowed only a taste of it when the sound of horse's hooves drew her eyes to the window, then the French doors.

Curious, she set the glass of milk back on the nightstand and went outside on the balcony just in time to see Paul and several of his men riding away from the premises.

"He's leaving!" Thalia whispered harshly to herself, her heart skipping a beat as a faint ray of hope sprang forth within her. "This is my chance to escape!"

The thought was too fleeting, for in the same moment she was breathing the word escape across her lips she was reminded of her sister.

No.

She could not escape.

At all cost, she must remain loyal to Paul Hathaway.

Her head hanging, her shoulders heavy with sadness, Thalia went back inside and closed the doors. She eyed the chest and then, emotionless, she settled down on her knees before the chest and turned the key. As she raised the lid, her heart leapt and she gasped when she found herself staring down at lovely dresses and undergarments of the finest fabrics, some even of silk and satin.

Then her gaze fell on a nightgown that was trimmed in white, delicate lace. She held the garment up for inspection, its sheer, transparent texture making her blush.

Rising to her feet, she held the nightgown against her and went to gaze into a mirror, envisioning just how she might look in such a shameful garment. It had the thinnest of straps and there were no sleeves. Its bodice was daringly low, surely meant to reveal most of the bust. She could see how every curve and dip of her youthful body would show through such thin material!

Giggling, feeling safe enough to wear this particular gown to bed, since Paul had said that he required nothing of her at night, Thalia hurried into the wondrously soft gown, then stared openly at her reflection in the mirror.

Again she blushed, for hardly anything of her body was left to the imagination. Even the nipples of her breasts were pronouncedly brown. Even the auburn triangle of hair at the juncture of her thighs was visible, drawing her hand to it and causing a sort of tingling heat to sweep through her at the touch of her fingers. She jerked her hand away, startled.

"Ian," she whispered, her face flushed. He had aroused similar feelings within her when he kissed her—feelings that were surely forbidden!

Shame engulfing her for her shameful thoughts, Thalia rushed to the nightstand and blew the candle out. She crawled into bed beneath the comforter, then remembered the milk that Paul had brought to help relax her so that she could get to sleep. Turning on her side, she shrugged. The milk would have been effective only when it was warm. It had sat too long. It was more than likely too cold to help her now.

"Goat's milk, indeed," she said, making a bitter face in the dark. "I didn't want to drink it in the first place."

Her eyes drifted closed. Unaware, she kicked the comforter from her body. The moon rippled and played down the full length of her sensuous curves.

CHAPTER FIVE

DREAMING, THALIA STIRRED IN HER SLEEP. IN
her dream she was feeling the wonders of a kiss.
Ian's kiss. He was holding her in his arms, protecting her from all harm. She emitted a soft
sob when he began backing away from her. She
beckoned with her arms for him to return to
her, but something was drawing him away . . .
away . . . away . . .

Her eyes flew open and her heart beat wildly.
Although in her dream Ian had turned away from
her, she could feel his presence even now. She
leaned up on an elbow and gazed at the moon-
splashed French doors, a tremor coursing through
her as her thoughts dwelled on Ian.

"Why can't I forget him?" she asked herself. "I
must! He forgot me, didn't he?"

Tired of fighting sleep and thoughts of Ian,

Thalia rose from her bed and began pacing the room like a caged tigress. Then, setting her jaw angrily, she took a shawl from the chest at the foot of her bed and wrapped it around her shoulders. She needed a breath of fresh air; she needed to walk off her frustrations. She would go outside, and if any of Paul's men got in her way, let them be damned! She was a prisoner up to a point. She was not locked in her room!

Opening the door slowly, Thalia peered out onto a dimly candle-lit corridor. She looked from side to side and saw no one. It was just as she had suspected. Paul felt smug enough not to leave guards. He knew that the threat he held over her head was enough to keep her at his ranch.

Oh, but if not for that . . . !

Stepping barefoot out of her room, she moved meekly down the corridor and down the steps to the first floor, then ran to the door and flung it open. She stood still for a moment, the moon and the stars overhead mesmerizing her. . . .

Two men stirred in the dusky shadows of night, hovering near the fence that snaked along pasture land. "Hawke, Hathaway's playing right into our hands," Ian said, tethering his stallion's reins to the fence. He watched Paul and his men riding at a good clip away from the ranch. "What do you bet the bastard's up to no good? What else would he be doing this time of night?"

"Hawke go after him?" Hawke growled, securing his horse beside Ian's. "My spear kill him fast!"

"No, Hawke," Ian said, giving his friend an

exasperated look. He placed a kind hand on Hawke's bony shoulder. "We've got to settle things in as peaceful a fashion as possible. Killing Hathaway would solve many of your people's woes, I am sure, but then you would become the hunted."

"Paul Hathaway no good," Hawke said flatly. "He kill many of my people when he first come to my land."

"Hawke, so did many other white settlers," Ian said, in his mind's eye recalling the slaughters that he had come across when he first arrived to Australia after graduating from college in America. It sickened him now to remember the dismembered bodies, flies and other insects covering and devouring them.

"Paul Hathaway turned sheep loose on my tribe's land," Hawke persisted, his English quite distinct tonight, his anger flaring. "My tribe was pushed into a corner. Food ran out, leaving us with two choices. Kill the sheep and in turn be killed for what white man calls crop and stock pests, or raid another tribe's territory for food and risk being killed for trespassing."

"And you chose to kill Paul Hathaway's sheep," Ian said, nodding. "In turn many of your people were killed."

"That is so," Hawke said, grabbing his spear from where he always kept it secured at the side of his saddle. "I kill many tonight. Hawke keep you safe while you steal the woman away from Paul's house."

"I most certainly hope you aren't given cause to kill someone," Ian said, spinning away from

Hawke to jerk his carbine from its gunboot. "That would mean that both Thalia and I were in danger. I hope to steal her away without any notice whatsoever."

He swung around and thrust the carbine at Hawke. "But if there is a problem, mate, use this instead of your spear," he said flatly.

"Spear my weapon," Hawke said, clutching more tightly to the spear. "It silent. It deadly!"

With his left hand, Ian eased the spear from Hawke's unwilling fingers and thrust the carbine there in its place. "Aye," he said. "Both are deadly, and perhaps your spear is the more silent of the two, but I put more trust in the speed of a carbine's bullet."

Hawke glowered down at the carbine. "White man's weapon no good," he said. "Aborigine's better!"

Ian leaned the spear up against the fence. "Hawke, I've taught you many things," he said, giving him a stern look. "And you, for the most part, have been an astute student. But you still fight me on which weapons to use." He slung a Colt from its holster and made sure it was loaded. "Trust me, Hawke. I'll use my Colt and you use the carbine if trouble brews while I am on Paul Hathaway's property."

"Carbine and Colt filled with thunder-like noise!" Hawke argued. "It will awaken even the dead!"

Ian chuckled as he flipped his Colt back into its holster. "Well now, mate, I wouldn't go so far as to say that," he said. "But if you are put in the position to use it, you will probably have more than one man to use it on."

Hawke laughed beneath his breath. "That is good," he said, his dark eyes gleaming.

Ian circled his fingers around the top rail of the fence and leaned his full weight on it. He peered toward the house, his eyes focused on one balcony in particular. His heart had melted when Thalia had stepped out on the balcony, fully clothed. With the moonlight on her, her hair blowing and lifting from her tiny shoulders, she had looked like some sort of goddess.

Just thinking about what she and Paul might have shared since then made jealousy gnaw at Ian's insides. There had been plenty of time for them to seek pleasures in bed.

"I'm sure she's being guarded inside the house," Ian said, more to himself than to Hawke. "Probably just outside her bedroom door. But I'll be damned if that's going to stop me."

He swung around and faced Hawke, his hand resting on his holstered Colt. "You keep watch for any movements in the courtyard," he said, smiling sardonically. "But I truly don't think we have guards to worry about. I've heard gossip that most who work for Paul Hathaway are here only to collect their wages. They don't give a hoot what happens otherwise." He looked toward the house again. "I would wager a' bet that none would gamble with their lives to see me dead. They more than likely will look the opposite direction if they see me."

"Hawke come with you," the Aborigine said,

taking a bold step toward the fence.

"No, Hawke," Ian said flatly. "You will be more useful here." He looked over his shoulder at the house. "From this vantage point you will be able to see anything or anyone that might be a threat to me. You know what to do."

Hawke lifted the carbine and practiced his aim. "Hawke shoot to kill," he said, laughing throatily.

Ian chuckled beneath his breath. "Just make sure it's not me," he said, placing his hands on the fence. Swinging himself over, he hunkered down low on the other side, looking up at the moon. It was his only true enemy tonight. There was a pure silver hemisphere of brightening moon, and the Southern Cross blazed overhead like a great brooch on a velvet canopy. He had stared into the unrelieved blackness of the sky many a night, as if something palpable and compelling held his eyes.

But tonight, his eyes held within them the wonder of a woman.

And time was wasting.

"You *rama rama* for wanting this woman in your life," Hawke scolded. "When you lose her like I lost my woman you will see. Hawke even lost daughter! It is too painful. Better not to care in the first place, Ian."

"*Rama rama*?" Ian chuckled. "All right, mate, call me crazy, and perhaps I am. But I must do what my heart tells me to do. And not only for myself, but for Thalia. I can't let her stay with Paul Hathaway. She is too sweet and innocent to live with a man with such a questionable reputation."

Ian's face clouded, wondering if Thalia was all

that innocent now. If Paul had taken her sexually, hadn't her life of degradation already begun?

This thought spurred him across the straight stretch of land, his Colt drawn and poised for action. His eyes darted from side to side, the shadow of the bunkhouse and barn giving him momentary cover as he slid his back up against one, then the other.

He took a moment to get his breath, then jumped with alarm when he felt something rubbing up against his leg. He jerked his Colt and aimed downward, then raised its barrel slowly up again when he saw that it was only a cat, purring and looking up at Ian with trusting green eyes.

"At least you're not a dog," Ian whispered, relief washing through him that a cat meowed, not barked.

He gently pushed the cat away from him with his foot and proceeded with his stealthy creeping across the courtyard, then hurried into the shadows of the house. He looked overhead, seeing the steeple of the old mission towering over him, then froze in his tracks when he heard soft footsteps approaching.

When Thalia came into view, going to stand beneath a tree to stare up at the star-flecked sky, Ian's breath caught in his throat. The moonlight illuminated her sweet loveliness, and so mesmerized was he by her that Ian could not move. If ever there was a woman who could change his mind about marriage, it was Thalia Drake. Lord, looking at her now made him realize that he would even die for her!

He took in a wild gulp of air when Thalia's shawl slipped down to rest in the crook of her arms and her breasts were all but fully exposed where the transparent fabric of her nightgown displayed their magnificence, their nipples hard and peaked. It would take every bit of Ian's willpower not to place his hands on her breasts, to experience the thrill of touching her.

But that would start a chain reaction. One touch would bring on much, much more than that. His body craved fulfillment and not with just any woman.

Only with Thalia!

Ian shook his head to clear his lusty thoughts, then focused his eyes on Thalia again. He had come to Hathaway's ranch for a purpose and too much time had already been wasted.

"It's now or never," he whispered to himself.

Slipping his Colt back into its holster, Ian circled around so that he was behind the tree Thalia was resting against. His heart thudded wildly as he inched around the tree and clasped a hand firmly over Thalia's mouth.

Thalia's knees grew weak with a sudden panic. Her shawl falling to the ground, she grabbed at the hand being held over her mouth, but with no avail. She couldn't budge it!

Then she stiffened and her eyes grew wide when the intruder in the night stepped into view. Ian! Ian Lavery!

Ian sensed her fear. "I'm not here to harm you," he whispered. "I'm here to take you away."

Thalia looked wildly up at him and again tried to

pull his hand away from her mouth. She could not leave! If Paul found her gone, he would think it was of her own initiative and Viada's life would be endangered!

"Calm down!" Ian whispered harshly, holding his hand firmly on her mouth even though one of Thalia's sharp fingernails pierced his hand painfully, surely drawing blood. "I've come to take you away from what could be a fate worse than death!"

Thalia was recalling how gentle Ian had been earlier when he had rescued her from the shark. Was it meant for him to save her from a human shark as well? From Paul Hathaway? Surely she could trust him now!

Yet, all that kept coming to mind was the safety of her sister!

Confusing Ian, she fought harder. He knew that she recognized him. How could she think that he could want anything but what was best for her? Surely by now she knew the sort of man she was married to. What woman could love Paul Hathaway?

"Thalia, I see that you aren't going to leave willingly," Ian grumbled, pulling a neckerchief from his rear pocket. "Though you may hate me for forcing myself on you like this, I have no choice but to do it. Please calm down. I only want what is best for you."

Thalia had a brief moment when her mouth was free and she could have screamed, but something kept her from it. Then that moment passed and Ian had gagged her. Tears rolled down her cheeks as he took a rope from his pocket and tied her wrists together before her.

"Ah, come on now," Ian whispered. A woman's tears always touched his heart. "Don't cry, luv." He smoothed tears away from her flesh with his thumb. "Soon you'll be safe from the scoundrel Paul Hathaway. When you left England and set out for Australia you surely did not wish for such company as his."

Sobbing against her gag, Thalia's eyes pleaded up at Ian. It was too late now for her to ask him to take her away with him so that she could be his wife or housemaid. Everything had changed the moment she had breathed her sister's name in front of Paul Hathaway. It was then that he had known he could hold onto her forever, for he had only to remind her about her sister's safety and she would be at his mercy—always!

Yes, Paul had planned it well. Now with Ian so close, Thalia wanting to lunge into his arms for protection, yet she could do nothing but fight her feelings—and him.

She pounded Ian's chest with her bound hands as he swept her up into his arms and began carrying her across the courtyard.

"Give up, Thalia," Ian whispered, leaning close to her face, her lips only a whisper away beneath the gag. "Damn it, it's going to be hard enough to carry you across this moonlit courtyard without getting shot, let alone have you wrestling me all the while."

Thalia's eyes locked with his, momentarily taken offguard by the feelings that had assailed her when she first saw him. Oh, up so close, was not he even more handsome? Beneath the thin layer of whiskers, his face was bronzed by the sun and his lips were full, his jaw tight in his determination to steal her away from Paul.

She so badly wanted to ask him what his plans were for her after he had taken her away from here.

Could he possibly even intend to marry her? If only she were free to go with him and spend the rest of her life loving him.

But she was not!

Torn with feelings, she looked away from him. But again her concern for her sister won out. She struggled a moment longer, then was surprised when Ian finally placed her feet to the ground.

"Now," he said bluntly. "I hope that makes you happy."

She gave him a puzzled stare, then turned to take this opportunity to run away from him.

"Aw, Thalia," Ian groaned, weaving his fingers frustratingly through his hair. "Why can't you trust me?"

He bolted after her and she soon found that his long legs were more than a match for hers. Again she felt herself being swept up into powerful arms and this time slung over Ian's shoulder as though she were no more than a sack of potatoes. She pounded her fists against his back as he began running with her again beneath the vast sprays of moonlight.

"I didn't know you were such a hellcat," Ian complained, stiffening his back to her blows. "God, Thalia, stop it. Can't you see that nothing you do will make me change my mind? I'll never return you to this damnable ranch."

Thalia fussed at him behind her gag, yet was glad when he set her across the fence to her feet. She turned and gasped when she found the dark eyes of an Aborigine looking at her, then grew cold inside when she discovered the dreadful short-barreled rifle held in his hands, aimed at her. She backed away from Hawke, trembling. One slip of the finger and she would be dead!

"Don't be afraid of Hawke," Ian said, climbing over the fence. He gently removed Thalia's gag and untied her wrists. "He's my friend and he will be yours, also, if you will allow it."

Thalia could not take her eyes from the carbine. "Tell him to turn that thing away from me," she pleaded. "Surely he has no knowledge of firearms. Don't the Aborigine usually fight with spears?"

"Well, luv, you are soon to find out that Hawke isn't just any Aborigine," Ian said smoothly, patting his dark-skinned friend on the back. "I've taught him several of my bad habits. Shooting a carbine is one of them." He eased the carbine from Hawke's grasp.

Thalia glared up at Ian. "You are also teaching him the art of kidnapping?" she snapped.

"Well, yes, perhaps," Ian said, chuckling. He cocked a hip and leaned his weight on it. "Whatever is necessary, luv. Whatever is necessary."

"Take me back to the house," Thalia ordered, wavering beneath Ian's firm stare, suddenly aware of her thin attire. Without the protection of the shawl that she had dropped during her scuffle with Ian, the moon beaming its silver light down upon her left nothing to the imagination. She hugged herself awkwardly, then dropped her hands to her side, knowing that no matter what she did, she was unable to hide herself from Ian or his friend.

"Take you back? Not on your life," Ian said flatly, walking past her to slip his carbine into its gunboot. "And we'd best be on our way if you don't want to witness several carbines in action at once. When Paul discovers you gone—"

"When he does he'll come after you," Thalia interrupted, tilting her chin stubbornly.

Ian took a step toward her and gazed steadily down into her eyes, avoiding looking at her ravishing curves and dips beneath the thin nightly apparel. He needed to keep his senses.

"Is that what you want, luv?" he asked, his voice soft, full of caring.

Thalia was at a sudden loss for words, knowing exactly what she wanted. She wanted Ian! To be with him forever! But she could not reveal this to him.

"Just let me go," she pleaded.

Ian grabbed her by the waist and lifted her into the saddle on his stallion. "No," he said flatly. He mounted his steed and held Thalia around the waist before him. "Now I suggest that you sit still or you might take a spill that would sting more than your pretty little fanny. We've a ways to go through the scrub. Just pretend you're on a tour of this lovely land, and the journey to Hawke's village won't be as unbearable for you."

Thalia paled. She turned to look at Ian. "You're taking me to an Aborigine village?" she gasped.

"That's our destination, all right, luv," Ian said, wheeling his horse around. He rode away in a steady gallop, Hawke riding alongside him.

The fight was gone from Thalia. She sighed deeply and relaxed against Ian as he guided his mount across the Murray River, the western boundary of the scrub. Beyond, the moonlight revealed a hanging brown haze through which she could see the outline of mountains, the scrub's northern wall.

As the stallion rode onward in an easy bounding gait over the ocean of land, a flight of white corellas threw a veil across the moon. A big red kangaroo, suddenly alert, bounded into a shadow and disappeared.

There was a deep silence.

Flipping the stub of his cigar on the ground and grinding it out with the heel of his boot, Ridge Wagner glared at a small, squat cabin with faint lamplight glowing at the window. He looked slowly around him, seeing the many tethered horses, then looked back at the cabin from which could be heard an occasional low drone of voices. In his mind he was going over what Ian had said about Honora having been abducted. His jaw tightened at the thought of her being sold in the underground slave trade.

Patting his holstered revolver, which he wore only at night on those occasions when he joined Paul Hathaway's bushranger activities, Ridge shoved the door to the cabin open. His cat-green eyes narrowed on Paul, who was at a desk, pointing to a map spread out before him. His gang stood around, obediently watching and listening.

"Tonight's caper shouldn't take long," Paul said, now folding the map and placing it in his vest pocket. "The gold shipment isn't guarded enough to discourage our attack." He leaned back in his chair and placed his fingertips together before him as he scanned his eyes over his men. "Do I hear any arguments? Or are you all ready to ride with me again and get richer?"

Ridge nudged the men aside and stepped up to the desk. He leaned his full weight on his palms as he rested them against the desktop, his eyes level with Paul's. "So it's a gold shipment tonight," he drawled. "You're not interested in abducting more natives for the slave trade?"

Paul's smug smile faded. He met Ridge's steady stare, his body stiff. "That's what I said, isn't it?" he commented back. "If you have a complaint, let's hear it."

Ridge didn't flinch. His voice was a hiss as he spoke. "You know that I joined up with you thinkin' all you were interested in was the gold shipments," he said. "I got tired of drifting and bein' poor, and the idea of gettin' rich quick appealed to me." He leaned closer to Paul. "You said you'd leave the Mount Gambier tribe of Aborigines alone. Did you lie? Or did you raid their village on a night I didn't show up to ride with you?"

Paul smiled slowly at Ridge. "What makes you think I may have?" he asked, a nervous twitch tugging at his left cheek.

"Because it's so low-down, I'd suspect you over anyone else," Ridge said, straightening his back and towering over Paul. His eyes grew haunted as he thought of Honora. He hadn't gone to see her since he had joined the bushranger gang. She deserved better than him.

"If you think so unkindly of me, what're you hanging around for?" Paul asked, rising from his chair. "Better yet, why don't you come to my ranch and check things over firsthand?" He reached a hand across the desk and placed it on Ridge's shoulder. "Why not come and stay at my ranch? I'm shorthanded. I can't trust any of the sonsofbitches who work for me there. Be one of my permanent station hands. You'd give my place class. Everyone who knows you respects you." He chuckled. "Even if you are just a *swaggie*."

Ridge reached his hand to Paul's and lifted it from his shoulder. "You're purposely avoiding answering my question," he growled. "You know that I can tolerate you just long enough to take occasional midnight runs with you for gold. Never could I stand seeing you every day." He glared at Paul again. "Now tell me, Paul, did you, or did you not, raid Hawke's village and take his wife and daughter away?"

Paul's eyes narrowed. He glanced around at his men, who had stood in stoney silence listening, their hands resting on their weapons at their hips.

Then he looked at Ridge and smiled widely.

"Hell, no," he said, stepping from behind his desk. He slung an arm around Ridge's shoulder. "I wouldn't do anything as stupid-ass as that. I gave you my word, didn't I?" He patted Ridge's shoulder. "Ridge, I'm going to change your feelings about me. Just you wait and see."

Ridge eyed Paul warily, then glared at Kenneth Ozier, who was standing in the shadows smiling crookedly at him.

"And another thing," Ridge said. "You'd best keep your eye on that lad over there. He was in *Joe's Pub* today. He almost got in a fracas with Ian Lavery. Now I don't think that's too smart, do you? If Ian or anyone else got the best of Kenneth, don't you know that he'd shout off his goddamn mouth about the gang to save his own hide?"

Paul kneaded his chin as he gazed at Kenneth. "Seems a smart enough fellow to me," he said. He shrugged. "I think he knows his place and where his loyalties lie." He looked slowly at Ridge. "The same as you, Ridge. You enjoy the profits made by bushranging too much to spoil it with loose talk— or worries of women, especially those with black skins."

Paul walked quickly away from Ian, his gang members following him outside to their horses. Ridge sauntered on outside, and as he mounted his strawberry roan he watched Paul mount his own steed. Paul had seemed convincing enough. And why should Ridge blame Paul? There were many bushranger gangs mixed up in the illegal slave trade!

As Ridge rode away with the gang, his gut twisted painfully at the thought of Honora living the life of a slave, only God knowing where.

Then his thoughts switched to Ian, his good and

trusting friend. If Ian ever found out about Ridge's occasional night activities, there would be hell to pay.

Kenneth rode up next to Ridge, his face lined with anger. "I didn't like you talkin' about me to the boss," he grumbled. "Don't you ever do that again. Or by God, Ridge, I'll find a way to make you pay."

CHAPTER SIX

HOURS HAD PASSED, MANY MILES HAD BEEN TRAVeled. His arm around Thalia's waist, anchoring her against him, Ian rode onward, leaving behind high sand dunes that had been shaped and formed by a constant, relentless wind. In this part of the scrub, the red, sandy loam produced mainly oddly shaped, dwarf eucalyptuses called *mallee*.

And then something else emerged from this blue-white hour of night—a reflection of orange in the dark sky, the signs of campfires up ahead.

"We're almost there, luv," Ian said, seeing the signs in the heavens. "Then we'll have us a little talk about your future."

"Yes, and so we shall," Thalia said, giving him an angry stare, her face bitter with fury. "And, kind sir, mine will not include you."

She glanced down at the golden ring on her finger, its deceit like a band tightening around her heart. It mocked everything that she had been taught about life—about what marriage vows meant to a woman, how cherished a wedding band was to a woman even as she lay on her death bed, how one should always tell the truths, for if one lie breathed across one's lips, it begat another and another.

She now knew that lies were sometimes necessary, no matter the web in which she would become ensnared. She was already trapped in something she did not understand, and which she feared with every beat of her heart!

"You will return me to Paul Hathaway's ranch," she told him, her voice thin and almost too revealing. She lifted her hand so that the ring was in the line of Ian's vision. "You see, I have a reason to want to return. I am Paul's wife."

The moonlight danced on the gold wedding band. Ian stared at it, the truth hurting him to the core. He looked away from it, envisioning Thalia and Paul in a lover's embrace. The thought made a strangling sort of bitterness rise up into his throat.

With fire in his eyes, Ian glared at Thalia. "You wasted no time, did you?" he accused. "You cared not even the sort of man you would be bedding with for the rest of your life. It's the vows that you want to brag about, is it not? Does it make you proud that you were chosen so quickly among the throng of women who arrive daily on Australia's shores? Is it something that you wish to boast about to your grandchildren?"

Ian's tongue-lashing caused Thalia to blanch. He

painted too sordid a picture of her, as though she were a conniving, sorry whore!

"How dare you speak to me in such a way," she said, hating it when her voice broke. "How dare you just sweep me away in the middle of the night without even asking me if this was what I wanted. Who are you to try and make my destiny yours? If you think so little of me, why do you even bother?"

Ian gazed at her, his face still and thoughtful. Something was amiss in her protestations, for he had not just imagined that her voice gave way while she had been trying to scold him. There was much that she was not saying. It was in her eyes—a quiet, sad sort of pleading.

Yet she was still adamant in her desire to return to her husband. How would her behavior change after she knew the common suspicions about Paul Hathaway? If only Ian had positive proof of Paul's illegal activities, then Thalia would surely turn her back on the villain forever!

Thalia looked cautiously around her as Ian drew rein in the midst of Aborigine activity, dismounted, then lifted her from the stallion. Tense, her gaze moved slowly around her. In the flat, gray sand behind a rough, half-circle hedge of broken bushes, nothing more than a crude windbreak, the Aborigines sat around an open fire, the moon's silver light glancing off their heads as if they were polished bronze.

Beyond the fire were a few bark *humpies*, houses constructed of simple strips of gum tree bark draped across tea-tree beams. From their doors peered several Aborigine children, giggling as they returned Thalia's stare. The glow from the fire revealed that none of the children was clothed, not even the girls whose breasts were blossoming into those of a woman.

Embarrassed, Thalia looked back at the adult Aborigines as Ian took her elbow and began guiding her toward a *humpie* that had no children standing in the door. Filled with wonder at these dark-skinned people, Thalia noted quickly their activities. None had greeted her and Ian, not even Hawke. Hawke had mingled quickly with his people, kneeling down among them in quiet conversation with one or another. Though they had only the light from the moon and fire, most were busy. One group was intently fashioning spears, paring them down tediously with the sharpened edges of stones. One of the patient artisans was holding a spear delicately in the fingers of one hand, at eye level, to test its balance.

Another group was busy shaping stone spearheads, chipping away at their work with other pieces of stone, or rubbing the spearhead along a larger stone to abrade it to a point.

At one end of the half circle of bushes, a middle-aged woman squatted. Suckling at one breast was a boy who appeared to be at least four years old. A dingo pup nursed at the other breast.

Startled, Thalia gasped and her footsteps faltered.

Ian followed her gaze. He smiled down at her. "Ay, I am sure you are shocked by such a sight," he said, guiding her inside a bark house, where a small fire burned in a firepit at the center. "The Aborigine women are generous with their milk because it will benefit them to keep the dingo pup alive, to be a part of their family.''

"Good Lord, do they go to this length just to have a pet?" Thalia asked, stunned at the thought.

Ian motioned toward a woven-grass mat. "Sit by the fire,'' he encouraged her softly. "This is my private hut, constructed before I came for you tonight.''

His gaze moved over her, his insides becoming inflamed anew at the sight of what the transparent garment she wore revealed to him. No more could be revealed, even if she were naked.

Thalia could tell that Ian was finding it hard not to look at her body through her thin apparel and she was torn between anger and humiliation. She eased down onto the mat and tried to position her arms so that her breasts were only partially exposed and she gathered the nightgown together so that the folds hid her thighs.

Ian removed his gunbelt and laid it on the floor behind him, then sat down beside Thalia. "The Aborigine women do not offer their breasts to the dingo pups out of mere kindness,'' he said, almost laughing at how comical Thalia looked as she sat in the most awkward position while trying to hide her bodily curves from him. He kept a straight face, making sure not to look at her, but into the fire instead. "That particular pup was brought to the camp to be reared and trained, like a game dog to help in tracking and hunting the tribe's foods.''

Ian glanced over at Thalia. He found her gazing at him, then frowned when she looked quickly away. "Luv, the little boy is the lucky one,'' he said. "He is the survivor of twins. The other, a girl, had her brains dashed to pulp against a gum tree the day after she was born."

Thalia flinched and placed a hand to her throat. She looked at Ian, mortified. "How could you be so devoted to such a people as these?" she gasped. "Why, they are nothing but uncivilized savages! How could they kill their own child? How?"

"Luv, it is not for me to condemn these people for their tribal laws that have been handed down through generation and generation," he said gently. "The slaying of their daughter was in accordance with a simple tribal law that either the last born of twins, or the girl of the pair, should be killed by either parent."

"How ghastly!" Thalia said, shuddering. "How inhumane!"

"Aye, and so it seems," Ian said, glancing down at her wedding band. "But I am sure, if questioned, these dark-skinned people would say that many of our habits and customs are just as questionable."

"Nothing could compare with taking the life of one's own child due to some ridiculous, ancient custom," Thalia said, flipping her hair back from her shoulders. "Nothing!"

"Though you are adamant in your feelings about their tribal law, they are, in truth, a very gentle people," Ian said, reaching for a log and placing it on the fire. "They cherish their surviving children. They have long, lasting love matches. It is common for a husband and wife to live out their lives together, faithful and loyal to the end. And when the first one dies, the other follows soon afterwards, fading away from the mere lack of a desire to live."

He reached for Thalia's hand, wincing when she

jerked it away from him. "Can you tell me that you have a love as true for Paul, your husband?" he asked, his voice low. "If he should die, do you truly feel that you would soon follow for the simple lack of a wish to live with your loss?"

Thalia's and Ian's eyes met and locked again. She swallowed hard. She so wanted to blurt out the truths to him, to tell him that she did not feel safe except while with him! She wanted to beg him to make all things right for her.

But she could not. She kept hearing Paul's threats to send orders to England to have Viada killed!

Ian was astute enough about people's feelings to see that Thalia was wrestling with something deep within her heart and soul. "Thalia, you did not answer my question," he said, wanting to draw her into his arms, to comfort her. "Is it because you are afraid to? You know that you can never love a man like Paul Hathaway. Admit to me that you made a mistake by marrying him so quickly. Tell me that you don't love him—that you never could!"

Thalia could not take anymore of his persistent badgerings about her marriage to Paul. Sobbing, she jumped to her feet and rushed toward the door. But she was not fast enough. Ian was there, his arm around her waist, stopping her.

Breathless, she turned and looked up at him, reveling in the magnificent strength of his arms as he held her close. It was in his expression that he was a breath away from kissing her, but she could not allow it. If he kissed her, all of her senses and reason would be stolen away, and she might confess all that she shouldn't to him in one rush.

"Please," she murmured. "Let me go."

With a tender touch, Ian smoothed a lock of her hair back from her eyes. "I so badly want to kiss you," he said huskily. "How could I not? You're so damn beautiful."

Her heart racing, telling her just the opposite of her brain, Thalia placed her hands to his chest and began gently shoving him away from her. "I am a married woman," she said, the words a treachery to her feelings. "Or do you make it a habit of kissing women who are already claimed, body and soul, by another man?"

The words cut at Ian's insides, as though someone had surely stabbed him repeatedly in the abdomen, so sharply that he took a wide step away from Thalia as though she were a hot coal that had burned him. "I tend to forget," he said hoarsely.

"Now will you please return me to my ranch?" Thalia asked, fighting back tears. "My husband will become alarmed by my absence."

"We can't leave just yet," Ian said. He took her by the elbow and urged her to sit down again beside the fire. "Though I know that you are married to Paul Hathaway, I have brought you here to tell you some suspicions I have about him and, by God, I refuse to take you back to him until I have said my piece!"

He glanced toward the door, hearing Hawke's voice suddenly speaking loudly to his villagers in his native tongue. "Also, Hawke has things to tell his people," he said, sitting down beside Thalia. "We must give him the time that is needed and then I must speak to them. They are troubled now and only he and I seem to be able to set their minds at ease."

"You?" Thalia asked, quirking an eyebrow.

"Aye," Ian said, moving to his feet. He leaned an arm against the top of the door and gazed out at his friend whose voice was rising in intensity as he spoke, so filled with rage about everything that had happened to his people, and fearing that which could happen. "They look to me as a sort of link to their future because I am always there, their advocate." He swung around and faced Thalia, his face haunted. "God. What if I let them down?

"As I feel I have let you down," he said as he sat back down beside her. He looked at her intensely. He touched a hand to her cheek, his insides paining when he felt her wince at his touch. "Luv, had I spoken up for you sooner, would you have chosen me over Paul Hathaway?"

Thalia's heart skipped a beat. Her throat went dry. Her pulse raced. Now would be the perfect time to tell him the truth! Did he not show sincere feelings for her? Could he make all wrongs right? Oh, could he?

She blushed as his eyes trailed down her body. Her breath was stolen when his hand followed his gaze and rested on a breast, cupping its heaviness in the palm of his hand. She bit her lower lip and closed her eyes. She could hardly bear the wondrous feelings of passion flooding her at his mere touch!

Oh, but what was she to do? He wanted her, and she was not free! She had to pretend that she belonged to another man—a scheming, evil man.

Knowing that she could not turn back the hands

of time and undo what had already been done, Thalia scurried to her feet. She turned her back to Ian, her breathing coming in short snatches. "You did not come for me at Odum House," she said softly, her voice quavering. "Paul did. And I am now his wife."

His insides burning for Thalia, Ian's rage against Paul building, he bolted to his feet. He placed a hand firmly on Thalia's arm and turned her to face him.

"Now you listen to me," he said. "It doesn't matter that you are wearing his ring, you have had time to share a bed with him only once. But that need be the only time! Stay with me. I shall see that you receive the proper papers that will state that you are no longer married to that cad. Just listen to what I have to say about him and then you will be ready to tell me that this is what you want."

"Nothing will alter my decision to be his wife," Thalia said, her own words like knives piercing her heart. In Ian she had found someone she could love forever. In his eyes she could tell that he felt the same about her. But it was a love to be denied. It just was not in their destiny to be together.

"Damn it, will you just listen to what I have to say?" Ian fumed. "Then if you still say that you want to be with that man, so be it! I would never keep a woman against her will, although I cannot say the same about Paul Hathaway. There have been rumors about him that women have fled from his ranch and have never been heard from again. Now I would wager a bet that those women had been held against their will before they found a way to escape. I would wager that Paul sent his men after the women and killed them for escaping.''

Thalia paled and a weakness encompassed her as she vividly recalled Paul's threats. She knew that what Ian was saying was true, yet she could not speak up and tell him everything! It was as though Paul were there even now with a pistol pointed at her and her sister's heads, smiling wickedly from one to the other. It would be so easy for a man like him to pull the trigger.

"Furthermore," Ian said icily, "though in the city Paul Hathaway appears to be a respectable, God-fearing man, it is suspected that he is the head of a bushranger gang. Thalia, those who are raiding the wagon trains are not only stealing and killing from them, they are mutilating people's bodies. Can you now say that you wish to live with a man who is suspected of stooping to such horrendous deeds as these?"

Thalia's knees grew weak with fear, truly understanding now that what Paul Hathaway had threatened her with could happen. His threats against Viada were real. Now, more than ever, she saw how important it was to pretend to be loyal to a man she not only despised, but feared with every fiber of her being! She knew now that she was dealing with a madman, a beast whose insane brain was surely so brutalized by crime and hate that no human consideration could ever penetrate it.

Yet she must pretend that she cared for him enough to live with him. She must perform better than any actor on a stage.

Or she and her sister would die!

"I do not believe one word of that," she forced herself to say. She tilted her chin stubbornly, hoping that she could hold back the tears she wanted to be shed for herself and Viada. "You said that you would not hold me against my will. You said that you would return me to my husband. Well, Ian, I am asking you to. Now. If I am lucky, he will not have discovered my absence. I am sure that Australia's courts hand out punishments to men who abduct women from their homes in the middle of the night."

Silently, Thalia prayed that Paul would not return home before she was safe and sound in her bed again—not only for her own sake and her sister's, but for Ian's did she pray for this. It would not be the courts who would hand down a punishment to Ian for what he had done. It would be Paul. And he surely did not have one merciful bone in his body!

Ian sucked in a great gulp of air, not wanting to believe what Thalia had just asked of him. After hearing what Paul really was, could she still wish to be his wife? Was she daft? No woman in her right mind would want to be returned to the arms of a man who was guilty of so many unspoken terrors! In the end, she could become one of those women whom Paul brutalized!

Yet Ian had given his word to her that he would return her if she wished!

He glanced down at her wedding band. Surely that was the only reason Thalia was asking to be returned to Paul. She was married and was loyal to her commitment. She was taking, quite literally, the words spoken in marriage ceremonies—that the man and woman are wed "until death do us part!"

"So be it," Ian said, grabbing her roughly into his arms, his insides melting as her breasts crushed against his chest. "I'll return you to your husband." He wove his fingers through her hair and drew her lips close. "But I have something to give you first. When you are in your husband's arms, think of this!"

His mouth seized hers in a hard, long kiss, his tongue probing her lips apart. Then he released her and silently looked down at her, his eyes charged with dark emotion.

Stunned anew by the passion that had just been exchanged between them, Thalia stepped away from Ian, touching her lips with her fingertips. She was so overcome with rapture that she felt lightheaded.

Yet she had to deny herself these wondrous feelings.

She had to deny herself Ian!

"I will take you back to your husband shortly," Ian declared, breaking his eye contact with Thalia long enough to reach for his gunbelt. He swung it around his waist and fastened it. "I must go out and add my support to what Hawke has already told his people." He firmed his jaw. "At least they listen to me when I talk." He paused, then added —"And they believe me."

He turned on a heel and left the hut.

Thalia swayed, then emitted a quivering sigh as she moved to the door and leaned against it. Her nightgown fluttered at her ankles as she listened intensely to Hawke, trying to make out his native language, yet unable to.

Then her insides grew warm when Ian stepped up beside Hawke, placed an affectionate arm around his shoulders, and began talking to the natives. Thalia was glad that he was speaking in English. What he was saying, and how he said it—so filled with concern for these dark-skinned people—touched Thalia deep into the core of herself. She listened to Ian speak to them of their past sorrows, and of the trouble that was facing them now. He explained that he had seen it in his own country of America—the dark-skinned people being treated as though they were not of the human race. After seeing so much injustice in America, he had become determined to do his best to set things right in Australia when he arrived in this country with his mother.

Thus far, the struggle had all been uphill. Perhaps it never would be better. But he was trying his damnedest to see that it was!

He looked over at Thalia. His eyes locked with hers. "Sometimes there is no way to alter the past, or the future," he shouted at the Aborigines. "There are so often too many obstacles in the way. And for the most part these obstacles are greedy, vicious men who do not look past their own needs—who are willing to kill anyone or anything to get what they want. Even innocent women."

Thalia grew cold inside, knowing that his words were meant for her ears only. And, oh, she understood that what he said was true! That he was speaking solely of Paul Hathaway!

Yet she was honor-bound to make sure nothing happened to her sister. She had promised Viada the world.

Viada would have it!

Thalia lowered her eyes, yet still listened.

Ian began moving around the group of natives, shaking hands with one and then the other, or patting the small children on the tops of their heads. "I know that the season of the swan's egg is near," he said hoarsely. "I understand your fear of your march to the sea so that you can participate in your yearly celebration. The swan's eggs are your favorite food and you want to feel safe gathering them along the beaches of the Indian Ocean. It is always a time of great rejoicing—the season of the swan's egg! Hawke has already given you his word that you will make the journey safely this year. I, too, will be near. You will gather your eggs! You will have cause to celebrate!"

So moved by the scene was she that tears streamed from Thalia's eyes. In Ian she saw a man who was gentle, who was revered by the Aborigines. Surely she should trust him to help her with her own problem, yet Paul's threat was too real to be ignored. She could not take the chance now, or perhaps ever.

Ian came to Thalia and took her by the hands. "It is time to go," he said. "That is, unless you have changed your mind."

Thalia looked solemnly up at him. "I haven't," she murmured. She followed him to his horse and let him lift her into the saddle. She glanced down at Hawke, who remained with his people.

Then she looked straight ahead, feeling as though she was being returned to the pits of hell.

The journey back to the ranch was made in silence. Fear filled Thalia as the sky began to lighten overhead. She had been gone for too long. Soon it would be day and there would be no way Ian could return her without Paul's knowing. Surely Paul had already returned and had discovered her absence!

She looked around her as the sun became visible along the horizon. In the crimson morning light, she felt too vulnerable, as though the whole world were seeing her in Ian's arms on his stallion. She was glad when they began making their way along the Murray River, and Ian soon reined in his steed at the fence that outlined the Hathaway Ranch.

Dismounting, Ian lifted Thalia from the saddle. "This could be a bit risky," he said, frowning. He patted his Colt revolvers. "Hawke stayed behind with his people. I've only my own skills with firearms to depend on this time."

"If Paul is home . . ." Thalia worried aloud, gazing at the old mission.

"If Paul is home and he comes shooting for me, that could solve your problem, couldn't it?" he asked, looking down at her, his reckless black eyes flashing. "You'd never have me to worry about again. You'd have Paul Hathaway, free and clear."

"No," Thalia gasped, placing a hand to her throat. "That is not what I want at all. Ian—"

Thalia stopped in mid-sentence, having come

110

close to confessing her true feelings to him.

"You were saying?" Ian asked, leaning down into her face, again trying his damnedest not to look at the dips and curves beneath her revealing silken attire. In daylight, her body was taking on a silken luster, so beautiful it nearly took his breath away.

"I must get back to my room," Thalia whispered. "I've been gone for too long as it is."

"I'll see to it that you get there all right," Ian said, peering toward the house, checking for any signs of activity.

"No," Thalia said. "There is no need. I can get there quite easily on my own. In fact, there is less danger in one person running across the courtyard. If I am caught, I shall say that I have just been out for a morning stroll."

Ian laughed throatily, his gaze sweeping over her. Her translucent gown whipped in the breeze. "And I am sure you would be believed," he said. He picked her up into his arms and set her bodily over the fence. "No. I'd best go with you."

Thinking of what Paul might do to Ian should he be caught caused panic to grip Thalia's insides. "No," she said, grabbing Ian's hand. "Nothing can happen to you. Nothing!"

Ian's jaw loosened and his mouth went slack with surprise. "You do care, don't you?" he gasped.

"Just leave," Thalia cried. "Now!"

She turned, lifted the soft fabric of her night-gown up into her arms and began running away from him. He stood his ground, stunned not so much by what she had said, but in the way she had said it. She did care!

Yet, she was willing to return to Paul Hathaway's bed!

Would he ever understand?

Watching her approach the mission, Ian patted a revolver nervously, then sighed with relief when she opened a door and slipped inside.

Then his insides grew clammy cold when he saw the dust of horsemen in the distance riding toward the ranch. "Hathaway!" he whispered.

He looked up at Thalia's room. When he saw her standing there, just inside an opened French door, he breathed much more easily and gave her a mock salute.

At least for the moment she was safe.

He mounted his stallion and rode briskly away.

CHAPTER SEVEN

THE DAY PASSED BY AS THOUGH IN SLOW MOTION for Thalia who was finding it hard to forget the previous night with Ian. How could she forget his maddening kiss? The strength of his arms as they held her to his muscled chest?

How could she forget the spinning sensation that had flooded her whole body, threatening to push all reason from her mind while she was with him?

When she thought of him she felt near to going over the edge into sheer ecstasy!

All day long, Thalia had struggled with these thoughts of Ian, moving mechanically through the old rooms of the mission, familiarizing herself with the furnishings which were for the most part plush and expensive, and with the chores that would be expected of her that the servants did not have the knowledge or skills to perform.

In Paul's library, she strolled slowly past row after row of leather-bound books, wondering about this man who seemed to have multiple personalities. He was intelligent. He was well-mannered. He was well-dressed. He was diplomatic—even enough to have fooled Daisy Odum!

But those who knew Paul Hathaway intimately surely realized that all of these character traits were a well-planned facade, for the man had learned very well the art of hiding behind all of these better qualities—in truth, he was surely a man put on this earth by the devil!

From a point high on the walls over the bookcases, stained glass windows cast their myriad of colors downward in hundreds of points of colorful light. Thalia turned away from the books and gazed at a massive oak desk that sat in the center of the room upon an oval braided rug. She eyed the desk warily, seeing many journals stacked high on the top, and loose, yellowed papers strewn about.

Her heart skipped a beat when she kept her gaze locked on the journals. Perhaps they revealed some of Paul's illegal activities?

She frowned, discounting this theory. He was not the sort of man who would leave anything lying around that might incriminate him.

Her gaze moved to the drawers.

She eyed them questioningly, wondering if she could discover any of Paul's secrets within them.

Today, Thalia had chosen from the chest in her room a cotton dress with a long, flowing skirt and a faint iris design embroidered on the lowswept bodice. The skirt of the dress rustled about her ankles as she moved determinedly to the desk.

Before proceeding with her detective game this late afternoon, she looked toward the closed door of the library and listened for approaching footsteps. When she heard none, she tried one desk drawer, and then, more frantically, another.

"I should have known," she whispered, stepping away from the desk angrily. "Locked. Every last one of them is locked."

She plopped down on a sofa that faced a stone fireplace and stared at the cold, gray ashes. Even if she had discovered something that could be used against him, what would she have been able to do with it? She could never tell anyone anything about Paul Hathaway. She was a prisoner. A virtual prisoner.

The tattoo of horse's hooves from somewhere outside drew Thalia quickly to her feet. She left the library in a rush and went to the parlor window. Drawing back a sheer curtain, she watched several horsemen riding away from the ranch, Paul at the lead.

"He just comes and goes all of the time and never says where," Thalia whispered to herself. "I wonder how long he'll be gone this time."

After Paul and his men were out of sight, she felt a reprieve of sorts. While Paul was gone, she was free to do as she wished—except escape. She craned her neck to see the Murray River and the scrub. In the splash of moonlight last evening, while she and Ian rode away from Hathaway Ranch, she had seen lovely flowers growing near the river. It would be such a delight to pick some of them and place them in a vase in her room. Surely they would cheer her up when she started feeling so alone, so empty. . . .

"I shall!" Thalia declared to herself, beaming. Walking briskly, she left the house. Lifting her skirt from her ankles, she rushed down the steps of the narrow front porch, then stopped with alarm when a burly, pock-faced man whirled around out of the shadows and into her path.

"Where you think you're goin', ma'am?" he asked. He folded his arms threateningly across his chest and spat a wad of chewing tobacco over his left shoulder. "I've been ordered to keep an eye on you." He smiled crookedly, revealing yellow, jagged teeth. "Now I have no trouble with that. It's much more pleasurable than ridin' a horse out in the scrub."

Thalia was very aware of his size and the brute strength such a man must possess, and her courage wavered. But only for a moment. She had to get away for a while or she thought she just might lose her mind. She had to fight back, or forever be at the mercy of not only Paul Hathaway, but his men as well.

"Step aside," she said, placing her hands on her hips. She looked up at the man and dared him with a set stare. "No matter what my husband says, I have the right to some privacy. If you do not comply, sir, I shall somehow see to your dismissal."

The man threw his head back in an outrageously loud laugh, startling Thalia from her head to her toe.

But she was not to be dissuaded that easily!

"I shall!" she reasserted, holding her ground, though every fiber of her being was afraid of this burly man. A thought came to her. There was one true defense where a wife was concerned. She would use the false title of 'wife' now for all that it was worth.

Taking a step closer to the man, Thalia placed a hand to her bodice. "Either you step aside or I shall rip my dress and swear to my husband that you raped me," she threatened, her eyes flashing. "Now what shall it be? Rape? Or a moment of freedom while I take a walk down by the river to pick a few flowers?"

Thalia knew that she was taking a chance—not only with the man, but also with Paul. Paul might not even care if one of his men had his way with her. Or it could enrage him, if he did not want his men to know that he cared so little for his wife.

Surely his men were not in on the charade!

Surely they did not know about the fake wedding vows, or the fake reason for her wearing the wedding band!

She felt a great sense of victory when she watched the man's eyes become filled with fear, utterly paling over her threat. She boldly took another step toward him when he took a step away from her. "Well?" she persisted. "What shall it be?" She cast her eyes upward. The sun was lowering in the sky. "Speak up now, for I will soon lose the daylight. I do not cherish the thought of wandering alone that close to the scrub after dark. I wish to go and pick my flowers and return soon to my house."

The man made a wild, loose gesture with a hand

toward the river. "Go on, then, damn it," he said. "I ain't one to argue with a woman of spirit. Damn it all to hell, I don't want to bend under the lash because of a rape I didn't commit."

Thalia's hands slipped down to her sides. "Bend under the lash?" she asked softly. "Do you mean . . . ?"

She did not get the opportunity to finish her question. The man spun around and walked hurriedly away from her. She stood watching him until he went into the bunkhouse and slammed the door after him. A chill soared through her. The man was afraid of Paul Hathaway. Paul surely whipped those who were disobedient to him—not only the Aborigine slaves, but also the men under his employ as well.

Would he use the whip on her if he ever became enraged enough with her?

The thought made her feel sick all over.

But, still, even that did not dissuade her from her planned escapade. She lifted her skirt into her arms and began running toward the river. When she reached the fence she scaled it awkwardly, flinching at the sound of the tearing of cotton as she finally got a foothold on the ground on the other side. She looked down and saw the hem in the front hanging by a thread, but shrugged her shoulders. There were many more dresses in the chest. She went on her way, lured by the beautiful trees and flowers that lined the Murray River.

Thalia was in awe of the towering, majestic red gum trees that were shading her moment of solitude. They were beautiful with their red and cream

118

trunks, and their thin, blue-gray eucalyptus-scented leaves.

Moving from tree to tree, she marveled at how some of their trunks extruded bright-red blobs of gum, like raspberry gumdrops. She had read in a book that these mottled-bark eucalyptus could live as long as fifteen thousand years, but that a spring flood every two or three years was essential for the germination of their seeds.

Too much water was as critical as too little, as Thalia learned on her journey from Adelaide to Paul's ranch. She had seen countless haunting graveyards of dead trees standing in great swampy areas.

A strong gust of wind bowed the pale, knee-high grass through which Thalia was walking. Her auburn hair whipped around her face, the ends stinging her cheeks. Brushing her wisps of hair aside, she inhaled deeply and searched with her eyes, for with the wind had come a sweet, aromatic fragrance of flowers.

Eagerly, Thalia followed the scent, thinking that these were the flowers she would take to her room. Their lovely fragrance would lull her to sleep tonight, even if the world outside her room was still wrought with danger, pain, and sadnesses!

She gasped when she found the source of the scent. Above her, the flowers of the acacia, a wattle tree known to her back in England as the mimosa, were as though a thousand sunbursts clung to the limbs of the tree. They were bright yellow, their scent peppery-sweet.

Stretching her back and arms, she tried to reach

a flower on the lowest limb of the tree, but found it impossible. Disappointment assailed her, for she so wanted this particular flower. Nothing could be as heavenly as its fragrance—not even an expensive French perfume sprayed from a fancy bottle!

"Could I lend you a hand, luv?"

The voice breaking through the silence startled Thalia, yet when she recognized it, she felt a sudden strange giddiness.

Ian.

It was Ian Lavery!

Spinning around, a surge of tingling heat flooded Thalia's insides when she found Ian casually leaning his weight on the trunk of another acacia tree beside the one she was admiring, his one leg crossed over the other, his hip cocked.

"You," she said, her voice lilting. "How long have you been standing there?"

"Long enough to know that you want a bouquet of flowers but are not tall enough to get them," Ian said, his eyes appraising her as he looked her slowly up and down, taken anew by her liquid curves, her flawless features. The bodice of her dress revealed her heaving breasts, a sign that she was anxious in his presence.

Anxious to leave?

Or to be kissed again by him?

Was he ready to be insulted again by her devotion to Paul Hathaway, her declared husband?

It seemed so, he thought, or he would not be there.

"Yes, it seems that I am going to have to search for my bouquet elsewhere," Thalia said, thrilling inside to see Ian, yet forced to be indifferent to him. If he persisted in coming around and Paul should find out . . . she did not want to think of the consequences.

For herself and Viada.

And for Ian!

"That won't be necessary if you truly wish the blossoms," Ian said, sauntering away from the tree he was leaning against, toward Thalia. When he reached her, he placed a hand above her head, into the foliage of the tree, and plucked a bright blossom.

Ian leaned over Thalia with burning eyes and placed the flower in the folds of her hair. "As you can see, I can reach as many flowers as you wish," he said, smiling down at her. "Just say the word, Thalia. I will pick enough to fill dozens of vases in your room."

Thalia reached and touched the flower, its petals silken. She was becoming quickly unnerved by Ian's presence. He was standing so close that she could reach up and touch his bronzed cheek. She could run her fingers through his toussled, rusty hair. She could lean up on her tiptoes and brush her mouth against his lips!

Oh, she so ached to do all of these things, for she could not deny to herself just how much she loved this man who stirred her insides into a sweet passion.

But again, she had to shake such thoughts from her mind. She must chide him into leaving! She had no choice but to convince him that she did not want to see him.

Ever again!

"Do not bother picking any more of the acacia blossoms," Thalia said icily. "There are other flowers growing along the riverbank. They will please me just as much."

Watching his expression, she plucked the flower from her hair and dropped it to the ground. When she recognized a sudden, searing hurt in his eyes, guilt washed through her. Throwing the flower away was the last thing that she had wanted to do. It had only been done to prove a point to him!

Though stung by her rejection, Ian disregarded her performance, for as sure as the stars were wed to the heavens, she was playing a game of pretense with him. Why? Would he ever know why?

"Then I shall walk along with you and help you pick the ones of your choosing," Ian said, placing a quick arm around her waist, walking her away from the acacia trees. He nodded. "Up just ahead, just past the trees that line the river, is a wild flower that might interest you. They have colorful blossoms that look like painted cardboard. They are so dry in their natural state they can be cut and kept not for only a few nights, but for years. Let me show them to you. I'm sure you'll be pleased with them."

Recalling how he so easily abducted her the previous night, Thalia's insides tightened. If he lured her far enough away from the ranch, would he not try it again? Had he had time to think over his decision to bring her back to the ranch and had he decided that it had not been wise? Oh, was he truly going to try it again?

Jerking free of him, Thalia turned and faced him, glaring at him. "Why are you here?" she demanded, placing her hands on her hips. "Are you toying with me on the pretense of being a friend, only to abduct me again? If that is your reason for being here, I shall fight you this time to the end! Never will you take me from Hathaway Ranch again. Never!"

Frustrated by her persistence and never believing that she could care this much for Paul Hathaway, Ian grabbed Thalia by the shoulders. "Luv, I just happened along and saw you at the river alone," he said, his voice deep and troubled. "Don't you know how foolish that is? You should never wander from the ranch alone."

"Ha!" Thalia said, tossing her head angrily. "You just happened along? I see no horse. If you just happened along, would you not be still on your stallion?" She peered through the foliage ahead. "I don't see Hawke either." She dared him with narrowed eyes. "You've come alone purposely to lure me away—if not to abduct me, to seduce me. Why else would you be alone? Hawke is your friend, isn't he? Doesn't he always ride with you? What have you been doing? Spying on me? Waiting for me to leave the house? Am I to have no privacy whatsoever, either from Paul or you?"

"Thalia, as for seducing you, that has crossed my mind more than once," Ian growled. "But as for abducting you—if I had wanted to, do you think I would be standing here, arguing about it? Damn it, I would just do it. And so could anyone else who might happen along." He looked her over, then stared into her eyes again. "I see no weapon. You are at the mercy of every two- and four-legged creature that stalks the scrub!"

"But, if this was not planned, and you just happened along, where is your stallion?" Thalia asked again, peering through the trees, her eyes searching. "Where is Hawke?"

Ian dropped his hands from her shoulders. "My horse? I tethered it in the trees, over there," he said, motioning with a hand toward a thick crop of red gum trees. "I did that and came by foot purposely to prove to you how easily it is for someone to sneak up on you. As for Hawke, he has stayed with his people to make plans for the march to the sea for the gathering of the swan's eggs. I may be riding alone more oft than not for awhile."

"Even if you did all of this just for my benefit, it is not necessary," Thalia argued. "I do not need a bodyguard. I have not survived to the age of eighteen by being a nitwit. I can most certainly take care of myself."

"Oh, you can, can you?" Ian challenged, resting a hand on one of his holstered Colts. He leaned closer to her face. "My little innocent one, let me tell you a few things about the scrub. It's a wicked place where packs of dingo dogs attack men head on and rip them to bits. There are escaped convicts who hide in the scrub who are savage, whose main relish is the whirr of the lash and the spurt of blood. Convicts break away from Adelaide Prison every day. They put down their tools and escape as soon as a supervisor turns his back. Luv, anything in the outback that hunts, is hunted. You should stay close to the house. Better yet, you should stay inside."

Thalia paled at hearing the dangers being described to her, yet she held her chin stubbornly lifted. "I need no lectures from you," she said. "Tell me the truth. You did not just happen by. You were spying on me all along!"

Tired of the bantering and knowing that he was getting nowhere with Thalia now that she was determined to be stubborn, Ian grabbed her roughly into his arms.

Thalia looked up at Ian, wide-eyed, held not only steadfastly within his grip, but also by the sudden throes of passion. His mouth was close, his breath hot on her face. His eyes seemed to grow smoke-black with passion as he gazed raptly down at her.

Yet he did not kiss her. It was as though an unseen force had made him change his mind, for he released her almost as quickly as he had pulled her close to him.

Remembering just at the most crucial moment how Thalia so cherished her wedding vows, Ian had decided that it was best not to kiss her after all. He turned and sauntered away from her. He went to the riverbank and sat down, picking up small pebbles to toss into the water.

Filled with such a strong desire for Ian and unused to these tumultuous feelings, Thalia hesitated for a moment, then went and sat down beside Ian. She plucked a blade of grass and began tearing it apart, piece by piece, feeling Ian's eyes on her.

"You're a hard one to figure out," he said. "Here

you are a stranger in a strange land and I am offering a hand of friendship and you act as though it would please you to cut off that hand. Why, Thalia? I have only good intentions toward you."

"I'm sorry," Thalia murmured, truly sorry from the bottom of her heart. But she did not dare say any more to him about how she truly felt. She had to change the subject quickly. If he delved into the inner depths of her heart, he would know that her every angry emotion directed toward him was false.

Oh, but what dangers there were in that!

She turned her eyes slowly to Ian. "Tell me something about yourself," she said softly. "Just anything. Perhaps about your parents. Truly I would love to know."

Ian quirked an eyebrow at her curiously. He had expected her to run away from him at her first opportunity; instead she had sat down beside him as though she truly wanted his company.

And to ask about his parents . . . ?

He scratched his brow idly, truly confused. "My parents?" he said, looking at her quizzically.

"Yes, please tell me," Thalia urged, wanting to establish some sort of peaceful bond between them, yet having to be cautious and not give him cause to pursue a closer relationship with her than that. "Ian, I shall never forget that you saved my life. I owe you the courtesy of friendship. But please understand that I am not free to offer more than that. My husband . . ."

"Aye, I know," Ian said, heaving a sigh. "You are married. Do you honestly think I could ever forget that? You've reminded me enough times."

Thalia lowered her eyes. "If friendship is not enough, then perhaps I'd best leave," she murmured. She became warmed clear through when she felt the pressure of his hand on her arm. She looked slowly over at him.

"No, don't go," Ian said hoarsely. He glanced up at the sky through the canopy of trees overhead. "But you can't stay long. Soon it will be dark."

"Yes, I know," Thalia said, fear creeping into her heart at the thought of the dangers that could be found this close to the scrub in the dark—and of Paul finding her gone. "I must leave shortly."

Her attention was quickly averted, drawn to a movement on the riverbank several yards from where she and Ian sat. She craned her neck and watched a flat, rubbery bill stick out of a hole in the ground. A fuzzy body emerged and waddled into the water and swam in circles before it dove beneath the surface. "Whatever is that?" Thalia asked quietly.

"A platypus," Ian said, also watching the activity of the mammal. "The platypus feeds at dusk. The hole it emerged from is the entrance to a tunnel which leads to its nest."

The platypus rose to the surface of the water and dove down again.

"It's diving to the bottom of the river where it feeds by probing the mud with its bill," Ian further explained.

"It is such a funny looking thing," Thalia marveled. "Its bill is shaped like that of a duck, yet its fur is like a beaver's."

"Aye, it's one of Australia's many unusual creatures," Ian said, laughing softly. "The platypus is a mammal, but its young hatch from eggs and they lap milk which secretes onto the mother's stomach, until they are old enough for worms and insects."

Thalia gazed at Ian. "You know so much about Australia, yet you are originally from America," she marveled. "You were going to tell me about yourself. Please do."

"If you insist, though I do not see the importance," Ian said. He was for the most part a private person. But with her, sharing seemed as natural as breathing.

"Aye, I was born in America," he began. "In Seattle. My father died when I was eight. When I was fifteen, my mother met and married an Australian who had come to America for medical treatment for a heart condition. She returned to Australia with him. I stayed behind. I lived with an aunt so that I could continue my education. I came to be with my mother a few years back when her Australian husband died of a heart attack. She wanted to stay in Australia."

"Ian, where do you live?" Thalia asked, somehow relieved to know that he did have a home to go to—his mother's. If Thalia could ever break free of Paul's bondage, perhaps she could have a decent life with Ian, after all.

Ian's jaw tightened. "I live no place in particular," he said, his expression guarded. "For the most part I live on my stallion. I keep in touch with my mother to keep a check on her."

Thalia's hopes waned. He had just explained to her how footloose and free he was! Surely no woman could ever totally penetrate the wall that he had built around himself, unless she . . .

Wanting to talk no more of himself, Ian turned to Thalia. He took one of her hands. "I'll never forget that shark circling you in the water," he said. "If I hadn't happened along . . ."

Thalia's doubts were cast into the wind, and she became dangerously aware of the passion inflaming her again as Ian scorched her skin with his touch where he held her hand so possessively. "But you did and you saved me from its terrible jaws," she murmured, his eyes mesmerizing her. She scooted closer to him. "I know I have thanked you before, but I must again. Thank you, Ian. From the bottom of my heart. Whatever can I do to repay you?"

Ian's eyes twinkled as he gazed down at her. "Luv, you might want to reconsider asking that question," he said thickly. "You just might not want to hear the answer."

Thalia saw a strange sort of light shadowing the depths of his eyes. He seemed to be looking into her heart. "What do you mean?" she asked innocently, her voice lilting.

Ian swept his arms around her and drew her close, oh, so close. "I am afraid that to ask for a kiss as a reward might cause you to condemn me as a rogue, especially since you are a married woman."

Unable to stop what was building between them, exquisitely dizzying Thalia, she blinked her eyes up at him. "Might you want to test this theory?" she asked, daring a situation to heat up that until now she had backed away from. She seemed to have no control this time. Her heart was prodding her forward.

"Why not kiss me?" she whispered. "You did before and it mattered not to you that I was wearing a wedding band."

"A wedding band does not a marriage make," Ian said, weaving his fingers through the soft glimmer of her hair. "The love between a man and woman and what they mutually share is how one knows whether the marriage is real . . . or false."

A slow blush rose to Thalia's cheeks, wondering if he somehow knew that all along she had been lying to him. Or was he astute enough to see it in her eyes and hear it in her voice that she was living this lie, hating it?

"Luv, I shall never forget that first kiss you shared with me," Ian said huskily. "Nor your lips . . . nor their utter sweetness."

In a swoon, as though in a magical trance, Thalia closed her eyes as Ian's mouth bore down upon her lips. Caught in his embrace, she felt her entire body becoming filled with yearnings. She had dreamed of—had fantasized about—this moment. She could not deny herself of it any longer!

Her entire being throbbed with quickening desire as he eased her to the ground. She was near to melting into a boneless surrender as his hand slid up the skirt of her dress, inflicting a sweet desire she had never experienced before.

But she became suddenly afraid when his hand reached the juncture of her thighs and began stroking her through her silk undergarment, softly, soothingly, kissing her now with just soft brushes of his lips.

She became afraid of this ferocious hunger within her—the sensations searing her, as though her entire being was aflame. She was wrong to have let this get out of hand. Oh, what was she thinking of? How could she have let herself forget Paul's threats?

Shaking herself free from Ian's embrace and shoving at his chest, sending him to his feet in alarm, Thalia rose quickly from the ground, sobbing.

"Please forget this ever happend," she cried, smoothing the skirt of her dress down. "I was wrong to allow it! So wrong!"

Crying so hard that she felt as though her heart was ripping in shreds, Thalia fled from Ian. She could feel his eyes branding her and she felt so ashamed, so wicked, so threatened by her intense feelings for this man. Because of this, she had almost made a fatal mistake—and with a man she could never marry. She could have made a mistake that would affect her entire life—even her sister's!

Blindly scaling the fence and running across the great courtyard, she stopped and hid behind the bunkhouse to get her breath. Peering around the corner of the building, she fingered her wedding band nervously. She could see Paul riding toward the house from the direction she had just come. She blanched. What if Paul ever found out that she had been with Ian in such a way?

She sighed with relief when Paul dismounted

and went inside the house. She went on to the house and up the back stairs, then to her room. She closed the door and threw herself across the bed, sobbing. She was so confused—so disheartened with life!

Ian shook his head with despair and mounted his horse. Not looking back, he rode away into the scrub.

Tanner McShane, a bald, tall, and wiry man, paced back and forth in his cell at Adelaide Prison. He tucked a rope beneath his shirt for later use and began sharpening a dinner knife stolen from the prison kitchen. He planned to escape tonight. Paul Hathaway would die soon. It was because of Paul Hathaway that Tanner was in prison. Tanner had been a leader of a bushranger gang. He and Paul had been of opposing forces of bushrangers. Paul had set Tanner up a few months back, and Tanner got caught while Paul continued to be free.

The authorities had paid no heed to Tanner when he said that Paul Hathaway was the leader of a bushranger gang and should be arrested, even hung for his evil deeds to humanity!

Tanner now knew why he had been ignored. It was said among those who were confined in the prison for life that Paul Hathaway paid the corrupted authorities well for their silence and protection.

Tanner had bent under the lash many times while in prison, cursing Paul as each spurt of blood splashed from his body. He was scarred for life because of Paul Hathaway.

Tanner would be more generous with Paul. Paul

would have only one scar—the scar on his neck made by a rope that would strangle his last breath from him.

"Aye, tonight," he whispered to himself, his eyes gleaming as he envisioned Paul squirming as he struggled to grab the rope from around his neck.

CHAPTER EIGHT

THE DAY WAS BRIGHT WITH SUNSHINE, FLOODING the parlor as Paul ushered Daisy Odum into the room where Thalia awaited her arrival. Appearing to be the perfect gentleman, Paul guided Daisy to a plush chair opposite Thalia.

"Why, Thalia, how nice it is to see you again," Daisy said, her tone pleasant. She tucked fallen locks of hair beneath her fancy straw hat adorned with ostrich feathers, and then arranged the skirt of her silk dress around her as she sat down, the cushion of the chair wheezing strangely beneath her weight.

Daisy patted the dress down on each side of her, darting her eyes from item to item in the vast, richly decorated room.

Then once again she looked at Thalia and smiled. "You seem content enough, luv, in these

134

surroundings," she murmured. She cast Paul a quick glance and gave him an appraising look, then focused her attention on Thalia again. "But of course, there is no reason why you wouldn't be." She glanced down at the wedding band on Thalia's finger. "It seems your husband is giving you the world."

Daisy averted her attention to Paul. She watched him go to Thalia, leaning over to give her an affectionate kiss on the lips, then sat down on the arm of Thalia's chair so that he could place an arm around her shoulders.

Then Daisy eyed Thalia closely, for something in her weak smile cast a doubt on all of this. "Thalia, you are happy, aren't you, luv?" she asked guardedly. "Things are all right, aren't they?"

The way Daisy was looking at her, as though she did not believe this charade being acted out before her, and the way she now questioned it, made a sudden panic seize Thalia. If Daisy was not convinced that everything was all right, then Paul would be given cause to retaliate! Viada could suffer because of it!

Thalia turned her face swiftly up to Paul and pretended to be looking adoringly at him. She touched his cheek gently, then placed her hand to the back of his head and encouraged his lips to hers. She kissed him passionately, putting everything in the kiss that she could, closing her eyes, pretending that Paul was Ian to make her act as real as possible.

When Thalia thought that she could not bear another minute of Paul's wet, slick lips, his probing tongue daringly close to entering her mouth, she eased her lips free and turned and smiled at Daisy. "Never have I been as happy," she said in a forced purr. "Paul is the perfect husband. I could never want for any more than he has given me." She glanced up at Paul and gave him another adoring smile. "I am so lucky."

Paul returned her smile, trying to hide the amused puzzlement in his eyes. He was quite taken by Thalia's act, thinking that she had missed her calling in life. She should be on the stage. No one could ever give such a grand performance as Thalia was achieving today!

"My dear, I am the lucky one," he said, cupping Thalia's chin in his palm. "You are the perfect wife. And you are so beautiful. Never have I seen anyone as beautiful as you. And you are my wife! My wife!"

Daisy sucked in a nervous breath of air, quite taken by these two people who were so obviously in love. She had been wrong to doubt them earlier. Their strained behavior had more than likely been because she was there, interfering in their passionate private moments together. When two people loved as intensely as they, surely they spent more time in bed than not!

With this thought in mind, and not wanting to interfere in what seemed to be a marriage made in heaven, Daisy pushed herself up from the chair. "I truly must go," she said, smiling from Paul to Thalia. "I've other stops to make today. I hope I find my other girls as happy as you are, Thalia. It gives me such satisfaction to find those content whom I have found homes for."

A desperation rose inside Thalia. She did not want Daisy to leave, yet knew that even if she stayed, it would not be a deterrent against what would happen later. Thalia was a virtual prisoner. She had no idea what to expect of the days and weeks to come!

Almost falling over herself, Thalia rose from the chair. "Daisy, surely you aren't leaving this quickly," she said, going to pour tea. "You have yet to take tea and cake with us. Surely you want to have refreshment before you go about your business of the day."

Daisy patted her large stomach. "Luv, I don't think refreshment is necessary for me," she said, laughing throatily. "My word, if I accepted tea and cake everywhere I stopped today I would not be able to board my buggy and return to the city."

Paul became wary, seeing Thalia's eagerness not to see Daisy off. Her performance of moments ago was threatening to become a quick failure and Daisy Odum's astuteness would pick up on any uneasiness that Thalia showed.

Working quickly, he went to Daisy and took her by an elbow and began walking her from the room. "Now, now, Daisy, do not be so anxious to condemn yourself," he said, his voice smooth and diplomatic. "You are a very attractive woman. Please place blame where blame is due. And we understand how busy you are." He gave Thalia a quick glance over his shoulder. "Don't we, darling?"

Thalia set the teapot down, boiling inside at his reference to her as "darling." Yet she knew what duty demanded of her. She must continue her role of perfect wife and hostess to the hilt.

Inhaling a nervous breath and lifting her chin bravely, she went to Daisy and walked alongside her toward the front door. "Please do come again soon," she said politely. "Perhaps then you can make time to take tea and cake with us. I enjoy your company immensely, Daisy." Her insides grew cold when Paul gave her a stern glance that Daisy did not see. "But I, too, realize that you are a busy woman and have more things on your mind than me and . . . and my husband."

Daisy sighed heavily, taking her purse as Paul ever so gently placed it into her hands. "Sometimes it gets too much for me," she said, frowning. "So I doubt if you can expect me to come and see you for a while, Thalia." She smiled at Paul, then at Thalia. "My dears, your love for one another warms my heart so! You do not need an interfering busybody like me getting in your way." She tossed the skirt of her dress as she stepped out onto the narrow porch of the mission, where her horse and buggy awaited her. She leaned a kiss to Thalia's cheek, then shook Paul's hand vigorously. "I'm glad I came today. Very glad."

Thalia forced a kind smile as Paul led Daisy down the steps and helped her up into her buggy. Thalia waved a good-bye, then went downheartedly back inside the house. Weary, her fingers trembling, she went into the parlor and poured herself a cup of tea. She fell in a near collapse onto the nearest chair, and began sipping the tea, growing tense when Paul came back into the room.

"You were convincing enough at first, Thalia,"

he said, stepping over to his liquor cabinet and pouring himself a shot of whiskey. "But you almost gave it all away by being so anxious not to let Daisy leave." He stood over Thalia, glaring down at her. "The next time, if there is a next time, you'd better be more careful." He gulped down the whiskey, then slammed the glass on a table. "I hope that is understood, Thalia."

Placing the teacup gingerly on the table, Thalia rose from the chair and glared back at Paul. "I hope this is understood," she said, and spat at his feet.

Without waiting for his response, she turned and fled toward the stairs, but she was not quick enough. He was behind her, his hand tightly on her wrist as he swung her around to face him.

"I shall overlook that," he said, his voice strained with anger. "But never let it happen again."

Defiantly, she spat at his feet again, then gasped painfully as he slapped her.

"That is a small punishment in comparison to what I hand out to the Aborigines when they show such disobedience," he growled, speaking into her face. "If you play with fire, you'll get burned!"

Thalia looked up at him, her eyes wild. She rubbed her scalding face as he began walking away from her.

"I have business to tend to," Paul said, going to the door. "Find something to do while I'm gone. Help Honora with the chores." He flung a wild hand into the air. "Go and gather the eggs. Anything to busy your mind and hands."

Thalia gaped after him as he left the house, banging the door shut loudly after him. Dispirited, her face stinging from the blow of his large hand, she went to the window and lifted the sheer curtain and watched him gather together several of his stockmen. After a short deliberation with them, everyone, including Paul, mounted their horses and rode away.

"Where is he going this time?" she whispered, recalling Ian's warnings of Paul and the sort of ugly pastimes he was perhaps involved in. "And he leaves me alone again? Damn his smugness. He knows that I won't try and escape. He has me right where he wants me and there isn't one thing I can do about it."

"Ian," she whispered. "If only I could confide in you. If only . . ."

As only a dim shaft of light filtered through grimy windows at Adelaide Prison, Ian's dark eyes watched an artist at work, his surroundings somber and gray. "How much longer is it going to take for you to sketch Tanner McShane's likeness?" he asked, resting his hands on his holstered Colts. "I can't go searching for the man until I see who I'm after. Hurry up with the sketch, will you?"

"The bastard only escaped from prison last night," the artist grumbled, his long and lean fingers moving across the paper as he sketched in ink an unpleasant face on paper, his fingers like limber branches blowing in a brisk wind. He looked up at Ian beneath a thick arch of blonde eyebrows. "Kind of anxious to get the reward money, ain't cha? Don't it ever get under your skin? Livin' off bringin' in carcasses of men?"

Ian's back stiffened and fire lit his eyes. His grip

on the handles of his Colts became so intense, his knuckles grew white. "You do the sketching, and I'll do the bringing in," he growled.

Turning, Ian left the artist to his job. He went to the magistrate and sat down across the desk from him. Familiar with the surroundings, he propped his feet up on the desk, crossing his legs at his ankles.

"Adam, tell me something about Tanner McShane," he said, drumming his fingers nervously on the arms of the chair. "Just what kind of man am I hunting this time? I don't recall his name. Is it his first time at Adelaide Prison? Is it his first escape?"

Adam, a striking man of thirty, offered Ian a cigar across the desk, then thrust it into his own mouth when Ian shook his head in silent refusal. He pulled a kerosene lamp close to him and leaned the cigar down its chimney and lit it. Taking several long drags from the cigar, he scooted the lamp back in place.

"Tanner McShane?" he said, leaning comfortably back in his chair and nodding. His fingers toyed with the gold buttons on the front of his crisp, blue uniform, his azure eyes intense. "He's a new one here at the prison but not to me. He's a dangerous man, one I hate to see loose out there again, wreaking havoc."

His interest in Tanner growing, Ian dropped his feet away from the desk to the floor and leaned closer to Adam. "So tell me," he said, looking at Adam over a pile of scattered papers. "What was he in for?"

Adam took his cigar from his mouth and flicked

ashes onto the floor. "It all had to do with Paul Hathaway," he said matter-of-factly. "Hathaway turned the sonofabitch in. The story is that Tanner stole some of his livestock. As far as I was concerned, Tanner McShane should've been arrested and thrown in prison for other reasons a long time ago. It was a well-known fact that he was the head of a bushranger gang, killing and maiming all across Australia. We just couldn't get proof."

"That's why I was never told about Tanner McShane so that I could go after him? You needed goddamn *proof*?" Ian said incredulously. "You've never needed any such proof before. Why this time?"

Adam became visibly annoyed with Ian's attitude and show of mistrust. He frowned darkly over at him. "Ian, I'm the law here, not you, so just mind your manners if you want me to continue supplying you with information about escaped prisoners so that you can continue lining your pockets with gold and silver when you bring them back to me for punishment," he lectured.

Ian leaned slowly back into his chair, his breathing shallow as he looked with more suspicion at Adam. He placed his fingertips together before him, and the room filled with a moment of strained silence.

Then he dropped his hands to his lap where he folded them together angrily. "All right, I'll not prod you anymore about this McShane fellow," he said, his voice slow and calculated. His thoughts were suddenly troubled by someone else. Thalia! If Tanner McShane was out for revenge on the man who'd turned him in, then he just might head for

Paul's ranch. Thalia could be caught and killed in the crossfire! "But tell me what you know about Paul Hathaway. Has any evidence of Paul being a bushranger been uncovered yet?"

"No," Adam said, placing his cigar between his lips. "Paul Hathaway's reputation is as clean as a whistle. Like I said before when you've asked about him—why worry about him when there are true criminals out there in the scrub killing and mutilating people?"

Again Ian became lost in silent wonder. It seemed to him that Adam was too convincing about Paul Hathaway. But this was not the time to pursue the matter any longer. Thalia was in danger from another man. Tanner McShane.

Springing from the chair, Ian nodded a quick and silent farewell to Adam and went back to the artist. He stood over him, impatience burning inside him as he watched the final touches being added to the likeness of Tanner McShane. When the artist thrust it up at him, Ian smiled through tight, angry teeth, then folded the drawing in fours and thrust it inside his shirt pocket. He left the prison in a rush and mounted his horse. Wheeling it around, he rode from the city, hoping that he would get to Paul Hathaway's ranch in time, for surely Tanner McShane would go after the man responsible for his being in prison.

CHAPTER NINE

THALIA WALKED CAUTIOUSLY INTO THE BARN. Her auburn hair was tied back from her face with a yellow ribbon that matched her yellow-print cotton dress with puffed sleeves and a lowswept neckline. Clutching the handle of a small wicker basket, she glanced around at the shadows inside the barn, knowing where the hens usually laid their eggs, but never sure if she and the hens were alone in this drab, cavernous place. She could never allow herself to trust Paul's cowhands, yet today they all seemed to have left on horseback with him. Surely she was safe to gather the eggs. It would be fun to take the time to sit down and watch the young, golden hatchlings that were scampering around pecking at seed close beside their mothers.

Hearing or seeing nothing that was threatening to her, Thalia's step became lively as she went from nest to nest, gathering up the warm eggs within the palms of her hands. Delicately, she piled the eggs into the basket, then stopped suddenly when she heard a noise overhead in the loft.

Fear grabbed her at the pit of her stomach as she turned her eyes slowly upward. She jumped with alarm, spilling some of the eggs from the basket, when some straw fell through the cracks in the flooring just above her, scattering across her upturned face.

Thalia spat and wiped her hand over her face in her attempt to get the straw away from her face and mouth, all the while keeping her eyes on the loft. She gasped and grew pale when Ian suddenly leaned his hand over the edge of the loft and smiled down at her.

"'ow's it goin', ma'am?" Ian asked, his eyes twinkling. "Many chickens layin' today?"

At first Thalia was at a loss for words. She was relieved that she had no true reason to be afraid any longer, yet was recalling vividly her moments with Ian beside the Murray River, when he had almost succeeded in seducing her.

Oh, why wouldn't he just leave her alone?

Yet, deep within her heart she didn't really want him to. Somehow his unexpected visits made her feel safer—at least for the moment that he was with her.

But there was the constant danger that Paul would find out and she would be blamed—and her sister could be harmed because of it.

Angrily, Thalia set what remained of her basket of eggs on the floor, and not wanting anyone to hear her scold Ian, she climbed the ladder to the loft. "What are you doing here?" she asked in a low hiss, reaching the top rung of the ladder and scooting onto the loft. She and Ian were both on their knees, face to face, eye to eye. Her heart was doing a slow melting, seeing how much more handsome he was, clean-shaven!

"Do you see what you caused?" she demanded, trying to mask her true feelings with a display of anger. She still had to convince him that she wanted no part of him. So much depended on her ability to do so! "I spilled half the eggs I gathered. Why can't you just disappear from my life? Why must you persist in annoying me?"

"I can help you gather the rest of the eggs if that's what's bothering you," Ian teased, his eyes dancing. He reached a hand to her cheek. "But that's not what's got you riled, is it?"

Thalia slapped his hand away. "Of course you know what else is bothering me besides the dratted eggs," she said, her resolve weakening as Ian took it upon himself to untie the ribbon around her hair.

Again she slapped his hand away, but not soon enough, for his hand came away holding the yellow ribbon. "You are bothering me. Always! How can I convince you that I don't want anything to do with you?" she demanded.

Ian tossed the ribbon aside. His fingers began to stir magical beams within Thalia as they traced her facial features, then dropped lower, creating passionate flames to envelop her as he swept a hand

146

beneath the lowswept bodice of her dress, fully cupping a breast.

Breathing hard, her eyes were wild as she was slowly becoming lost to Ian again.

This time, oh, this time, the melting sensation was so beautifully sweet.

It was overtaking her.

Body and soul . . .

"Thalia, I don't believe you when you say that you don't want anything to do with me," Ian said huskily, easing her down, to lie on the soft straw spread out on the floor of the loft. "Kisses don't lie. Do you remember how it felt when we kissed? I felt passion. Hot and hungry passion. Tell me the truth. You felt it also."

"Let me go," Thalia pleaded, his hands holding her wrists securely to the floor. "I do not want this. You were spying on me again. Oh, how can you expect me to think anything but bad of that?" She paused, biting her lower lip, then blurted out, "And how can you always forget that I have a husband?"

Ian's eyes were dark and knowing. He laughed throatily, his mouth grazing Thalia's lips. "So there is that same argument," he said, moving his hand to her breast again and kneading it through the fabric of her dress. "You speak of a husband who bought you for a price? How can you take him or his vows seriously?" He twined his fingers through her hair and drew her lips closer, his other hand lowering her dress down from her shoulders. "I am the only one you should be taking seriously, Thalia. Everything I do is sincere. My darling, let me show you what true love is all about. Here. Now."

147

His mouth came down over Thalia's. The kiss was all-consuming, drowning Thalia in an exquisite ecstasy, his palms moving seductively over her breasts that were now bared to him. His fingers taunted her, teasing her fiery flesh. Without even being aware of it, her body strained closer to him, her nipples taut with desire.

Ian's body hardened, his muscles tightened, reacting to the tantalizing cleavage of her silkenly soft breasts and her lips that were not denying him any longer. His hands worked slowly to remove the rest of her clothes, his lips now brushing against her throat, evoking a soft moan from deep inside her.

Thalia now fully unclothed, Ian leaned away from her and gazed down upon her slim and sinuous body, her tiny waist, her long and tapering calves and silken thighs. Seeing her made his heart pound inside his chest, almost threatening to take his breath clean away from him.

"Why can't you forget about me?" Thalia asked, trying to draw from whatever senses she still had. She reached for her dress but Ian's hand pushed it farther away. "Oh, Ian, please don't. It's not right."

Ian leaned over her and gathered her into his arms. His fingers ran down her body, caressing her, making her shiver. "Thalia, kiss me again, and then, if you want me to leave, I shall," he whispered, his breath teasing her ear, his hands continuing to awaken her to an intense rapture. He bore his mouth down upon her lips and kissed her hotly.

When she reached out for him, and her fingers began unbuttoning his shirt, Ian's whole body quivered with the sensation this aroused within him. She was responding in kind. She was not going to fight this thing that they had discovered between them any longer.

Finally she was seeing the rightness of what he was saying, what he was doing. . . .

Enveloped in a drugged passion, Thalia eased her lips from Ian's and devoured him with her eyes as he knelt down close beside her. Her fingers trembled as she slowly undressed him, this the first time, ever, for her to be so brazen with a man. All thoughts of Paul, of even her sister, were swept from her mind by the intense love of this man who had entered her life and refused to leave it. She never wanted to let him go. She would take from him this moment that he offered and would cherish it forever, for this would be the only time she would allow it.

As Thalia removed each of Ian's garments, she became enthralled with the expanse of his sleekly muscled chest, the curling hair that tapered down to his waist, and his hard, flat stomach. His was a body of tight muscles, lithe and well-aroused.

When he reached for her hand and placed it gently on his manhood, she blushed and swallowed hard. As though guided by some unseen force, her fingers circled his hardness. Slowly she moved her hand up and down on the stiff shaft at the guidance of Ian's hand which circled her own.

Ian sucked in a wild breath and closed his eyes, the need for Thalia scorching his insides. When he could bear no more and the end was too near, he moved her hand away and rolled her over so that he was atop her.

An explosion of ecstasy was exchanged between

them when Ian covered her lips with another heady kiss. Thalia's pulse raced when she felt the velvet tip of his manhood touch her inner thigh, then move slowly along her flesh until he positioned himself at the very core of her womanhood and began to press into her very slowly.

Panic suddenly seized Thalia. Her eyes flew open wildly. She shoved at Ian's chest, for if she let him continue he would soon discover that she was a virgin! He would then know that, although she professed to being married to Paul Hathaway, she had not shared a bed with him!

What would Ian think?

What would he do?

He would forever persist in trying to get her away from Paul, a man she so obviously cared not a jot for!

"Ian, I can't," she cried, tears streaming from her eyes. "I . . . just . . . can't."

He kissed her with a soft brush of the lips, again stealing her thoughts and worries away. He stroked her body with an exquisite tenderness. She drifted toward him and hugged him to her, burying her tearful eyes against his chest. "Oh, but do love me," she whispered. "Please . . . love . . . me. I don't think I can bear it if you don't."

Their bodies strained together hungrily. Ian kissed Thalia softly. He kissed her sweetly. His fingers digging softly into her buttocks, he lifted her to himself and entered her with slight, slow movements. His body hardened and tightened as he thrust home—to the depths of her as she opened herself to him.

The pain of Ian's entry was intense for Thalia,

but brief. She then received him willingly and enclosed his hard shaft within the warm, moist cocoon of her womanhood. She lifted her legs around his waist and moved with him, meeting his eager thrusts with her own.

Molded into the contours of his body, she kissed him long and hard, lost in passion's promise. The wondrous feelings that were filling her were drenching her with something akin to torment, yet it was so deliciously beautiful that she worked with him, now anxious to reach that ultimate release that would momentarily quench this wild desire.

Ian could not keep his hands in just one place. They wandered feverishly along Thalia's curves, feasting on their softness, as though he were caressing velvet. A spinning sensation inside his head was making him aware that he would not be able to hold back much longer. Every nerve in his body was screaming for release.

Ian's ragged breath became slower as he eased his mouth from Thalia's lips. He looked down at her. Their eyes met, locked in an unspoken understanding, promising ecstasy. The air was heavy with the inevitability of intense pleasure.

Tremors cascaded down Thalia's back as Ian's fingers traced circles around her stomach, up to her breasts, and then back down again, stroking her throbbing center. She closed her eyes, becoming mindless. She moaned sensually when again he began his strokes within her, but this time more demandingly. Wondrous passion suddenly exploded within her. She clung to him as she felt his body stiffen, then make one last maddening plunge within her.

Only a moment later, his groans proved that he had reached the same pinnacle of joy as she, and she knew that she could never find the same sort of bliss with any other man, ever again.

Only with Ian.

The sensual vibrations were gone. Thalia clung to Ian, one of his hands cupping her breast. Withdrawing himself from inside her, he breathed hard, sweat pearling his brow. "You can't be sorry for what we shared," he whispered, brushing a kiss against her lips. "Tell me you're not sorry."

The magic of the moment gone, reality staring Thalia straight in the face as she realized just how foolish these past moments had been and what they could cost her, she shoved Ian away from her and, sobbing, gathered up her clothes. She started to dress but stopped when Ian grabbed her by a wrist and turned her around so that he could look at her. She recognized a shocked look on his face and wondered about it. She wiped tears from her eyes and looked where his gaze was locked and she gasped and teetered from shock when she saw blood between her thighs.

"You . . . were a virgin," Ian gasped, looking quickly up at her, dismayed by the discovery. He jerked Thalia closer to him. She fell to her knees in front of him, her eyes wild. "Why didn't you tell me?" He grabbed her hand and looked at the wedding band, then looked intensely into her eyes. "You're married. You're wearing his ring. Why hasn't he . . . ?"

Fearing the questions more than she had been shocked to see the blood, having never been told that her first lovemaking meant bleeding, Thalia jerked free and placed her back to him. In her hungers of the flesh, she had let herself forget the welfare of her sister. She had let Ian feed her hungers!

She turned to face him again and slapped his face, then began tearing into her clothes. "All along you have been pursuing me not to rescue me from Paul Hathaway, but for your lust for my body," she cried, glad to get her dress buttoned so that the sight of her nudity no longer tempted Ian's further lustful approaches. She plopped down onto the cushion of straw at her feet and jerked on one shoe and then the other. "I don't know what I was thinking! I was raised with strict morals. How could I have become a loose woman so quickly?"

Confused to the core over everything about Thalia, yet worried more about her state of mind than his, Ian slipped into his breeches, stopping Thalia just as she started to descend the ladder to leave the loft. "Thalia, stop," he said, gently grabbing her by a wrist. "Don't go away from me filled with such guilt. You aren't a loose woman. Never could be. You are—are sweet and innocent. I am a rogue for having placed you in such a position as this."

He lifted her chin with a forefinger. Tears splashed from her eyes as she looked up at him— oh, so adoringly. "But never believe that I did this only because of my lust for you. Darling, somewhere between saving you from that shark and now I fell madly in love with you. I now know for certain that you feel the same about me."

He cleared his throat nervously and momentarily lowered his eyes. "The fact that Paul Hathaway slipped the ring on your finger first cannot stop our love for one another." His eyes lifted and he drew her close and embraced her. "What we shared today was beautiful. It was meaningful. Please do not feel dirty because of it."

Thalia's heart was soaking up his every word, so wanting to believe that he could care that much for her without having an ulterior motive. There were many women for him to seduce. The arrival of ship after ship of women to Australia's shores attested to that!

Yet she was finding it hard to believe that he truly wanted her for herself alone.

If so, why had he not claimed her at Odum House instead of Paul?

Oh, why?

"Unhand me," she said, stiffening beneath his grip. "I don't want to hear any more of your meaningless words. Haven't you done enough? Am I not stained for life, both heart and soul, because of you?" She sniffled loudly as tears rushed from her eyes in torrents. "I never want to see you again. Oh, please just leave!"

"Thalia, you must know before I leave that I came here for a purpose other than seducing you," Ian said, digging his fingers into the flesh of her shoulders as he held her away from him, so that she was forced to meet his eyes. "And by damn, you are going to hear me out."

"Do you do everything by force?" Thalia asked, lifting her chin defiantly.

"Only when I deem it necessary," Ian said, glowering down at her. "It is necessary now,

Thalia. I'll say my piece, then I'll let you go."

"It matters not when you let me go, for I shall always hate you, Ian Lavery," Thalia spat, her own words tearing at her heart. She lowered her eyes, finding it almost unbearable to look at him. Loving him so much, she ached unmercifully.

"Thalia, my reasons for being here were not to see you, but to keep an eye out for an escaped convict who may be gunning for Paul Hathaway," Ian told her.

Thalia turned defiant eyes up to him. "Now do you honestly think that I can believe that?" she said, laughing bitterly. "What is it to you that someone is gunning for Paul? Wouldn't it make it simpler for you to get your hands on me more often if Paul were dead? For you to abduct me and keep me as your love slave?"

Ian dropped his hands from her shoulders. He raked his fingers through his hair nervously. "Love slave?" he gasped.

Thalia continued her verbal assault. "Anyhow, you are a prospector," she said icily. "Why would you be concerned over escaped convicts?"

She leaned her face up into his, smiling cynically. "Just how successful have you been in the gold fields?" she mocked. Her eyes raked over him as he stepped away from her and slipped his fringed buckskin shirt on. "It looks to me like you are as poor as a church mouse."

Ian looked at her questioningly; he had never told Thalia that he was a prospector. Then, seeing how her eyes were moving over him, he realized, by his attire, just how she could have come to that conclusion. And until today, hadn't he been unshaven while with her? Aye, he could see how she might take him as a prospector down on his luck.

His eyes wavered. Though so many women of fine breeding looked to bounty hunters as heartless heathens, he had no choice but to reveal the truth to her. "Thalia, I am not a prospector," he said. "I'm a bounty hunter. I came today to watch for an escaped convict—for Tanner McShane, but not so much for the two-thousand pound reward on his head, as to make sure that you don't get caught in the crossfire between Paul and the convict."

Thalia looked at him incredulously. "My, but aren't you skilled at thinking up tall tales," she laughed. She placed her hands on her hips. "You are a liar. I was foolish ever to have believed that you were anything but a rogue!"

She started down the ladder before he had another chance to stop her. When she reached the lower floor, she grabbed her basket of eggs and rushed toward the house, while Ian descended the ladder and watched her quick escape. He wanted to go after her but feared that some of Hathaway's men might return and discover him.

His thoughts returned to his moment of discovery, when he realized that he was the first man she had ever lain with. He shook his head slowly back and forth. Perhaps he had been wrong about many things—about Paul Hathaway, for one, who apparently hadn't taken advantage of Thalia after all.

And what of Thalia? What accounted for her dedication to a husband whose commitment did not go as deep as to include loving her? It was in her embrace and lovemaking that she felt far more for Ian than Paul, so much that she gave herself to him. Yet she refused to leave Paul! Why?

Perhaps Paul Hathaway was a decent sort after all!

For now, Ian decided to leave Paul and Thalia be. It seemed that Tanner McShane wasn't headed this way, so Ian would search for him in the scrub. That should take his mind off his confused feelings for a woman who had stolen his heart.

He moved stealthily across the land until he reached his stallion. Without looking back, he rode away, into the wonders of the scrub.

Thalia left the basket of eggs in the kitchen for Honora to see to and fled to the privacy of her room. She threw herself on her bed, sobbing and pummeling her fists into the mattress. She was confused. She was ashamed! She had let a man who was no better than a drifter, a skilled liar no less, make love to her. She had returned the love!

Oh, how could she have?

Now wouldn't Ian expect more of the same?

He would never leave her in peace now. Surely Paul would find out, and it would soon be over not only for Thalia, but also her sister.

Thalia turned on her side and fingered her ring nervously, hating it with a greater passion even than that which she had shared with Ian! At this moment, she wished that Paul were dead and that Ian had never, ever entered her life!

Oh, but if her parents could only be alive and she

could just be back in England where things were much simpler!

"Viada, things aren't working out as I planned," she whispered to herself. She rose from the bed and went to the window, staring pensively at the brilliant blue sky. "We may never see each other again, baby sister. And perhaps you would be better off because of it. I am nothing but a bungler." She choked on a sob. "Perhaps no better than those whores who frequent the night streets of London, lifting their skirts for any amount of coins paid them."

She bowed her head, Ian's image dashing before her mind's eye and sending her into a tailspin of passion with just the thought of him.

If loving a man so intensely was whorish, God pity her, for there was no denying that she loved Ian with all of her heart and soul.

Paul gazed from the cabin window at his hideout, running his eyes over his lounging gang members. One among them had to be trusted enough for Paul to go to him with an offer he would not like, but could not refuse, for the payment would be too tempting to say no to.

Taking his spectacles off and wearily rubbing first one eye and then the other with the back of his hand, he eased down into his chair behind his desk. Heaving a heavy sigh, he held his head back and closed eyes. Of late, he was beginning to feel as though his world, which was once so secure, was pressing in on him, as though his life was in the midst of a slow transition, and he didn't like the direction it was taking.

He rubbed his eyes again, trying to blot Thalia from his mind's eye, fearing that she was the cause of his uneasiness—as though she alone were the threat to his total existence. Yet he could not summon the courage to order her sent away, or killed. So much about her reached deeply into his soul, touching that part of him that once was good and God-fearing. Through her, he could feel almost human again!

"There are too many dangers in feeling like that about her," he whispered, opening his eyes to stare into space. "But still I cannot kill her!"

He laid his spectacles aside on the desk and set his jaw angrily. "But should I die, she must die also," he whispered harshly to himself. She must not be allowed a lifetime with Ian Lavery, and Paul knew that she would go to him, if she were free from him. Ian was never far from her mind since that kiss they shared on the wharf the day of her arrival. Paul was sure she was not far from his either.

His brow knitting into a frown, Paul reached for a bottle of whiskey and poured himself a shot. He must set his plan in motion. He must choose who would kill her after he was dead.

He gulped down the whiskey and poured himself another shot. Who of his men had become the most greedy—the most willing to do anything for a little gold?

He rose to his feet and looked out the window again. His gaze locked on Kenneth Ozier, and then his thoughts strayed to Ridge Wagner, who had left for Sydney for a short respite from bushranging. Both men were prime candidates for this assignment that could make them richer than either ever could imagine!

Aye, soon he would choose which one he would ask to carry out this mission.

CHAPTER TEN

CLUTCHING HER GOWN AROUND HER, THALIA SAT ON the edge of her bed. She trembled inwardly as she looked at the glass of goat's milk that Paul held clutched in his hand, then up at him. The candle on her nightstand cast only dim light in the bedroom and created strange dancing shadows on his face, giving him the sinister look that was due him. Thalia was unnerved enough over her sensual moments with Ian not all that long ago without having to face Paul Hathaway so soon after. She had not left her room since she had fled from Ian. She had hoped to have at least a small measure of privacy so that she could ponder her careless behavior with the man she could not help but love.

But she could never forget that she was Paul's prisoner, at his mercy always. Total privacy was something that she had kissed good-bye the instant she had left England.

"Your face is strangely pink tonight, Thalia," Paul said, a twitch tugging nervously at his left cheek. "Did you have too much sun today? Did you do more than gather eggs?"

Fear grabbed at Thalia's heart. Could Paul know the true reason her face was flushed? Was he toying with her? Had . . . had Ian been caught as he left the barn?

The thought made a strange sort of sickness spiral through her. Yet, if Ian had been caught, there would have been a commotion outside and she would have heard it. Never would he have let himself be captured without a gunfight, and there had been no gunfire anywhere near the ranch this afternoon or evening.

No. Paul was just fishing for answers, again demonstrating that Thalia was never to have any sort of private life while she was with him. If it were up to him, he would know her every move, her every whim, her every desire. . . .

"I did much today around your dreaded ranch, thank you," Thalia snapped, her voice filled with loathing and sarcasm. "I am your slave, aren't I? I mingled with your other slaves. I worked from dawn to dusk. Does that please you?"

Paul's jaws tightened. His eyes filled with rage. "It would please me most if you would be more accepting of what I have offered you here at my ranch," he gritted through his teeth. "You are not a slave. Slaves do not sleep in a master suite, nor do they have silks and satins to choose from for their daily apparel."

Thalia looked up at him questioningly. "And why do you offer me these things if all you want from me is the same that you want from your slaves?" she asked, her voice quavering. Then she folded her arms across her chest and gave him an angry stare. "You don't need to answer that. For a moment I forgot that I am here only to make you look respectable in the eyes of the community. Daisy Odum was fooled. So shall everyone else be fooled. I wish that I could tell them all what a crazed man you are! I wish I could return to England!"

"You know what would happen if you told anyone the reason you are here," Paul spat, leaning down into her face. "You would return to England all right, but in a pine box! So would your sister greet you in a pine box!"

He thrust the glass of milk toward her. "Now, damn it, drink this milk and go to bed," he ordered hotly. "I've had enough of you for today. And tomorrow you had better be on your best behavior or—"

Thalia paled. "Or what?" she gasped.

Paul forced the glass into her hand. "Just drink this," he growled. "I've got things to do."

Thalia took the glass. She held it to her chest and watched Paul leave in a huff. Then she set the glass down on her nightstand and slowly removed her robe. Disheartened, she lay down on the bed and curled up under the sheet. Watching the flames of the candle hypnotically flickering, tears strolled down her cheeks as she tried to force Paul and his threats from her mind. Again she became consumed with thoughts of Ian. Except for Paul's interruption, she had hardly thought of anything

163

but the moments spent in Ian's arms and what had transpired there. Oh, but she was so in love with him!

But what were his true feelings for her? Why did he persist in bothering with her? Was it only to get what he could from her? Had he chosen her over all of the other women in Australia because she was a challenge? Because she belonged to another man? Did making love to her today become more pleasurable because he felt victorious over stealing another man's woman?

All of that could so easily be true! There were many women arriving each day in Australia who were seeking male companions. Ian, as handsome as he was, could have his pick.

Trying to blank out memories of how Ian's lips and hands had drugged her into total surrender, Thalia closed her eyes tightly. Yet nothing could make her forget. Even now, as she let herself be caught up in the wondrous desire of those moments, her heart soared to the heavens, and her stomach felt strangely, sweetly queasy. Ian had taken her to paradise. Caught up in the throes of romance she knew that she could, if given the chance, succumb to his passions again and again and again.

Tossing over to lie on her back, Thalia stared up at the ceiling. "Ian," she whispered to herself. "Who are you? What are you?"

He had said that he was a bounty hunter.

Was he?

He had sounded convincing enough!

If so, she had mixed feelings about knowing that he hunted men and took them to Adelaide for pay.

A part of her abhorred a man who would make a living in human flesh, yet a part of her admired his courage for going after the vicious convicts who were the most dreaded men in Australia.

She most of all felt deeply thankful for such a man as he. He was not only a protector of the dark-skinned people, but also of the white!

That is, if he was a bounty hunter at all!

She was so weary, so torn with feelings! Thalia looked at the glass of goat's milk. Perhaps it was the answer to her restlessness. Hadn't Paul said that its warmth would relax her? Hadn't he said that it would help her go to sleep?

Desperate enough to try anything to blot her misery from her mind—especially the memory of how her body had reacted to Ian today—Thalia sat up and reached for the glass. She peered down into the milk for a moment, not sure if she wanted to drink milk that had come from a goat, but the warmth of the glass to the palms of her hands felt comforting. It was the warmth of the milk that could give her the blessing of sleep. Surely it would be no different than drinking milk from a cow!

Placing the glass to her lips, Thalia took her first sip, shuddering and screwing her face up with distaste. The goat's milk was nothing at all like any other milk she had ever drunk before. There was something intensely bitter about it. Her tongue seemed to curl up with the bitterness.

But the warmth of the milk was at least welcome, and she practiced something her mother had taught her long ago when she was ill and had been forced to take certain medicines. Her mother had instructed her not to breathe in while drinking—to hold her breath as she let the liquid flow down her throat. Then she would not taste or smell the vile liquid, yet would still get the full benefits from it.

Tipping the glass to her lips, she followed her mother's teachings as though she were there now, looking over her as she had so often when Thalia was a child. She drank the milk in fast gulps, and again she shuddered. She set the empty glass on the table and wiped the excess milk from her lips with the back of her hand, then blinked her eyes nervously when she began seeing two candles on the nightstand instead of one. She rubbed her eyes and looked again. Now she was seeing three candles and her stomach felt like some strange empty pit!

As her head began to spin she peered at the empty glass. "Did he drug me?" she whispered, slipping down to the bed, her eyes closing involuntarily. Her body became limp, yet strangely heavy at the same time, her breathing even and tranquil as she fell into a deep sleep.

And then she began to dream. She was in the ocean. Many sharks with sharp teeth dripping with blood were circling her, their eyes empty sockets, their bodies stripped clean of their flesh, revealing only the skeletal remains of sharp, jagged bones. Ian was beyond the sharks, his arms moving wildly in the water, trying to swim toward her, yet getting nowhere. It was as though there were some evil, unseen force holding him there, immobile.

Thalia tried to scream, but it was as though her throat were frozen.

And then her nightmarish dream transported

her to land. She was being held captive by more bloody, sharp teeth, but this time they belonged to a pack of dingo dogs. They had encircled Thalia in the scrub, snarling, their eyes red and squinting. Beyond the dogs, Ian was trying to draw one of his Colt revolvers from a holster, but it wouldn't budge! He couldn't remove it! He looked back at Thalia, his eyes wild with fear as the circle of dogs moved in closer. . . .

Suddenly Thalia was catapulted from her nightmares and lay somewhere between sleep and waking when a harsh scream rang out through the silent Australian night. At first she thought that the scream was hers, but then she heard it again and knew that it was not. She was awake enough to know that the sound had come from somewhere close by, outside the mission. Her whole body jerked when she heard another blood-curdling scream, then another and another.

"I . . . must . . . see who . . ." she whispered, trying to will her limp legs to move from the bed. As she hung them over the sides, her head began to swim, her eyes no more able to focus now than before she had fallen asleep.

She glanced at the empty glass on her nightstand. "Damn him!" she whispered. "He did drug me!"

Determination swam through her. She lifted a leg with her hands and placed a foot on the floor and repeated the arduous task until finally both of her feet were firmly on the floor.

Trembling and staggering, weakness engulfing her, Thalia pushed herself away from the bed, her feet shuffling as she directed her attention to the window across the room.

Another throaty, shrill scream sent goosebumps rising along Thalia's flesh. She reached for the windowsill, but she was too lightheaded to go any farther. She crumpled to the floor and breathed heavily, the hard wood cold against her cheek.

Slowly she turned her eyes back toward the bed. She had to get back to bed. She must sleep this off! She had no choice!

Scooting an inch at a time, she finally reached the bed. Grabbing the sides of the mattress, she pulled herself slowly upward. Finally on the bed, she collapsed and let the euphoria of sleep claim her again.

This time she slept without nightmares.

She was in a pleasant void, where everything was dark. . . .

The moonlight silhouetted a lone horseman watching the Hathaway Station from a close-by bluff. Tanner McShane leaned over his saddle and peered down at the ranch, his lean fingers stroking his bald head as he smiled wickedly.

He chuckled beneath his breath, realizing that Hathaway was up to his same old tricks when he heard that damn, dark-skinned woman scream as the whip cut into her sleek, black flesh. He knew that bastard Paul Hathaway better'n he knew 'imself. That damn idiot got more delight in hurtin' women than humpin' 'em. As far back as McShane could recall, he didn't ever remember Hathaway takin' a woman to bed. His pleasures came in all ways other than the normal ones.

Dismounting, his tall and wiry figure making

hardly a shadow as he tethered his horse to a limb of a eucalyptus tree, Tanner knelt down to one knee, continuing to observe the activity at Paul's ranch. He had dodged Ian Lavery more than once today and had arrived at the outskirts of the Hathaway place just in time to see Thalia doing her chores. He had even seen her flight from the barn, Ian Lavery emerging shortly after her.

Tanner chuckled again, his gray eyes gleaming, knowing beyond a reasonable doubt what had transpired inside the barn. He would have paid plenty to have witnessed the beautiful young woman lifting her skirts to the handsome bounty hunter. Even now he was getting a raw itch in his loins, picturing the two together, coupling like dogs in heat.

"It's for sure she ain't here for that sort of pleasure with Paul Hathaway," Tanner whispered, watching with keen interest someone being dragged from the barn, lifeless.

In the flood of moonlight he recognized the dark flesh of an Aborigine girl. She was nude, her body striped red with blood streaming from wounds. "Nor do I suspect she's at the ranch for that sort of treatment," he said, shuddering as he watched the body being dumped into a shallow grave behind the barn. "I wonder just how many graves there are now?"

He shifted his gaze and peered toward the house, where soft candlelight still glowed through lacy curtains at the French doors on the second story. He had observed the house long enough to know that was Thalia's room. He smiled slowly. Thalia was one of many young women who had slept in that room. He wondered how long she would last? Time and again the women had disappeared and were never heard from again.

"Well, it's time for another young woman to disappear," he chuckled. "And so she shall."

He became consumed with memories of the days when he and Paul Hathaway had been buddies. They had been inseparable. They had ridden together, members of the same bushranger gang. They had wreaked havoc everywhere they went. Together they had stolen more Aborigine women than all other bushranger gangs put together, and their pockets had filled with coins because of it. The slave trade back then was profitable. Today it was less, yet it appeared tonight that Paul was still practicing it!

But he got too greedy, Tanner remembered, doubling a hand into a tight fist. He quit splittin' everything down the middle with his buddy, and began keepin' most of the loot himself. He forced Tanner's hand, and Tanner had no choice but to leave and start up his own gang.

His eyes gleamed. It had been damn fun to go up against Paul—be his competition. He laughed. Then he glowered. But he couldn't stand the competition. He made sure Tanner got caught, hoping he would rot in jail while he continued to become richer and richer.

He rose back to his feet and placed his hands on his hips, laughing throatily. A new idea had come to him. "I've come for revenge, Paul," he said in a low hiss. "But I don't plan to kill you quite yet. First, I'll steal your latest white filly away from you. I can't think of anything that would frustrate you

170

more. You're runnin' out of excuses for the missin' women. What will you tell Daisy Odum now? Huh?''

He took his bedroll from his horse—a horse stolen from another station, along with a gun-holster well supplied with revolvers and bullets—and clothes that made him look respectable, not like an escaped convict. He spread the bedroll on the ground, placed the pistol close beside his head and stretched out on his back.

Crossing his feet at his ankles he became relaxed, even sleepy. Yeah, stealin' that pretty woman from Hathaway would be enough revenge for now. Tomorrow, when Paul and his gang left to do their day's dirty work, he'd grab 'er. He smiled crookedly. Who could tell? Maybe she'd be glad of his company. Anything had to be better than being saddled with a man like Paul Hathaway. She chose a quick roll in the hay with the bounty hunter, didn't she?

He laughed again, then drifted off into sleep, content for the moment.

CHAPTER ELEVEN

GOING THROUGH THE MECHANICAL MOTIONS THAT got her through her days at Hathaway Ranch, Thalia turned the washtub over on the ground right outside the back door and watched water splash from it, leaving a circle of suds behind as the water seeped into the sun-baked earth. Thalia righted the washtub. Groaning, she placed a hand to her back and leaned against the house for a moment of rest. Her eyes widened and her gasp was lost against a powerful hand as it covered her mouth, and an arm snaked quickly around her waist.

"Don't fight back or I'll break your neck faster than a frog catches a fly on its tongue," the voice threatened in a hoarse whisper. "Just come along easy like." Tanner McShane laughed throatily. "There ain't no one left here on the ranch 'cept black skins, anyhow, to hear you scream. The sucker sure trusts you, don't he, and everyone else who happens along! Bet he's blackmailin' you into stayin', ain't he? Why else would you so willingly wash Paul Hathaway's breeches in that mangy washwater? As I see it, you're too pretty to join in with the natives, workin' alongside them."

Tanner McShane gave a hard yank on Thalia's waist, causing her to emit a loud groan of pain against his hand. "But I didn't come here to give you a talkin' to," he grumbled. "I come here to steal you away from that damn sonofabitch. I'd like to see him when he discovers you gone. He'll be out for blood. I'll send word later who it was that took you. That ought to get a holler or two outta him."

Thalia had no choice but to go with the man as he carried her bodily from the premises. She was immobile against his tall, wiry frame, and he was too strong to fight off.

Her eyes darted desperately around her, hoping that someone might see her being abducted.

But the man was right. It seemed that the entire ranch was deserted!

Where were Paul's help? They always seemed to disappear into nowhere when he left. Surely he left someone behind to keep an eye on things!

But where were they?

Though she wanted to flee the clutches of Paul Hathaway, she did not wish to trade him for this stranger! One was no better than the other! Where she was concerned, neither of their intentions were good.

Finally she got to see the man who had abducted her as he reached his tethered horse and lifted her into the saddle. He looked ordinary enough, like so many of the men she had seen on the wharf in Adelaide. He was dressed in kangaroo hide breeches and shirt, which hung loosely on his thin frame. Bald, he had a hawklike appearance, his nose crooked and sharp at the end. His eyes were deep gray and looked kindly enough up at her.

But it was the drawn expression around his narrow lips that gave him away as a man who was troubled.

Her gaze shifted, resting on the massive revolvers holstered at each hip, and she turned cold inside.

"Who are you and why do you see a need to abduct me?" Thalia asked weakly, wincing as he swung himself into the saddle behind her. "Paul will come for you and kill you."

"So you see yourself as so important to the sonofabitch, do you?" Tanner said, grabbing the reins and wheeling the horse around. He sank his heels into its flanks, sending it off into a steady gallop. "Now I don't think I can count on my fingers just how many women Paul has fooled into thinking they were so important to him." He cackled. "Pretty little thing, aren't you? He'll be infuriated because you're gone, but I bet he'll have you replaced in no time flat."

Thalia grew pale. She leaned back against the man involuntarily as his arm drew her closer to him. "Are you the one who is responsible for the other missing women from Paul's ranch?" she asked, breathless as the horse broke into a hard gallop at the man's command, causing the wind to whip her hair back from her eyes and her dress up past her knees. "He blamed it on the Aborigines. But was it you? Did you carry them all away?" She swallowed hard as she turned her eyes slowly to him. "If so, what do you do with them? Did you kill them? None were ever heard from again."

Tanner threw his head back into a boisterous laugh. "Me? Steal women from Paul Hathaway?" he said, sobering as he stared down into Thalia's eyes. "My time is more valuable than that to me."

"But, sir, you have abducted me," Thalia said, her eyes innocently wide.

Tanner's lips quivered into a sly smile. "And so I did," he said, chuckling low. "And so I did."

"But why me?" Thalia pleaded, turning her eyes away from him, fear gripping her. "And who are you?"

"Never mind why I took you or what my name is," Tanner said, riding farther and farther into the scrub. "But now that I have you, I intend to have some fun. It's been many a month since I've had the soft flesh of a woman against my hard body." He snickered. "Seems I need some revitalizin', don't you think?"

Panic flooded Thalia's insides. She began to claw at Tanner's arm but it didn't budge from around her waist. She turned and began pounding at his chest, but also to no avail. He just looked down at her, laughing all the while.

Soon Thalia gave up. She watched the beauties of the scrub pass her by as the horse thundered onward. Not any too soon, when Thalia's bones were aching from the long, hard ride, her abductor drew rein beside the Murray River, well beyond the stretch that ran peacefully past the Hathaway station.

As Thalia was helped down from the horse, she stretched and eyed her surroundings, knowing that if she did not manage to escape, she would be raped, then possibly murdered. She was most surely one of a long line of innocent women who fulfilled this man's lusts!

Tanner led his horse to the water and left it to drink at its leisure. He then turned to Thalia, his eyes gleaming. He loosened his gunbelt and laid it down on the ground, then began lowering his breeches, a sheathed knife becoming visible where it had been hidden beneath them, at his waist.

"Come here, sweet thing," he said, beckoning for Thalia with a hand. "Let me give you the sort of thrill that you got in the barn yesterday. Let me teach you a few lessons that you couldn't get from Ian Lavery. I'm full-blooded Australian, ma'am. We Aussies know ways to love a woman that no mere American could ever know."

Thalia's face flooded with color. She placed her hands to her cheeks, feeling the heat of her embarrassed blush. "You saw me yesterday?" she gasped. "You know that I was with Ian in the barn?"

"You thought you were getting away with something, didn't you?" Tanner mocked, laughing a choked sort of laugh. "Honey, I've got eyes in the back of my head, don't you know?" He kicked his breeches away from himself, revealing his aroused, stiffened manhood to her fearful eyes. "Come here, pretty thing. Let me give you a thrill."

Thalia was numb with fright. She started backing away from him but he leaned to one knee and withdrew one of his revolvers and aimed it threateningly at her.

"I wouldn't consider escapin', if I were you," Tanner said, motioning with his revolver toward her. "I've got the reputation of being quick with a gun. Now I wouldn't test the theory, if I were you."

Thalia stood her ground. She eyed the gun, then the knife that he still had sheathed at his waist. A germ of an idea began to form within her troubled mind. The knife. If she could just get hold of the knife! And the only way possible was to play up to him, make him think that she was giving in to his demands. She would even have to force herself to act as though she was enjoying being kissed and touched by him.

The chances were, though, that he might not begin with preliminaries of kissing and touching first. He just might grab her and rape her!

But that was a chance she would just have to take.

Forcing herself to smile, flicking her hair back from her shoulders so that it lay in a copper sheen down her slim back, Thalia moved slowly and seductively toward Tanner. "You have a reputation of being quick with a gun?" she purred. "Why, sir, I have the reputation of being quite cooperative with a man if I like him enough. I'm beginning to like you lots. You're strong. You're virile. Why, sir, you are all a woman ever wants in a man." She laughed sarcastically. "Why, that Ian Lavery is nothing compared to the likes of you."

Her gaze lowered. She felt close to retching when she watched his free hand stroking himself.

She was not sure if she could continue with this charade. Everything about him now made her stomach feel as though it was turning inside out.

But she had to get his full attention, and to do that, she had to pretend to be something she wasn't.

"Just look at you," Thalia said, stepping up so close to him now that she could touch him. She reached her hand to his hardness and cupped her fingers over his moving hand and became a part of his game. "Why, I have never seen such a well-developed man. I am sure you will thrill me over and over again when you make love to me."

Tanner gulped hard, the sexual tension building within him feeling as though it might snap at any moment, spilling over within him that which he wanted to save until his body was locked with Thalia's.

But, damn it, he was finding it hard to ask her to stop. Her hand moving with his felt like nothing he had ever felt before. He sucked in a wild breath as the edge was almost reached. His whole body was flooded with pleasure. He stiffened and shuddered and closed his eyes, no longer caring about anything but that surge of ecstatic energy that was ready to envelop him. . . .

"That's the way, baby," Tanner said huskily, licking his lips. "Keep that up and Tanner McShane'll return you the favor. Tanner'll be good to you. You'll see."

Thalia was momentarily caught off guard when she heard his name, wondering where she had heard it before, but the opportunity to make her move had arrived. He had closed his eyes. She had to forget everything at this moment but the importance of making the right moves, and quickly. She unbuttoned his sheath and grabbed his knife from inside it. Without much thought as to whether or not she should kill or wound him, she raised the knife and lowered it into the muscled, meaty flesh of his upper right arm. The blood left his wound in wild spurts.

Tanner yelped and spilled his revolver from his hand. Thalia grabbed it and thrust it into its holster, then picked up his gunbelt that was heavy with revolvers and began running through the scrub away from him. She could hear him cursing her but knew that he could not follow her all that quickly. He would have to see to his wound. He was losing too much blood too quickly! If only she could get far enough away from him to hide, and then if he came after her, she had the guns!

The guns weighed her down, and the skirt of her dress impeded her as it wrapped clumsily around her legs. Thalia fell suddenly to the ground. Panting, she lay there for a moment, getting her breath.

But fearing that her abductor's horse might come barreling down on her at any moment, she grabbed up the holster and started to rise to her feet when she became aware of something growling. She turned her head with a start and every bone in her body seemed to grow weak with fear when she saw that she was surrounded by a pack of wild dingoes, growling and snapping at her.

Terror-stricken, recalling her nightmare and wondering if it was coming true, she watched as the dingoes grew closer, their teeth bared. The weight of the gunbelt in her hand reminded her of the weapons that were available to her.

She looked down at the revolvers. She had never discharged such a large firearm before. Could she now? Or would the time taken to draw the firearm be time that could be used to scramble away from the dingoes?

She knew that escape was not likely now. The dogs could get her in one leap should they so desire. Perhaps if she shot one dog, the others would flee. Or perhaps even the sound of the gunfire might scare them away!

Her fingers trembling, Thalia yanked one of the revolvers from its holster. She tried to steady it in her hands as her forefinger found the trigger. Not taking the time to aim, she pulled the trigger. The report of the gun caused her to lose her balance. Again she found herself lying on the ground, but she righted herself quickly and watched as all but one of the dogs scurried away, yelping.

The one that remained lurked closer and closer to her. She had no time to raise the revolver to shoot it again. The dog jumped on her, its sharp teeth grinding into the flesh of her left hand.

Pain shot through Thalia like white heat. She screamed, then flinched with alarm when a sudden gunshot rang out. She screamed again when the impact of the bullet entered the dog's body and caused it to bolt like a horse kicking its hind legs, landing on the ground with a loud thud beside her.

Dazed and nearly hysterical, her hand paining her as it bled, Thalia watched Ian step into view, his Colt hanging in his hand, smoking, the sharp tang of powder prickling Thalia's nostrils.

"Ian?" she gasped, holding her hand. "You shot the dingo?"

Ian slipped his revolver into its holster and hurried to Thalia. Bending to one knee beside her, he took her hand and inspected the wound. "That's a vicious bite," he said shallowly. "We've got to get it seen to." He reached beneath Thalia's dress and ripped a strip of her cotton petticoat away. He gave her a half glance, then proceeded to bandage the hand. "This should do for now."

Thalia winced every time Ian pressed the cloth against her hand while wrapping it, overwhelmed that he had been there again to save her. "Thank you, Ian," she murmured, tears sparkling in the corners of her eyes. "As before, you happened along just in time to save my life. And why would you? I have been nothing but horrid to you."

"Yes, you've given me a few hateful moments," Ian said, continuing to wrap her hand. "But, Thalia, I know when someone is lying to me. Little darling, you're damn good at it, but not that good. I guess I'm just going to have to be patient and wait to discover why you are indifferent to me more than not."

Not wanting him to realize how his presence truly affected her at this moment—and always— Thalia quickly changed the subject. "The man who abducted me—that horrible Tanner McShane— had planned to—to rape me," she said, shuddering.

"So it was that sonofabitch McShane who is responsible for this, is it?" Ian said, his dark eyes boring down on Thalia.

"You know him?" Thalia said, then gasped softly. "Oh, Lord. Now I remember where I heard the name before. Isn't he the man you told me about yesterday? He's the escaped convict you said you were watching for. You were there yesterday, truthfully, to protect me from him?"

"That's what I said," Ian grumbled, tying the bandage, securing it. "That's what I meant."

"But, Ian, if you were watching for him, how did you allow this to happen today?" she asked, searching his eyes for answers. "Where were you?"

"I wasn't anywhere near the ranch when he abducted you," Ian said, helping Thalia to her feet. "I've been on McShane's trail but lost it in the scrub yesterday. I was just happening along here when I heard gunfire." He glanced down at the wild beast, its eyes staring ahead in a death stare. "It's a good thing I did. You were a bad shot. This thing would've made a meal out of you, for sure."

Thalia shuddered at the thought. She eased from Ian's grip, but leaned into his embrace when a lightheadedness swept over her. "I don't feel so good," she said softly, closing her eyes as she rubbed her brow.

Ian looked across her shoulder deep into the scrub, wincing at the thought of having to forget about Tanner McShane for now. Thalia's welfare came first. The two thousand pounds offered for bringing Tanner in would have to go to whoever found him. He looked quickly down at Thalia. "How did you manage to escape from Tanner McShane?" he asked, lifting her fully up into his arms and carrying her toward his horse. "Where is he now?"

Thalia smiled sheepishly up at Ian. "I used the oldest trick in the book," she confessed. "I pretended I wanted him to make love to me." She laughed softly. "When his breeches were removed, momentarily disabling him, I grabbed his knife and stabbed him in the arm." Her smile faded. "And then I ran as fast as I could." Again she smiled up at Ian. "After I stole his gunbelt, that is. I have no idea where he is now. Perhaps bleeding to death?"

Ian chuckled. "So you wounded the bastard, huh?" he said, setting her easily in the saddle.

"Yes, but not badly enough," Thalia said, grabbing at her hand as she hit it against the pommel of the saddle. "But I could not gather up enough courage to—to plunge the knife into his heart."

"What you did at least stopped him for the moment," Ian said, swinging himself up in the saddle behind her. "That took a lot of courage, Thalia."

"But not enough, it seems," she argued. "Now we've still got him to worry about." Again a dizziness swept through her. She bent her head low. "I truly don't feel so good. I feel . . . sort of . . . sick to my stomach."

"I'll get you back to the Hathaway station," Ian said, holding on to her as he sank his heels into the flanks of his stallion, urging it into a steady lope across the land.

"You will take me there without an argument this time?" Thalia asked incredulously. She turned and gazed up at him. "Truly? Without any hesitation you will take me there?"

"It is the closest house around," Ian said, his

voice flat. "I have no choice but to take you there. You need that nasty bite doctored as quickly as possible."

"But what if Paul sees me with you and shoots you without asking questions?" Thalia prodded.

"Now why would he shoot me when he will see quite clearly that I am bringing you to his ranch, not taking you away?" Ian argued.

He gazed down at her, then reached a hand to her chin and urged her lips to meet his. "This time, for a little while, Thalia, both Paul and I will forget our differences. Your welfare is all that is important."

Their lips met in a sweet kiss, then Thalia leaned into his embrace as they rode on past eucalyptus trees, koala bears feasting on their leaves.

CHAPTER TWELVE

PAUL STOOPED OVER THE WASHTUB AND RAN HIS fingers around inside it. "Dry," he said, his voice drawn. He looked up at the men standing around him and glowered at them. "It's damn dry."

He knocked the washtub aside and knelt to the ground, then ran his fingers over the bleached-white ground where the wash water had been dumped. His fingers again came away dry. "Thalia's been gone long enough for the ground to dry," he said, rising to his full height. He wiped his hand on his breeches and looked into the distance, to the beginnings of the scrub. "But she couldn't have gotten far. You've checked the barn and said there are no horses missing. She must've gone by foot."

His brow became creased with a deep frown. "Unless she was taken by someone," he said, again looking from one man to another. "Those of you few who stayed behind to do your chores—did you see anything out of the ordinary while I was gone? Did you hear anything?"

Everyone shook his head anxiously, meaning they hadn't seen or heard anything. Paul removed his spectacles and wiped his eyes wearily with the back of his free hand. "No one ever hears or sees anything when I'm gone," he grumbled. "It's mighty suspicious to me."

Paul eased his spectacles back on his nose. "But I'll tend to that problem later," he said, walking angrily toward his reined horse.

"Get your mounts, gents. We've some riding to do," he said over his shoulder. "We're going to go and find that little lady and bring her back here."

He placed a boot into a stirrup and swung himself up into his saddle. He wheeled his horse around and faced his men as they mounted. "We'll separate," he shouted, gesturing with a hand toward the scrub. "Kenneth Ozier, you go with the men that way and if you come across Thalia, shoot your gun once into the air, and then a second time. Wait there until I arrive. I've a thing or two to teach my—ah-hem, wife, and I'd rather do it away from the watchful eyes of the Aborigines in my house. They've got enough tales to tell about me, as it is. No need to add fuel to the fire should any of them ever manage to escape."

"Aye, sir," Kenneth responded heartily. "It's as good as done."

Having said his piece, and anxious to get on with

the search, Paul snapped his reins and shouted at his horse. Dust flew behind him as his steed rode hard away from the mission. Cattle scattered. Sheep bawled noisily as they scampered across the land away from the thundering hooves of the horses that soon followed Paul's.

Thalia flinched when Ian's horse jumped a low bush, causing her hand to throb unmercifully beneath the tight bandage as she clung to Ian with all of her might.

"Are you all right?" Ian asked, slowing his stallion's pace. "Did the jump hurt you?"

Thalia forced a smile, yet knew that it must be a grim one. "I'm fine," she lied. She peered ahead. "How much farther?"

"Eager to see him again, are you?" Ian taunted, frowning at Thalia as she turned to look up at him. "Can't stay away from him?"

Thalia gaped openly at Ian, knowing that by now he must realize just how much she did *not* care for Paul, no matter how hard she pretended that she did. But Ian's voice was thick with sarcasm; his eyes were lit with points of fire as he glared down at her.

Yet she could not reassure him of her hatred for Paul any more now than before. Too much depended on her silence. Even now she wondered what Paul must be thinking. Surely he knew better than to believe she would escape of her free will. He held the trump card, it seemed—the welfare of Viada! He had to assume that Thalia had been abducted.

But by whom? That would be the true puzzle for Paul Hathaway. He would leave no stone unturned to find her and her abductor.

"I am only eager to get off this horse and into a warm bath," Thalia said, sighing. "Of course, I am anxious to have my hand seen to." She shuddered. "The dingoes . . . they just came out of nowhere. . . ."

The sound of approaching horses caused Thalia's words to fade. She clutched Ian's arm when she spied the horsemen and the man in the lead.

"Paul Hathaway," Ian said, drawing his reins tight to stop his stallion. He rested a hand on a holstered revolver.

Paul wheeled his horse to a stop beside Ian's and glared from Thalia to Ian. "Well, now, ain't the two of you cozy?" he said, a twitch tugging at his left cheek. He leaned closer. "Ian Lavery, as I figure it you can't be the one responsible for stealin' my wife or you'd be riding in the opposite direction. Where'd you find her, Ian? Who with?"

"I think you've heard of Tanner McShane, haven't you?" Ian said slowly.

Paul was taken aback by the name. He straightened his shoulders. "Who hasn't heard of that bastard?" he said, squinting his eyes in thought as he recalled the night he had set Tanner up to get caught. Tanner had been helping round up Paul's cattle, which Paul had purposely sent astray so that he could point an accusing finger at Tanner, saying that he was stealing them.

Paul had thought that by now Tanner would have

rotted away in prison. Apparently there wasn't any prison that could hold the likes of Tanner McShane for long.

"Well, he's the one who came on your property in broad daylight and took Thalia," Ian said, looking past Paul, at the somber men on horseback behind him. "Seems your men were a bit lazy, don't you think?"

Paul looked over his shoulder, glowering at his men, then focused his attention back on Thalia. He saw the bandage on her hand, blood seeping through it. "Is Tanner responsible for that hand?" he asked, his spine stiffening. "Where is Tanner now?"

"I stabbed him and while running away from him I was attacked by a pack of dingoes," Thalia offered.

She lowered her eyes, hating her next words. "Paul, please take me home." She could feel Ian tighten up, and understood why. Again she was choosing Paul Hathaway over him, even though this time it was obvious that she had good reason for needing to go with Paul—her hand needed tending to.

Paul's eyes lit up. He inched his horse closer to Ian's. "Give her to me," he said, giving Ian a smug smile. The transfer was made. Thalia's insides grew cold as Paul locked his arm around her waist as he situated her snugly on the saddle before him.

"And you say you stabbed Tanner?" Paul asked, peering intently down at Thalia.

"Yes, but only in the arm," she said, regretting that she had not aimed better and sunk the knife into the depths of his evil heart! It was enough to have Paul to worry about, much less Tanner McShane! Now she would always have to be on watch for him. He would surely not rest until he had her in his clutches again, but this time more than likely to kill her!

Paul laughed. "You struck a powerful blow by only wounding him," he said, drawing Thalia closer to him. "Everyone will know that a woman got the best of him, and for a man like McShane that could be worse than death. I doubt if I have to worry about him showing up at the ranch again. He'd fear bein' laughed at."

He looked slowly over at Ian. "As for you," he said, "I guess you just happened along out of nowhere?"

"I had many reasons for being in this part of the scrub," Ian said, shifting his weight in his saddle. "And none that I wish to spell out to you." He gave Thalia a wistful stare, then looked darkly at Paul. "Hadn't you best get her back home? That hand needs immediate attention."

"I don't need you telling me what to do, or how to do it," Paul said between clenched teeth. He jerked his horse's reins and rode away from Ian. "Lavery, keep your distance from my station, do you hear?" he shouted over his shoulder. "There ain't nothin' there that belongs to you!"

Feeling as though she were being thrown back into the pits of hell, Thalia blinked tears from her eyes.

Paul's throaty laugh as he rode away with Thalia made Ian's flesh crawl. He watched for a moment longer, then turned his horse in the opposite direction. Again he was being forced to forget Thalia.

"But only for a while," he whispered. "Only for a while."

For now he would go and search for Tanner again. He couldn't have gotten far in his condition. And then back to Adelaide Prison. This time the two thousand pounds would be well deserved. The damn outlaw would be lucky not to be shot by Ian before being taken back to the prison for the reward.

He rode hard until he arrived at the spot that was familiar enough to him—where he had found Thalia cornered by the dingoes. He rode slowly now, watching for any signs of where Tanner had been stabbed.

And then he saw it. A great pool of red ahead in the grass.

"Tanner's blood," Ian whispered to himself. "This is where he was wounded." He scratched his brow idly, looking slowly around him. "But where is he? Did he get on his horse and ride away? Did he have the strength?"

He cupped a hand over his eyes and peered intensely into the distance. He gasped and his hair rose at the nape of his neck. "Christ!" he uttered harshly, his eyes glued to a gruesome sight. He did not dare approach the scene ahead, where several dingoes were feasting on a horse.

"That must be Tanner's horse," he mumbled, placing a hand over his mouth and feeling as though he might retch. "Does that mean they have already feasted on Tanner?"

Ian decided it was best to ride away. He would

not last a minute with the dingoes if he went snooping around while they were eating. There was no way to tell Tanner's true fate.

No chance in hell.

Paul stood just inside the barn, Kenneth Ozier close beside him, listening intently. "So you understand what's being asked of you, lad?" Paul said, placing a hand on Kenneth's shoulder.

"You want me to try and infiltrate Ian Lavery's group of friends so that I can question around and see what he's doing at all times," Kenneth said, his hands resting on his holstered pistols. "You want me to tell you if he's got eyes for your wife?"

"Aye, something like that," Paul grumbled. "If necessary, ride side by side with Ian or some of his bounty hunter friends, pretending to be his friend, too. Anything, Kenneth, to get to the core of his plans."

Kenneth frowned. "I've heard that Ian usually rides alone except for that black-skinned man," Kenneth worried aloud. "For the most part he's a private man."

"Aye, for the most part," Paul said, nodding. "But he has a network of very loyal friends who are ready to ride with him at a moment's notice, if needed. You become one of those loyal friends, Kenneth. Do you understand?"

"A friend to that bastard?" Kenneth said hotly. "Why, he ain't nothin' but an insulting sonofabitch, someone I'd like to—"

Paul interrupted, laughing. "So you did have that run-in with Ian at the pub that Ridge told me about, did you?" he said, his eyes gleaming. "Good. That'll give you reason to go after him with all your energies."

"He may not want the likes of me near him," Kenneth said, doubts filling him.

"He's got a soft spot in his heart for anyone down on his luck," Paul said flatly. "Act like you haven't got a friend or a cent in the world. He'll react accordingly. You'll be in his circle of friends before you can bat an eye."

Kenneth slung a pistol from its holster, grinning smugly.

The night air swept through the opened French doors in Thalia's bedroom, bringing with it the sweet fragrance of flowers. Her hair still wet from shampooing, clinging in wisps of curls around her face, she lay on the bed in the moonlight, pondering the day's activities. If Ian hadn't arrived when he had, she would be dead now. Her throbbing hand was a continuous reminder that she owed him so much—and all that she could give him was sarcasm! If not for him, the dingo would not have stopped at her hand!

Turning on her side and curling her legs up beneath the cotton nightgown, she was most aware of something else tonight. Her brow was hot with fever. She had not gotten the dingo bite cleansed and medicated soon enough. It was surely infected!

Closing her eyes, she drifted into an uneasy sleep. Nightmares quickly claimed her. She was running. Hundreds of dingoes were chasing her, their teeth dripping with blood. Breathless, too tired to run any longer, she fell to the ground and waited for the dingoes to pounce on her. . . .

Thalia was drawn awake from her hideous nightmare when a soft hand touched her brow. The moonlight was flooding the room enough for her to make out the eyes and face. She welcomed the smile and gentle touch. Quickly her nightmare was forgotten.

"Honora has come to make you feel better," the Aborigine girl said, turning to a basin of water that she had brought into the room. She took a washcloth from it and wrung it free of excess water, then placed it gently on Thalia's brow. "You are hot. This cool compress should help."

Thalia arched an eyebrow. "Honora, you speak English almost as well as I," she said incredulously. "Who taught you? Paul? Did he take the time to teach you?"

"Paul Hathaway not teach Honora. Honora is friend of Ian," the girl said gently, smoothing the soft, wet cloth back and forth across Thalia's brow. "He taught me English. I tell you that he is my friend because I now know that you are also his friend."

Thalia leaned up on an elbow and gazed intensely up at Honora. "How do you know that?" she asked guardedly, not sure whom she should or should not trust.

Honora's dark eyes twinkled. "Honora sees everything," she said, smiling down at Thalia. "I see Ian take you away from the mission, then bring you back. I see you meet Ian in the barn."

Her face flooding with a blush, Thalia looked away from Honora. Lord, it seemed that everyone knew about her rendezvous with Ian in the barn! First there was that dreadful man Tanner McShane, and now Honora! How could Paul possibly not know?

"My father is Hawke, Ian's very best friend," Honora continued, drawing Thalia's eyes quickly up again. "I was abducted by Paul Hathaway's men and brought here against my will."

Honora dunked the cloth back in the water and brought it out again. "I know Paul Hathaway killed my mother," she said, wringing the cloth out and looking as though she wished it were Paul's neck.

Thalia brushed Honora's hand aside as she tried to place the cloth on her brow again. She sat up and came eye to eye with the lovely creature. "Honora, why don't you flee into the scrub?" she asked. "You know that it's possible. Paul's men are very lax in their duties. All of the slaves could escape if they tried." She placed a hand on Honora's thin arm. "Why didn't you make yourself known to Ian when he was here?"

Honora's eyes were innocently wide, yet hiding deeply within them a great fear. "You have escaped and you always return," she said. "Why do you, Thalia? I think it is for the same reason that none of my people try to leave. Because of fear. We fear to risk death! As you must know by now, Paul Hathaway is a mean, crazed man. He hates all women, especially the Aborigine. He blames my people for many things—even for his impotency."

"Impotency?" Thalia said, gasping. "Paul is impotent? This is why he has never made sexual advances to me?''

"Nor to any women," Honora said, sitting down on the bed beside Thalia. She stared out at the moon-washed night. "One day not so many years ago, while Paul Hathaway was fighting and killing Aborigines, one hit him in his vital parts with a club. He was rendered impotent. His hate for the Aborigine has worsened since then. He takes his hate out more on the women than the men, embittered because he cannot perform as a man.''

Honora looked at the spellbound Thalia. "His anger drives him almost to madness," she said, shivering. "Not many know this secret about him. I only recently discovered this while he was viciously flogging an Aborigine girl." She placed a hand to her mouth; tears flooded her eyes. "While he viciously whipped the girl, he screamed this truth at her as he hit her—and hit her, and hit her.''

Stunned by the discovery and filled with sympathy for Honora and what she had witnessed, Thalia was for the moment at a loss for words. This man whom she pretended to be so devoted to, who even acted as though he were her husband, was a sick and twisted man. Each day this was proven to her in worse ways. She was finding it harder and harder to look to tomorrow!

Perhaps there would be none for her!

"Honora must go," the native said, rustling quickly to her feet. "I have said too much. Should Paul ever find out, I would be beaten unmercifully.''

She was gone from the room before Thalia could even reach out to her, to try and comfort her. As a sharp pain stung her hand, she grabbed at it, groaning. Then she grew coldly numb inside when Paul was suddenly at the door, a glass of goat's milk in his hand.

His eyes were narrow slits behind his glasses as he moved toward her.

CHAPTER THIRTEEN

GRABBING A BLANKET, THALIA SWEPT IT OVER HER up to her chin and clung to it as Paul came and stood over her at the side of the bed. She wondered if he had seen Honora leave the room. If so, would he suspect that Honora had confided in her?

His cold, stony stare made Thalia realize that this was not a polite visit to assure himself of her welfare. Although he had seen to her dingo bite quite efficiently, it had only been because he wanted her alive to use her for his selfish purposes —thank goodness, at least, none of those was sexual.

Paul bent over Thalia and placed a hand to the back of her head and lifted it up from the pillow. He placed the glass of milk to her lips. "Damn it, I'm going to be sure that you drink the milk tonight," he said, his tone threatening. "I'm tired of wondering where you'll be next. Tonight you're going to be asleep for the full night."

"No," Thalia begged, then almost choked as he began forcing her to drink the milk. She gulped and sputtered, and then, afraid of being drugged and what might occur while she was, Thalia overcame her fear of Paul long enough to raise a hand and knock the glass from his hands. It flew to the foot of the bed, milk splashing across the blanket and soaking it.

Paul straightened his back and looked down at Thalia, his mouth agape with surprise. Then he struck her on the face, so hard that she was jolted sideways. She crumpled to the bed, sobbing.

"You are giving me cause to regret that I chose you from the others at Odum House," he growled, his teeth clenched as he grabbed up the empty glass. "But I'll be damned if I'll fool with you any more tonight. You drank enough of the milk to make you drowsy." He doubled a fist and placed it in Thalia's face. "Damn it, Thalia, go to sleep or I'll come back here and hog-tie you to the bed. I've got things to do besides babysit you."

Thalia cowered away from him, again clutching the blanket up to her chin. She watched, wild-eyed, until Paul left the room. Then she tossed the soaked blanket aside and turned on her stomach and began pummeling the mattress with her fists.

"I hate you!" she cried. "Oh, how I hate you!"

A lethargic drowsiness began claiming her senses. She felt relief wash through her when she closed her eyes and found escape as she drifted

. . . drifted into sleep. . . .

But she did not sleep for long. A scream awakened her. She bolted upright in the bed and stared toward the opened French doors as another scream pierced the night air. Though disoriented and dizzy from whatever Paul had put in the milk, Thalia was able to recall worrying about Honora. Had Paul seen the girl leave the room? Was he punishing her now? Was Honora the one who was screaming?

Her legs feeling no stronger than a feather, Thalia eased herself gingerly from the bed. Her knees wobbling, her feet not wanting to follow her command to move, she finally succeeded in getting to the French doors. Leaning her full weight on one of them, she inched herself out onto the balcony. Standing in the shadows, out of the moon's glow, she watched the activity below.

She could not believe her eyes. She rubbed them, thinking that perhaps she was still asleep and the drug was causing her hallucinations.

Yet the more she watched, the more she was aware that what she was seeing was real enough. The knowledge made a slow ache circle her heart and a loathing for Paul Hathaway build to extreme proportions within her. He was standing just outside the barn with a huge whip clasped in his hand as several Aborigine women were being ushered into the building, their hands tied behind them.

Suddenly one of the women refused to go and showed her contempt for Paul by spitting in his face.

Fear and revulsion grabbed Thalia at the pit of her stomach when one of Paul's men instantly stabbed the woman.

Breathing hard, Thalia turned her eyes away from the ghastly scene. "I've got to get out of here!" she cried to herself. "I have to escape! Paul is wicked! This place is wicked!"

Managing to get to the bed, she sat down on the edge and tried to stop the crazy spinning of her head. She glared at the milk-soaked blanket. She had been right to suspect that Paul had put something in the milk again. Had she drunk the whole glass, what then . . .? She was certain that Paul had drugged her so that she would not see what was going on at the ranch.

The murders.

The beatings . . .

"Escape," she whispered to herself. "I must escape!"

She held her face in her hands. "But what of Viada?"

The door squeaked as it opened. She turned her gaze slowly toward it, relieved when she discovered that it was Honora.

"I cannot bear staying here any longer," Honora sobbed, rushing to Thalia. "I saw my cousin murdered tonight! I must escape! You must go with me!"

Thalia moved shakily from the bed, her eyes wide with fright. "Yes, yes," she said anxiously. She looked heavenward. "Oh, please forgive me, Viada," she whispered. "I must escape. I have taken all I can of this place. What I saw tonight . . . was horrendous!"

"Paul and his men are gone now," Honora said, grabbing Thalia as she momentarily wavered. "I waited to be sure they were gone before coming to your room. If we are ever to get away from this place, it should be now." She hung her head and cried even more remorsefully. "My cousin. My dear cousin . . ."

Thalia's head spun crazily. She clung to Honora. "Paul put something in my milk," she said. She raised her hand and looked at it. "And my hand throbs so."

Honora touched Thalia's brow gently. "Yes, I know," she said. But your fever is gone." She faced Thalia. "We must hurry."

Thalia swallowed hard. "But where can we go?" she asked, removing her nightgown and taking the kangaroo-hide dress that Honora had brought for her to wear.

"We will go to Ian's house in the scrub," Honora said. "He will protect us!"

Thalia smoothed the soft dress over her head, and down the curves of her body, then gazed incredulously at Honora. "Ian?" she said. "You say that Ian has a house in the scrub?"

"Yes, and we will be safe there," Honora said confidently, bending to a knee to fit moccasins on Thalia's feet.

Discovering that Ian did have some sort of roots surprised Thalia, yet she did not think more on this discovery, because this house that Honora spoke of was surely no more than a thatched-roof hut, much the same as Hawke's.

But it would be a place of refuge—a place where she would be protected from Paul Hathaway. It seemed now that only God could be Viada's protector, for things were out of control for Thalia.

Honora scampered to her feet. She went to the balcony and looked slowly around the grounds beneath her, then rushed back to Thalia and took her good hand to lead her toward the door.

"The time is good now for escaping," she whispered. "Paul is gone. He is busy now with his bushrangers. They are evil raiders. They raid my people's villages and carry off women to use as slaves. Or they are sold. Paul and his men are part of the underground slave trade. I was carried off in such a way from my village. I did not fight them. I have cooperated with them. If not, I would be like the others. If the slaves don't do enough work, they are tied to trees and flogged. If they are stubborn, they are killed."

"How could you have stayed so long?" Thalia whispered as they stepped cautiously out into the corridor.

"It has not been easy," Honora whispered back. "But when you see so much pain, your fear becomes heightened to the point of doing anything to merely survive." She gave Thalia a pensive stare. "You understand. You returned to Paul when you could have gone with Ian."

"Only because Ian could not help me," Thalia murmured. "He is a drifter, a bounty hunter. With him I saw no way to save my—"

She stopped short, having almost revealed the truth of her fears for Viada to Honora. Though she was leaving Paul's sheep station and was possibly placing her sister's life in jeopardy because of her decision to escape, she still could not find it within herself to confide freely in anyone about Viada's welfare.

Then fear for her sister suddenly overwhelmed Thalia. She turned away from Honora and started back toward her room. "I can't," she whispered harshly. "I can't leave!"

Honora stopped her with a firm grip on the wrist. "Please?" she pleaded. "I do not believe I have the courage to leave unless you go with me. Please go with me. Never have I come this close to escaping! If I don't leave tonight, I may never get the chance again. Paul is killing more and more of us. If I displease him over the smallest thing he may kill me just as quickly!"

Thalia looked at Honora, seeing the desperation in her eyes and hearing it in her voice. It was only an assumption that Viada would be harmed. It was a fact that Honora's and Thalia's lives lay in the balance each and every day they stayed at Paul's ranch.

"I know that you are right," she said, her sister's face so vivid in her mind's eye that it tore at the core of her being to have to admit once again to herself that she did not have the means to fully protect her. Thalia had been wrong to ever believe that she could.

She took Honora's hand. "I will go with you," she murmured. "But you must realize what the chances are of being caught. You know the punishment if we are!"

"We must chance it," Honora whispered. "I cannot stay here any longer and watch my people be slaughtered. I must spread the word to Ian. He must see that something is done!"

Stealthily, like two ghosts in the night, they crept down the stairs and outside. They hugged the mission wall with their backs as they looked from side to side, to see if anyone was near. And then they broke into a mad dash and made it to the barn.

Breathless, Thalia leaned against the barn door. "We've made it this far," she whispered, giving Honora a questioning look as the other girl took her hand and led her around to the back of the barn, instead of inside to steal horses.

"What are you doing? We don't have time to do anything but get the horses and get out of here."

"I must say good-bye to my cousin," Honora whispered. "Please, Thalia? I must take time to say good-bye to my cousin."

Thalia's eyes widened when the spill of moonlight revealed several mounds of dirt behind the barn. They were all in the shapes of bodies. "Lord," she gasped, paling.

"The freshest one will be my cousin's," Honora said, spying the fresh mound of dirt among the others. She crept on away from Thalia and fell to her knees beside the grave. She bent lower over it and kissed the dirt. "Honora sorry. Honora did not know you were among those brought to the ranch tonight. Even if I had, I could have done nothing. I am so sorry."

Thalia's heart ached at the sight and at the remorse in Honora's voice. She turned her eyes away and was glad when the girl's hand slipped into hers and they were once again moving away from the gruesome sight of graves.

"Just how many do you think have been murdered here?" Thalia asked, her voice choked.

"Many," Honora said bleakly. "Many too many."

"I'm sorry, Honora," Thalia said softly.

"You are sorry, I am sorry," Honora said, giving Thalia a wistful look. "But that does not save my people."

They moved inside the barn. A lantern was casting faint light around inside. Thalia's breath was stolen away when out of the shadows stepped a large, burly man, a revolver filling his right hand.

"Well," he said, chuckling. "What have we here?"

CHAPTER FOURTEEN

THE MAN WAS SO THREATENINGLY LARGE, AND HIS revolver aimed so steadily at her, that Thalia froze inside. Paul's warnings were like claps of thunder going off inside her brain. She had to think fast.

"What do you think you are doing?" she asked heatedly, everything within her rebelling against the courage she was mustering up. Her fear made her legs feel like jelly, as though they might melt beneath her! "Can't I go into the barn whenever I please with my servant? I—I failed to collect the eggs today. I've come to collect them now. Honora is going to assist me because of my injured hand."

The man looked menacingly down at her bandaged hand, then slowly up at her. "The boss never allows that wench to leave the house, and he told me that you'd not be leavin' your bed tonight," he growled. "He said you weren't able. So how is it that you recovered so quickly?"

Thalia held her throbbing hand out before her, wincing as the pain soared up, through her arm. "I personally gave Honora permission to accompany me to the barn to gather the eggs, and as for myself—I am not a weakling who needs bedrest over a—a mere dingo bite," she said, forcing her voice not to quaver, to give herself away, although she wanted nothing more at this moment than to be able to lie peacefully in bed with no frets or woes. But the world was not that kind. Most certainly its people were not!

The man moved closer to Thalia. The color of his eyes was so washed out that she could hardly tell if they were blue or gray.

They were most certainly threatening, however, and within their depths she could see lust.

"Sir, you are excused," she said thinly, glancing at Honora, momentarily forgotten, who was inching around behind the man. "And I will be sure and tell Paul that you did your duty well tonight— that you confronted me with what you thought was an escape."

"Do you think I can be fooled so easily?" the man said, chuckling. He held his aim steady. "Do you think I'm a damn idiot? The boss gave us all lectures today about being lax in our jobs. There'll be no more strangers comin' and goin' from these premises without their heads gettin' blown off." He placed the barrel of his pistol to Thalia's abdomen, prodding her with it. "I sure as hell ain't goin' to let you get away with anything. If I did, I'd be no better off than those blackies buried behind the barn. I'd be deader'n hell."

"You don't understand," Thalia said, her heart pounding. "My husband gave me permission to do what I pleased around here. He just did not know that I felt good enough tonight to gather eggs. Now please let me do my job or I will be the one who is punished. Paul does not know that I did not get my chores done today."

"I'd like to be in on that punishment," the man said, laughing boisterously. Then he sobered, his eyes squinting as they traveled up and down Thalia. "Missie, I could make you a deal. Give me what's beneath your skirt and I won't tell the boss that you left your room tonight." He poked her with the pistol again. "You see, I know you weren't supposed to go nowheres. That's why I was left behind to keep watch on you. I was the one Hathaway depended on. I won't let him down." He laughed throatily. "I'll even service his woman for him. He won't never find out."

"You wouldn't dare touch me," Thalia said, her voice weak, her eyes wary. She glanced at Honora, sucking in a wild breath when she saw what Honora now held within her hands—a pitchfork! The man, so caught up in his games with Thalia, had completely forgotten about Honora!

She was raising the pitchfork.

Just as the man lifted the skirt of Thalia's dress, the pitchfork came down.

Thalia muffled a scream behind her hand when the pitchfork stabbed into the man's back with a loud crunching sound. Wide-eyed, she watched his body lurch with the impact and his face turn into something grotesque as he breathed out a strangled sort of noise. His hand loosened its grip on the pistol, and it dropped to the floor. Crumpling to the floor beside the pistol, on his stomach, the man's body convulsed. Then he lay quiet. His eyes stared blankly, yet saw nothing. He was dead.

Honora trembled as she looked down at the man, her hands curled into tight fists at her sides. She turned an imploring gaze to Thalia.

Then they ran to one another and embraced.

"Honora never kill a man before," the slight woman cried. "But I had to! I had to! He would have raped you. He would have soon remembered me and raped me, also, then later told Paul about our escape attempt. We would have both been severely punished."

Thalia hugged Honora reassuringly. "You did what was right," she murmured, avoiding having to look at the man again. "But, Honora, we'd best get out of here. Who is to say when Paul and his men will return? Perhaps others are guarding the premises. Let us take our leave while we can and not think another thing about what had to be done to achieve the escape."

Honora crept from Thalia's arms. She wiped tears from her eyes and looked down at Thalia's hand. "How are you feeling?" she asked softly. "Is all of this too much for you?" She reached a gentle hand to Thalia's brow. "You are hot again. Your fever has returned!"

"I'm fine," Thalia tried to reassure her, yet she was quite aware of how miserable she was. Her skin burned with fever, and her hand pained her more than ever. She moved away from the death scene and began searching in the stalls for available horses.

Then she stopped, awe-struck over what her search had uncovered. "Camels?" she said, stepping closer to a stall and eyeing one inquisitively. "I don't remember seeing camels in the barn before."

Honora stepped to her side. "They were brought here today while you were gone," she said, reaching a hand to touch the snout of the curious-looking creature. "Paul probably stole them from a caravan traveling in the scrub. They've been brought to Australia because they're able to penetrate deeply into the scrub better than horses."

"I am sure the best-trained horses are with Paul and his men today," Thalia said wistfully.

Honora quickly opened the stall and yanked at the reins attached to the camel. "We shall ride the camel," she said flatly, leading it past the dead man to the outside. She gave Thalia a glance over her shoulder. "Thalia, come. You get on first. I will follow."

Thalia moved to the camel's side. "But how do I get on this thing?" she asked, still eyeing the camel speculatively.

Honora worked with the camel for a moment, finally getting it to its knees. "You get on now," she said. "It is your height now."

Thalia laughed nervously, then grabbed hold of the hump with her good hand and pulled herself atop the camel. "That wasn't hard at all," she said, smiling victoriously at Honora. "Hurry. We've got to get out of here."

Honora mounted the camel behind Thalia and gave the reins a flick against the beast's side as she nudged him with her knees. "Giddyup!" she cried, turning to look at Thalia with despair.

"He's not going to budge!" Thalia cried. "Perhaps we'd better try one of the horses instead." She shifted her weight from side to side. "It's uncomfortable, anyhow."

"No," Honora said stubbornly. "We travel on this camel. He's just being mean!"

"Arrogant is a better word for it," Thalia said, nudging her own knees into the sides of the camel. "Move, you wretched beast! Get up on your feet and move!"

"Giddyup!" Honora cried, furiously snapping the reins against the sides of the camel. "Giddyup!"

Thalia could hardly help but laugh when the camel yawned lazily. Her eyes gleaming, and for the moment forgetting the dead man in the barn and the dangers of lingering at the ranch, she enjoyed the contest between Honora and the camel. Honora had slipped from the beast's back and was standing, fuming, eye to eye with it. Then she marched around to its backside and kicked it.

When the camel produced another yawn, Thalia giggled. Then she grew pale with fright when the beast made a strange hissing noise through its huge yellow teeth. "Honora, I don't know if it's safe to stay on the camel," she said.

Honora ignored Thalia and scampered back onto the camel's back. She slapped him at the side of his head with a loud whack of her hand.

"Oh, no—!" Thalia cried as the camel erupted

with even stranger noises. She clung hard to the camel's hump when it began snorting and spewing and then honked like a goose.

With a lurch, the camel got up.

"Well, finally," Thalia said. She turned and smiled at Honora who sat behind her, balancing herself on the camel's back. She held a stick with one hand and clung to Thalia's waist with the other. "What are you going to do with that stick, Honora?"

Honora's dark eyes twinkled. She giggled. "I have been on camels before," she said. "If you want to turn right, you hit camel's right side with the stick. If you want to go left, you hit left side." She whacked at the camel's right side and he turned north. "You see? He no longer mean. He take us to Ian's!"

"I certainly hope so," Thalia said, dreading the journey on this uncomfortable, arrogant beast.

"You soon be with Ian and never have to see Paul Hathaway again," Honora said as the camel carried them into the scrub. "Honora be with father and cousins! Honora be happy again."

Thalia was aware of Honora heaving a deep sigh. "Honora, you will be happy, won't you?" she questioned softly.

"Honora's heart has grown used to missing Ridge Wagner," she murmured. "For a while my happiness meant being with him. But he fled. He love me no more. I must learn not to love him and be happy living life without a man."

"This Ridge Wagner," Thalia prodded. "Who is he?"

"He is a friend of Ian," Honora said, her voice

tremuluous. "He is called a *swaggie*. He is a man who never wants a wife. Honora did not know this when she gave him her heart!"

Thalia wanted to ask what a *swaggie* was, but the despair in Honora's voice made her realize that this was not the time for further questions about the man who had rejected this lovely Aborigine maiden. That he did so at all made Thalia dislike him sight unseen. Even if he was Ian's friend, she hoped that she would never have to meet him.

Thalia looked cautiously around her for signs of Paul and his men. But the farther the camel traveled through the scrub, the more confident she became that the escape was successful.

Groggy, weakness assailing her as the pain of her hand and the soaring temperature overwhelmed her, Thalia slumped back against Honora. For hours they traveled like that, Honora devotedly cuddling Thalia close to her. The Australian scrub was dense and unyielding. It was an ominous place with an incredible, frightening emptiness. The camel struggled alternately through heavy mud and blowing sand drifts.

Then Thalia awakened and felt as though she was in a dream, for she was staring up at a house that was so tall and magnificent it was like a castle in the sky. It was big and spacious, like the scrub itself.

"We are at Ian's," Honora said softly. "In his house you will find comfort and safety."

"This house is Ian's?" Thalia asked weakly, dizziness once again claiming her. "I thought he—he was poor."

"Ian is not the sort to boast of his riches," Honora said, slipping down from the camel. "Ian is a man who is filled with much kindness."

In a feverish haze, Thalia closed her eyes, unable to comprehend these truths about Ian. She went limp when strong arms lifted her from the camel. "Ian?" she whispered, then looked up and found the dark eyes of an Aborigine brave gazing down at her.

She was so tired and worn out that she was only half aware of being carried into the house and up a steep flight of stairs. Through a strange sort of haze, she felt the wondrous softness of a bed as she was placed on it. She could feel Honora's gentle hand touching her brow.

She could hear Honora conversing with a lady, but something was keeping Thalia from emerging from the lethargy that was trying to claim her again. Perhaps it was the effect of the drugged milk that had been forced down her throat. Perhaps there had been enough drug in it, mingled with the effect of the temperature and her tiredness, to make her only half aware of what was happening around her now. She strained to listen and comprehend what was being said.

"Honora, everyone thought that you were dead," the soft voice of a lady said. "Where have you been? Your father will be thrilled to know that you are all right."

"I am eager to see my father," Honora said, dabbing Thalia's brow with a wet cloth. "Also your son, Ian." She paused, then added. "Donna, now is not the time to tell you where I have been, or with whom. That I am away from there is all that is important."

"I will send for both Ian and Hawke," Donna said. "They have been riding separately these past few days. Hawke is with your people, trying to keep them safe from the bushrangers as they prepare for the march to the sea. Ian has been close by, I swear surely preoccupied these days by a woman. I have never seen him behave so erratically as now. When you see him, you will recognize this in him, also."

There was a pause, then Donna spoke again.

"Honora, who is this young lady you brought here today?" she asked. "Why did you?"

"She is a very special lady," Honora said, affection evident in her voice. "Her name is Thalia. Like you and Ian, she has a kind heart."

"But where did you find her?" Donna persisted.

"In a place of sadness and death," Honora said glumly.

"Where on earth are you talking about?" Donna asked in a low gasp.

"The same place I have been since I was abducted from my people," Honora said, again placing a hand to Thalia's fevered brow. "At Paul Hathaway's ranch."

"Paul Hathaway?" Donna said guardedly. "Why, he is a much admired man in the community."

"Admired falsely," Honora hissed.

"Then what you are saying is that Paul Hathaway keeps slaves?" Donna asked. "You were his slave?"

"He has many slaves. He kills many of my people when they do not cooperate! He is evil! It is good to be free from him!"

Honora sighed heavily and dropped the cloth in the water. "Now that Thalia safe with you, I must go back into the scrub and find appropriate herbs to make her well," she said, her voice fading from Thalia as Honora walked out into the hallway, Donna at her side.

Honora turned and eased into Donna's arms. "It is good to be here with you again," she murmured. "Ian is so lucky to have such a sweet and caring mother."

"Your mother was as sweet and caring," Donna said, stroking Honora's dark hair. "I'm so sorry about her death, Honora. It was so—so useless."

"So are all deaths of my people useless," Honora said, leaning away from Donna. "If all white people like you and Ian, there be no more tragedies wrought upon the Aborigines by the dreaded bushrangers."

"Ian is doing what he can to help your cause," Donna said, placing an arm around Honora's waist as they walked down a graceful spiral staircase.

"And I will repay him by getting his woman well again," Honora said, giving Donna a half-glance. "Thalia Ian's, not Paul Hathaway's."

Donna's eyes widened. She gaped openly at Honora, filled with wonder. "What do you mean?" she said, her voice shallow.

"Ian and Thalia in love," Honora said matter-of-factly. "I bring her to him. Both will be happy now."

"How did this happen?" Donna prodded. "My son and—and that young lady?"

Honora shrugged. "Honora only know they in

217

love," she said. "That is enough, is it not?"

Donna shook her head wearily, never knowing what to expect from her son next. "And how about you?" she murmured. "How long has it been since you've seen Ridge Wagner?"

Honora's eyes misted with tears. "Forever," she murmured. "Forever—and never." She cast her eyes downward. "And I do not understand. He vowed to always love me."

Donna patted Honora's back. "My dear, men can be so fickle," she said. "So fickle."

His finger on the trigger of his drawn revolver, Ridge Wagner crept stealthily along the wall of the barn, eyeing Paul Hathaway's house cautiously. He had returned from Sydney purposely to come to Paul's ranch to check things out for himself. There was only one chance in hell that Honora could be there, but that was motive enough to investigate. Chances were greater, though, that if Paul had abducted her, he would have sold her in the underground slave trade. Except that Honora was skilled enough in the English language that Paul may have kept her on at his ranch as his own slave and personal servant.

"And she's so damn pretty and sweet," Ridge uttered to himself. "If that bastard so much as touched her . . ."

He held his gun hand steady with his other hand, poised for firing should someone suddenly appear before him. Breathless, eyes alert, he inched toward the barn door, having decided to post himself there to keep watch on the premises for a while. If

Honora was there, surely he eventually would get a glimpse of her.

Springing like a panther, Ridge rushed into the barn, then stopped stone cold in his tracks when he discovered the dead man, a pitchfork in his back.

"My God," he gasped, every muscle in him tightening. It was Thomas, one of Paul's gang members. He moved to a knee beside the man and reached a hand to his throat. Searching for a pulsebeat, he found none. "Dead." He looked over his shoulder, then up at the loft. "Who did it?" he pondered.

Ridge straightened to his full height. Whoever did it had done him no favor. He couldn't stick around now. Once Thomas was discovered, every inch of this place would be searched.

Irritated that his plans had been foiled by some low-down murdering fool, Ridge hurried from the barn. He glanced momentarily at the old mission. He would have to come back later to see if Honora was there.

Ridge made a quick turn and fled to the back of the barn, stumbling over a mound of dirt. Steadying himself, he stared in disbelief at the mounds. They looked like graves!

His gaze moved around him, silently counting the graves, and his newest discovery made him grow ill. He now realized that he had made a mistake by not taking Paul up on his offer to come to the ranch earlier on the pretense of working for him. He could have seen the murder! Perhaps he could have stopped it!

Tears flooded his eyes. "Honora, are you in one of those graves?" he whispered. "God, Honora, are you?"

Ducking his head, he ran blindly from the scene of death, cursing beneath his breath. He had let Honora down. He had let everyone down! And perhaps it was too late to ever make things right again.

CHAPTER FIFTEEN

SOMEONE SPEAKING HER NAME BROUGHT THALIA out of her peaceful sleep. In a quick flutter of eyelashes she looked up and saw a familiar figure sitting on the edge of the bed beside her. "Ian?" she whispered, her lips parched.

"Well, finally our sleeping beauty has awakened," Ian said, bending to kiss her gently on the brow.

Thalia smiled awkwardly at him as he drew away from her. She looked slowly around the room, trying to recollect what had led her to this place she did not recognize. She was in a plush bedroom on a bed with comforters trimmed with fine lace covering her. Honora was standing beside the bed, smiling widely down at her, her eyes dancing.

"Where am I?" she asked, leaning up on an

elbow. She gazed up at Ian. "How did you know that I was here? How did I get here?"

Then she was flooded with recollections. She and Honora had fled from Paul Hathaway's ranch on a camel. During the journey to Ian's house, Thalia's temperature had returned and soared, making her feel as if she were losing her mind. The last thing she could remember was a powerful Aborigine taking her from the camel and carrying her up a steep flight of stairs.

After that, she must surely have fallen into a deep sleep.

Holding her left hand up before her eyes, she discovered that it was no longer bandaged, the wound now only a slight puckering of skin. It was almost healed. The pain was gone!

But how?

She placed a hand to her brow. It was cool. She no longer had a temperature!

But how?

"Honora performs magic with her herbs, doesn't she?" Ian said, seeing the wonder in Thalia's eyes as she examined first her hand, and then her brow. "You're going to be all right, Thalia. Everything is going to be fine."

"Herbs?" Thalia gasped, looking from Honora to Ian.

"The Aborigine know many things magical," Ian said, sweeping fallen locks of hair back from Thalia's brow. "Healing is only one of them. Because of Honora's skills, you are well much quicker."

"Thank you, Honora," Thalia murmured. "I so appreciate your attentiveness to me." She swallowed hard, her throat so dry she found it difficult to swallow.

Ian saw her discomfort and rose from the bed to pour her a glass of water from a pitcher. He held the glass to Thalia's lips. "Drink it slowly," he urged. "You've been asleep for quite a while. Too much water too quickly might make you ill."

Nodding in understanding, Thalia took slow sips from the glass, looking over the rim at Ian. She was beginning to remember too much that Honora had told her that made her wonder about Ian and his true feelings for her. This house—it was Ian's. Just from this room and its rich decor Thalia could tell that Ian was a rich man, yet he had held this truth from her.

Why? Because he had never truly intended for her to know? He had never truly wanted to marry her? He had not planned for her, ever, to be a part of his life? Surely he had made love with her only because she had made herself available!

The pain of regret stabbed at her insides. She turned her lips from the glass, her eyes from Ian. "How long have I been here?" she asked softly.

"One day and one night," Ian said, sitting back down beside her. He tried to take her hand and was puzzled when she pulled it away from him.

"I can hardly believe that we're no longer at Paul Hathaway's house," Thalia said. The touch of Ian's hand had awakened so many wonderous memories that wanted to chase away all of the doubts that now assailed her.

Suddenly new, more fearful thoughts terrified her. Had Paul already set plans into action to kill Viada? Was he searching for Thalia even now?

"Yes—and by God, I'll never let you return to that hellhole again," Ian said, his eyes dark pits as he looked down at Thalia. "Honora told me all about what goes on there."

"She told you everything?" Thalia said, stiffening.

A great streak of lightning criss-crossing the heavens outside the window lighted the room with a silver-white light. A loud clap of thunder followed, shaking the floor.

Ian ignored the threatening weather outside. The atmosphere inside the room was almost as unsettled as any storm. "Yes, she told me everything about Paul and his unethical activities," he said solemnly. "I have always suspected Paul Hathaway of being guilty of many things. But never had I thought he was involved in the slave trade."

He forked his fingers through his hair, his jaw tight. "I have seen it in America—how the slaves are the very reason that that country is torn apart. A civil war is being fought to protect the black people's rights. There aren't enough people in Australia who care enough about the Aborigines to fight for their rights. I have tried, but I have failed them." He doubled a fist to his side. "Christ. I am only one man!"

Another flash of lightning lighted the room. A dark figure emerged from the corridor into the bedroom. All eyes turned to him.

"Hawke," Ian said. He started to go to him, but stopped when Honora emitted a loud cry and dashed into her father's beckoning arms.

"Father!" Honora cried, hugging him tightly. "Oh, Father. Honora so glad to see you!"

Tears sparkled in Hawke's eyes as he looked down at his daughter. His long, lean fingers stroked her dark hair. "My daughter," he said, in his clipped English. "When word came to me that you were alive and well I came hurriedly." He framed her face between his hands and gazed in wonder down at her, tears making paths of silver down his dark cheeks. "You are well. I see that. That is good, daughter. That is good."

"Father, I go home with you," Honora said, sniffling. "Never will evil white man take me away again. I will keep a weapon with me at all times. I kill whoever comes near me that I do not know!"

Hawke smiled proudly. "My daughter speaks boldly," he said, chuckling.

"Your daughter knows much about the world and its people that she did not know before," Honora said.

Hawke drew her into his arms. "Evil white men make you a bitter person," he said, hugging her. He gave Ian a stern look over his daughter's shoulder. "The storm is going to delay our plans, Ian."

Ian gave Thalia a troubled glance. "Hawke, proceed whenever you see the time is right," he said, his eyes now locking with his trusted friend's. "You know what to do. Do it."

Hawke nodded. "As you say," he said flatly.

Arm in arm, Honora and Hawke left the room, leaving Thalia and Ian alone. Their eyes met. There was a moment of silence, and soon Thalia felt herself becoming unnerved beneath Ian's steady stare. So much was being said without words.

"Plans?" she blurted out, breaking the momentary tension between them. "What plans, Ian? You seemed so—so secretive with Hawke."

"It is nothing for you to concern yourself about," he said, his hands going to her throat and framing her face. "God, Thalia, when I think of what could have happened to you at Paul's ranch, I almost get ill."

Thalia grew weak inside as his lips traversed her face, raising heated passion in their wake. She knew the dangers of letting him be so gentle, so loving, yet she could not shake herself away from him this time. It felt too wonderful. His touch gave her a peace of mind that had eluded her of late. If only for a while, she could feel needed. . . .

Then she suddenly recalled where she was and whose house she had been brought to! Ian's! He was not a poor prospector—he was rich! She jerked away from him and gave him a pensive stare.

Confused by Thalia's suddenly changed attitude toward him, Ian laughed awkwardly. "To what do I owe this close examination?" he asked, taking her hand and then wincing when she yanked it away from him.

"Ian Lavery, do you have an honest bone in your body?" Thalia finally asked, squaring her shoulders angrily.

"What do you mean?" Ian asked. "I've given you no cause to question anything I do. I do everything for you for one reason and you know it."

"And that is?" Thalia said, her eyes snapping.

Ian placed his hands gently on her shoulders and refused to budge them as she tried to squirm free. "Because I love you, damn it," he growled. He yanked her next to him, straining his body against hers. Crushing his mouth to her lips, he kissed her heatedly.

Then he released her, leaving both himself and Thalia shaken. She backed away from him on the bed, wiping her mouth with the back of her hand.

"You just won't give up, will you?" she cried. "Even though you know that I understand how much you have deceived me, you persist in trying to convince me that you love me. Ian, please don't treat me as though I am a mindless ninny."

Ian shook his head and frowned. "Unless you tell me, I guess I'll never know what you're talking about," he said.

Thalia made a wide sweep with her hand as she looked around the plushly furnished bedroom. "This!" she accused. "You are obviously a rich man and you led me to believe that you were dirt poor! A man who is anxious to marry a woman is usually more honest."

Her voice faded, then she spoke softly, in a confused tone. "Usually a man who is rich will use those riches to win a lady," she said. "But not you, Ian. Why? I can only assume you did not share the truth with me because you never truly planned to have anything to do with me except—except . . . in bed."

Ian's face became red with anger. He grabbed Thalia by the shoulders again and yanked her close. His eyes gleaming, he looked down at her. "Do you forget so easily?" he said, his voice filled with a low, measured anger. "You have never let me forget your wedding vows. Though both you and I know the circumstances, you continue to stay true to those damnable vows which represent nothing but a mockery of a marriage! Why should I confess the truth about myself to you when I continuously run up against the obstacles that you place between us?"

Ian's voice broke. "And, Thalia, would it have made a difference had I told you about my riches?" he asked. "Would you have left Paul then, to be my bride? Are you only after money, Thalia? Nothing more than money?"

A loud burst of thunder and the splash of rain on the windows made the atmosphere suddenly ominous in the bedroom. An involuntary shiver raced across Thalia's flesh as her eyes remained locked with Ian's, her ears filled with the tortured sound of his voice. Oh, but surely he could not think her capable of being so conniving—that all she wanted was money!

"Oh, Ian, the only thing that would have changed, had I known you were wealthy, was that I would have confided in you and asked your assistance preventing Paul from harming my sister," she blurted out, the words suddenly on her lips without thought. "You could have used your wealth to send for her before Paul had a chance to."

Ian's lips parted in surprise, then he took her hands and gripped them tightly. "What are you talking about?" he asked. "What sister? You never mentioned a sister to me before."

Thalia blinked tears from her eyes. "No, I didn't," she murmured. "And I don't know how I kept it to myself for so long. Oh, Ian, all that I have done since I came to Australia was because of my sister, Viada."

"Tell me everything, Thalia," Ian softly encouraged her. "Everything."

And so she did, and never had she felt so good—so relieved once the words were out!

"Ian," she said, once she had spilled out all of her feelings to him, "do you now see why I thought that you could not help me? Why I felt I always had to go back to Paul? It was because of my commitment—not to him, but to my sister." She swallowed hard. "Oh, Ian, you would have helped my sister had you known, wouldn't you?"

He drew her into his arms and held her close. "You know I would have," he said thickly. "If you had trusted and confided in me, so much of the hell you've put yourself through would have been unnecessary."

He laughed softly. "And thank God, it's good to know that your interest in me goes beyond the riches I possess."

"Ian, I love you and never could I love you more because of your money," she sobbed. "I fell in love with you that moment I saw you, vowing to save me from that dreaded shark! The very moment I saw you, I knew you were the man I had searched my entire life for. Oh, but if only you had gone to Daisy and asked for my services instead of Paul! Everything would have been so wonderful, Ian! Oh, why didn't you, if you say you love me so much? Didn't you love me as instantly as I loved you?"

He held her away from him and peered intensely into her eyes. "I know, now, that I should not have waited to go to Odum House," he said. "But please try and understand when I tell you that I hesitated only because I thought I did not want to lose my freedom—the freedom a man has only if he is not married. Bounty hunting has become my life. It is a damn exciting life, Thalia, one that I would surely have to give up if I gave myself wholly to a woman."

A sudden thought came to Thalia. She had told Ian everything except that she was not married to Paul. "But you changed your mind?" she tested. "You went to Odum House. I was gone. Had you decided that you wanted me more than anything else? When you came to Paul's to abduct me, even then you had decided to change your life—for me?"

"Thalia, don't you know that you are now life itself for me?" Ian said huskily, brushing soft kisses along her lips. "I want you. You say that you love me, so you must want me as badly. Stay with me. You will be happy. I promise."

"Ian, there's so much that I should . . ." she attempted to say, but Ian stole her thoughts and breath away when he swept her into his arms again and began raining her face with gentle kisses.

"Darling, I can think of better things to do on a dark, stormy spring day in Australia," he whispered. "Let me make love to you, Thalia. Forget for the moment anything but how it feels to be totally loved."

Kneeling down over her, he kissed her long and hard, his hands gliding up her gown, setting her aflame everywhere he touched. "Let me love you, Thalia," he whispered as his mouth gently parted from her lips.

Then, briefly, he pulled away. "Unless you are too weak from your recent ordeal . . . ?"

"I am weak, but not from my ordeal," Thalia said, closing her eyes and heaving a shaky sigh as

Ian kissed the hollow of her throat. "My darling, it is because of you—because of you!"

"Then you wish to be loved?" he whispered. He gazed down at her, his face a mask of naked desire. Tremors cascaded down his back when she bashfully nodded her head, her face flushing red with color.

"Then you shall be," Ian said, smoothing her gown slowly up her legs, revealing her long, smooth thighs and then the supple broadening into the hips with their central, auburn muff of hair.

His desire a sharp, hot pain in his loins, Ian raised the gown higher, revealing the slimness of her body and then the magnificence of her breasts. He lifted the gown away from her, then cupped a breast within the palm of one of his hands and brought the taut nipple to his lips. He flicked his tongue over the nipple, then circled the soft mound of her breast with his tongue, tasting the sweetness of her flesh.

When Thalia moaned and twined her fingers through his hair, urging his mouth closer, his hands made their way down her body. Her breathing became ragged when he rested a hand over her soft triangle at the juncture of her thighs. Slowly he inserted a finger inside her. His mouth moved from her breasts to her lips. He kissed and sucked on her mouth while his finger moved within her, drawing from somewhere deep inside her contented, soft purring noises.

"I love you," she whispered against his lips.

"You are so beautiful," Ian said, a gasp echoing like thunder from deeply within him when Thalia lowered a hand to touch the hard swell of his manhood that strained against his breeches. He gritted his teeth with desire as she moved her hand over him, the kangaroo-hide material a barrier that impeded her full touch.

Thalia smiled sheepishly up at Ian as he reached for her hand that was pleasuring him and encouraged it at the front of his breeches where leather thongs tied the fabric together.

Understanding his silent bidding, seeing his eyes now smoky with emotion, she untied the thongs and began lowering his breeches across his powerful hips. Very soon his hard, flat stomach with its fine spray of hair was revealed to her, and then the curling of hair which led down to the part of him that was well aroused.

Blushing, the sight of his arousal causing desire to rage and wash over her, Thalia continued to undress him. After she tossed the last of his garments aside, she laughed and sucked in a wild breath of air as Ian rose above her, one of his knees nudging her legs apart.

"You can't know how much I want you," he said, his voice husky. "I doubted that it would ever be possible again. You were so determined . . ."

Thalia silenced further words by feathering sweet kisses across his lips. "Shh," she whispered. "Please let us not ruin this moment with any more talk that upsets us. You say that you love me. Love me now. Love me long."

Ian glanced down the full length of her, his gaze burning upon her liquid curves. She looked up at his sun-bronzed face and ran her fingers over his strong chin and the slope of his hard jaw.

And then their lips met in a frenzied kiss, Ian's

tongue plunging inside her mouth. His hands cupped the soft, round flesh of her buttocks, moulding her curves into his as he plunged his hardness deep within her.

Caught in his embrace, Thalia felt her body become warmed, all senses yearning for the same rapture she remembered so vividly from that first time with him. Surges of tingling heat flooded her as she worked her body with his. Each stroke within her spoke to her heart more sweetly, more endearingly, than the last. A wondrous sort of curling heat was spinning through her, his lips now at the nape of her neck, his hands awakening her breasts to a keen throbbing.

"Ian," she whispered, moaning with ecstasy. "You are wonderful . . . wonderful . . ."

Ian stopped his strokes within her. He leaned back and smiled down at her, his hands smoothing some damp tendrils of her hair back from her brow.

Then his mouth bore down upon her lips and his hips moved, filling her again with his hardness. His strokes within her were demanding. She met the demands with upraised hips, locking her legs around his waist. Together they rode, body to body, heart to heart.

Soon the passion crested and exploded, leaving them clinging, their world melting away. . . .

A great flash of lightning and crash of thunder drew them apart. They looked out the window and at the heavens as lightning danced in white, heated zigzags across the sky. Thalia turned woeful eyes to Ian.

Ian gazed back at her. "Something besides feeling good about what we just shared is on your mind," he said, placing a hand to her cheek, then looking down at her wounded hand. "Did I hurt your hand? Is that why you look so sad?"

"It has nothing to do with my hand," Thalia said, turning her eyes away and breaking the spell that had woven them together during their intimate embraces. She left his side and moved from the bed, grabbing a robe to throw around her shoulders. She went to the window and watched the lightning play in the sky.

"It's the storm," she murmured. "I am sure that out there in the storm, Paul is searching for me. He won't stop until he finds me."

She turned slowly and faced Ian as he stood beside the bed, drawing his breeches up his powerful legs. "Ian, the search could bring Paul and his men here," she said. "If they find me here, you could be accused of abduction. I fear what Paul might do. He has many men who ride with him. None would think a thing of burning down your house and killing everyone in it."

A low rumble of laughter emerged from Ian's throat. "Let him try," he said, slipping into soft moccasins. "I'd welcome him on my premises with volleys of gunfire. He would never have the opportunity to get even close to my house." He wove his fingers through his hair, straightening it. "And he knows this, so I doubt he will come. He knows that I value the safety of my mother. No one dare come near her, to harm her."

"Your mother?" Thalia said, now recalling another voice in her room right after she was brought to Ian's house. It surely was his mother!

"She lives here? In this beautiful house?"

"Yes, my mother," Ian said, going to stand beside Thalia. He placed an arm around her waist. Together they watched the play of elements in the heavens. Ian knew that the time had come to be totally honest about himself with Thalia, especially about how he had become so wealthy.

CHAPTER SIXTEEN

"I DID NOT INTENTIONALLY CONCEAL THE TRUTH about myself from you," Ian said, slipping an arm about Thalia's waist. He drew her close to his side and talked quietly as he watched the fierce flashes of lightning in the sky. "In time, had I managed to get you to leave Paul, I would have told you everything then."

He looked down at her, at her eyes gazing up at him, luminously blue. "I love you so," he said. "I want nothing more than to share everything with you. My life—my past, present, and future."

He swung her around to face him. "But even though I do not have any promises yet from you," he said, gripping her shoulders gently, "I will explain to you just how I possess so much, while so many in Australia have so little."

"You earned it as a bounty hunter," Thalia said, her voice shallow.

"If that were true, would you love me less?" Ian asked, frowning down at her.

Thalia turned this over in her mind. She swallowed hard, then looked back up at him. "I could never love you less," she murmured. "No matter what I may hear that I find unpleasant."

"Rest easy, darling," Ian said, his lips curving into a slow smile. "I did not come by my riches from being a bounty hunter. It was all inherited— every last penny, every mile of the estate, every stick of furniture in the house—the house, too, for that matter."

"Inherited? Your father was rich?" Thalia asked, a gush of warm relief blossoming inside her. Although a part of her admired Ian for protecting the citizens of Australia, another part of her would have abhorred the thought of everything he owned being, in a sense, tainted by the blood of those he had killed.

She sighed, again glancing around the plushly furnished room. It was so grand, so very, very grand.

Ian placed an arm to Thalia's elbow and led her to a velveteen settee before a roaring fire in the fireplace. He urged her to sit down, then sat beside her. He draped an arm around her shoulders and drew her close. "No," he said, his voice drawn. "I did not inherit anything from my true father. It is all a gift from my step-father. My mother and I share everything equally."

Ian went on, "You see, Thalia, although my mother should have inherited everything, my step-father did not trust her judgment in being able to manage the wealth because she was a woman. The reason I hold claim to half of his vast fortune was because he wanted to make sure that everything would be seen to properly. He was the sort of man who looked to—let's see, now what did you accuse me of thinking you were a moment ago? A mind-less ninny? Well, that is exactly how my step-father thought of all women. He always said that women were only good for one thing."

He paused. Thalia smiled weakly up at him and said nothing. Now that she had gotten Ian started talking about his past, it seemed there was no stopping him. She listened, glad that he cared enough to confide his most private affairs with her. His doing so proved just how much he cared for her.

Her thoughts drifted momentarily to Paul Hath-away. She hated him even more than before, for he was standing in the way of her true happiness—a happiness she had always sought and dreamed of.

Then she brushed these thoughts aside and absorbed Ian's words, feeling his anger, his frustra-tion, his determination.

Ian rose to his feet and leaned an arm against the mantel, staring down into the flames. He spoke with quiet, controlled anger. "I have not enjoyed an inheritance achieved by a step-father who killed and maimed many Aborigines in order to possess land to build this, his vast empire," he said. "I am here only on brief occasions. My mother and her servants live here. I want no part of this sort of life. I have chosen the rebel life of a bounty hunter over that of a rich land owner."

"Your step-father did that?" Thalia asked, rising to her feet. She stood beside Ian, looking up at him. "Ian, this must have been before your mother met and married him, for it is obvious that she does not share his feelings about the Aborigines. Honora brought me to this house without hesitation and—and it was surely your mother who welcomed her here." She placed a finger to her lower lip in contemplation. "I am sure it was your mother who was talking with Honora when I lay in this room only half conscious. There seemed to be so much love shared between them. Am I right, Ian?"

Ian turned and faced her. "You are right, of course," he said, smiling down at her. "Before my mother married my step-father, he had already amassed his riches. She had no idea how, Thalia, or I doubt she would ever have married him."

He looked past her, over her shoulder, out the window at the gloom of the stormy day. "When she met him and fell in love with him he seemed such a decent sort," he said. "Never would my mother or I have believed that he had such a cruel side to him. But I learned all about it from Hawke and his people. Every last dirty detail."

He looked into her eyes again. "Thank God, Mother never saw the ugly side of her husband. Shortly after they married and she came with him to Australia, he became too ill to wreak havoc on the Aborigines any longer," he said, his jaw tight. "He was forced to live out the remainder of his life in bed, my mother coddling him as though he were a child."

"You speak so endearingly of your mother," Thalia said softly. "It is good to see a man love a mother so much. It shows that the man has a warm and generous heart."

"This man has a heart big enough to make room for two women in his life," Ian said, sweeping his arms around Thalia and drawing her to him. "My darling, you and my mother are the special loves of my life."

There was a soft knock on the door. Ian and Thalia jerked apart, smiling awkwardly at one another.

"Who's there?" Ian asked, slipping his fringed shirt over his head. He watched Thalia scramble quickly into her robe, tying it securely in front; then she ran her fingers through her hair, her face flushed.

"Ian, it's your mother," Donna said through the closed door. "Is everything all right? The door is closed. Does Thalia need anything?"

Ian brushed a kiss of reassurance across Thalia's lips, then went to the door. Smiling, he opened it and embraced his mother, then led her into the room.

Thalia stood stiffly, her eyes wide as she found herself being closely scrutinized by a lovely lady in her early fifties. Only faint wrinkles creased her brow and the corners of her eyes. There were sprinklings of gray in the golden hair that hung loose over her shoulders, pulled back from her temples with lovely, jewelled combs. Her bosomy figure was encased in a breathtakingly beautiful low-swept, purple satin dress, and diamonds sparkled at her throat and ears. Her fingernails were long and carefully manicured; her facial features were finely chiseled. There was so much about her that spoke of Ian, causing Thalia's reserves to melt. She knew that, given the chance, she could grow to like this woman immensely.

Donna went to Thalia and gently lifted her injured hand and inspected it closely. She smiled at Thalia as she released her hand. "My dear, I see that Honora has performed another one of her miracles," she said softly. She touched Thalia's brow, then drew her hand away. "As I see it, you are almost as fit as a fiddle. Your hand is healing nicely and your temperature is gone. You are a lucky girl. A very lucky girl."

Donna stepped back to stand beside Ian, locking an arm through his. She looked up at him with pride. "Now do you want to tell me just what your feelings are for this young lady?" she asked straight out, not one to mince words. "It is obvious, son, that there is more than a mere acquaintance here."

She looked at Thalia again and cocked her head to one side. "Young lady," she resumed, "Honora says that you are married to Paul Hathaway. Yet I see so much in the way you look at my son. Why is that?"

Thalia glanced quickly at Ian. She had still not told him the full truth about herself—especially that she was not truly married to Paul. Her lips parted to break the news to Ian and his mother, but she hesitated when Ian came to her, drawing her close to his side and speaking before Thalia had a chance to say anything.

"Mother, Thalia's marriage to Paul was a grievous error and is only temporary," Ian said, causing Thalia to look quickly up at him, her lips parted in surprise. He gazed raptly down at her. "Soon I hope to talk her into being my wife. But it seems that for now, there are a few obstacles in the way."

At a loss for words, Donna placed her hands to her cheeks, trying to comprehend all that she had discovered these past two days—the horrid tales about Paul Hathaway, and now a son who loved the woman married to the vicious man.

"Well, Mother?" Ian said, unnerved by his mother's unusual silence. "Don't you have anything to say? You are usually more opinionated about things that concern me."

Donna squared her shoulders and lifted her chin. "Son, you have to know that I would prefer things to be simpler for you, concerning the woman you love," she said, clasping her hands together before her. "But be that as it may, all I can advise you is to be careful. From what Honora has told me about Paul Hathaway, he is not a man to cross. One more killing will not make the hangman's noose any tighter about his neck once the authorities arrest him."

She looked pityingly at Thalia. "When there is a woman involved, a man's wrath increases tenfold," she said softly.

She moved to Ian and Thalia and hugged one and then the other. "Most normally, I would scold you, Ian, for loving another man's wife," she said, stepping away from them, looking troubled. "But I shall refrain and try to understand."

Thalia began to intercede in another attempt to

explain her marital status, but again Ian spoke too quickly.

"I'm glad, Mother," Ian said, moving away from both Thalia and Donna. "For you may not understand what I must do once the storm passes." He went to the window and peered out at the sky. It was still heavy with rain clouds, and occasional streaks of lightning silvered them in a white sheen.

The skirt of Donna's satin dress rustled as she went to stand beside Ian to also study the sky. "Ian, what is your adventurous heart leading you to do now?" she dared to ask. "Yet, perhaps I don't want to know. It might frighten me too much."

Ian cast Thalia a glance over his shoulder, then looked with a tight jaw down at his mother. "I've got to go and find Paul Hathaway and put a few things straight in Thalia's life for her," he said, hearing Thalia's tight gasp from across the room.

Donna paled and stepped back from Ian, looking up at him incredulously. "You cannot mean that," she gasped. "Ian, Honora told me that Paul—"

Ian placed a hand gently to his mother's mouth, silencing her argument. "I know all about Paul Hathaway," he assured her. "I'm going to see to it that everyone else does. Justice will finally be served when I take him in to the Melbourne authorities with proof of his guilt."

He dropped his hand to his side. "Then I will find a way to convince Thalia that it is with me that she must spend the rest of her life," he said, his brow constricting into a frown as he gazed at Thalia.

243

Donna shook her head as she glanced at Thalia, then moved toward the door. "I guess in time I shall understand what this is all about," she murmured. She turned and gave Ian a wistful stare. "I will leave you two alone to iron out your differences. But now that I see that Thalia is able to dine with us, be prompt, Ian, to bring her to the dining table to join us for a nourishing meal." She gave Thalia another questioning stare, then left the room, closing the door softly behind her.

Thalia gave Ian a look of wonder. "You are going after Paul?" she said, her voice quaking.

"I and a few of my friends are going to stop that bastard dead in his tracks," Ian grumbled. "I should have done it long ago, but I had no solid proof that he was the dastardly criminal that he is."

"I want to go with you," Thalia begged, looking up at him with pleading eyes. "I've got to know, first-hand, if he has put plans in motion that could harm my sister."

"A manhunt is not the place for a woman," Ian said, weaving his fingers through her hair. "Especially not my woman."

"If you don't agree to take me, I will follow anyhow," Thalia said stubbornly, reaching to remove his fingers from her hair. "Now would I be safer traveling alone? Or with you?"

"You are fresh from the sick bed," he argued. "You'd best return to it and forget this foolishness of becoming a female bounty hunter."

"Ian, after I eat a nourishing meal I will be as fit as a fiddle," Thalia persisted.

Surprising Thalia, Ian shrugged and suddenly

agreed to let her go.

"Truly?" she gasped. "I can go? You will allow it?"

"Would you rather I throw a fit when you persist at stubbornly refusing to listen to reason?" Ian said, yet knowing damn well that she would not be a part of any actual fight. "Honey, if you insist, you insist." He would take her to his hideout and after she fell into a sound sleep, he would leave with his men.

Then she would have no choice but to wait for his return—with Paul Hathaway!

Thalia choked back a sob and flung herself into his arms. "Oh, Ian, thank you," she cried. "I am glad that you understand."

Ian stroked her hair, then moved a hand to the belt of her robe and untied it. "Darling, before long Paul Hathaway will be only a sordid memory," he said huskily. "Let me show you what you can expect of me every day, my love, once we rid him from our lives."

He swept the robe from her shoulders, revealing her magnificent breasts. He lowered his lips and sucked at a taut nipple, aware of her shoulders suddenly swaying in her passion. His hands moved over her glossy skin, down over her ribs, and lower, finding the moist channel at the central chasm of her desire.

Thalia closed her eyes, lost in the agony and bliss of rapture as his fingers awakened her to pleasure again. "Ian, how can you promise so much, when —when your days are filled with danger and uncertainty?" Her gasps became long, soft whimpers.

"Darling, never before have I had you to fill the void in my life that I have up to now filled with my work," he said, easing her down on the bed. He rose above her and quickly undressed.

"But, darling, we don't have time for this now," she argued feebly. "Your mother expects us soon at the dining table."

"My mother has grown used to waiting where I am concerned," Ian said, laughing softly. "But never you, darling. Never you."

He stretched out above her and his hands moved beneath her. His whole body quivered with sensation, for cupping her buttocks was a sensual ecstasy all its own. He guided her hips in at his and entered her moist channel with one wild thrust. Her buttocks were smooth and hard as she strained into him, meeting his strokes with abandon. Their naked flesh seemed to fuse, their bodies sucking at each other, flesh against flesh. He kissed her, his tongue flickering in and out, moving it along her lips. As Ian's passion rose, his whole body seemed fluid with fire.

Once more they gave themselves over to a wild ecstasy, all woes and cares momentarily forgotten.

His horse whinnying as it fought the deep mud at its hoofs, Paul Hathaway leaned against the cold and driving rain, his sheepskin cape drawn close around his face. He peered up into the sky and raised a fist. "You cursed storm!" he shouted. "Why now? I can pray for rain and never get it! When I don't want it, the heavens open up and it's like a river turned upside down in the sky!"

"Let's head back!" one of Paul's gang begged as

he rode up beside Paul. "No woman is worth this. Forget her, Paul! There are others just like her at Odum House who're willin' to lift their skirts to live the life you offer at your station!"

Paul slapped the man across the face with the back of his hand. "Just keep your opinions to yourself!" he shouted. "I intend to find Thalia! She can't be allowed to escape! Do you hear? There's more at stake here than a mere lifting of skirts!"

The man recoiled with the blow, then edged his horse away from Paul's, glowering. He joined the others following behind Paul. They all exchanged ugly stares, but rode on relentlessly into the storm.

CHAPTER SEVENTEEN

THE DAY WAS BRILLIANTLY CLEAR WHEN IAN AND Thalia bade Ian's mother good-bye. Clasping her reins tightly as she rode beside Ian away from the mansion, Thalia gave him occasional nervous glances. Something was amiss with him. He still had not tried to talk her out of going with him to capture Paul. It was as though he were playing some sort of silent game with her. Even in his eyes she could see a quiet amusement when he caught her glance with one of his own.

Thalia turned her eyes away, unnerved.

Ian smiled to himself when he saw Thalia's tight lips. He knew that she was confused by his easy capitulation, yet it would not be long when she discovered exactly what his plans were for her. Damn it, he was just as good at keeping secrets as she was. Soon she would see just how good.

The sun was a flood of infinite fire saturating earth and sky and sending heat billows almost as palpable as smoke wavering upward from the blinding landscape. The breeze felt good to Thalia, as it lifted the travel skirt which Donna had lent her up above her knees, and billowed her cotton shirt away from her. Her hair blew in wisps around her face and across her shoulders. Her injured hand lay on her lap while the other clasped the horse's reins.

Determined not to let Ian know that she was puzzled by his attitude, Thalia focused her attention on things other than him. As she looked around her, she was impressed anew by exactly how much Ian did own jointly with his mother. The mansion, with its series of rambling pavilions linked by wide verandas, was behind them, and she and Ian were traveling on a winding graveled driveway along the hilly countryside past rows of pines and eucalyptus. Lilacs, dogwoods, and azaleas washed the hillsides. Down a gentle slope of land, symmetrical plantings and box hedges, like the formal geometrics of a French parterre garden, were laid out near fine examples of the topiary art, hedges shaped into all manner of animals.

In another corner of the estate, a Japanese garden, complete with waterfall, Japanese maples, azaleas, and tulips caught her eye.

Farther away still, along the hillsides, cows and sheep grazed placidly, hares darting by.

"You see now why I do not choose to return home that often," Ian said, catching Thalia offguard, for she had not known that he was observing her.

She turned with a start and looked at him, her lips slightly parted. Then she spoke. "Ian, it is absolutely breathtaking," she said, not understanding how anyone could not want to enjoy such beauty.

Ian swept a hand around. "Two hundred and seventy acres," he said bitterly. "And all taken by force. My step-father had a dream, and he made sure no one got in its way." He dropped his hand to the pommel of his saddle and grasped it so hard, the knuckles of his hand were rendered white. "Many an Aborigine's blood was spilled on this land. To me, it is a place of mockery."

"But if you feel this strongly against it, why not move away form it?" Thalia asked.

"Because of my mother," Ian said. "Her husband, my step-father, is buried on these grounds. She promised him, on his deathbed, that nothing would ever desecrate his grave, or the land that he loved." His eyes narrowed. "I cannot do anything that would make my mother unhappy. She has had enough unhappiness in her lifetime." He cleared his throat. "Anyhow, the Aborigines would not want the land now. They see it as unholy. They, too, know the amount of blood that was spilled there."

"How sad," Thalia said, shuddering. She shook her windblown hair back from her shoulders.

"Yes, sad and unfortunate," Ian agreed. He looked at Thalia and admired her suppleness in the saddle. In so many ways she was like his mother.

They each adapted well, no matter the hardships. Would Thalia understand when he chose not to live in the mansion with her after they were married?

He wanted to settle on a sheep station—a simple place for their children to play and run freely. This was the environment that best suited children —not a ghostly, oversized mansion on land that had been shaped by greed and death!

This was the environment that best suited him— and he hoped fiercely that it would suit Thalia too.

Thalia looked up at the sky. As she and Ian rode deeper into the scrub, the sun swept slowly across the huge archway of heaven, and the shadows shifted. "At least the weather is in our favor today," she said, recalling the fierceness of the storm the previous evening. "I'd much prefer this heat to a storm while traveling in the scrub."

Ian nodded, yet did not tell her that he doubted their journey would be free of storms. He had no choice but to lead himself and Thalia along a trail that was also a watercourse, where flash floods were known to roar down at a moment's notice. This was the way to the hideout where Ian and his men would band together before going to Paul's ranch to overtake him and his men. Earlier, before Thalia's escape from Paul's sheep station, it had also been planned to steal Thalia away permanently. He was glad that she was no longer a part of that perilous plan. She was safe now—under Ian's protection, she would be safe always!

The trail dipped up and down, and then the ground leveled out as the watercourse passed between two lines of gum trees that ran due east, a

251

hundred yards apart. Between the trees grass grew two feet high and pure white, sprouting to infinity. It was smooth traveling between the gum trees, their leaves dark and so crisp they would turn to powder under a gentle squeeze.

Everywhere Thalia looked she saw signs of flooding. On one side was an uprooted tree and nestled in the branches was the trunk of another gum tree. On her other side, dead logs and trees were caught in the branches of the trees that had remained rooted.

"What is this place?" Thalia asked suddenly, facing Ian for the truth. "Where are you taking me?"

Ian's dark eyes wavered. He did not want to answer her yet—not until they had reached the hideout!

He started to speak, but sighed with relief when an approaching horseman drew Thalia's attention away from him. Ian inhaled a nervous breath as he watched Hawke approach quickly, then wheel his horse to a stop alongside him.

Hawke eyed Thalia warily, then looked at Ian, his jaw firm, his eyes flashing. "It is done, Ian," he said in his gravelly tone. "The mission has been completed. Word is being spread to all parts of the scrub. All of your bounty hunter and rancher friends will be waiting for your arrival. A young man who calls himself by the name Kenneth Ozier volunteered, also, to ride with us. Hawke gave him permission." He gave Thalia a nervous glance, then looked at Ian again. "I must move onward, my friend, and go in different direction. My people are already on their march to the sea for the season of

252

the swan's egg. There will be many attempts to stop them. I must depart and go to guard my people."

Ian nodded. "I understand," he said. "What about Ridge Wagner? Did you find him and ask if he wanted to lend us a hand?"

"Swaggie Ridge couldn't be found," Hawke said. "Sorry."

"That's all right, mate," Ian said, nodding. "I wasn't counting on his help, anyhow. He's chosen a wandering sort of life, and I'm sure no one can ever change him."

Ian leaned over to Hawke and embraced him. "Ride with care, my friend. Let nothing happen to you, do you hear?"

Hawke patted Ian on the back. "Nothing happen to Hawke," he said gruffly. He clasped a hand to Ian's shoulder. "Let nothing happen to you. You are best friend in the world to Hawke!"

Ian laughed softly. "Hawke is Ian's best friend, also," he said, then grew serious. "Go. I hope I can join you soon to help your people. I know the importance of the swan's egg season to you all. This year, you must be allowed to celebrate it!"

Hawke held his bare, bony shoulders squared as his eyes filled with pride; then he spun his horse around and rode away.

"Ian, Hawke said that your friends would be awaiting your arrival," Thalia said, inching her horse closer to Ian's. "Where? What are your plans? Please tell me. I am a part of this. I should be kept informed of everything."

"Thalia, you insisted on coming with me," Ian said, his jaw tight. "So I suggest that you just don't worry yourself about all the particulars."

A sudden anger flared in Thalia's eyes. "Do I detect a bit of your step-father has rubbed off on you after all?" she said. "You are treating me as badly as your step-father treated your mother—as if I don't have the sense of a magpie!"

Tears streaming from her eyes, Thalia forgot the pain in her hand as she grasped the reins with both of her hands, slapped them against the horse, and rode away from Ian in a hard gallop.

Knowing her so well, Ian was not all that stunned by her reaction to his cool attitude. Now he cursed himself for not being open with her. He sank his heels into the flanks of his stallion and flicked the reins; leaning low over the horse's flying mane, he followed Thalia in a mad gallop. Suddenly, ominously dark puffs of clouds scudded across the sky overhead. Drum rolls of thunder shook the earth as lightning flashed across the heavens in great forces of light.

"Thalia!" Ian shouted, riding hard toward her. "Damn it, Thalia, wait up! It's going to storm! You don't know the dangers!"

Ignoring Ian, Thalia flicked her reins more angrily. Yet she could not help shivering with fright when a strong wind came up, blowing hard against her and threatening to topple her from her horse.

Clinging to her reins, Thalia rode onward, guiding her horse around the fallen trees. She felt small and alone as the rain began to rush against her in torrents, and the lightning continued to rip open the sky, sending thunder to deafen the scrub.

But she would not stop and accept any sort of comfort from Ian. She would not humble herself to him again, ever!

"Thalia, damn it, stop!" Ian shouted, aware of the grinding rocks and moving earth being ripped up and hurled away up ahead where a flash flood was roaring down the watercourse, already uprooting trees in its path.

He poured leather into his horse. Finally he caught up with Thalia and rode up close to her. He reached an arm out and wrapped it around her waist, then jerked her from her saddle and placed her on his lap.

With the rain pounding against her face, her hair knotting wetly, Thalia turned and pummeled her fists against Ian's chest. "Let me go!" she screamed, squirming. "My horse! The storm will frighten it away! Let me down to catch it!"

"There's more to lose here than a damn horse!" Ian argued, holding her tightly against him. He gave her a hard glance as he turned his horse and began riding back in the direction they had just come. "Don't you hear it? It's almost upon us!"

Sudden terror was in Thalia's face as she listened to the rumbling and grinding of rocks and the distinct splash of water rushing toward them from behind. She looked over Ian's shoulder and gasped. She no longer just heard the danger! She saw it! Behind the waterfall of rain, a four-foot wave showed itself, blowing brown globs of foam, rocking forward on its wide, even track—directly along the watercourse!

Then the water hit Ian's horse. Not under, but up! The horse was lifted up in the air by the force of the wave that had engulfed it. Drawn apart by the impact, Thalia and Ian fell on opposite sides of the animal. Thalia screamed as she fell into the water. She clawed the air, looking for fingerholds, then crashed back into the water, bobbing up and down, swirling.

"Ian!" she screamed, swallowing a wild gulp of water as she looked frantically around and could not see him.

She was sucked under the water, battered with rocks, shoved upward and sucked back down, back down and forward, rammed forward by the speed and tremendous power of the flood waters. Along with the water, she was tumbling, twisting, spinning and floating.

Suddenly she found herself flung into the air, then diving into the earth—into mud. . . .

The sun was sliding out from behind retreating clouds. The flood was gone. The watercourse was a foot deep with mud. The earth had been dry and porous and had soaked the water up like a sponge.

Surrounded by mud, Thalia sat up and began scooping mud out of her eyes, her nose, and her ears. Then she heard a rumble of laughter behind her. Blinking her mud-heavy lashes, she turned and saw Ian standing knee-deep in the mud, not one inch of him spared from the brown, clinging wet earth. His dark eyes looked down at her through the mud, still twinkling. His lips quivered with a slow laugh that emerged from deep within him. Thalia looked down at herself and quickly understood what Ian found so funny. Even she could laugh, now that she and Ian had come out of this frightening ordeal without broken bones.

Thalia looked up at Ian again and started giggling, then broke into a fit of laughter as she tried to rise to her feet but fell again and again back into the brown mire. Even when Ian tried to grab her hand to help her, it slipped free and she would fall on her bottom again. She flopped over and over again back into the mud, trying to get a foothold.

Finally Ian managed to draw her completely up; he held her close, and each steadied the other. Their laughter died and their eyes met and held. Ian lowered his mouth to her lips. He kissed her, the taste of the mud lost in the wonders of their renewed passion.

CHAPTER EIGHTEEN

THE WHINNY OF A HORSE DREW THALIA AND IAN quickly apart. They steadied themselves in the mud and looked around them. Thalia clasped a hand over her mouth as a sick feeling grabbed her insides. Not far away she saw Ian's beautiful stallion hanging tangled in the branches of an uprooted gum tree. A dead wombat was jammed against him where the tree was lodged between large rocks. Blood gushed from a wound in the horse's belly where it had been pierced by the sharp, jagged ends of the broken tree.

Thalia looked quickly at Ian. Incredulity changed to belief and pain in his face as he gazed somberly at his faithful mount.

"God!" he said, wavering at the sight. Suddenly there was nothing humorous or romantic about the situation he and Thalia had found themselves in.

Without much thought, but knowing that he must put his faithful horse out of its misery, Ian drew his pistol from its holster and aimed—but his gun would not fire. He turned it around and looked into its barrel. Mud was impacted into it.

The horse whinnied again and shuddered violently, then went limp, its eyes staring ahead in a death lock.

"Ian," Thalia said, placing a hand on his arm. "I'm so sorry."

Ian grumbled something unintelligible to Thalia and slammed his pistol back into its holster. He stared at the horse a moment longer, then looked down at Thalia, his eyes showing the depth of his emotions. "This is one hell of a mess I've got us in," he said, looking her mud-smeared figure up and down. "Let's find a waterhole and get cleaned up. Your horse is long gone by now, and mine is dead, so we've a ways to travel by foot."

"Just exactly where are you taking me?" Thalia asked, trying to keep her anger at bay. At this moment Ian did not need any more problems. He had just lost his wonderful horse. Thalia would choose another time to scold him—if that opportunity ever arose. Many dangers awaited them in the scrub without a horse!

"I guess I have no choice now but to tell you what I have planned," Ian said, looking into the distance, squinting his eyes against the brilliant rays of the sun. "But first, let's find us that waterhole. We'll bathe and wash our clothes and

259

while they are drying, I'll explain everything to you. Then if you wish to hate me, that's beyond my control."

"You just keep me so confused," Thalia said, unable to stifle a giggle when he lifted her up into his arms, for she slipped and slid all about within them as he carried her from the watercourse. She clung around his neck, her eyes dancing as she looked up at him. Even covered with mud, his handsomeness showed through.

Thalia would never forget the kiss they had shared—a kiss all slippery with mud!

"Honey, confusion seems to be our middle name," Ian said as he stepped to dry ground. Behind him the mud was beginning to dry. He was familiar enough with the watercourse to know that in an hour, the mud would be gone. All that would remain would be the havoc it had wreaked.

He looked at his horse and his saddlebag and his carbine thrust into the saddle boot at the side of his stallion. He must remove them from the horse. Their survival depended on them. Thalia did not know it, but there were many miles to walk to get to his hideout. They might just not make it alive.

"Thalia, I'll get the things from my horse," he said, setting her on her feet. "You go on and start looking for that waterhole." His lips quivered into a smile as his gaze swept over her. "I'd be lying if I said you were as pretty as a picture now."

Thalia's fingers went to her hair, thick with mud. Then she ran her hands over her face, shivering with distaste when she discovered that the mud was dried and cracking, surely making her look like a witch out of a storybook!

"Lord," she gasped, now taking the time to look down at herself and the way her mud-caked skirt and blouse were drying to her body like a second skin. "I do look horrible. I must find a waterhole."

Her boots heavy from the caked mud, Thalia began stumbling along. She was amazed at how everything was so dry so soon after such a rain. It was even bone-dry where the banks of the water-course had overflowed!

Ian caught up with her, weighted down with his saddlebag, firearms, and the other equipment he had rescued from his horse. "It may be a while before we find water," he said, his face dry and drawn beneath the mud. "Out here in the scrub, the earth soaks up every bit of the water as quickly as it rains."

"If I could just wash my face," Thalia complained, running her tongue over her parched lips. "I don't think it will ever be the same again. I feel as though the mud is cracking even through my skin!"

Ian fought against laughing. He gazed down at Thalia, seeing her genuine concern. A tear was trickling down her cheek, making a path through the mud and revealing her luscious pink skin.

He waited a moment, then thrust a canteen of water toward her. "There," he said, his eyes twinkling down at her. "That ought to take care of your worries for now." He forced the canteen into her hand. "Use some of the water to wash your face." He chuckled. "I think we can spare it. Anything to set your mind at ease about that lovely face of yours."

Thalia's eyes wavered. "But, Ian—should we not

261

find a waterhole, this could be all that we have to drink for Lord knows how long," she said, her voice breaking. She thrust it back at him and lifted her chin stubbornly. "No. I shan't use it. I am not so vain that I would rather wash my face than have water to drink."

Ian chuckled and slipped the canteen back inside his saddlebag. "Whatever you say, luv," he said, moving relentlessly onward with her trudging along at his side. "Whatever you say."

Ian did not want to alarm Thalia by saying that perhaps she had just made the wisest decision of her life. The storm had thrown him off course and had changed the terrain too much. He was disoriented. Nothing looked the same. He would have to wait for night to find his direction by the stars. Until then, though, he must keep pushing relentlessly onward.

Traveling by foot, he and Thalia were the prey, the intruders to the scrub. . . .

The day had become timeless. Thalia stumbled alongside Ian, his arm around her waist. Cupping a hand over her eyes, she looked into the distance and spotted a dust cloud being given off by a herd of *brumbies*, wild horses that ran free in the scrub.

She moved her hand over her eyes to shield them and looked directly at the sun. It seemed to be jiggling all over the sky, looking as though there were many fiery discs in the heavens, not one. When she looked away she still saw the discs— bright yellow circles dancing everywhere!

The heat shimmered and swayed above the long, brown flats. The atmosphere was airless and depressing. Her mud-tight skin stretched her face painfully, and Thalia's eyes ached from the glare. All she could think about was water. If only she could have at least a trickle of cold water down her aching throat.

Looking at the saddlebag hauled across Ian's shoulder, Thalia thought of the canteen that was now empty. She and Ian had shared the last drink.

Had that been an hour ago? Or two? Or more?

"Luv, are you going to be all right?" Ian asked, breaking the silence. He stopped and turned Thalia to face him. "When I decided to take you to my hideout, I never thought I would be endangering your life by doing so. I was going to take you there and, when you were safely asleep, leave with my men without you. Now I regret that I did not demand that you stay with my mother."

Her throat so dry she found it hard to speak, Thalia forced the words between her lips as she gazed up at him. "Your hideout?" she gasped. "You were taking me to a hideout to abandon me there?"

She placed a hand on her hip. "I knew it!" she stormed. "You have been lying to me ever since we left your mansion. You never had any intention of letting me be a part of Paul's capture. You are a deceitful, lying man. It would serve you right if you died in the scrub. I would laugh at you while you were dying!"

"I guess I deserve that tongue-lashing," Ian said, sighing heavily. He licked his parched lips and placed a gentle hand on Thalia's mud-cracked face. "But, Thalia, there is no need for you to be with me when I capture Paul. The fact that he is stopped is all that should matter to you."

"I must know about my sister," Thalia said, biting her lower lip in frustration.

"We must believe that he has not done a thing about your sister," Ian said. "God, Thalia, it takes months for a ship to get to England. I doubt very much if Paul has even thought about sending word about your sister to anyone. He has been too busy wreaking havoc across the countryside. He is a bushranger. He deals in the underground slave trade. Heaven help us whatever else he deals in."

A choked sob rose from deeply within Thalia. "I know you are right," she cried. "How foolish I have been! But he frightened me so when he began threatening me about Viada! All I could think about was that I had vowed to keep my sister safe after our parents died. Had I been the cause of her death at the hands of a madman such as Paul Hathaway, I would have wanted to die also!"

"That you married the man is something hard for me to grasp," Ian grumbled, his eyes dark pits as he gazed down at Thalia. "But of course, he was the only recourse at the time."

"Ian, I'm not married to the man," Thalia confessed. She smiled weakly up at him as his lips parted and he was speechless for a long moment.

Then his eyes lit up and some of the mud cracked on his face when he broke into a fit of laughter, his eyes watering from the force.

Then he sobered and stared incredulously down at her. "You went that far to protect your sister?" he said softly. "You pretended to be his wife? This, too, was a part of his crazed plan?"

"Yes, and every minute was pure torture," Thalia said, relieved to have finally told Ian the full truth. But her throat felt as though it were on fire from having said so much already. She was so thirsty. How could she stand it much longer?

She coughed and grabbed at her throat.

Ian understood. His throat was raspy and aching also, feeling as though it was swollen double its size. "We'll talk some more once we reach a waterhole," he said, turning around to peer into the distance.

"*If* we find a waterhole, shouldn't you say?" Thalia said, moving in step alongside Ian again.

Little by little they moved east. Ants an inch long tried to crawl on their shoes but were just as quickly shaken off. A tiny red lizard scampered in front of them, then disappeared quickly beneath leaves. Spirals of dust twirled by, pulsating. Dirt rained down on them. They spat out what they could and rubbed their eyes clear.

And they trudged endlessly onward.

A short while later, the thump of emus on the run and the bounding of kangaroos in the distance startled the silence of the land. A great shadow on the ground a few feet ahead of Ian grabbed his attention. He gasped and stopped, grabbing Thalia by the hand.

"Look!" he exclaimed, looking skyward.

Thalia looked quickly up at the sky. A huge wedge-tailed eagle was passing overhead, its shadow seeming to chase itself on the ground.

"Why, it is a most lovely bird," Thalia said, her voice raspy.

"Yes, it's lovely," Ian said, excitement showing in his tone. "But that isn't why I'm so happy to see the eagle. A bird in the scrub means that water can't be that far away."

Hope finally within reach, Thalia's eyes widened when she now saw more birds flying overhead. There were so many, it was one big black patch in the sky!

"By damn, there is water ahead!" Ian said, breaking into a shaky run. He looked over his shoulder at Thalia, then stopped. He went back to her and placed an arm around her waist. "If not for this damn saddlebag and everything else loading me down, I'd pick you up and carry you. But as it is, luv, you'll just have to do your best to keep up with me."

"Ian, with water up ahead, I'll have no trouble keeping up with you," she said in a parched whisper, laughing almost hysterically with happiness. "I'm going to throw myself in it and stay there forever! My whole body is screaming with thirst!"

Ian gave her an understanding look and kept running with her. The wind stirred up the dust, veiling the sun; the pale grass bowed low. When they arrived at a salt-encrusted swamp, known to Australians as clay pans, they realized that they had not found water after all.

Thalia broke into tears. She leaned into Ian's embrace. "It can't be," she cried. "It just can't be! Where were those birds going? Where?"

Ian held her and comforted her, his eyes darting overhead, watching the birds flying farther still than he and Thalia had come. "Don't give up," he urged. "We must continue to follow the flight of the birds. I swear to you, Thalia, that water can't be all that far away." He grabbed her hand and began walking east again, this time up a rise of land. "Come on. Keep your faith. We've only a little way to go now. I give you my word, Thalia. Trust me."

Thalia wiped the tears from her eyes and gave Ian a pinched, sour look. "Trust you?" she said, hardly recognizing her scratchy voice now. "How can I? Look where my trust has got me. I've never been so miserable in my life, Ian, as I am now. And I have only you to blame!"

"Thalia, this isn't the time to argue," Ian said, casting her a harried look. "Blame me all you want, but later. Let's get out of this mess first."

"Hah!" Thalia snapped, tossing her head haughtily. "You can't be serious."

"Never have I been more serious," Ian said, frowning down at her. "I got you into this mess. I'll get you out of it."

"And then?" Thalia persisted. "Will you leave me with your bounty-hunter friends while you go and get yourself killed fighting Paul and his gang?"

Ian's lips parted with a slight gasp. "You say that as though you care about what might happen to me," he said. "You *do* truly love me."

Thalia looked away from him, not wanting to reveal her inner feelings. "I'm just so thirsty," she whined. "All I want right now is a drink of water." She glanced down at herself. "And a bath!"

"Luv, you need wish no longer," Ian said, their persistent walking bringing them up from the parched, dry land.

Seeing the promise of water ahead, they broke into a soft run. They passed under ghost gums and over fields of spongy grass. An occasional koala clung to a gum tree. Kangaroos bounded away, their babies in their pouches. The air was becoming humid, smelling alive and sweet.

Suddenly they saw the shine of an emerald lake, white swans dotting the water. Thalia left Ian behind as he stopped to unload his gear. Laughing, she ran into the water, then dove in headfirst, swans scattering to the land on the opposite shore.

When she broke back to the surface, she cupped her hands and drank greedily as Ian splashed into the water and soon was lost from her view. As he bobbed to the surface beside her, mud streaming from his hair and face as it washed from him, Thalia almost choked on the water as she felt the urge to laugh again at his comical appearance.

Oh, Lord, it felt so good to laugh!

To have something to laugh about!

CHAPTER NINETEEN

THALIA'S SMILE FADED AND SHE LOOKED AWAY from Ian when a kookaburra bird emitted peals of loud laughter from somewhere close to the lake. This startled her back into the reality of the situation she and Ian were in. They were lost in the scrub without a horse. Somewhere out there, Paul Hathaway was surely searching for her, perhaps planning to kill her on sight since he had probably guessed that she had escaped and told Ian the whole story.

She shivered when she recalled Paul's many threats.

"Don't be frightened, Thalia," Ian said, swimming to her when he saw the sudden fear in her eyes. "What you're hearing is only a laughing bird."

He reached for her and drew her through the

water and into his arms, their mud mingling as it streamed from their bodies. "Everything is going to be all right," he said, cradling her close. "I'll get you back to civilization. It's just going to take some more walking. We need to bathe, eat, and get some much needed rest."

"It all seems so useless," Thalia said, sobbing. She clung to Ian. "Ever since I made that fateful decision to come to Australia, nothing has gone right for me."

"I hope that you don't mean that," Ian said, framing her face and turning her eyes up to meet his.

"Why wouldn't I?" Thalia asked, tears streaming from her eyes. Then her lips quivered into a smile. "Of course, you are referring to our meeting." She reached her hand to his cheek and ran her fingers through the reddish-golden stubble of whiskers that were just appearing. "Ian, you have to know how I feel about you. Though I have fought with you over so many things, for the most part it has all been out of pretense. In truth, my darling, you are the only good thing that has happened to me. Thank God there is you."

Ian brought his lips to hers and kissed her long and sweet, then drew away from her. "As much as I would like to devour you, luv, this isn't the time," he said, looking up at the sky through the over-hang of sweetgum branches. "It soon will be dark. We should be settled in before then. We have much worse than laughing kookaburras to fear."

Thalia hugged herself beneath the water, look-ing guardedly around her along the banks of the lake. At present it seemed so innocent—even beautiful. Rock lilies, red-petaled flannel flowers, and sweet-scented boronia with its tiny purple blossoms lined the shore. The fragrance wafting through the air was exquisite.

Ian splashed himself with water, smoothing the mud off his body and out of his hair. "Luv, we've got one thing in our favor," he said, trudging through the water toward shore. He looked at her over his shoulder as he pulled himself out of the water. "The rifle. In its leather gunboot it was protected from the mud. We have it for protection and for shooting our supper."

Thalia's stomach growled. Until now she had forgotten about food. Water had been the most prominent thought on her mind. But now that everything looked more promising, she realized that she was famished!

Eagerly, she splashed the water over her body and washed the mud from her hair as best she could, then joined Ian on shore. She smiled a thank-you to him when he offered her a sheepskin cape that he had taken from his saddlebag.

"You'd best get out of those wet clothes," Ian said, looking her slowly up and down, his loins growing warm at the sight of the clinging blouse and skirt. Everything about her was defined sensually, even to the dark points of her breasts.

"Seems I have some laundry to do," she said, wrapping herself in the cape. She went to Ian and ran a hand over his wet breeches. "It looks like you will have to go hunting for our supper in the nude, darling, if you want your clothes washed while I am washing mine."

Ian stiffened when her fingers brushed against his manhood. He let out a long, quavering sigh. "Luv, if you don't stop what you are doing you may not have any supper," he said, chuckling. "You'll be all I need." He reached for her and pinioned her against him, causing her to drop the cape to the ground. "I'll devour you, luv. Devour you."

Their lips met in a frenzied kiss. Thalia ran her fingers across his back, then down to his buttocks and clasped tightly to them. She held onto him as he lowered her to the ground. She was faintly aware of how the grass smelled like lemons. Her breath was stolen from her as Ian swept her clothes away, his hands touching her every vulnerable, sensitive spot, awakening her to desire as only he knew how to do.

Their lips parted. Thalia watched Ian undress. "Ian, have you forgotten that I must do the wash?" she teased. "That you have to hunt for our supper?"

Ian did not reply. Now shirtless, he stepped out of his breeches and tossed them aside. His gaze burned along her bare skin, causing great gushes of feeling to soar through her. It was incredible to her that she could feel this lighthearted after what they had been through.

But after a brush with death in the swirling, raging waters of the watercourse, she could not help but want Ian more than anything else at this moment. She wanted to cling to him and never let him go! Though they could not know what fate had in store for them, all that mattered was this moment—this paradise found and shared with the man she adored and loved with every fiber of her being.

Ian lay down over her and nudged her thighs apart with a knee. He surged into her with a sensation of hot relief mingled with a passion that made her moan. His fingers went to the nape of her neck and urged her lips to his. Ecstasy whirled inside Thalia as they shared a dizzying kiss.

Slowly, powerfully, he moved within her, their flesh brushing lightly together with exquisite agony. Ian's hands cupped her breasts, his thumbs circling and teasing the nipples with light strokes, causing them to rise into taut, hungry peaks.

Thalia's hips responded in a more rapid rhythmic movement. She locked her legs around his waist and drew him more deeply inside her, moaning against the corded muscles of his shoulder as he took his mouth from her lips and buried his face in her breasts.

Ian groaned with the pleasure that was building . . . building . . . building. . . .

Overwhelmed with ecstasy, Thalia shuddered and cried out against Ian's heated flesh as the rapturous feelings dissolved into a tingling, fierce heat. She clung to his sinewed shoulders as the wondrous explosion of their needs overtook them.

Afterwards, they lay clinging, having once more found the splendid joy that loving one another granted them.

"I love you more than life itself," Ian whispered, reveling in the sweet warm press of her body against his as he moved to her side, enfolding her within his arms. He kissed her hungrily, then rose away from her, to his feet.

Ian gave Thalia a steady smile as she turned on her back, looking the picture of contentment as she smiled lazily up at him. "Well?" he said, forking an eyebrow. "Do I get my breeches washed or not? Or do you dare force me to stay naked? As you have just seen, I have no control over my lust for you when fully unclothed."

"But, Ian, even after I wash them, they will take forever to dry," Thalia teased, curling up on her side as she leaned on her elbow. "I guess I will just have to take my chances with you, won't I?"

Moving briskly around, Ian began plucking dried fallen limbs from the ground beneath the gum trees. "If we are to get anything else done, I'd best build a fire," he said, giving her a rueful smile. After collecting an armful of limbs he lay them aside and cleared a place for a campfire.

Thalia moved to her feet and helped stack the firewood in the center of the firepit, then eyed Ian quizzically. "All right, we have the wood, now where is the fire?" she asked.

Ian had already found two stones that would serve to kindle a spark. He began rubbing them together, the friction causing sparks. Thalia gathered dried leaves from beneath the trees and positioned them between the branches in the firepit. Ian moved the rocks close to the leaves and continued making sparks.

After a few minutes of patient effort, flames jumped from leaf to leaf, and then the wood began to sizzle and pop.

Thalia sighed with relief. She grabbed their clothes and carried them to the lake and began splashing them in the water. Over her shoulder, she saw Ian tramping away, looking almost comical carrying the rifle at his side, his bare body glistening in the evening sunlight.

Entranced by the sight, Thalia locked her gaze on Ian's muscled buttocks and how they flexed and unflexed as he took each step. It caused a sensual tremor to soar through her; then, embarrassed by her reaction to her nude lover, she turned her eyes away and concentrated fully on the task at hand. She worked hard at getting the clothes washed, although her sore hand interfered with the arduous task, then hung them on limbs over the fire.

Feeling the chill of evening closing in on her, Thalia placed the sheepskin cape around her shoulders again and huddled close to the fire. Fear was beginning to set in. Ian had been gone for longer than she had expected he would be. The sun was a red rim slipping over the western horizon, and the shimmering afterglow was too quickly fading into night's darkness.

As time passed, and Thalia became more wary, she trembled and looked heavenward. As white as the bark on the eucalyptus, the moon was large. If she had not felt so alone, so vulnerable, she would have thought everything around her was unreal—too beautiful. The air was too fragrant. The stars were too shiny in the dark sky, where an eagle circled high above her, then circled and soared across the moon.

A stirring in the water drew Thalia's gaze away from the sky. A swan that was as black as the night suddenly glided across the lake, smearing the reflection of the moon and making the water shimmer like white velvet blowing in a gentle breeze.

The sudden blast from a gun jerked Thalia quickly to her feet. Clutching the cape closely around her shoulders, she looked in the direction of the sound, but there was only silence in its wake.

"Ian?" she whispered, trying to see through the night, yet seeing nothing but blackness distorted strangely by shadows made by the moonlight.

Hovering closer to the fire, she waited for Ian to return, hoping the gunfire meant that he had shot something for supper. She would not let herself think for one minute that someone else could be out there this close with a gun, and that Ian had been shot . . . !

"No," she whispered to herself, sinking back down close to the fire. "It was Ian. He's all right. He'll return soon. There's no one else here. Lord, Ian and I haven't seen any signs of civilization since we left his house."

The minutes dragged into what seemed hours to Thalia. Tears misted her eyes. If Ian was all right, he would have returned by now. Perhaps he fell on his own rifle by accident! Should she go searching through the darkness for him?

"But I'd get lost for sure!" she argued with herself just beneath her breath. "I must stay put. Ian would want me to stay by the fire. Surely I am safer here. The fire will discourage any savage animal attacks."

Weary, weak from hunger and anguish over Ian, Thalia looked up at her skirt and blouse. They would be dry by now, and she would be much better off dressed if tragedy did strike tonight.

Tossing the cape aside, she rose to her feet and jerked her clothes from the limb. She winced when she felt their stiffness as she hurried into them, for the mud had been too stubborn to wash completely out.

Sitting back down beside the fire, she pulled on her boots, then sprang with alarm back to her feet when she heard the rustling of feet moving toward her through the scrub.

Her heart pounded as she stared into the darkness, damning Ian's mud-clogged pistols, leaving her weaponless.

Oh, but surely the person approaching was Ian! There was too much of a determination in the step. If it were a stranger, he would be more hesitant— more cautious.

"Ian?" Thalia whispered, her voice weak. "Darling? Is that you?"

Ian stepped into view, carrying his rifle over his shoulder. The moon spiraling down through the leaves overhead silvered his nudity, making him look like an approaching ghost.

Giggling, then laughing from relief, Thalia ran to him and threw herself into his arms. "You're safe!" she cried jubilantly, hugging him tightly. "Oh, Ian, you were gone for so long!"

"I'm sorry, luv," Ian said, hugging her with his free arm. "I walked much farther than I thought."

He eased her away from him and looked down at her with a quiet amusement in his eyes. "But while I was gone, I found something," he said, walking away from her. He lay his rifle down beside the fire and grabbed his clothes, hurrying into them. "Gather up what you can carry. I have a surprise for you."

Thalia's eyes widened. "A surprise?" she questioned. She just then realized that Ian had returned without having captured an animal for their evening meal "The gunfire, Ian. It was you who fired the shot, wasn't it?"

"You'd bloody better believe it was me," Ian said, bending to a knee as he began scooping dirt onto the fire, extinguishing it. He gave Thalia a sideways glance. "Who else, luv?"

Thalia placed a hand to her throat. "Ian, why on earth are you putting the fire out?" she gasped. She eyed him quizzically. "And if you fired the rifle, where—where is—?"

Ian went to her and placed a forefinger to her lips, stopping her questions. "Trust me, Luv," he said, chuckling. "Just come with me and let me show you there is no need for any more questions tonight."

Thalia sighed. "If you say so," she said softly. For a moment she watched Ian move around, putting things in his saddlebag.

Then she helped him until all that was left of their visit by the lake was the campfire that emitted tiny traces of smoke.

"Well? Are you ready?" Ian asked, giving Thalia another amused sort of smile.

"Ian, I wish you would tell me what this is all about," Thalia said, falling into step beside him. "I'm not sure if this is the right time to be playing games. I'm hungry. I'm tired. I'm sleepy!"

"I guarantee you that soon you will be fed and

278

you will have reason to enjoy a full night of restful sleep," Ian reassured, smiling down at her.

"On, no—don't tell me that you have another mansion hidden in the scrub that you didn't tell me about," Thalia said, giving him a look of frustration.

Again Ian chuckled and locked his free arm around her waist, helping her along through the night filled with moonlight and stars.

CHAPTER TWENTY

AN AROMA OF SOMETHING COOKING WAFTED through the air, taking Thalia off-guard. Her footsteps faltered as she inhaled deeply, then eyed Ian suspiciously. "You never did say," she began slowly. "When you fired your rifle—what were you shooting at?"

Ian's eyes twinkled as he looked down at her. "Just a little farther and you'll see," he said. "Didn't I tell you to trust me?"

"Ian, please don't say that to me again, ever," Thalia said, her voice drawn. "So much has happened to me since my parents' deaths, I may never learn to trust again."

Ian's smile faded. His jaw grew tight, hate for Paul Hathaway seething inside him. Now that he and Thalia had been sidetracked by the storm, would his plan go awry because of it?

What of his men awaiting his arrival at his hideout? What must they be thinking now?

Surely they were searching for him, realizing that he had run into trouble.

Thalia resumed her steady gait beside Ian, her hunger now almost overwhelming her. The wondrous aroma of something cooking was getting stronger, making her insides gnaw unmercifully!

What was cooking? Where?

Oh, why did Ian have to make a game of it?

She was tired of being a part of a game—all games!

That cat-and-mouse game she had shared with Paul Hathaway had been the worst!

"Well, there it is, luv," Ian said, motioning with a hand. "Food and shelter, just as I promised you."

Thalia stopped in her tracks, numb, when she saw the bright glow of a campfire up just ahead beneath the ghost-like gum trees splashed with moonlight. Her gaze shifted and she gasped when she discovered something else—a grass hut!

Laughing beneath her breath, Thalia was relieved and amazed that Ian had found something in which to make residence for the night. Just perhaps she could get a full night's sleep without being bothered with the worry of beasts slipping up on her, dragging her away!

The wondrous aroma drew her attention back to the fire. She was close enough now to see that something was cooking on a makeshift spit over the flames. She looked up at Ian, her lips parting with surprise.

"Aye, I did shoot something with my rifle," he said, catching her looking skeptically up at him. "A hare. It should almost be ready for eating."

He glanced at the hut. "And that abandoned Aborigine hut, my darling, is the biggest of my surprises," he said, chuckling. "Grant you, it's not a mansion, but it should do for the one night we will be spending in it."

Thalia gazed at him for a moment longer, then broke away and ran to the campfire, where she dropped to the ground before the fire. Using two sticks instead of a fork, she tore a piece of meat from the roasted hare. Only half aware of Ian laughing softly as he placed his saddlebag and gear aside and sat down beside her, she started to take a bite, then stopped.

Looking at Ian, feeling guilty for her greed and selfishness, she smiled sheepishly and handed the meat to him. When he took it, she focused on her own hunger again and ripped another piece of meat away and tore into it with her teeth. They both ate silently until all that was left of the meal was a stack of bones.

"I made an absolute pig of myself," Thalia said, stretching out on her back on the ground. "I feel as though my insides might burst!"

She yawned and wiped a hand across her eyes. They were heavy with the need of sleep. "Now if only I could just float away into a peaceful sleep, perhaps then tomorrow might be bearable."

She opened her eyes and looked up at Ian. "Is that possible, Ian?" she murmured. "Can tomorrow be better than today? Do you truly believe you know where you are and can get us back to civilization?"

"I've finally got my bearings. The stars are my map. Aye, I can get you to my hideout, if that's what you mean," Ian said, tossing the last stripped bone from the hare onto the pile of other discarded bones beside the fire. He eyed her warily. "Do I have any arguments from you about that now, Thalia?"

Thalia yawned again. "No arguments, Ian," she sighed. She scooted over and sat beside him, relishing the feel of his strong arm around her waist as he drew her against him. "I know you are doing what you think is best for me."

"I should've done it a long time ago," Ian growled. "But you seemed so committed to Paul Hathaway. What else could I do?"

"I hate that man with a passion," Thalia hissed, shivering with her intensity of hate. "And I regret so much, Ian—so much!"

"You needn't," he tried to reassure her. "You were frightened of the man. You had no choice but to pretend that you cared for him." He turned to her and brushed a lock of hair from her brow. "But you need pretend no longer." He took her hand and glared down at the ring. "That damnable ring."

Thalia gazed at the ring, her eyes narrowing with disgust. Very determinedly, she slipped it from her finger. Smiling, her eyes flashing, she tossed it into the tall, waving grass. "I am now free," she said, her voice trembling. "I hope I shall never have to look that man in the face again."

Then her eyes wavered as she looked at Ian. "Lord help me if I have made the wrong decision and anything happens to Viada," she murmured.

She drifted toward Ian as he wrapped his arms around her again. She closed her eyes as he gently rocked her.

"Everything is going to be all right," Ian tried to reassure her. "I'll do everything in my power to make it right for you."

"As you have from the beginning," Thalia said, snuggling closer. "Oh, Ian, you are everything good on this earth. How could I have ever doubted you?"

"Let's not talk anymore about doubts," Ian said. "I think it's time to call it a night."

Thalia leaned away from him and stretched her arms over her head, yawning heavily. "I don't think I've ever been so tired," she murmured. She watched as Ian placed more wood on the fire, then grabbed his saddlebag and sauntered toward the hut.

"Coming?" he said, looking over his shoulder at Thalia.

Nodding, Thalia followed him. Bending low, she moved into the hut, finding it barren of furniture, the floor nothing but bare earth. Ian searched in his saddlebag and soon withdrew two blankets. He spread one out on the ground then settled down beside Thalia on it, covering themselves with the other one.

Thalia cuddled close to Ian, then looked overhead at the cracks in the ceiling where the moon spiraled its silver light through them. Feeling at peace with herself, she kissed Ian on the cheek.

"Darling, I am so glad that we found the lake, and now this hut," she whispered. "If not, where would we be now? I'm so glad to be here with you, Ian. So glad. We may have never found another lake for days! We would have died of thirst!"

"Sometimes I think all of the lakes and ponds of Australia are one big mystery, like Lake George that I have heard so much about," he said, gathering her closer, whispering into her ear. "Lake George keeps disappearing and reappearing. When explorers first saw the lake, it was so huge they thought they had reached the sea. By this time last year, the lake had almost disappeared. No one knows how."

Ian's words drifted off when he became aware that Thalia was breathing steadily, having fallen asleep. Reaching behind himself to make sure that his rifle was close, he closed his eyes and let sleep claim him, also.

But he did not sleep for long. A scampering noise overhead on the roof drew him awake. His eyes squinted in the darkness and his pulse raced as he now recognized the sound of scratching and clawing and he saw silhouetted in the moonlight the shapes of rats!

Ian inched his hand toward the rifle and circled his fingers around it, his finger finding the trigger. Slowly he raised the rifle and aimed toward the roof, but while moving it he had accidentally scraped it against Thalia, awakening her with a start.

Thalia leaned up on an elbow, then gasped with fright when, in the shadows of the moonlight filtering down through the cracks in the ceiling, she saw Ian aiming his rifle at something above them.

285

And then her heart seemed to stop still when she heard the scratching and clawing and the most identifiable squeal of rats as they began to tumble through the cracks in the ceiling, one falling on Thalia's shoulder.

Thalia screamed and frantically brushed the rat away. The explosion of gunfire momentarily deafened her as Ian began shooting at the small scampering animals as they multiplied in strength overhead.

Still screaming, chills racing up and down her spine at the sight of the rats continuing to tumble through the holes in the ceiling, Thalia rushed to her feet and dashed outside, discovering that she was no better off than if she had stayed inside. Rats were everywhere. The bones of the hare seemed to have attracted them, for the rats were swarming over them, thankfully ignoring Thalia and Ian for the moment.

Ian ran from the hut. He shot into the bunched-up rats. Some flinched as the bullets entered their bodies while the others scattered, leaving a deathly sort of silence behind.

Thalia hugged herself with her arms, her teeth chattering as she looked cautiously around her, now seeing no signs of rats, nor hearing them. She looked slowly up at Ian. "Are they gone inside, as well?" she asked, her voice weak.

"Except for those I shot," Ian said, frowning toward the door. "I'll get them out of there and clean up the mess. You stay by the fire."

Thalia inched closer to the campfire. "I'm not sure I can go back inside," she said shallowly. "What if they return?"

"They are far gone by now," Ian said, sweeping a comforting arm around Thalia. "They move in swarms like that through the scrub. By now they have more than likely traveled half a mile. They'll find a dead carcass out there somewhere and stop to feast on it, then go on their way again. They seem never to have a true destination. It's like the devil is in them, and they are fated to keep moving until they die."

"I wish they had traveled on past us," Thalia said, shivering. "They've ruined my night, that's for sure!"

"We'll see about that," Ian said, kissing her softly on the tip of the nose, then handing her the rifle. "Keep watch just in case while I clean out the hut."

Thalia's hand trembled as she held onto the rifle. "So you aren't all that sure they won't return after all," she said.

Ian walked on away from her. "Luv, you worry too much," he said.

Stiffening her back and tightening her jaw, Thalia turned around and faced the fire. She jumped with alarm when Ian stepped up beside her with two dead rats dangling by their tails from his fingers. "Ian, what are you doing?" she gasped, then flinched when he dropped them into the fire. He picked up the other dead rats beside the pile of hare bones and dropped them into the fire also.

Thalia turned her eyes away quickly.

"We don't need dead carcasses of anything bringing any other unwanted visitors in the night," Ian growled. He splashed water from his freshly-filled canteen onto his hands and washed them.

"The bones of the hare must have drawn them," Thalia said, looking gloomily down at the pile of bones. "Perhaps we should burn them, also?"

Ian glanced down at the bones. "There's not enough meat left on them to attract anything," he said. "The rats stripped them clean."

"I'll be so glad to leave this ghastly place," Thalia said, going to Ian to shove the rifle back into his hands. "Even Australia! It is a most unpleasant, wild place! I should have never come!" She lowered her face in her hands. "Oh, why did I?"

Ian laid his rifle on the ground. He turned to Thalia and took her by the elbow and guided her back inside the hut. "Darling, what you need is that good night of sleep I promised you," he said. "I'll stand guard outside so that you can sleep in peace."

Thalia nodded, wiping tears from her eyes. "Thank you, Ian," she murmured, settling down on the blanket. She looked up at him adoringly as he spread the other blanket over her. "I so love you, Ian. So very much love you."

Ian knelt over her and kissed her softly on the lips, then left the hut and settled down just outside the door, his rifle resting on his lap. He focused first on the black sky set with stars, studying them, in awe of the Southern Cross again as though it were the first time he had seen it.

Then his eyes were drawn to a pond not far from the hut. Their heads curled around and tucked beneath a wing as they slept, many swans looked like large white flowers against the backdrop of the water.

And then Ian nodded his head, his eyelids growing heavy with the need to sleep. For a moment he drifted off, then bobbed his head up and blinked his eyes wildly and stared off into space, now so sleepy he was seeing nothing but what seemed a lazy sort of haze before his eyes.

"This is ridiculous," he moaned, shaking his head to clear his vision. He needed to get some sleep too. He would need all his strength to get Thalia safely to his hideout tomorrow. They had a long way to go, by foot.

His rifle tucked beneath his arm, he rose to his feet and placed more wood on the fire until its light reached high above the trees, casting golden reflections on the dark sky. That ought to take care of any animal that wanted to come snooping around. He glanced around, frowning. At least for a little while, he thought, he'd go inside and take a cat nap. That ought to do it.

Stretching and yawning, he went inside the hut. Placing his rifle close beside him he crawled beneath the blanket beside Thalia. He curved his body into hers and hung an arm over her, his fingers brushing against her breast. Sighing leisurely, he drifted into sleep.

Thalia awakened as faint morning light began to shine down on her from the cracks in the ceiling. She ran her tongue over her lips and yawned, then was aware of a body pressed against her from behind, and smiled.

"Ian?" she whispered, turning to look over her shoulder at him. "Darling? It's morning."

Then she remembered what had happened the previous night and Ian's promises to keep guard outside. Guilt flooded her, wondering if he had just crept into the hut after staying awake all night.

She turned her eyes slowly back around and tried not to breathe heavily, now hoping that he wouldn't awaken. She must allow him to get some sleep. He needed his rest as badly as she did. She had been selfish not to have realized that earlier!

Taking advantage of this opportunity to rest longer herself, Thalia closed her eyes and sighed heavily, reveling in Ian's closeness, asleep with her. How wonderful it would be to wake up every morning with him at her side! Was she wrong to hope for this?

Or would Paul still stand in her way of happiness forever?

A sound outside the hut made Thalia's eyes jerk open widely. She caught her breath when she heard it again. It was a strange sort of sound, as though someone were eating something. She could hear sucking and biting noises!

She grew cold all inside.

Oh, Lord, had the rats returned?

Thalia turned quickly to face Ian and shook his shoulders violently. When his eyes popped open and he stared in wonder up at her, she leaned down into his face. "Something is out there!" she whispered harshly, nodding toward the door. "Ian, surely it's the rats! They've come back!"

Ian groaned. "Those rats are long gone," he said, raking his fingers through his hair that lay down across his brow. "You're imagining things."

Then he jolted with alarm as he realized that it was morning and he had slept the entire night away. He rose to a sitting position, reaching for his rifle. "Damn it," he growled. "I didn't mean to sleep so long."

Then the hair seemed to rise at the nape of his neck when he heard the same sounds that Thalia had described. He eyed the door warily, unable to see anything that might be on the other side of the fire, away from the hut.

"Didn't I tell you?" Thalia whispered, grabbing Ian's arm, her fingers digging into it. "You heard it also. Ian, I'm frightened!"

Ian placed his finger on the trigger of his rifle and eased Thalia's hand from his arm. "You stay here," he ordered calmly. "I'll take care of this."

"No!" Thalia whispered harshly, crawling on her knees beside him toward the door. "You're not going to leave me alone for the rats to fall through the ceiling on me again. I'm coming with you, Ian."

Side by side they went to the door.

Both gasped when they looked outside and discovered who the intruder was.

CHAPTER TWENTY-ONE

"**T**ANNER MCSHANE?" IAN SAID, AIMING HIS rifle at the man. His gaze swept over Tanner, aghast at his condition. Thin, his clothes filthy, his right arm dangling limp and gangrenous at his side, Tanner continued to suck hungrily on the bones of the hare, glancing wildly from Ian to Thalia.

"My Lord!" Thalia said, shivering disgustedly as Tanner tossed one of the bones aside and grabbed up another one to gnaw at it. She turned her eyes away, recalling the swarm of rats on the bones only a few hours before. She gagged as a bitter bile rose up into her throat.

A gun's blast made Thalia turn her head back around with a start. Horrified, she gazed at Tanner as he grabbed at his chest, blood rolling from a wound down the front of his shirt. Her eyes followed him to the ground and watched as he clawed a while longer at his chest, groaning, then was suddenly still, as death claimed him.

Stunned, Thalia turned and gaped at Ian disbelievingly, wondering how he could have so cold-bloodedly killed the defenseless, starving man who could have been no threat to anyone. Was this the way he had killed the escaped convicts? Did he give them no chance at all? What Ian had just done was the same as shooting a man in the back!

Puzzled, Ian stared down at his rifle, then gaped at Thalia with parted lips. "Thalia, I . . ." he began, but a familiar voice speaking up behind them caused him to flinch, understanding what had just happened. Paul Hathaway!

"Drop the rifle, Ian," Paul ordered. "Now! Drop it or you'll get a dose of what Tanner just got, 'cept that you'll get yours in the back."

"Paul!" Thalia gasped, paling. She gave Ian an apologetic look, feeling guilty for having thought that he could kill a man so heartlessly. She was so glad that she had not voiced this accusation out loud. He may have never forgiven her.

Trembling, she watched Ian ease the rifle from his fingers and let it drop to the ground. Parting with the rifle could be the same as parting with their lives!

A feeling of helplessness overtook Thalia, yet she kept her chin firmly lifted. She would not let Paul see her cower! Never!

Paul inched around Ian and Thalia and faced them, a smoking pistol aimed at Ian. He moved closer, his eyes squinting behind his spectacles. "I guess I get to kill two birds with one stone this morning," he said, his lips quivering into a smug smile. "I've taken care of that sonofabitch Tanner and now I'll get just as much pleasure in seeing that you two get what you deserve." He chuckled low as he motioned with his pistol. "Of course, it won't be each other."

"Paul, let me explain," Thalia pleaded, eyeing the pistol warily as its aim stayed on Ian. "Ian isn't responsible . . ."

"And you expect me to believe that?" Paul hissed, his face reddening with anger. He glanced from side to side. "Where's your horse, Ian?"

"I'd say it's beginning to rot about now in the tangles of a gum tree," Ian said, waiting for Paul's concentration to lapse for just a second. Then Ian would jump him.

"I found the camel you stole from my barn, Thalia," Paul grumbled. He smiled coyly at Ian. "Of course, I couldn't get it back without a fight. It pleasured me lots, Ian, to kill those men guarding your mother." He chuckled. "I enjoyed watching the bonfire your mansion made after my men torched it."

Ian felt a sick feeling grab his insides. He doubled his hands into tight fists and took a brave step toward Paul. "My mother," he said between clenched teeth. "If you so much as laid a hand on my mother, so help me you'll—"

"Don't take another step," a loud, gravelly voice said from behind Ian. "Or it'll be your last."

Thalia turned slowly and grabbed for Ian's arm fearfully when she saw a dozen men moving into view on foot. She swallowed hard and turned her eyes away, looking up at Ian for courage, and perhaps answers.

Ian's spine stiffened and his eyes were blazing. "Hathaway, you'd better tell your men not to take their eyes off me for one minute, for I swear to God, I will kill you if I get even half the chance."

Paul ignored the threat. He holstered his pistol now that his gang was there to protect him, and knelt down over Tanner McShane. "You bastard," he said in a low hiss. "You should've stayed in prison where you were safe. As it is, you've just made me two thousand pounds richer."

He rose to his feet and motioned to one of his gang to come to him. Removing his glasses and cleaning their lenses with a handkerchief that he flipped out of his trouser pocket, he continued to glare down at Tanner. "You know what to do with him," he grumbled to the man who had stepped to his side. "You just make sure you show up at my ranch with the money or you'll be the next man to get one of my bullets in him."

"I hear you well," the man said, tipping his wide-brimmed hat back from his brow with a forefinger. "I'll take him to town and hand him over to the authorities, then I'll meet you back at the ranch."

"Fine," Paul said, slipping his glasses back on. He gave Tanner a kick in the side, causing the body to jump, then fall back to the ground. "Now get him outta here. I can't stand the stench of him."

Paul walked back to Ian and smiled smugly at him. "Now what was that you were saying about your mother?" he said, his eyes gleaming.

"You sonofabitch," Ian growled, taking all of the willpower he could muster not to lunge into Paul and tear him apart. Thalia's grip on his arm was a reminder that should he do anything careless, she would be the one who would pay in the end.

"Your mother has taken a journey through the scrub with some of my men," Paul said, rocking back and forth from his heels to his toes and back again. He clasped his hands together behind him. He was enjoying toying with Ian. "I'm taking you to her, Ian. Just be patient. You'll see her soon enough."

Rage splashed through Ian. His jaw became tight. Yet he had no choice but to do as Paul Hathaway said. He silently prayed that his mother had not been harmed. She was a gentle woman used to gentle ways.

What if she had—been raped . . .?

The thought torturing him, Ian turned his back to Paul. Thalia drifted into his arms, so frightened she felt faint.

"What can we do?" she whispered as Ian's fingers stroked her hair. "Oh, Ian, surely we are going to be killed. And, oh, what of your mother?"

"For now we must do exactly as we are told," Ian whispered back to her, his lips pressed against her ear. "But, by damn, I'm going to get you out of this mess. I must get to my mother and help her!"

Paul yanked Thalia away from Ian. "There'll be no more whispering between you two!" he shouted, drawing a hand back and slapping Thalia across the cheek. He shoved her toward the waiting men. "Start walking, wench. Follow my men!"

Ian's blood was boiling. He clenched and unclenched his fists, his gaze settling on his rifle on the ground. It was so close! So very close! If he could move quickly enough, he could have it!

After that, only the good Lord would guide them. . . .

Taking a deep breath, then exhaling shakily, Ian bent to his knees and stretched his hand out for the rifle.

But he cringed and stifled a cry of pain behind closed lips when a heavy boot came down on his hand, crushing his fingers into the ground.

"Now that was a bit stupid of you, wasn't it?" Paul said, grinding his boot harder against Ian's hand. "Get up, Lavery. Slow and easy. Start walking toward Thalia. But don't ever get close enough to her to talk to her." He jerked his foot away, chuckling beneath his breath.

Ian lay there for a moment longer, his hand throbbing with pain. Then he sucked in a long breath and drew his hand slowly toward him. He inspected it. The skin was already yellowing with contusions, yet it was not broken.

Determined not to let Paul see him show any signs of discomfort, Ian pushed himself up from the ground and walked boldly toward Thalia. When she looked at him over her shoulder, tears shining in her eyes, he vowed to get even with Paul if it took his last deed on earth to do it! He watched a horse being led to McShane's body and Tanner being tied across its back. Then he saw up ahead the horses that had been left tethered while the bushrangers had come by foot to the campsite.

Paul walked at a brisk gait past Ian to his horse and mounted it. He wheeled it around and rode back to lean down to speak into Ian's face. "We don't have any spare horses," he said. "Seems you and Thalia are going to have to walk."

"How'd you find us, Hathaway?" Ian asked in a low growl.

"It's strange as hell, Ian," Paul chuckled. "I was having no luck looking for Thalia so I thought I'd look for the man who'd gone to her rescue. While lookin' for you who do I come across on the trail? Tanner. And wouldn't luck have it that he led me right to you? Now I'd say that I'm livin' right, wouldn't you?"

"You'd best enjoy it while you can, Hathaway," Ian said, his eyes narrowing. "Because soon I'm going to see you rotting in hell."

Paul's eyes wavered, then he wheeled his horse around and began galloping away, laughing boisterously.

Ian held his chin high as he looked ahead and saw the dozens of bushrangers riding with Paul Hathaway. And then everything changed. The men circled around, following Paul's lead, and Thalia and Ian were at the front of them.

The bushrangers started taking turns tormenting first Thalia, then Ian. One of the men would ride slowly beside Thalia and poke at her ribs with the butt of his rifle, or pull at her hair. Another bushranger would go past Ian, kicking at him, laughing. Others hit him with their rifles until blood was trickling from his brow.

Thalia was dying a slow death inside as she watched Ian being humiliated, her own humiliation forgotten. She wiped tears from her eyes and stumbled along, Ian's helplessness affecting her too.

But she knew that if Ian ever got the chance, all of these men would pay for what they were putting them both through!

Yet, how could he get the chance? He was weaponless. He was powerless against so many!

The sky grew lighter as dawn awakened fully into day, and its purple shadows were captured in the folds of the mountains in the distance. Thalia jumped aside when a snake crawled out of a hole close to her, then darted back inside when Thalia screamed.

Sighing heavily, she then trudged onward, too far from Ian to draw any sort of comfort from him. If they got too close, a bushranger would move his horse between them.

The heat was becoming intolerable, shimmering along the ground and distorting distance and size. It was a sticky, humid morning, airless and depressing.

When a wedge-tailed eagle passed overhead, turned back, and circled again over Thalia—so lovely, so free—the horror of being held captive became almost too overwhelming for Thalia to bear.

But then Ian would look at her and give her hope. Up to now he had always protected her. She had to keep faith that he would find a way to do so again.

Yet she was reminded of her plight of only yesterday and of the thirst that she had felt.

Again! She was as thirsty again!

It was as though she had not had water for days. Her tongue was so dry it kept sticking to the roof of her mouth.

And the sandy orange earth stretched out before her, the solitude and heat creating ghostly images which continually danced in the air ahead of her. Beyond, the horizon seemed too far to imagine. The mountains rose spectacularly in sharply tilted sandstone peaks. Jagged and bizarrely eroded, they looked like rogue waves endlessly breaking against the sky.

Thalia and Ian were forced to move endlessly onward, lizards with whippish tongues darting past them on the ground. There were water holes grown over with hibiscus ablaze in color, and termites in mounds taller than a man.

"Water!" Thalia suddenly cried, reaching her hand toward a water hole. "I need . . . water . . . !"

Paul rode up to her and pulled her up onto his horse. "I'll take you to get a drink, but Ian gets none," he said, holding tightly to Thalia as she began pushing and shoving at him to get free.

"Let me down!" she cried. "If Ian can't have a drink, I won't drink either!" Her insides cried out against her declaration of loyalty to the man she loved, but she fought against the thirst with all of her might.

Paul threw her from the horse. "If you think I'm going to force water down your throat, you're daft," he said, glaring down at her. "Die with your lover and I'll dance on your graves!"

He wheeled his horse around and rode away

from her, leaving Thalia on the ground, stunned. She leaned up on an elbow, her head swimming.

"Go and get a drink, Thalia!" Ian shouted at her. "Don't be foolish! You may not have a second chance!"

Thalia rose slowly, raking her fingers through her hair to draw it back from her face. She looked at Ian, anguish filling her for what they were being forced to endure at the hands of the madman Paul Hathaway. She felt responsible. If she had listened to Ian in the first place, none of this would have happened!

Yet there was Viada. Everything had been done for the love of Viada! Even now she did not know her sister's fate.

And what of hers and Ian's?

Placing a hand to her aching back she walked away from the water hole. "I shall drink when you are granted the same opportunity," she said, giving Ian a stubborn stare. "Only then, Ian. Only then."

They were forced to march onward. The water holes and everything that seemed promising was left behind again. Then Thalia felt a sudden dizziness grip her when she saw in the distance a sight that tore at her consciousness. When a loud cry broke the silence, she looked quickly over at Ian. He too had seen the sight too grotesque, surely, to be real!

"You depraved maniac!" Ian shouted, waving a doubled fist at Paul. Then he broke into a mad, crazed run toward his mother, who was tied to a stake, her clothes hanging in shreds, her eyes haunted and staring.

Thalia's screams echoed across the land when she watched, helplessly, as Paul rode up beside Ian and hit him over the head with the butt end of his rifle. She felt a blackness seize her, and she crumpled to the ground in a dead faint.

CHAPTER TWENTY-TWO

THALIA FLUTTERED HER EYES OPEN. A DRONE OF voices somewhere close by outside had awakened her. She paled and jerked herself to a sitting position when she discovered Ian close beside her, still unconscious, blood dried on a wound at the side of his head. Suddenly it was all coming back to her! Where she was—and why!

She looked around her. She had been taken to a grass hut after she had fainted. She knelt down low over Ian, sobbing, glad at least that they had been imprisoned together.

Gently placing Ian's head on her lap, she cradled him close. "Ian," she whispered. "Oh, Ian. Please be all right. Please wake up!"

She felt a tiny shred of hope when Ian moaned and licked his lips. "Ian?" she said, giving his shoulders a soft shake. "Can you hear me? We've been brought to Paul's bushranger camp."

Then she sickened at heart when she suddenly recalled what she had seen that had made her faint. She bit her lower lip and turned her eyes away from Ian to hang her head. His mother! His mother was tied to a stake! More than likely she had been raped or tortured—or that was the intention before she would be set free.

Thalia looked down at Ian. Would he be able to bear any of this when he awakened? He would feel so helpless! He might even blame himself should his mother die.

Paul Hathaway's voice came to Thalia from those who were laughing and talking outside the hut. She leaned her ear toward the door that had only a veil of blowing sheepskin hanging there. Hate swelled inside her as she listened to this voice that she had grown to loathe. When she heard his mockery of the Aborigines and what he had planned for them, she was glad that Ian was unable to hear. Again he would feel helpless, and in the end, would possibly blame himself for what happened to his friends. She had heard him promise to look out for them.

They had listened trustingly!

Paul lifted a mug of ale to his lips and drank greedily, some of the ale splashing from the sides of the drinking vessel and running down his chin onto his shirt. He knelt down before the campfire, as the members of his gang stood around him, smoking, eating, or drinking.

"Just think of it," he said, looking around the

circle of his men. He wiped some ale from his chin with the back of his hand. "We're finally going to have the opportunity to stop those dark-skinned bastards in their tracks."

He looked over his shoulder at the hut in which Ian and Thalia were held captive. "With Ian Lavery out of the way, we'll stop those Aborigines before they gather even one of those damn swan's eggs," he bragged.

He looked at Ian's mother, smiling crookedly. "Then we'll return victorious and whoever wishes to can have fun with that woman over there," he said, then chuckled. "But we must first make sure her son is conscious enough to watch."

He glanced over at the hut. "And then we'll kill that sonofabitch," he said in a low growl.

"What of your wife?" one of the men asked, his voice filled with lust. "What're you goin' to do about her?"

Paul looked over at the man, smiling. "You damn idiot," he drawled. "She ain't my wife. Don't you know? I hate all women!"

The man's eyes gleamed. "I kind of thought so," he said. He looked at the hut, snorting strangely as he laughed throatily. "I don't hate women. I'll have lots of fun with her."

"Come around close, men," Paul said, rising to face them. He tossed his mug aside and placed his doubled fists on his hips, looking from man to man. "Here's the plan. We're going to attack the Aborigines while they are marching to the sea. We'll rid Australia of every last one of Hawke's tribe."

He smirked. "But we're not doing it for Australia," he continued. "We're doing it for ourselves. It will be the same as going on a buffalo hunt. We'll slaughter the Aborigines because it'll be great sport!"

Loud shouts of approval reverberated from man to man, fists held victoriously in the air. Paul puffed his chest out proudly. "Get your horses and weapons ready," he said, dropping his hands to his sides. "I've got something to take care of before we leave."

He muscled his way through the throng of men and stopped just outside of the small hut, smoothing his hair back from his brow with the palm of a hand. He cleared his throat nervously, then bent low and entered the hut.

Thalia's eyes narrowed with hate and her shoulders grew tight as she glared up at Paul. "You are truly a fiend," she hissed. She cradled Ian's head protectively closer to her on her lap. "When will your murdering days finally end?"

"Nothing can stop me," Paul bragged, resting a hand on the holstered pistol at his right hip. "Not Ian. Not the Aborigines. No one."

Thalia wanted so badly to blurt out to Paul that Ian's men were out there somewhere planning to foil his plans, but she would not give him any clue as to what his future might be. Hopefully, even without Ian as their leader, his men would follow through on their plans to search for, find, and stop Paul Hathaway and his thieving, murdering gang.

"If I could, I would stop you," Thalia said, glaring up at Paul. "I would so enjoy watching you squirm before I shot you!"

Paul chuckled. He stooped to one knee beside

Thalia and reached a hand to her cheek, flinching when she tossed her head so that he could not touch her. "My little spitfire," he said. "If ever I would find a woman who could accept my way of life, she would be just like you. We would ride side by side and be partners in crime. Perhaps I could even grow to love a woman like you, yet I couldn't . . ."

A strange sort of pain entered his eyes as he stopped his words in mid-sentence and momentarily looked away from Thalia. Even if he could love a woman, it would never be consummated. His masculinity had been robbed from him with one carefully-aimed crude blow from a club—just as his love for mankind had been robbed from him at, surely, the moment of his birth!

Paul turned his head slowly back around and his gaze stopped on Ian. "As it is, I've much to do," he grumbled. "Much to prove."

He jerked himself up and walked to the door, throwing aside the sheepskin covering. He looked over his shoulder at Thalia, his eyes wavering. "I could have loved you," he said thickly. "Perhaps I do."

Stunned by his words, her lips parted, Thalia stared openly at Paul as he stepped out of the hut. It seemed that she had somehow managed to touch a vulnerable part of him, yet not deeply enough to make a difference. He was evil, through and through. Nothing could ever change that. Not her. Not anything!

"Damn it," Ian mumbled, stirring from unconsciousness. His hand reached for his throbbing head. He moaned as his eyes opened slowly. "What happened? Where am I?"

Thalia leaned into his face, smiling radiantly now that she knew that he was all right. "Ian," she said, kissing him on the brow. "Oh, darling, finally you are awake."

Ian gazed in wonder up at Thalia, then leaned up on one elbow and looked slowly around him. It was like a stab in his gut when he remembered where he was, and why, and who besides himself and Thalia was being held captive.

"God," he said, rushing to his feet, yet teetering with lightheadedness. "My mother!"

Thalia saw how unsteady he was on his feet and pushed herself up from the floor to place an arm around his waist. "Ian, there's nothing you can do," she said, her voice breaking. "Paul has many bushrangers with him in this camp. I am sure we are under heavy guard." She shook her head. "Even when he leaves to—to go after the Aborigines, I am sure he will leave us heavily guarded."

Ian glanced down at her in alarm. "What do you mean, he is going after the Aborigines?" he asked, his voice drawn. He jerked away from Thalia and clasped his fingers to her shoulders. "Tell me. What do you mean? What does that sonofabitch have planned?"

Thalia gazed wearily up at him, then spoke. "Ian, Paul and his bushrangers are going after the Aborigines and stop their march to the sea," she said in a rush of words. "He plans to slaughter all of Hawke's tribe before they reach the sea for the season of the swan's egg celebration."

His jaw tight, Ian moved his hands from Thalia and began pacing the hut floor. "I knew it!" he exclaimed. "And here I am, unable to help them!"

Then he looked at the sheepskin covering at the door, as if seeing beyond it. "And my mother," he said desolately. "I am even helpless to go to her rescue."

In one wide stride he was at the door and had the sheepskin drawn aside. He peered outside at the bushrangers mounting their steeds, Paul at the lead, and then at his mother, who still hung helplessly on the stake, her head bent, her long golden hair hanging in waves across her face and shoulders.

All reason, all caution was forgotten. Ian burst from the hut and began fighting off the guards as first one pounced on him, and then another. Fallen men scattered everywhere as Ian found hidden strength in the courage it took to reach his mother.

But it was not enough. He was wrestled to the ground and held immobile, a bushranger with a thick, red beard and golden-brown eyes glowering down at him. Ian inhaled several erratic breaths and then gathered a large gob of spit on the tip of his tongue. His eyes dark with fury, he spat on the man's face.

The man gagged and let go of Ian long enough to make a wide swipe across his face with his hand. That was enough time for Ian to knock the man off him sideways. Ian jumped to his feet but stopped instantly when he recognized the distinct feel of a rifle barrel thrust hard against his back.

"That's enough entertainment for this morning," Paul said, chuckling behind Ian. "Perhaps when we return from killing your friend, Hawke, you can give us a repeat performance. But for now, Ian, get back in the hut with Thalia."

Ian doubled his hands into tight fists, glancing over at his mother again, dying a slow death inside when he saw her helplessness. "Hathaway, somehow you'll pay for all of this," he growled. "Somehow!"

"I'm scared to death," Paul mocked, slowly moving around Ian so that he was facing him. He smiled smugly up at him. "But as it is, son, you've got hell to pay. Not me."

"We'll see about that," Ian said between clenched teeth. "Once the news spreads to Adelaide of your activities, there will be a large bounty on your head. Someone will take you to the authorities to collect the reward."

Paul threw his head back and laughed, then looked smugly at Ian. "You aren't as smart as you think you are," he said. "You should go back to America and get yourself some more schooling. You see, Ian, anyone who thinks he's as smart as you do should have figured out a long time ago that I have many friends in high places who vouch for me and pretend that I am a God-fearing, respectable man. I pay my friends well for their silence and cooperation so that I can ride with my bushranger gang. It's only you who have been a threat. Because of you, I've been forced to keep an eye on my back."

He nodded, pushing his spectacles back farther on the bridge of his nose. "Yes, son, for all your schooling, I'd say I've outsmarted you where it matters the most," he boasted. "You've always been a threat to me because of your cunning ways in the scrub. But now our game has ended and I have won."

Paul then motioned with his rifle toward the hut. "Get back inside with Thalia," he said flatly. Then he smiled crookedly, his eyes squinting as he looked up at Ian. "You should thank me, Ian. I've given you a private hut so that you and Thalia can wile away the hours in one another's arms. You can't ask for much more than that, now can you? Ain't I just too generous?"

Ian stumbled as one of Paul's men reached out and gave him a shove inside the hut. He fell against Thalia. She steadied him, and they clung together as Paul entered and stood glaring from one to the other.

"Thalia, a while ago I said things that I'm already regretting," Paul said icily. "In truth, you are nothing but a disappointment to me. You are no better than the other girls Daisy Odum let come work for me. When they saw me kill slaves and then ran away into the scrub, I found pleasure searching for them and killing them."

Rage lit his eyes behind his glasses, and he spoke in a low, threatening hiss. "I hate all women. White and black-skinned. It makes me no difference. Now, not only will you die, but also your sister. Viada is on a ship bound for Australia even now."

Laughing, Paul turned on a heel to leave, then spun around and faced Thalia and Ian again. "Me and my gang are leaving for the Aborigine kill," he bragged. "I know where the swan's eggs can be found in massive amounts—on a peninsula that is only a half mile wide. It will be a simple thing to draw a cordon across it and cut off the Abos' retreat. I will capture and kill them at my leisure!"

He started to leave again, but as before, turned around to voice more threats as his eyes gleamed and a twitch tugged at his left cheek. "I plan to bring many spoils of war back to the camp," he said huskily. "Mutilated, of course. I'll show these off to you both and then—who knows? Perhaps you will meet the same fate once I have finished with you."

This time he turned and finally left the hut. Thalia trembled, Paul Hathaway's threats about the Aborigines and Viada haunting her. She clung harder to Ian, tears streaming from her eyes. "It's like one of those nightmares I've recently had," she said, leaning her cheek against his chest. She could feel the rapid thudding of his heart, and knew that it was because he felt cornered by Paul, unable to prevent his mother's dying—perhaps she was even already dead—or his friends, the Aborigines, from facing sure death.

Thalia's own heart was beating as loudly, but more for her sister now than anyone else.

If Paul got his hands on Viada—oh, what of her? What would be her fate?

"Will it ever end?" she sobbed.

Ian held Thalia close and burrowed his nose into her hair. He was momentarily lost in remembrance of their sensual, sweet moments by the lake when they had made endearing love. That now seemed a whole lifetime ago!

"We must never give up," Ian whispered. "My friends will surely not wait around my hideout for long when they realize that we are not going to show up. They'll find us, Thalia." He swallowed hard. "I just hope it is soon enough."

Easing away from Thalia, Ian began pacing again, like a caged tiger. "When I think of Hawke leading his people into a trap it sickens me!" he said, wincing when his head resumed its throbbing. "They could all be gone so quickly. Hawke, Honora—all of those beautiful, innocent people!"

The sound of departing horses made Thalia's breathing grow shallow. Her shoulders heavy, she sat down beside the fire. Ian still paced . . . fitfully paced . . .

The minutes dragged by. Ian and Thalia lay side by side, gazing with longing into the fire, then bolted to their feet when gunfire exploded outside.

Ian drew aside the sheepskin covering at the door and watched a battle raging on all sides of him. He smiled widely when he saw that his men had come and were fast doing away with the bushranger guards left at the camp.

Then his heart turned to ice when he saw the guard just outside the door raise his pistol and aim at one of Ian's oldest friends, who was riding past at a gallop, firing at those bushrangers who had not yet been shot.

"No!" Ian shouted, lunging for the bushranger and knocking him to the ground. They rolled over and over, grappling for the pistol. Thalia stood at the door, horror-stricken, knowing that the gun could go off at any moment and Ian could be killed.

She looked wildly around her for something to hit the man over the head with. Her heart skipped a beat. Close enough for her to grab, a rifle was resting against the hut. She reached for it and aimed it at the man's back as Ian became pinned to the ground, then felt a weakness claim her knees when she began pulling the trigger and stopped just in time as Ian suddenly was on top on the man, pinning him to the ground, the pistol now knocked away from them both.

"Ian, I've got him covered!" Thalia shouted, stepping closer.

Ian smiled at Thalia as he began to rise, but froze again when out of the corner of his eyes he saw the bushranger make a mad lunge for the pistol.

Thalia's heart leapt into her throat. She stepped quickly away from Ian and pulled the trigger. The bushranger screamed and grabbed at his back, then fell over onto his stomach, dead.

Feeling suddenly ill, for this was the first time Thalia had actually killed a man, she dropped the rifle.

Ian realized the shock she had suffered and grabbed her as she teetered, threatening to faint. "Thalia, this isn't the time to get weak on me," he said hoarsely. "You did what you had to do. If you hadn't, that man would've—"

"I know," Thalia murmured, looking up at Ian through tearful eyes. "Please don't say it."

Kenneth Ozier wheeled his horse to a halt beside Ian and Thalia, a triumphant smile across his youthful face. "Am I glad to see you!" he said, slipping his pistol into his holster. "For a while I thought we had arrived too late."

Ian questioned Kenneth with his eyes, something deeply within his consciousness recalling having seen this young man before. But he had forgotten where, and that the young man was riding with Ian's friends was enough to prove he could be trusted. Ian reached a hand to Kenneth.

"Thank you, friend," he said, shaking Kenneth's hand. The gunfire was over. He looked at the rest of his friends circling around him on horseback. "Thank you all. I knew that I could depend on you."

"I think we've done a fair amount of riddin' the earth of bushrangers here, don't you, Ian?" Kenneth said, his gaze sweeping around the ground at the dead bushrangers. A part of him felt as though he had betrayed so many that he had ridden with, yet another part of him realized that his hide was all that ever counted. He had plans that included no one but himself!

Kenneth gazed at the stake, where one of Ian's devoted followers was cutting Ian's mother free. "Who is that?" he asked. "She don't look like she's got much life left in 'er at all."

Ian ran to his mother just as she was being covered with a blanket, except for her face, which meant that she was still alive. A sob tore from his throat as he knelt over her and held her close to his chest. "Mother," he whispered. "Thank God you're alive. But God damn him all to hell, Paul'll pay for what he's put you through!"

Donna's eyes opened slowly. She reached a hand to Ian. "Don't trouble yourself about me," she said, her voice weak. "Go and stop Paul Hathaway. I heard all of his plans. He intends to kill Hawke and all of his people! I'll be all right. Go and save Hawke! Ian, save sweet Honora!"

Thalia knelt down beside Ian. She slipped an

arm around his waist and smiled at Donna. "I'll see to your mother, Ian," she said, running a gentle hand over Donna's brow.

"If you think I'm going to leave the two of you here without my supervision, you're wrong!" Ian said, rising briskly to his feet. "Mother, are you well enough to travel? You've got to be. I must take you and Thalia with me."

"Ian, son, do what you must," Donna whispered, smiling gently up at him. "I have been through an ordeal, but I think if I ride with someone on a horse who can steady me, I am fit enough to travel."

"That's good enough for me," Ian said determinedly. "You see, I personally want to accompany you out of the scrub to assure myself that you get to Adelaide unharmed. The only other alternative is to take you with me in pursuit of Paul Hathaway. Too much time has already elapsed since Paul and his gang left to kill the Aborigines. I must take you and Thalia with us."

Donna grabbed Ian by the arm. Tears were in her eyes. "My beautiful home," she sobbed. "They burned it, Ian."

"Yes, I know, mother," Ian said thickly. "Paul enjoyed bragging about it."

"Ian, I want to return home," Donna sobbed, her fingers digging into Ian's flesh.

"But, mother, you can't," he said, his eyes wavering. "You just said that you saw it burning. There's nothing left to go home to."

"No," Donna said, slowly shaking her head. "Not that home."

"Then where?"

"America. I want to go to America."

Ian looked at her, taken aback by her declaration. "America?" he gasped.

"I have had all I want of Australia, son," Donna said, running her tongue over her parched lips. "And, son, I want you to return to America with me." She looked at Thalia. "Bring Thalia with you. Let us share a home together in Seattle."

Ian sighed. "We'll talk about it later, mother," he said, then turned to Thalia. "Darling, are you ready to go after that sonofabitch Paul Hathaway?"

Thalia smiled at him, and nodded.

Ian rose and faced his men. He sorted through them with his eyes, then stopped at Kenneth. "Lad," he said, placing a firm hand on his shoulder. "I'd appreciate it if you'd see to my mother's welfare—let her ride with you."

"It's the same as done," Kenneth said, smiling crookedly. "Proud to be of further service to you."

"Thanks," Ian said, then grouped his men together, shouting out orders to them.

A shiver soared through Thalia, knowing the dangers that awaited the man she loved.

A gentle hand wove around Thalia's. "My son will not be harmed," Donna murmured as she rose slowly to her feet. "He is a courageous man—a man whose goodness follows him everywhere. God will not let him be harmed."

Thalia choked back a sob, then flung herself into Donna's arms. "I hope you are right," she said, knowing how filled Paul was with vengeance and hate. "Paul Hathaway stops at nothing when he hates someone. He will do everything within his power to kill Ian if he sees that he has escaped

317

imprisonment."

"As I said, Thalia," Donna reaffirmed. "God will not let Ian be harmed."

Then Donna crept back into Thalia's arms, hiding her fears from the vulnerable, innocent girl whom Ian seemed to love with all of his heart. Donna had never before been subjected to the cruelties of the world. Her husband had sheltered her well. So had Ian tried to do. But events had overwhelmed even him.

CHAPTER TWENTY-THREE

THALIA WAS CLINGING AROUND IAN'S WAIST ON HIS stallion as he led his men at a fast gallop toward the sea. Locusts swarmed overhead with a pillar of wheeling hawks over them. Wallabies scattered through the high, lush greenery at the approach of the horses. Glancing over her shoulder, Thalia tried to reassure Donna with a smile as she rode with Kenneth Ozier, her golden hair flying, her face pale.

But Donna was unresponsive, and within her tired eyes was a deep, haunting sadness as she stared ahead.

Thalia looked away from Donna, her own battles raging within her. She tried to block out worry over Viada. There were more pressing concerns. Ian would soon be fighting a battle that could cost him his life. Even hers. . . .

Her chin held firmly, too stubborn to let doubts completely consume her, Thalia accepted fate as it was handed to her. The horses passed through creek beds overflowing with lavender flowers, then followed a broad trail that led straight to Ian's destination—a wide, smooth cliffhead that overlooked the vast blue expanse of the Indian Ocean.

Drawing his stallion to a stop, Ian was intensely viewing everything within range. Thalia's eyes followed his steady gaze. In one direction, she saw towering rock pinnacles that the relentless waves had cut away from the sheer cliffs. She gasped when, in the other direction, she found herself looking down at a peninsula where numerous swans were resting in their nests, their white bodies like snow against the gleaming brown sand of the beach.

"Thank God the Aborigines have not arrived at the peninsula yet," Ian said, more to himself than anyone else.

Then he looked over his shoulder at Thalia. "How are you doing?" he asked softly. "We still have a way to go."

"I'm a bit weary, yet fine enough," Thalia said, relaxing her hold on his waist. "Don't worry about me. I'll just be glad when this is all over."

Ian made a wide sweep with his hand toward the land just below the butte, where the sight of anything that might lie beyond was cut off by a thick cover of trees. "The Aborigines are there somewhere," he said. "So are Paul and his men. But Hathaway does not have the advantage he wished for. He can't cut off the people on the peninsula if they aren't on it to make an easy slaughter for him. As fair as the fight can be with the Aborigines for the most part fighting with spears and clubs against Paul's guns, this fight will be much fairer fought away from the peninsula."

Thalia reached for Ian's hand and clasped it tightly. "Please be careful," she said, her eyes wavering. "Promise me that you'll be careful."

"With so much to live for?" Ian said, squeezing her hand affectionately. "No way in hell will I let anything happen to me." He smiled warmly at her. "Nor to you."

Then he drew his hand away and raised a fist in the air, looking over his shoulder at his men. "We've wasted enough time," he shouted. "Let's ride!"

Thalia clung to him again as his stallion began leading the way down the steep sides of the butte, the land smoothing out soon into a great forest of gum trees. Her skirt flying up above her knees, her hair lifting in the breeze, Thalia held onto Ian, but still almost fell off the horse when he drew it to a quick halt.

Thalia steadied herself, then found herself in Ian's arms as he reached up and took her from the horse. She ran with him to his mother, who was already standing on the ground, looking limp with fear.

Ian swept an arm around his mother's waist, then Thalia's, and led them both to cover behind a thick stand of red gum trees. The sound of a confrontation was just up ahead through the trees.

There was gunfire and loud shouts and screams, and horses whinnying.

Ian took one of Thalia's hands, then his mother's. He looked sternly down at one, then the other. "I've got to leave you here for the time being," he said. "I'll be back as soon as I can."

Thalia's mouth went agape when Ian turned and began running back toward his horse. "Kenneth, stay behind and guard my women with your life," he shouted. "I'm depending on you."

"It's my pleasure," Kenneth shouted back. "Go and butcher those sonofabitch bushrangers!" He smiled smugly to himself. It had been as simple as pie to get on Ian's good side. Now he had to give Ian cause to take him totally under his wing. His eyes danced when he envisioned Paul Hathaway being shot by Ian and his friends. With Paul Hathaway out of the way . . .

Thalia looked wildly at Donna, then back at Ian. How could he expect her to stay behind and just wait to hear whether he had lived or died?

She had to go with him!

She would fight alongside him!

Turning to face Donna, Thalia held her hands and beseeched her with her eyes. "I can't stay here with you," she said in a rush of words. "I must go with Ian!"

Hearing the thundering of the horses as they left, Thalia gasped and looked over her shoulder just in time to see Ian's flying hair as he rode away from her. Panic seized her. She turned away from Donna and began running after Ian, waving her hands frantically.

"Ian, please don't leave without me!" she

shouted, a sob lodging in her throat when he did not respond.

Winded, feeling more alone now than ever before in her life, Thalia stopped and leaned against the trunk of a tree and held her head in her hands.

"Ma'am, you'd best come back here with me and Ian's mother and stay out of sight," Kenneth said as he stepped up beside her. He took her by the elbow and began walking her to the cover of the trees. "You're my responsibility now. I cain't let anything happen to you."

Thalia looked up at Kenneth and could not help but smile at him. He looked as though he might be one of the youngest of Ian's friends, perhaps her same age, with freckles spotting his nose and cheeks and golden hair that hung to his shoulders. Thin and lanky, his kangaroo hide outfit hung away from him like a loose skin.

He was probably the sort who would take a scolding quite badly from Ian should anything happen to the women he was guarding. But that was not Thalia's concern. She had to follow Ian. If she did not do everything possible to help him and he should die, she would have that to live with for the rest of her life. Ian was her life. Without him, she would want to die also.

She looked at the horse that was tethered close by. Slyly, she looked up at Kenneth. She clung to his arm and batted her eyelashes at him seductively. "You are so kind," she murmured. "If not for you, I would be so frightened. Thank you, Kenneth, for being here. I shall never forget your kindness."

Kenneth squared his shoulders as he gave Thalia

a look that she did not quite understand. It was somewhere between being appreciative and cautious.

"If there's anything, ever, that I can do for you, ma'am, just let me know," he said, his white teeth flashing as he spoke. "You're one beautiful lady. It pleasures me to make you happy."

Thalia eyed Donna warily, seeing that she was standing as though in a strange sort of swoon, her eyes staring blankly ahead, her body swaying gently. She rushed to her side and placed an arm around her waist.

"Kenneth, please get Donna a blanket so that she can sit comfortably on the ground while we await Ian's return," she said, giving him her most alluring smile. "Then, perhaps, you could fetch her some water from the creek I saw through those trees over there. Ian's mother does appear faint."

"Yes, ma'am," Kenneth said. "Just give me a few minutes and I'll get a blanket and fresh water."

Thalia was getting impatient with this game. The sounds of fighting up ahead seeming to be getting worse; blasts of gunfire reverberated through the air, and screams of pain and death reached her ears.

But other than grabbing Kenneth's firearm and holding him at bay while she escaped from him, Thalia had no choice but to take her time to be sure that she was able to go to help Ian.

For the moment she would try and give Donna comfort. She held her close, then eased her down on the blanket after Kenneth spread it out on the ground for her. "Donna, Ian will be back very soon," she tried to reassure her. "Then we'll leave this horrid place."

Donna smiled faintly and reached a hand to pat Thalia's cheek. "I wish that we could have met under different circumstances," she murmured. "As it is, Thalia, you are seeing all of my weaknesses instead of my strengths." She sobbed as tears began to flow down her cheeks. "But I've experienced such tragedies in so few hours!" She grabbed Thalia by the arm and held tightly. "If I should lose Ian—oh, Lord, that would mean that I have lost everything!"

Thalia glanced up as Kenneth rushed through the trees with his empty canteen, toward the creek. Then she looked down at Donna. "Neither of us is going to lose Ian," she said, her chin firm. She bent low and brushed a gentle kiss across Donna's brow. "I'm going to him, Donna. Now. We'll both return soon."

Donna's eyes widened with horror. She tried to reach for Thalia as Thalia began running toward the horses, but she did not cry out. Deep within her she knew that Thalia was doing what she felt was best.

She lay back down, sighing wearily. She closed her eyes and placed the back of a hand over them, blocking out the light and at least some of the pain of her present existence.

Her fingers trembling, Thalia unwound the horse's reins where they had been secured around a tree limb. Keeping watch over her shoulder for Kenneth, she swung herself into the saddle. Digging the heels of her boots into the flanks of the mare, she rode away in a strong gallop toward the continuing sounds of battle. Kenneth's shouts faded as she rode harder away from him.

Soon Thalia wheeled her horse to a stop and dismounted. Over the trees ahead drifted a choking cloud of white powder smoke and she could hear the spitting, snarling chorus of gunfire.

When she reached the break in the trees, she became witness to an explosive battle. Horrified, her face white with the chill of fear, she watched the flurry of shooting and the frenzy of horses as they were led into the fight. Some of the men were shooting from their horse's backs, others had sprung to the ground. She could see their crouched forms as they knelt to get a steadier aim.

On her knees behind a scattering of bushes, Thalia trembled as she searched the faces of the men, looking anxiously for Ian. She saw homely, taciturn, daring and stubborn faces.

Then her heart seemed to stop still when she found Ian fighting gallantly upon his horse, his men scattered around on all sides of him, fighting the bushrangers, Paul at their lead. She gazed proudly at Ian. He was leaning low in the saddle, firing his revolver, his magnificent horse responding quickly to all of Ian's commands.

All around Ian, lead slugs kicked up little smoking clouds of dust on the ground. Close to him a gelding went from a thundering run to a long, sliding fall, the rider pitching over his neck, hitting the ground, his legs jerking, dead before he struck.

Not far from where Thalia was hiding, feeling helpless in this maddening battle, a thoroughbred took a fall, spilling its rider. She scarcely breathed, recognizing the rider as one of Paul's bushrangers.

For a moment he was stunned, then he moved shakily to his knees, his hand grasping a pistol, his angered gaze following Ian.

Thalia's world seemed to stop still, realizing what the man's intentions were. He was out of eye range of Ian and his men. No one was even looking his way. He could get a clean shot at Ian and no one would be the wiser!

"I must do something!" Thalia whispered to herself, looking quickly over at Kenneth's horse and at the rifle in the holster under the stirrup leather.

Scurrying to her feet, she ran to the horse and grabbed the rifle. She knelt low as she moved within firing range of the man who was just raising his pistol to take aim.

Thalia placed the rifle to her shoulder and balanced it. Snuggling her cheek against the stock, she felt a sob rising and choked it back. Fighting away the tears, she held her breath and steadied the rifle barrel. She swallowed hard as she pulled the trigger, her shoulder jolting at the report.

For an instant a white puff of smoke blotted out everything before her eyes, but when the smoke drifted aside, her heart gave a great leap. The bushranger lay dead.

Slowly she lowered the rifle, inhaling a jagged breath, still suffering right along with Ian as he continued to fire at the bushrangers, knocking others from their horses to be trampled beneath the hooves of others.

Farther away still, on the far side of the fighting, the Aborigine children and women stood in clusters, their men standing protectively before them, their spears poised, ready for throwing.

Thalia soon recognized Hawke. His dark eyes were narrow and filled with fierce anger, his jaws clamped tightly.

Suddenly, in a burst of fury, Hawke led his men into the battle and it became a war of spears against guns as the long, narrow, sharp weapons whizzed through the air. One by one, Paul's men began dropping from their horses, clutching at spears in their chests, or lurching when a spear entered a man's back, sometimes coming on through the chest.

The sight sickened Thalia, yet she would not look away. She was afraid that if she did, something would happen to Ian. She watched him, then Paul Hathaway, seeing how they seemed to be working through the grappling men and horses, closer to one another, only to be torn in the opposite direction again when another horseman got in the way.

Thalia looked to the heavens. "Please, God, let this be over soon," she whispered. "Please let nothing happen to Ian—Please!"

She was stunned speechless when the rifle was knocked from her clutches and a sudden bony, dark hand clamped around her mouth. Then an arm snaked quickly around her waist, dragging her away. She clawed at the arm and hand, kicking wildly as she was lifted from the ground and held immobile against the thin body scarcely clad in a loincloth.

When she saw that it only weakened her, Thalia stopped struggling. She was taken to a cave and dropped to the ground away from the battle.

Turning to her side, she stared up at an Aborigine who had his spear poised in the air over her.

Thalia breathed more easily when he lowered his spear, then her breath caught in her throat when several more Aborigines emerged from the bushes and came into the cave, peering down at her.

Realizing how devoted Ian was to these people, and that he was fighting for their rights even at this moment, Thalia looked into the dark, accusing eyes of her abductor. "I am a friend," she said slowly, fearing that these particular Aborigines might not know the English language as well as Hawke and Honora. She motioned toward the scene of the battle. "I am Ian's friend. He soon will be my husband!"

The men did not move or speak. They held onto their spears as they glared down at her.

"You're making a big mistake," Thalia cried. "I am here to help you! I even shot one of the bushrangers. Why can't you understand? I . . . am . . . a friend!"

Her words were falling on deaf ears. She breathed shallowly when one of the men knelt down beside her and tied her wrists with thin leather thongs. She tried to get up and run away when he reached for her ankles, but was knocked down again by one of the others. She fell to the floor of the cave, numbed by the impact, then sighed heavily and watched as her ankles were also bound.

And then Thalia was alone. The Aborigines left just as silently as they had arrived. Her eyes wide with fright, she looked around her at the dark, dank walls of the cave. Somewhere behind her, more deeply into the hollow of the cave, she could hear strange squeaking noises.

"Bats?" she thought to herself, cringing at the thought.

But her mind did not dwell on bats. Her fears were for Ian. She listened to the intensifying of the battle—to the rifles' sharp, peremptory reports echoing through the trees outside, the echo immediately drowned in the long, spattering roll of a fresh volley of gunfire.

CHAPTER TWENTY-FOUR

THE CRUNCH OF ROCK OUTSIDE THE ENTRANCE of the cave made Thalia's heart pound as she waited for whoever was approaching to reveal himself to her. Afraid that it might be the Aborigines returning, possibly to harm her since they had not understood that she was Ian's friend, she began scooting backward on the sandy floor. Her breathing became shallow as the figure of a man became silhouetted at the entrance. The cave was too dark for her to make out the face.

But she felt at least a measure of relief when she realized that this man was fully clothed and so not an Aborigine.

Could it be Ian?

Yet, closer scrutiny told her that this man was not tall and slender like Ian. This man's stature was more like . . .

Paul Hathaway!

Shivers of fear raced across her flesh. She tried to get to her feet so that she could run farther into the cave. But her bound ankles made her body lurch forward and she fell clumsily back to the sandy floor, panting.

"So you thought you had escaped from me, did you?" Paul said, walking toward her. "Perhaps for a while—but no longer."

He slipped a knife from a sheath at his side. Its blade glinted as it picked up the light from the cave entrance. "I plan to take care of you, Thalia, this time for good." he said.

Kneeling before her, Paul leaned his face down into hers. He snickered as he ran the cold flat side of the steel blade across her brow, then down one cheek and up the other. "I'm going to cut you in little pieces and feed you to the dingoes," he threatened. "Not a trace of you will ever be found."

Nervous perspiration beaded up Thalia's brow. She tried to move away from Paul, but he grabbed her by the shoulder and held her still.

"Let me go," she begged. "I meant you no harm, ever. I came to Australia to find employment with wages enough to eventually send for my sister. I wanted nothing more. Nor do I now."

"You wanted a husband more than mere employment, isn't that right?" Paul said, smiling devilishly down at her. He gave her a wet kiss, then drew away from her, chuckling. "Why, darling, I gave you a wedding ring and a beautiful home. What more could you have wanted?"

He lifted her bound wrists and looked down at her ring finger. "The ring," he said, rage lighting his eyes. "Where is the ring? It was my mother's. I planned to take it back after—"

"After you killed me?" Thalia said, choking back a sob of fear. She found some reserve courage and lifted her chin defiantly. "I threw that damnable thing away. It meant nothing to me but mockery."

Paul drew back away from her a fraction, looking disbelievingly down at her. "You threw . . . my mother's ring away?" he gasped, then raised a hand and brought it down across Thalia's cheek with a loud whack. "You shouldn't have done that!"

Thalia's head jerked with the blow and pain tore at her flesh, but she refused to react in any way. Perhaps these were the last moments of her life and she wanted to be brave and strong to the end.

She looked defiantly up at Paul. "How did you know that I was in this cave?" she asked in a hiss, suddenly aware that the rolling roar of rifle fire in the distance had degenerated to quick, sharp throbs in twos, threes, and ones, then ceased altogether. It seemed that Paul was so intent on harming her that he had not noticed that the fight was over outside.

Thalia wondered if she would ever know who the victor was.

Or would she be dead before she learned the truth?

Oh, if only Ian were the victor and he arrived to rescue her! Yet he did not even know that she had been taken to the cave!

She was at Paul Hathaway's mercy.

"I saw the Aborigines abduct you," Paul said, forcing her to stand as he held the knife to her ribcage. "No one saw me leave the battle. It's one hell of a jumbled-up mess of men fighting—one more or less made no difference at all."

"You're wrong," a voice said from behind Paul.

Paul was so startled, he dropped his knife. He turned around just as Ian pounced on him, dragging him to the floor of the cave.

As they wrestled, Honora rushed suddenly into the cave, carrying a long and deadly spear. She hurried to Thalia and fell to her knees beside her, laying her spear aside.

"Those from neighboring tribes who did not know you were a friend and who do not speak or understand English bragged to me and father that they captured and brought you here," Honora said, her fingers loosening the bonds at Thalia's ankles. "Honora sorry. Honora come to set you free."

"Honora—oh, thank you, thank you," Thalia said, her eyes never leaving Ian. She winced as Paul sank his fist into Ian's jaw, then sighed with relief when Ian grabbed Paul around the neck and forced him down to the floor of the cave on his back, straddling him.

But too soon, Paul had the best of Ian and had him pinioned to the floor.

"Hurry, Honora," Thalia said, Honora now struggling with the bonds at Thalia's wrists. "Oh, please hurry."

She paled when Paul began choking Ian with one hand, his other hand creeping along the sandy floor of the cave toward his knife.

A sudden, overpowering fright seized Thalia when Paul's fingers circled the handle of the knife. She looked desperately around for a weapon, and just as the leather thongs fell away from her wrists, freeing them, her eyes locked on Honora's spear lying only a few inches from her feet. Her pulse raced as she stared at it for a moment, then stooped and grabbed it up. Without further thought she plunged it into Paul's back just as he had his knife poised for the fatal descent into Ian's chest.

Paul's body jerked as he emitted a loud gurgle of pain. He dropped the knife and fell away from Ian. As he tried to reach behind to take the spear from his back, his spectacles dropped from his face.

Ian bolted to his feet, crunching the spectacles beneath them. He placed his fingers to Thalia's shoulders. "Thalia—?" he questioned, her continued acts of bravery astounding him.

"I had to, Ian," Thalia said, as Ian looked incredulously into her eyes. "He was going to—to stab you." She sobbed. "I couldn't just stand there and let him."

"You saved my life," he said. "How can I ever repay you?"

"Ian, do you forget so easily the times you have saved my life?" Thalia asked, reaching a hand to his face. "I just paid you in kind, that's all."

She glanced down at Paul and shivered at the sight of him lying on his side in his own blood, his body trembling, his face etched with pain as he looked up at her.

Then she was seized with another cause for

panic. Viada! What would be Viada's fate if Paul should die? Had he already given the orders to have her sister killed?

Wrenching herself away from Ian, Thalia fell to her knees beside Paul. She placed a hand beneath his head and lifted it up.

"Paul, please tell me what you have done about Viada," she pleaded. "Oh, please tell me. You know that you're dying. Don't die without first telling me what you have done about my sister. Have you really sent for her? Have you?"

Paul looked up at Thalia with a smirk on his lips, even as blood curled from their corners. "Your sister?" he managed to say in barely a whisper. "Ah, but I have taken very good care to see that she will arrive in Australia just as you intended when you came here—in search of some sort of future."

A cold numbness washed over Thalia. She leaned closer to his face. "She can't be on a ship," she said, her voice quavering. "There hasn't been enough time."

"Before you can do anything about it, your sister will be on a ship and she will be with several of my men," Paul said, wheezing. "By the time she reaches Adelaide, she will be a woman instead of a girl—many times over."

Sickened by the picture Paul painted in her mind, Thalia turned her eyes away. When Paul gasped, she looked slowly around at him again, hating him so much that she wanted to take the spear from him and thrust it into his flesh—over and over again!

She recoiled when Paul grabbed her hand and looked desperately up at her. "Everything I just told you is a lie," he confessed, his features marked by nearing death. "Everything!"

Hope rose within Thalia, then changed to confusion. "Are you trying to say that my sister is safe?" she pleaded. She moved closer to his lips as his breathing became erratic, his body convulsing. "Tell me, Paul. Tell me the truth about Viada!"

Paul smiled crookedly up at her. "The truth?" he whispered harshly. "The truth is that you will pay for what you have done to me. Not your sister, but you, Thalia! In time, you'll see what I mean." He coughed and grabbed at his throat as he began gagging. His eyes were locked on Thalia. "In time! You will . . . pay . . . Thalia."

Silence fell as Paul's body convulsed and writhed for the last time and his breathing ceased. Thalia felt sick to her stomach as his eyes stared blankly up at her accusingly. She choked on a sob as she turned her face away, glad when Ian's strong arms were there, drawing her to her feet away from the dead man.

"What did he mean?" Thalia asked, shivering as she looked up at Ian. "Did you hear his threats? What did he mean?"

"Nothing, damn it," Ian said, sweeping an arm around her waist and quickly whisking her from the cave. "He just wanted to make sure he left you as tormented as when he was alive." He swung Thalia around to face him. "Damn it, Thalia, you can't let him put doubts in your mind like that. The sonofabitch is dead. His threats are empty now."

Thalia pleaded at him with her eyes. "But he had so many faithful followers," she said, her voice faint. "What if he had it all planned? How I would die if anything should happen to him?''

"I wouldn't put anything past him," Ian said, his eyes narrowing with hate. "But we won't dwell on the possibilities. Darling, I'll be there, forever, to protect you. Please take some comfort from that."

Thalia slipped into his embrace and hugged him tightly. "And what of Viada?" she murmured. "Was he lying or telling the truth about her?"

"We shall travel to England soon ourselves and see about your sister," Ian reassured her. "We'll bring her back to Australia. She will live with us. I shall be more than happy to share my home with my wife and sister-in-law."

"Oh, Ian, really?" Thalia cried, suddenly radiant with happiness. Then she questioned him with her eyes. "And what of your mother? Will she live with us also?"

"No, my mother will be going back to America," he said, looking over her shoulder, into the distance. "Unless we can talk her into staying with us." He looked down into her eyes again. "That is, if you wouldn't mind."

"I think it would be marvelous," Thalia said, smiling up at him. She stepped away from him when Hawke came into view, walking proud and tall. He went to Ian and clasped his hands onto his shoulders.

"It is over," Hawke said. "The victory is ours."

Thalia could see a sparkle of tears in Ian's eyes and was touched to her soul by this. She flicked tears from her own cheeks as Ian and Hawke embraced fondly, then broke free, a gentle peace on both their faces.

"My people are anxious to resume the journey to

the sea," Hawke said, squaring his shoulders. "You come now? You bring Missie Thalia?"

Ian smiled at Hawke. "Yes, I will bring Missie Thalia," he said, then looked over Thalia's shoulder again, into the distance. "And also my mother. She would enjoy being a part of the celebration." He smiled down at Thalia, his eyes gleaming. "How on earth did you get here? Where was Kenneth? Did you manage to escape from him?"

"Darling, I am quite cunning—or hadn't you noticed?" Thalia teased.

"Hadn't I noticed?" Ian said. He threw his head back with laughter, then sobered when he and Thalia were surrounded by admiring Aborigines. Suddenly he found himself being lifted onto their shoulders.

Tears welled up in Thalia's eyes, pride for Ian flooding her insides, as the Aborigines pranced around with him on their shoulders, and the others clapped, sang, and shouted as they looked up at him with deep admiration.

Hawke stepped up to Thalia on one side, Honora on the other. "My friend Ian is a hero," Hawke said proudly. "He treat my people well! They treat him well! We celebrate more than the season of the swan's egg this year. We celebrate Ian Lavery!"

"That is so lovely," Thalia said, wiping a tear from her cheek. "So very lovely."

She looked at Hawke, then at Honora. "I hope not too many of your people were killed in the battle," she said softly.

"Only a few brave men die," Hawke said, frowning. He looked down at Thalia, his thick, dark lips lifting into a smile. "But many bushrangers die!"

"But not all of them?" Thalia asked guardedly, recalling Paul's threat against her.

"No, not all of them," Hawke said matter-of-factly.

"But they run away afraid," Honora interjected. "We never see them again."

Thalia swallowed hard as a sudden fear pressed in on her heart.

CHAPTER TWENTY-FIVE

THALIA RODE WITH IAN ON HIS STALLION TOWARD the ocean, where the great gum trees soared over them, their stringy bark peeling off in long fronds. She could hear the surf smashing in with a deep booming noise and then she caught her first glimpse of the peninsula where the eggs were to be gathered. It was barren of any swans now, the recent gunfire having frightened them from their nests.

Soon the peninsula was a frenzy of laughing and shouting Aborigines, filling their kangaroo-hide bags with the delicate, white swan eggs.

Ian reined in his horse before reaching the nesting site. He dismounted and lifted Thalia from the saddle, then swung around when he heard the arrival of horses and his mother's voice behind him. He nodded a silent thank-you to a friend who had gone to collect Kenneth and his mother.

He gathered his mother into his arms as she came to him in a rush, tears streaming from her eyes.

"Son, I'm so glad you aren't harmed," Donna said, hugging him tightly. "All the while I heard the gunfire I prayed that none of those bullets would hit you. My prayers were answered."

"I couldn't be finer," Ian said, smiling down at his mother as she stepped back from him to devour him with her searching eyes. He nodded toward the Aborigines. "So is Hawke. So is Honora."

He gazed down at Thalia. "And so is Thalia," he said proudly. "Because of her, I'm alive."

Donna lifted a quizzical eyebrow. "Because of Thalia?" she asked, looking over at Thalia. "My dear, what did you do?"

Thalia lowered her eyes and blushed, then looked up again when Ian lifted her chin with a finger. "She'll tell you about it later, Mother," he said. "For now, let's join the celebration. We have much to celebrate."

His smile faded. "Paul Hathaway is dead," he said, his jaw tightening. "He'll be causing none of us any more problems."

He looked at the excited natives. "And look at them," he said. "Finally, they have a measure of peace *and* they have the opportunity to enjoy the season of the swans' eggs. They have been forced to wait too long."

Honora ran up to them. Her dark eyes wide and filled with excitement, she grabbed Thalia and

Donna each by a hand. "Come," she said breathlessly. "We join other women preparing the meal for tonight's celebration. By moonlight tonight, we will have a great feast."

Donna laughed lightly and rescued her hand from Honora. "You two young things go on and I'll be there shortly," she said, smoothing a hand over her tired back. "You will have much more fun without me to slow you down."

"Aye, you two go on," Ian said, snaking a comforting arm around his mother's waist. He held her as she rested herself against his solid, steel body. "I'll see to mother's comfort."

Thalia gave Ian and his mother an understanding sweet smile, then giggled as she ran, hand-in-hand, with Honora toward one of the many fires that were already burning on the peninsula.

"This is a time of great joy and thanks for my people!" Honora said, half-dragging Thalia down beside her on the beach close to the fire. "Since I was a small child it has been my desire to participate in such a celebration as this. My people have been kept from the peninsula by evil white men for many years." She began tossing more wood into the fire. "But not this swan's season! We will take back to our village many eggs! They will feed many people the nourishment that has been lacking for too long!"

Thalia rested herself on her knees, facing the fire in a shallow pit packed around with stones. She touched a stone, then jerked her hand away when she felt how intensely hot it was. "You do not plan to cook the eggs over the fire? You will not eat the eggs tonight?" she asked, then turned her head and watched an Aborigine man approach with a slain kangaroo.

She jumped with alarm back to her feet when the man was joined by another as they stood on the other side of the fire from her and Honora and held the kangaroo over the flames, turning it quickly several times until the fur was singed off.

"No, we not eat eggs tonight," Honora said, hopping to her feet. "Tonight we eat kangaroo and other—how do you English say it—delicious, fine things. We share the eggs in our village later with those who were unable to make the march to the sea."

Thalia watched in fascination as Honora emptied a small bag of *nardoo* seed onto a rock, then with another rock pounded it into flour. Honora then spat into the flour until it was moistened enough to pat it flat and put it into the ashes to bake.

Brushing her hands on her kangaroo-hide skirt, Honora moved to her feet. She grabbed Thalia's hand again. "Come," she urged her. "We watch the preparation of the kangaroo."

"I'm not sure if I want . . ." Thalia said, cringing when Honora urged her to follow the men who were in charge of the kangaroo. She was just getting over the fact that Honora had spit into food that soon would be offered her, wondering what the others would do to prepare their food. A sick sort of feeling enveloped her when the kangaroo was opened up with stone ax-heads, and its entrails tossed into the fire.

What followed was more intriguing than disgusting. Thalia stood beside Honora as the men juggled some of the hot stones that had been taken from around the fire, and placed them inside the carcass of the kangaroo. She followed them back to the fire where the animal was thrown into the flames. The ashes and sand were then raked across it.

Thalia looked around her. Those who were not hunting the eggs any longer, whose bags were already bulging with the delicacies to be savored later, were tending to smaller animals and birds cooking over the other fires. There was already a hint of celebration in the air—the chatter amongst the Aborigines became an incessant hum as the afternoon light began to wane and turn to night.

Ian moved up behind Thalia and nuzzled his nose into her hair as he snaked his arms around her waist. "Beautiful, isn't it?" he said, then turned her around to face him. "The happiness, the joy is beautiful, isn't it?"

Thalia crept her arms around Ian's neck and drew his face down close to hers. "My darling, I feel it deep inside my soul," she murmured. "I am so glad to be a part of the rejoicing. I shall never forget this day. Nor this night."

"For many reasons, I hope," Ian said, smiling down at her. "The night has just begun, darling. Before it's over, it will belong to just you and me."

Smiling mischievously up at him, Thalia drew Ian's lips closer. "And how can you arrange that?" she whispered, her lips brushing his. "There are so many who will demand your attention. You are special, Ian, to many more than just me."

"Luv, never doubt my ability to find ways to be alone with you," he teased, flicking his tongue across her lips.

A tremor of ecstasy overtook Thalia, and she looked around her, embarrassed. "But we are not alone now," she whispered, slowly looking back up at Ian again. "We'd best join the others, wouldn't you say?"

"I'd say that is a damn good idea," Ian said, chuckling as he stepped away from her.

He took her by an elbow and walked her toward the Aborigines, who were gathering in one group around the largest of the fires. He reached a hand out to his mother, who had been waiting for him there, and helped her down to the sandy beach on one side of him, Thalia on the other.

The tide was full, the moon not yet risen. The waters of the Indian Ocean rushed at the shore in long rollers out of the darkness, only to ebb down the sand in a froth of frustration. The prevailing west wind blew strong and intrusive on Thalia's cheeks, yet brought with it the wondrous aroma of all sorts of foods that were cooking.

She was so hungry that even kangaroo meat sounded good to her.

"You will find everything very tasty," Ian said, trying to reassure Thalia who looked horrified as the Aborigine women raked the cooked carcass of the kangaroo from the fire and hacked it up with large hatchets. Eager dark hands reached out for the meat as it was distributed to the men and women squatting around the fire, waiting.

"The flesh of the kangaroo is tough and sinewy, but tasty," Ian tried to reassure Thalia as she accepted a hunk of meat from Honora.

Thalia gave him a quizzical glance, then bit into the meat, discovering that her teeth sprang back from it, unable to penetrate it. She watched Ian, her lips parting in surprise as his teeth tore without hesitation into the meat that had been offered him.

"My Lord, how did you do that?" she asked, eyeing the hunk of meat that remained in his hand, then his jaw moving as he chewed the meat as though it were as tender as the chickens that Thalia's mother had always served every Sunday at dinner after church.

Thalia eyed his piece of meat speculatively, then her own, then suddenly noticed the difference in the textures. She laughed as she looked back at Ian. "You scoundrel," she said, grabbing what was left of his meat from his hand and replacing it with her own. "You aren't eating kangaroo meat at all. You are eating some sort of bird!"

Giggling, she took a bite of the delicately sweet and tender meat, savoring the taste on her tongue, ignoring Ian now struggling with the kangaroo meat as he tried to tear bits and pieces of it away with his teeth.

Then she almost spat back up what she was enjoying so immensely when she caught sight of Hawke stooping behind her, plucking something from the sand. In the light of the fire she could see that he had captured a sugar ant between his fingers and she almost gagged when he pinched the sugar bag from the underside of the ant and popped it into his mouth, throwing the rest of the ant aside.

Turning her eyes quickly away, Thalia placed a hand to her mouth as she found herself gagging again.

Ian tossed what remained of his meat into the fire and grabbed for Thalia's hand. "I thought you were enjoying your meal," he said. "Aren't you?"

"Hawke. He ate . . . a part of an ant."

Ian threw his head back and laughed, then drew Thalia closer to his side. "Aye, I'm sure he did," he said, still chuckling. "The sugar ant is his favorite." His eyes danced as he told Thalia, "You might want to try it sometime. Nothing compares with its sweetness. I'm sure not even the pies your mother made for your Christmas meals."

Thalia turned angry eyes to Ian. "I do not wish to hear anymore about Hawke or what he eats, or why," she said. "Please, Ian. Let us just stop speaking of food altogether."

"Aye, let's," Ian said, his gaze moving to Hawke. "But let us not ignore Hawke. Look at him. I have never seen him happier." His eyes followed Hawke's hand movements, seeing what he was reaching for behind him, then he glanced down at Thalia. "Hawke is quite a talented musician. Just watch and listen, Thalia. You will find yourself quite entertained."

Thalia looked at Hawke, at the shadows of the fire playing in his dark eyes, making them appear golden. Her gaze settled on the object in his hand, a sort of hollow club of wood. Her eyes widened when he placed this to his mouth and began blowing the end, bringing forth from it strange, yet enjoyable, sorts of twangs and buzzes. Through this long, hollow gum bough, he continued blowing low, mournful notes, while a couple of drummers beat out a rhythm with the clack of sticks on sticks.

"He's playing a *didgeridoo*," Ian quietly explained. "Mystifying, isn't it?"

"Yes, very," Thalia said. The music caused a strange sort of sensual tremor to soar through her. "Very mystical."

The fires were all burning low now with a kind of sullen ardor, though sometimes one flared up unexpectedly to illuminate the shiny bodies of the men and women clustered around it.

Accompanying Hawke's music now were the voices of his people, a new sound now joining in from a piece of wood swung through the air by means of a rope made of hair.

"What sort of instrument is that?" Thalia asked, moving closer to Ian so that she only whispered. "I find its sound almost as pretty as the *didgeridoo*."

"That is a *churinga*," Ian whispered back. "The Aborigines call it *singing wood*, or a bull-roarer, because it roars when you get it going fast enough. It is swung only by the Aborigines, and only at an important ceremony. To them, it is a very sacred object. *Churinga* not only means singing wood, but also sacred."

"I find the customs of the Aborigines so very interesting," Thalia whispered, looking up at Ian. "Almost as interesting as the American Indian."

"The Aborigines are called simple savages by most Australians," Ian said, nodding. "They are concerned purely with survival."

Thalia began to sway her body in time with the music. "I find their songs so beautiful and touching," she murmured, closing her eyes as she enjoyed this moment of true peace and fellowship.

"Their songs are of the myths and faiths handed down to them through the ages," Ian quietly explained. "Thalia?"

"Yes?" she murmured, seeing a strange sort of light in his eyes, then recognized it as one she had seen before. He wanted her. At this very moment, he wanted her.

"We can hear the music as easily away from the campfires," Ian said, his lips lifting into a slow smile. "No one will notice our absence. Shall we?"

Thalia swallowed hard, then nodded, accepting his solid hand in hers. Together they escaped to a sandy knoll closer to the ocean, from behind which they would be protected from anyone who might have noticed their flight.

As they flung themselves down on the sand, Ian's fingers wove through Thalia's hair and he drew her mouth to his. Trembling lips met, tongues flicked together. Ian's free hand crept up Thalia's blouse and cupped her full, round breast, drawing quivering sighs from deep within her.

Afraid of being seen, Thalia drew her lips from his and pulled his hand from her breast. "We mustn't," she whispered, her breathing ragged with passion. "Someone might come."

"Everyone will remain by the fire until the music ends," Ian said, drawing her lips close to his again. "It is a time for celebration. They have waited too long not to enjoy every minute of it now."

"But you and I left, Ian," Thalia argued softly.

"That is because we wish to have our own private celebration," Ian chuckled. He eased her down onto the sand on her back. His mouth brushed her lips with a soft kiss. "Will you just relax? Darling, I cannot wait until we reach Adelaide to have you." His tongue swept across her lower lip. His hand snaked up her blouse again, his thumb circling her nipple, causing it to harden against his flesh. "I must . . . have you now."

"I want you just as much," Thalia whispered, becoming breathless. "But I am afraid that should we undress, we will be caught . . ."

"Then we shall remove only what is necessary," Ian said, his eyes twinkling down at her. "I'm sure you know which garment of mine that will be, but only down to my knees."

Thalia's face became awash with a blush. "Ian, that is so shameful," she said, giggling. "I will feel more wicked now than that first time with you!"

"That should make the pleasure twofold," Ian said, his free hand working its way up her skirt. He began to caress her at the juncture of the thighs. "Let me love you, Thalia. Put everything else from your mind. Let your feelings take hold—your feelings for me, darling. Nothing else."

"Yes, yes," Thalia whispered, trembling beneath his sensual caresses. "Love me. Love me now."

The sky was a velvety purplish-blue sprinkled with stars. A tremendously full moon gave an eerie silvery sheen to the landscape, like daylight turned inside out. The ocean was quiet, ebbing upon the shore in a gentle effervescent foam, the air deliciously cool and calm.

Thalia's insides were purring as she moved towards Ian. The flesh of her thighs rippled in sensuous hollows as he forced her hips in at his, crushing her against his manhood. She placed her hands on his buttocks. They were smooth and hard as he strained into her, their naked flesh fusing. They moved together, her body absorbing the bold thrusts, accepting them and the wondrous pleasure it was building within her.

"I love you so much," Ian whispered against her cheek, then kissed her with a fervent fire, his fingers moving down her body, caressing her. He could feel his body hardening and tightening, the rapture growing and growing, almost to the bursting point.

Thalia could barely wait for that moment of intense relief that her body was crying out for. Her head was reeling, her insides feeling as though what had been a slow breeze of excitement was now like the deep rumblings of a volcano before it erupted. She sucked on Ian's tongue, she lifted her hips in eager submission, overcome now by the unbearable sweet pain that was encompassing her.

Drawing in her breath sharply, Thalia gave herself over to the wild ecstasy and sensual abandonment as their bodies quivered together, Ian's soon subsiding exhaustingly into hers.

They lay there for some time, Ian stroking her neck gently. "Marry me when we reach Adelaide?" he whispered.

"Yes, yes . . ." Thalia whispered back. "Oh, Lord, yes. . . ."

She snuggled close to him. "That we are free to wed is nothing short of a miracle, Ian," she murmured. "Up to today there have been so many obstacles."

"Yes," Ian whispered. "Yes."

A strawberry roan shook its mane and pawed at the ground as its rider sat quietly in the saddle. Well hidden behind a cluster of bushes, Ridge Wagner watched the Aborigine celebration, his gaze singling out Honora. As her supple body swirled and danced in time with the music, the campfire cast a golden glow on her dark skin. Ridge became entranced with her, as though it were the first time he was seeing her. His eyes followed her, his heart bleeding with loneliness. He had relinquished all claims on her long ago when he had chosen Paul Hathaway and the life of a greedy bushranger over her and his best friend Ian.

Aye, he was bought by Paul Hathaway more than once and now it was too late to turn back the hands of time.

He sighed resolutely, thanking God that he had not taken part in Paul Hathaway's attack on the Aborigines today. He had not even known about it. Only by accident had he come upon the battle after it was over.

And now Paul was dead.

Ridge looked toward the moon-washed beach. He had observed Ian and Thalia's escape there alone. Aye, Paul was dead and Ian and Thalia were very much alive.

Wheeling his horse around, Ridge rode away, his heart heavy, his future no brighter than his past. Greed had changed him into a person he no longer knew—or liked.

CHAPTER TWENTY-SIX

THE RAUCOUS NOISE OF MEN AND WOMEN'S LAUGH-ter and the tinkling of pianos wafting up from the saloons below and through the hotel window made Thalia quite aware that she was no longer in the scrub, but instead safely back in the city of Adelaide. Bath water dripping from her body, her hair hanging in a silken auburn sheen across her shoulders and down her back, she stepped from the copper tub onto a braided oval rug.

The lamplight was low in the room. Thalia grabbed a towel from the bed and began drying herself leisurely, looking slowly around her at the richness of the decor. Ian's. This hotel was Ian's, proving to her again just how rich he was. When he, his mother, and Thalia had arrived in Adelaide directly from the scrub, they had gone to this hotel where the fourth floor was always reserved for Ian and whomever he chose to share it with.

Jealousy swam through Thalia when she looked at the wardrobe overflowing with beautiful women's dresses and thin, silken finery. This reminded her of another aspect of Ian's life she preferred not to think about. He most certainly could have his choice of women—and had, as was evident by the clothes that hung in the wardrobe.

"And he intends for me to wear them after Lord-knows-who has had them on?" Thalia grumbled to herself, tossing the towel aside. She reached for a silk robe and eyed it angrily, getting a faint whiff of perfume wafting from its folds.

But she had no choice but to wear it. Her own clothes that she had worn in the scrub smelled to high heaven. And she couldn't go naked!

Slipping into the robe, she moved to the dresser and gazed into the mirror. She ran her fingers over her face, bronzed from the sun these past few days. Picking up a brush, she began drawing it through her hair. Though relieved that her long ordeal with Paul Hathaway was over, she could not seem to fight off a strange sort of loneliness that was assailing her. At this moment, alone in a strange room, it felt as though she had not experienced any of these past days with Ian at all. If she could be with Ian, now, then the reality would be there, for her to reach out and touch. As it was, he had felt more comfortable placing her in a room alone away from his own, since his mother was there in the hotel able to see Thalia and Ian together.

Thalia did not like the arrangement, yet she understood. She did not want to begin a relationship with Ian's mother by demonstrating to her that she was the sort to lie with a man before marriage. Even Thalia had had guilt-ridden moments because of her loose behavior. She could not believe that she had let herself be so free with him.

Yet, even now, she was considering going to Ian's room to find escape within his powerful arms from loneliness and building despair over Viada.

Laying the brush down, Thalia tiptoed barefoot to the door and inched it open. She peered down the dimly lighted corridor, where candles burned low in wall sconces outside each door.

She eyed one door in particular—Donna's. Ian's mother was in the room between Thalia's and Ian's, and Thalia dreaded having to pass it to get to Ian.

What if Donna opened the door and found her sneaking past it barefoot, attired only in a robe?

Smoothly and quietly, Thalia slipped out into the corridor, the wood floor cold against the soles of her feet. She eyed Donna's door again, relieved when she did not see any light reflecting from beneath it. She concluded that, as exhausted as Donna had been, she had already gone to bed.

Sighing, Thalia moved with less caution toward the aroma of cigar smoke, which grew stronger as she got closer to Ian's room. When she reached it, she leaned an ear against the closed door. She giggled when she heard Ian singing a ballad quite out of tune; then he stopped, his room now stone quiet.

Thalia slowly turned the doorknob and opened the door, seeing him immediately, although he was still unaware that she was there. Thalia stifled a soft laugh behind her hand at the sight of him. He was sitting in chin-high, sudsy water, a cigar hanging loosely from the corner of his mouth, a glass of whiskey in a hand resting on the side of the massive copper tub. His head was hung, his chin almost resting on his chest, looking as though he had drifted off to sleep.

"Perfect," Thalia thought to herself. "Just perfect."

Her eyes dancing, Thalia closed the door behind her and tiptoed across the room to the tub. Kneeling down beside it she slowly dipped a hand into the sudsy water, then quickly splashed it onto Ian's face.

Startled, Ian raised his head and opened his eyes wildly, his cigar falling into the suds, sizzling. The whiskey glass fell from his hand to the floor and shattered into minute pieces, spilling whiskey on Thalia's bare toes. She squealed and started to rise, but Ian was too quick for her. He grabbed her by the waist and pulled her into the tub atop him.

"Ian!" Thalia shrieked, the water soaking into her gown and clinging to her body, revealing her dips and curves. She winced when the cigar floated up next to her skin. "Get that nasty thing away from me," she said, struggling to get up. "Ian, let me go. I didn't come here to take a bath with you!"

Ian scooped up the soggy cigar and tossed it on the floor beside the tub. "Should I ask why you did come?" he teased. "My dearest darling, don't you know that mother is in the next room? The walls are like cardboard. Surely she will hear us."

Thalia's face flooded with color as she glanced at

the wall that separated her from the woman she so admired. "I hope she didn't hear me let out that horrid scream," she whispered, settling down onto Ian's lap, reveling in his closeness. "What would she think of me?"

"You should have thought of that before you came here," Ian teased unsympathetically. His hands were moving caressingly beneath the wet gown, along Thalia's wet flesh to cup her breasts. "You knew that should I see you in that tempting garment I could not just share idle gossip with you." He smiled warmly at her. "But of course I would prefer you with nothing on at all." His hands slid up past her breasts and began smoothing the gown down from her shoulders. "You'd be much more comfortable, Luv, without that wet thing on, don't you think?"

Thalia closed her eyes and sucked in a wild breath when Ian leaned his mouth to a breast and his tongue swirled around its taut peak. "Ian, you are not letting me concentrate on a thing you are saying to me," she whispered, her pulse racing. "Oh, Ian, I came to you because I need you. Darling, I felt so alone in my room. So alone."

"You could've found companionship with my mother," Ian teased, whisking the gown away from her until it lay in a pool of white around her in the water, suds clinging to it.

Thalia opened her eyes and gazed in rapture up at Ian. She placed her hands on his cheeks and drew his mouth down to her lips. "But my darling, that is not the sort of companionship I was seeking when I left my room," she murmured. "My need is for you, Ian. Tell me that you need me as much."

"Always," Ian said huskily, taking one of her hands and leading it beneath the water to his swollen manhood. "There. You feel my need. It belongs to you. Only you."

"Forever?" Thalia asked, her lower lip forming a pout. "Can you forget all those other women the clothes in my room belong to?"

"To me, none of those women exist anymore," Ian said, his heart pounding as Thalia began caressing him slowly, making the heat rise within his loins. "They are nameless. They are faceless."

"Will it be the same one day for me, Ian?" Thalia persisted, momentarily drawing her hand from him. "Will you also forget me?"

He guided her hand back to his hardness and cupped it around him, his hand moving with hers, leading the way for her. "How could I ever forget you?" he said, the flames growing brighter within him as the passion built. "I imagine the only way I can prove my sincerity is by standing in front of a preacher." He kissed her softly, then leaned a fraction away from her. "And that will be soon. Thalia, you will become my wife as soon as arrangements can be made."

Tears streamed down Thalia's cheeks. She looked adoringly up at Ian. "I will be the happiest bride," she murmured.

"You will be the loveliest bride," Ian said huskily. He swept her up into his arms and stood to his feet in the tub, then stepped out onto a towel that he had spread there earlier. "Tonight I hope to make you the happiest fiancée."

"Tonight I am the happiest fiancée," Thalia whispered, clinging around Ian's neck as he carried her to the bed. She pulled him down atop her when he lay her on the bed on bright red satin sheets, and she felt the tightness of his muscled body and the strength of his manhood against her thigh.

"All of your doubts of me are gone?" Ian asked, kissing the hollow of her throat.

"Yes," Thalia murmured, then laughed softly. "Darling, these satin sheets are cold to my back," she said, squirming. "And so slippery."

"But you like them?" he asked, kissing the gentle curve of her neck, his knee gently nudging her thighs apart.

"Should I?" she asked, sighing languorously as she felt his hardness enter her and he began his slow but sure thrusts. "They are for the rich, you know. My darling, my family was simple. My father worked very hard to make a living. But we had all the necessities to make us comfortable enough. We . . . were happy."

Ian snuggled her close within his arms. "Darling, I did not mean to cause you to think back to anything that might make you sad," he said, cradling her face in his hands. "And I know that when you are reminded of family, you become sad. Tonight, darling, let us not think of the past or the tomorrows. Let us concentrate on now. On us."

"Kiss me, Ian," Thalia said, her lips seeking his mouth. "Please kiss me. Then I shall forget everything but the paradise that you always transport me to."

An incredible sweetness swept through her when his mouth touched hers in a gentle and lingering kiss, and his fingers began making a slow, sensuous descent along her spine. The thrusting of his pelvis unleashed a trembling weakness in her lower limbs; the press of his lips was warm and soft, yet demanding.

Ian reveled in the touch of her creamy skin against his flesh and felt a tremor deep within him as his tongue surged between her lips, coaxing from her a soft cry of passion. He placed his hands on her buttocks and lifted her closer to him and anchored her more fiercely still so that he could reach his manhood more deeply within her.

A wild, exuberant passion overtook him as a golden web of magic began to spin around them, making them one. He drew his mouth away and reverently breathed her name as he ran feathery kisses across her brow and then her breasts.

Her eyes glazed with desire, and a curl of heat tightened inside Thalia. And then a searing, scorching flame shot through her. She arched and cried out, laughing and crying at the same time when she realized that Ian had reached that peak of passion at the same moment she had.

It was as though he had been waiting for her, wanting to share, totally, in the pleasure.

She sought his mouth and kissed him with a strange yearning, soaring with joy, then laughed softly up into his eyes as he drew away from her and left the bed, his fingers combing through his hair to straighten it. She watched him in silent admiration as he went to a cabinet across the room and took from it two long-stemmed wine glasses and a bottle of port, bringing these back to set on the nightstand beside the bed.

"Ian, even wine?" Thalia said, leaning up on an

elbow. "You never cease to amaze me."

"I know that I told you that I did not chase the opulent ways of life," he said, cocking an eyebrow as he poured the wine. "But I never said that I actually ran away from it, either. After being in the scrub sometimes months at a time, searching for escaped convicts, I must admit this is nice to return to."

"But you had such a wonderful place to go home to," Thalia said, smiling a thank-you to Ian as she took her proffered glass of wine. "It's so terrible that Paul burned it."

"I can't say that I regret all that much that it burned," Ian admitted. "It had become a prison to my mother. Now she has, in a sense, been set free. I hope with all of my heart that she does catch a boat to America, and soon. That would be the best thing for her."

"You said that she wanted you to go with her," Thalia said, sitting up to make room for Ian to sit down beside her. "You won't, will you? I don't like Australia, but I doubt if I would like America any better. It's a large continent. How does one not get lost there?"

Ian chuckled and took a sip of his wine, then set his glass on the table. He stretched out on his back, looking contemplatingly up at the ceiling as he rested his head on his hands behind him. "Perhaps I will take you to America one of these days and show you the loveliness of its forests, rivers, and mountains," he said. "It is a place you would not mind getting lost in. Yet I have just begun to make a life for myself here in Australia, and I am not one who gives up a challenge all that easily." He sighed, then smiled at Thalia. "Here in Australia, you and I shall live on a spread of land where everywhere you look you see nothing but sheep. Do you like sheep, Thalia?"

"I think they are lovely creatures," she said, setting her glass beside Ian's. She scooted over and snuggled up beside him. "Even Australia will be lovely in my eyes if I am here, with you."

Then she looked away from Ian, sad. "I would be much happier if Viada were here, also," she murmured. "As it is, it will be some time before I even know how she is."

Ian kissed her cheek gently. "Luv, soon we shall board a ship and head for England to see, first-hand, how your sister is," he reassured her. "But first I must see to making arrangements for my mother's passage." He kissed her again. "And we can't forget our marriage plans, can we?"

Thalia beamed up at Ian, hope always there when she looked at him. "Do you think I ever could?" she said, her voice lilting. "I will soon be Mrs. Ian Lavery. How lovely that sounds."

"It is the same as done," Ian said, easing away from her. He rose from the bed and slipped his fringed breeches on, then his shirt. Sitting on the edge of the bed he worked his feet into his boots.

"Why are you dressing?" Thalia asked, drawing a blanket around her shoulders as she sat up, watching Ian. "Where are you going?"

"I have a few errands to run," he said.

Thalia scampered to her feet. "I'd best get to my room, then," she said, and winced when she looked in the tub and saw the robe that she had worn to Ian's room still floating around, silvered with suds. "But how can I? I have nothing to wear. And I'm afraid your mother would catch me sneaking from your room to mine with this skimpy blanket."

Ian guided Thalia back to the bed. "You stay here for the night," he said. "No one will be the wiser."

"But your mother?"

"I'm going to go and talk with her now about her voyage to America and to break the news to her that we will not be accompanying her," Ian said, helping Thalia back on the bed. "You are safe here, luv. Once I leave my mother's room after our talk, she will think that I am not returning to my room just yet, so she will have no cause to come here for anything."

"Where are you going after you leave your mother?" Thalia asked softly, plumping a pillow behind her head as she stretched out on the bed.

"I have a preacher to see and something else to do that will come as quite a surprise to you," Ian said, his eyes twinkling.

Thalia rose up on an elbow. "A surprise?" she said, her eyes wide. "Oh, Ian, what sort?"

Ian chuckled and circled his hand around the door knob. "Darling, if I told you, then it would no longer be a surprise, would it?"

He left the room and closed the door behind him, knowing exactly the man to go to, one who had been trying to sell his fleet of ships without success. Ian would lighten the man's financial burdens quickly. With a wife and children in the future to care for, he would have to give up his wandering, carefree life of bounty hunting.

But he did not want to settle down with just one

business just yet. It would be a mite too boring.

Ships. He would invest in ships.

He would make sure that no one who traveled from England to Australia on his ships would arrive with horror stories of ill treatment while on the voyage.

His fleet of ships would be luxury liners!

CHAPTER TWENTY-SEVEN

As Thalia left the church, the bright sunlight danced and shimmered on her golden wedding band. Holding her wedding bouquet in her right hand, she gazed down at the lovely ring on her left, hardly able to believe that she had just exchanged wedding vows with the man she adored. How could she be so lucky not only to have found a husband, but also to love him with every fiber of her being?

Ian was her soul! Her every breath!

A strong arm sweeping around her waist urged Thalia to gaze rapturously up into Ian's dark eyes, then at his finely chiseled, sun-bronzed face. "Tell me that I'm not dreaming," she murmured, placing her hand gently on his smooth, freshly shaved cheek. "I never knew there could be such a feeling of calm, of peace, as I am feeling now. Ian, it is because of you that I feel these things. Because of you, my future is filled with love, not bitterness."

Ian gazed down at Thalia. Never had he seen her so vibrant and glowing. With the soft glimmer of her auburn hair blowing in the gentle breeze across her shoulders, she looked exquisitely pretty in the traveling dress that he had purchased for her early this morning before the wedding.

Pale blue, the smoothness of the velvet fabric revealed the perfect curves of her breasts and her narrow and supple waist. The style was not all that appropriate for a wedding ceremony, but it suited the boarding of a ship well.

Ian's lips quivered into an anxious smile. Thalia was not yet aware just exactly what sort of ship she would soon be boarding. She had spoken of her dread of traveling by ship again, not knowing that there could be such extremes in conditions on sea vessels. He had made sure that she would never fear a sea voyage again!

"Darling, none of this is a dream," Ian said, his hands framing her face. "And soon I hope that all of your dreams will come true. Once Viada is with you, you will never have cause to worry again. Everything in the world will be right for you and I intend to see that it stays that way."

Thalia lowered her eyes sadly. "Oh, but I did, for a moment, forget the welfare of my sister," she sighed, then looked anxiously back up at Ian. "But I do have faith, Ian, that we will find her unharmed. It is true, isn't it, that Paul didn't have time to send word to harm her?"

"Darling, I have to be truthful about this," Ian

said, afraid that if he wasn't, and they arrived at England shortly after another ship that had carried one of Paul's henchmen, they might be too late by only that too brief twist of fate. "You must prepare yourself for whatever we might find in England. Paul was an evil, conniving man. He had time to do whatever he damn well pleased. I just wish I had known earlier about Viada. I would've stopped that bastard. But as it is. . . ."

Paling, Thalia turned her eyes away again. "If I had been truthful from the beginning, you mean," she murmured. "If anything happens to Viada, I will be at fault. Only I."

"Damn it," Ian grumbled. "Now I've gone and spoiled our wedding day by putting doubts in your head again. What could I have been thinking of?"

Thalia felt as though she were the one casting a shadow of gloom and despair on their beautiful day of shared vows. She smiled reassuringly up at him. "Everything is too wonderful today, Ian, to think of what might transpire tomorrow," she said, forcing a lightheartedness she could not totally feel.

She spun around as Honora and Donna came walking toward her and Ian from the church, Hawke beside them, looking quite handsome himself in a suit that Ian had taken hours to talk him into wearing for the wedding.

"And who shall be the next one to wed?" Thalia asked, raising her bridal bouquet in the air and waving it. Her eyes danced as they met and locked with Honora's. Honora was mystically beautiful in a fully gathered, white silk dress, its bodice lowswept, its long sleeves puffed, hiding the scars and remnants of her tortured past beneath them. In her dark hair she wore pink roses, almost as delicately pretty as she.

"Honora?" Thalia said, giggling. "Will it be you?"

Honora blushed. She was not used to these strange customs of the white people—wearing such fancy clothes, or standing in a church listening to a preacher saying words that made a man and woman husband and wife.

But she did know that not long ago she had realized the promise of such a happiness as Thalia was feeling today.

Memories of Ridge Wagner tore at her heart. For a while, she had known much happiness with him, and then he had stopped loving her. She did not ever want to make the mistake of loving a man again. Ever!

"No!" Honora said, her shoulders squaring proudly. "Honora does not want a husband. Ever! Honora live for her people's destiny only!"

Thalia's eyes wavered, then she thought she understood what had prompted Honora's denial of men. It was because she had loved and lost! And Honora had chosen never to love again because of this man—this Ridge Wagner. She would be wed, instead, to her people.

Thalia wanted to understand this commitment, and thought that she might. She had seen Ian's devotedness to the Aborigines, and his skin was white. To be dark-skinned, one's devotion must run as deeply as their soul!

"The bouquet is yours anyhow!" Thalia said, tossing the flowers to Honora. She giggled when

Honora caught them and looked down at them, smiling, yet most surely not understanding what the true meaning was behind catching them. Honora had stood with quite a puzzled look throughout the wedding ceremony, and, of course, she would. It was her first experience in a church, much less as a witness to a white couple's wedding.

Thalia broke away from Ian and went to Honora. She gave her a warm hug. "I'm going to miss you on the long voyage to England," she murmured. "Please take care of yourself while I'm gone."

Honora slipped from Thalia's embrace. "My time will be filled working for my people," she said proudly. "Now that the worst of the bushrangers are dead, we all can live in peace and fellowship."

Hawke moved to Honora. "My daughter," he said, placing a hand to her shoulder. "Already you have sacrificed enough for our people."

"Honora's sacrifice never enough for the Aborigine," she cried, lunging into her father's arms. She hugged him tightly. "Our people suffer too much too long."

"They are now happy," Hawke said, leaning away from her. "Seeing you happy is what measures my own happiness."

"Then you have reason to smile, father," Honora said. She stared up at her father for a moment longer, then turned to Thalia. "I hope you find your sister alive and well," she said softly.

Thalia sniffled as tears threatened to spill from her eyes. "Me too," she murmured. "Me too." She welcomed Ian's arm around her waist, and smiled at Donna as she stepped up to her in a stiff-looking black dress and hat with a veil hiding her eyes.

"My dear, Thalia, it seems that we just did not get the chance to know each other well enough," Donna said, looking from Thalia to Ian, then back at Thalia. "Ian was able to book passage on the ship bound for America this morning, and I will soon be back where I belong." She looked sadly around her, over her shoulder at the city of Adelaide, then past the city at the mountains outlined in the far distance. "I never truly belonged here. I shouldn't ever have come."

She gazed at Thalia again. "But things will be different for you here," she said, her voice drawn. "You have an advantage I never had because you have a strong man at your side." She cast her eyes downward. "My late husband was once as strong as Ian, but after his heart attack, not only his body wasted away, but also his mind."

Ian stepped forward and locked his fingers on his mother's shoulders. "Mother, there is no benefit in regretting the past," he said earnestly. "Once you are back in America with all of your old friends and my aunts and uncles to spoil you again, you will forget all the sadness brought on you by marrying that—that—"

Donna reached a hand to Ian's lips. "Shh," she said softly. "Don't say things you will regret. It is enough to know how you felt about your stepfather. Please let's not speak it aloud again."

Thalia locked an arm through Ian's and glanced toward the ships moored at the quay across the street from the church. One in particular caught her eye, its smokestack taller and grander than the others. She had never before seen such a stately oceangoing vessel. Compared to the one she had traveled on from England, this ship was surely a haven for the very rich! It was of a full-rigged design and had a broad bow, its toprails and stanchions made of mahogany, ruddy with refracted beams of light. In this hour of early morning, when the sunlight was on her in a russet gold radiance, she glistened.

Thalia studied the ship, whose decks were filled with men at work. The wharf where it was moored was a turbulant waterfront scene, men pushing and shoving as they lugged huge bags of provisions on board the large, intriguing vessel.

And then Thalia's gaze stopped at the side of the ship, where, in bold black letters against its white hull, was painted the name . . .

"Thalia?" she whispered, paling. "That ship is called the *Thalia*?"

A warm sort of feeling encompassed her, realizing that somewhere a man loved a woman enough to give his ship her name. She was touched that it was her own name. It made her feel as though she was a sort of kindred spirit with the ship and the woman it had been named after.

Thalia was drawn back to the present when Ian walked her toward the moored ships, his mother at his other side. "Mother, we'd best get you aboard your ship," he said, only glancing over at the *Thalia*, which was also being readied for departure. He could hardly wait to see Thalia's eyes when he took her aboard and told her that it was theirs!

His gaze swept over the name on the side of the ship, wondering if his wife, as astute as she had proven to be, had noticed it yet.

Even if she had, though, she would never associate it with herself! She expected Ian to become a ranch owner only. Little did she know that even she could never quell his restlessness entirely!

"I'm going to miss you so, Ian," Donna said, looking pensively up at her son. "I'm afraid you will never come to America and see me. I shall die, I am sure, before ever setting my eyes on you again."

Ian glanced at his ship again, his eyes dancing, then looked devotedly down at his mother. "I assure you, mother, that Thalia and I will come to America," he said. "It may not be for another year or so, but we will come and spend several weeks with you, perhaps around the Christmas season, when families should be together."

Thalia had been listening intently and her heart lurched with excitement at the mention of going to America. Oh, how could all of these good things be happening to her? Was it the good before the ugly? Was all of it going to be spoiled once she reached England and found out that her sister's fate was not a pleasant one?

Closing her eyes tightly, she tried to block out all uglinesses from her mind's eye at this moment when everything should be so perfect.

"When will you be leaving for England, my son, to look for Thalia's sister?" Donna asked, her insides tightening as she now stood in the shadow of the large ship that would carry her back home, feeling downcast over all that she had lost in Australia.

Her beloved husband. Her beloved home.

Everything but Ian. Thank God she had been spared him!

"Today," Ian said, trying to hide the eagerness in his voice as he once again glanced toward his waiting ship. "We board our ship for England almost as quickly as yours departs for America."

He looked down at Thalia. "And while we are gone, Hawke and my friends will build my wife and me a house on a spread of land I've already purchased close to the Murray River. When we return, we shall have a wonderful life together."

Donna gazed up at her son, tears near. She lifted her veil and reached her lips to Ian's cheek and kissed him, then grabbed him away from Thalia and hugged him desperately. "My son, my son," she cried. "Please be careful."

"Mother, please don't worry," Ian said, running his hands across her back in a gentle caress. "You know that everything is going to be all right." He leaned her away from him and with a finger flicked a tear from her cheek. "You tell Aunt Rose and Uncle Matthew that their wandering nephew and his lovely wife will come to Seattle to see them as soon as possible. Will you do that for me?"

"Yes," Donna said, choking on a sob.

Thalia moved to Donna and hugged her. "Have a safe journey," she murmured. "I will always remember your kindnesses to me."

Donna hugged her back, then swung away from them both and, with a lifted, proud chin, walked toward the ship and up the gangplank. Almost the very instant she was aboard, the anchor was heaved in and shadowy sails filled and carried the vessel away from the land.

Thalia and Ian waved at Donna until they could no longer make her out in the crowd on deck, then Ian turned to Thalia and placed his hands to her waist. "I think it's time to find our own ship before it leaves us behind," he said, unable to stop a gleam from surfacing in his eyes. "Is my bride ready for another long sea voyage?"

"If you weren't going to accompany me, I would say a fast no to that question," Thalia said, sighing heavily. "But with you at my side? Yes, Ian. I'm ready." Then she frowned. "But first, Ian, I would like to see someone—that is, if we have the time."

"Oh?" Ian said, idly. "I thought we had said all of our good-byes. Who is it you need to see?"

Thalia looked over her shoulder and down the street. "Daisy Odum," she said, her voice drawn. "I'd like to see Daisy Odum."

Ian's eyes darkened with memories of the last time he had been at Odum House. He had been too late then, he thought. Too late.

CHAPTER TWENTY-EIGHT

DAISY ODUM?" IAN ASKED. "WHY DO YOU FEEL IT'S so important to see Daisy now?"

"I can't forget the mistake she made by letting me go with Paul Hathaway," Thalia said, looking at the ships at the quay again and recalling the day she had arrived from England and how she had been swept away by Daisy, and why. "She must be told what happened to me so that she will be more careful in the future."

"And you insist that you must tell her now?" Ian asked, slipping an arm around her waist to guide her away from the bustling wharf.

"I am sure that more than one ship will arrive from England while we are gone," Thalia said. "If what I tell Daisy can save even one of the innocent women who arrive here from the hardships I was forced to endure, then I will rest easier on my voyage to England."

"Then so be it," Ian said, leaning to kiss her cheek. "We want your long journey to be as care-free as possible. I will do my best to see that it is."

"I know that you will," Thalia said, smiling up at him.

She grew tense as she stepped up to the door of Odum House. The last time she had been there was the day she had been introduced to Paul and had left with him. At the time, she had felt that he was all the hope she had for a decent life in Australia. Her hopes of Ian being the man to claim her had been dashed too quickly.

If she had waited!

"Thalia?"

A tiny voice behind her and Ian filled Thalia with a different sort of memory of that last time she had been at Odum House.

Ava. Sweetly innocent, deformed Ava.

"Ava," Thalia said, turning quickly around. "How are you?"

"Just fine," Ava said, standing with her back all hunched over, carrying a laundry basket filled with dried clothes just taken from the clothesline out back. "Daisy is so very good to me, always." She smiled awkwardly up at Ian. "Hello, Ian," she said, squirming as she tried so very desperately to straighten her back. She had had a crush on Ian as far back as the first day he had arrived in Australia.

Then she looked from Ian to Thalia, seeing their total happiness and how wonderful they looked together. Her smile widened and her eyes twin-

378

kled, especially when she looked down at Thalia's ring finger and caught sight of the wedding band. "My, oh, my," she sighed. "You two are married?"

Then she lost her smile in a frown. "No, I apologize," she murmured. "You can't be married. Thalia married Paul Hathaway. That's Paul Hathaway's wedding band. I'm sorry."

Thalia giggled. "Ava, I am married to Ian," she said. "I never was married to Paul Hathaway."

"What is this you say?" Daisy said, suddenly appearing at the door. She stared disbelievingly down at Thalia. "Did I hear you say that you were never married to Paul?"

As she looked up at Daisy, Thalia's eyes wavered, recalling the day that Daisy had visited Paul's ranch to visit her, and Thalia had been forced to lie to her. "Daisy, it was all a farce," she said. "It was all in pretense—the marriage to Paul, my role as a loving wife, everything. It was all forced on me by that—that evil man. He had his reasons for doing this, Daisy, and all were ugly and diabolical. I'm sorry I could not be truthful with you, could not confide in you that day you came to call. I had to play my part well, for there was more than one life at stake had I not."

Paling, Daisy placed her hands to her throat. "My word," she said, her voice weak. "Had I paid more heed to my feelings about that man, then none of this would have happened to you."

Daisy's face became drawn with quick, deep regret. "Oh, God, no!" she gasped. "He did not— take advantage of you?"

"No," Thalia murmured. "He never forced himself on me. In fact, he—he never approached me at all in that way."

Thalia could feel Ian's eyes on her and suddenly realized that she had never explained to him why Paul had left her alone. After they got on the ship, on their way to England, she would tell him everything that she had left out originally.

Everything.

Daisy sighed with relief. "Where is Paul Hathaway?" she asked, directing her questions at Ian now. "How is it that Thalia is married to you, Ian?"

Ian circled his arm around Thalia's waist possessively. "Paul is deservedly dead," he said flatly. "Thalia and I just got married. We are on our way to England to see about her sister Viada."

Thalia intervened. "I wanted to take the time before we boarded our ship to warn you about men like Paul Hathaway," she said solemnly. "Please screen your clients more carefully, Daisy. What I went through before Ian rescued me was pure hell. No one should be forced to endure what I did."

"I have always tried my best," Daisy said softly. "But in the future, I shall try even harder."

"Thank you," Thalia said, then turned to Ava. "Ava, when Ian and I return from England, I would like for you to come and live with us. You would so enjoy it out at our sheep station with so many sheep you could never count them for wearing your poor mind out from trying."

Thalia blinked back a tear when she saw how gratefully humble her offer made Ava. "Please, Ava. We'd love to have you," she said, wanting to tell Ava that far from the city, she would also be far away from the mocking jeers of drunken idiots.

But Ava knew that without being reminded. Living on the sheep station, clear of all abuses, she could finally feel like a human being, a person with feelings.

Ava sobbed tears that had been welling up inside of her for an eternity—tears of gladness!

"I'd love to come and live with you," Ava said, placing her laundry basket on the ground. She wiped her nose and eyes with the back of her hand. "I will keep your clothes washed and ironed. I will cook. You'll see. You won't be sorry you invited me there."

Thalia laughed and hugged Ava. "My darling friend, I would not want a maid in you," she murmured. "I do not want a maid at all. I plan to do my own chores. I love to see the rewards of my day's work, just as a man enjoys seeing his. But if you want to work alongside me, I won't argue with you over that."

Ava nodded anxiously. "Anything you say I'll do," she said, then slipped from Thalia's comforting arms and turned to Daisy. "Mu'm, can I go?"

Daisy's lips parted in surprise, touched that Ava felt she had to ask her permission. She gathered the small thing into her arms. "My dear, I would never keep you from what I believe will be the best thing that has ever happened to you," she said, her voice breaking. She looked at Thalia and Ian over Ava's shoulder. "Thank you," she mouthed beneath her breath so that Ava could not hear. "Thank you."

Choked up, not wanting to cry and get her face all red and bothered since she had a ship to board at any minute now, Thalia coughed into the palm of her hand, then slipped her arm through Ian's. "I think everything has been taken care of here, Ian," she said, lifting her chin proudly. "I'm ready to board the ship."

"May God be with you two, always," Daisy said, waving.

Beaming, Ava waved the tail of her apron.

Thalia and Ian waved, then walked away toward the wharf. Ian chuckled as he slipped his arm through Thalia's. "I think you'd best prepare yourself for that surprise I promised you," he said, pushing himself and Thalia through the milling crowd and the men thronging toward the *Thalia*, lugging bags and packages.

Thalia's eyes widened in wonder. "Surprise?" she said, her voice lilting. "Oh, Ian, what sort?"

"Just take a look yonder," Ian said, gesturing with the swing of his free hand toward his ship. "Do you like it?"

Now in the shadow of the large ship that Thalia had admired earlier, she stopped and gazed up at the name again. She smiled. "Oh, that," she said, shrugging. "Isn't that nice? Some man loved a woman enough to name his gorgeous ship after her."

Ian chuckled as he guided her toward the gangplank. "Not just any man, nor just any woman," he said. "Darling that man is me and the woman is you. I named the ship *Thalia*. I hope you approve."

Her footsteps faltering, Thalia gaped openly at the name on the side of the ship again, then looked quickly at Ian. "What?" she gasped. "This ship is yours? How, Ian? How can that be?"

Ian shrugged. "I thought it was time for me to

spend some of my inheritance," he said, ushering her up the gangplank to the deck of the ship. "This is one of many ships I have purchased. I have my own fleet. They will allow those who travel between England and Australia to avoid the hardships that you encountered on your voyage here."

"My Lord!" Thalia said, her face coloring pink with excitement as she stopped and looked around her. Everything was new. Everything was wonderful! The decks were white. The brass and the copper that was abundant everywhere had a lick of fire from the reflection of the sun in them. The sails just now being unfurled looked like great white ghosts in the sky!

A distinguished man with a blue uniform, resplendent with gold braid and buttons, stepped forward, his hand outstretched. "Good day, sir," Victor Connors said, his thin mustache as gray as his abundant head of hair. "And is this the bride? This is Thalia?"

Thalia smiled up at the man who looked down from an even taller height than Ian's, seeing a polite appreciation in his blue eyes. She offered him a hand. "Yes, I am Thalia," she said, almost shyly. "I am Ian's bride."

Victor took Thalia's hand and raised it to his lips, kissing the back of it suavely. "I am pleased to make your acquaintance, ma'am," he said, reluctantly releasing her hand.

He cleared his throat and focused his attention on Ian. "I trust that your quarters have been made comfortable enough for you. If not, please do not hesitate to send for me," he said smoothly. His mustache quivering, he smiled saucily down at

Thalia. "The champagne is in your cabin. The—ah-hem—comforter has been turned down on your bed."

Ian swept an arm around Thalia's waist and led her away from Victor. "Much thanks, mate," he said over his shoulder. "And I doubt I will have need to see you again, I am sure, until tomorrow at breakfast?"

"That is good, sir," Victor said, making a slight waving gesture with a hand. "Your evening meal will be sent to you. But do not fear—you will not be disturbed. It will be placed just outside your door and the cabin boy will knock and leave."

"Thanks, mate," Ian said, then bent low, into Thalia's face. "Now. Tell me what you think of my surprise."

"My, but you are quite a master of deceit," she said, giving him a slow smile.

"Me?" Ian said, his eyebrows raising. "You call me a master of deceit? Look how long you pretended that you were that bastard's wife. You played the role well, luv."

"I had no choice," Thalia said. "And you know the reason why."

"Aye, I know," Ian said, guiding her to the rail. The anchor had been heaved in, the ship had embarked with a favorable wind, and the sails creaked and groaned overhead. "I know."

Thalia circled her fingers around the ship's rail, watching the land and sea flitting by.

"This ship, the *Thalia*, is far better than the average sea vessel," Ian bragged, drawing Thalia close to his side. "Most are built for only cargo, and passengers are crowded into makeshift bunks in the hold. Mine is a passenger ship with state-rooms. It also has windmill ventilators which give the passengers constant currents of fresh air."

Thalia was only half listening to Ian, for she was thinking back to their bantering about who was the true master of deceit. This reminded her that she must tell him about Paul and why he had never made sexual advances toward her.

With the full intention of telling him now, she turned to him, but her gaze was drawn back to the water and the dangers that lay there now that they were far out to sea from Adelaide. The helmsman of the *Thalia* seemed to have incorrectly taken the ship off course, and they were now dangerously close to a coral reef.

"Ian," Thalia gasped, pointing. "My God, look. We may capsize!"

CHAPTER TWENTY-NINE

THALIA LUNGED FOR IAN AND GRABBED HIS ARM AS the ship began inching past the coral reef. "Ian, the ship is going to scrape any moment now," she gasped. "Hold me! We may be thrown overboard! Oh, Ian, I shall never forget the time that I fell into the water. The shark! Oh, surely there are even more sharks here than in Adelaide Harbor!"

Looking frantically around her, Thalia was stunned to find that no one else seemed bothered by the danger. The crew were working normally, the crowd on the topdeck were pointing at the lovely coral, oohing and aahing instead of shrieking with fear.

"Darling, one can tell that you are not a seasoned passenger of an oceangoing vessel," Ian chuckled, caressing her back as she pressed her cheek hard into his chest. "Just relax. Do you think I would hire a sea captain and helmsman that would take me to my death the first time I journeyed on my new ship? No, I think not."

"But, Ian, one can never be sure about anything in life," Thalia argued softly. "Especially strangers who you think you might be able to trust. Never forget Paul Hathaway! Was he not a stranger in whom I put my trust?"

"Luv, in matters of the sea, there are endless tests and procedures the owner of a ship goes through to choose the proper crew," he said, his hands on her throat, framing her face and forcing her eyes to meet and hold with his. "The man I purchased my fleet from chose only those with the highest of recommendations. I kept the same crews, trusting his judgment since he has lived with the sea for the biggest part of his life. Now, darling, this is our honeymoon. Can't you give me just a little smile?"

Thalia sucked in a wild breath, so aware now of his nearness and how he had a way of mesmerizing her. As she gazed up at him, even now she could see strange lights moving in the depths of his eyes, and understood the meaning. His love for her was deep and he needed her now, just as her need for him was rising within her like the sun, blossoming into something deliciously warm and wonderful.

"You ask for a smile?" she whispered, reaching a hand to trace the line of his jaw with her fingers. "Why, darling, I think I can manage that and can promise even more than that, should you ask."

"Here? For everyone to see?" Ian teased, his

thumb caressing her flushed cheek. "Has marriage turned you into some sort of shameless hussy?"

"Ian, don't tease me here," Thalia scolded. "Everyone will see me blushing."

"Then are you saying that you wish to retire to our quarters?" Ian asked, his lips a feather's touch from hers. "Perhaps you need a bit of champagne to soothe your nerves?"

He chuckled beneath his breath. "Or should I say—to cool your ardor?"

With Ian's lips so close that she could feel the warmth of his breath on her own, Thalia could hardly control the erratic beat of her heart. She drew away from him, breathless, and turned to the ship's rail and clasped her hands tightly onto it again, shifting her attention back to the reef that the ship was still inching past.

"It is fascinating, isn't it?" Ian said, stepping up beside Thalia again. He ran a finger around the edge of his collar, which seemed to have gotten tighter—damn sure hotter—during his moments of teasing his wife. Being so near her always lit him up inside like heat lightning. The long voyage with her would be like something out of a dream. They would awaken in the morning and retire each evening alone in their stateroom making love. His desire for her was never quenched. Never would it be, ever!

"It would be lovely except that one can't forget that many lives must have been lost because of it," Thalia said, shivering at the thought.

Yet she could not help but admire the reef. It was a horseshoe-shaped piece of coral, edged with a sparkling white sandy beach. The reef was covered in part by coarse grass and big, gray shrubs that looked like cabbages. Dead trees, battered by the storms, leaned askew against the few that still lived. Morning glories grew among the trees. Sandpipers traced the beach in delicate, linked patterns. Booby birds slumped in the sun, too lazy to watch the sandpipers.

The ship groaned, the masts nodded and swayed and bent as the vessel finally cleared the reef. Ian swept an arm around Thalia's waist and walked her away from the rail. They made one turn around the crowded deck, where couples roamed about, men stood about in small knots, talking or gambling, women stood in clusters, gossiping.

Thalia silently admired the ship again—the teak balusters and stanchions, the curved, ornamented stern emblem, the rails that were bound in brass. It was enough to fill one with wonder!

Then Thalia was glad when the topdeck was left behind and they were below in a stateroom that took her breath away.

"My word!" she said, her eyes widening at the richness of the suite. Candles flickered from wall sconces, their golden light revealing a red plush settee and matching overstuffed chairs flanking it, a teak sideboard, a chart table, cabin mirrors and bird's-eye maple panels, with great scrolls of mahogany on the door frame. A bed, large and inviting, was at the far end of the room, a red velveteen comforter drawn back to reveal two red satin pillows trimmed with white lace. A bottle of champagne and two-long stemmed glasses awaited the newlyweds on a nightstand beside the bed.

"This is something I would expect to find in a

hotel suite, perhaps in London, but never on a ship," Thalia said, in awe of it all. "But, of course, the staterooms are not all this exquisite on this ship. This is your private master cabin."

"Correction," Ian said, lifting her suddenly up into his arms, carrying her toward the bed. "This is *our* stateroom." He nuzzled her neck with a kiss. "And, darling, we can do anything we wish to each other and it is all damn legal."

Thalia locked her arms around Ian's neck. She drew his lips to hers and gave him a long, sweet kiss, hardly aware of being placed on the bed. She was becoming dizzy with desire as Ian's hands began quickly disrobing her, moaning with pleasure as he soon cupped her breasts within the palms of his hands and squeezed and fondled them until her nipples were points of throbbing need.

"Ian, my love," Thalia said in a gurgle of ecstasy. She ran her hand over the slope of his hard jaw, his eyes smoke black with passion as he gazed down at her. "Please undress. I want to see you. All of you, my darling."

Ian rose from the bed. Thalia's breathing became steadily harsher as she watched him disrobe and she hastened out of her own clothes.

Piece by piece, Thalia watched Ian toss aside his clothes, revealing to her his magnificently wide shoulders which tapered to his narrow hips—his hard, flat stomach, his long, firm legs—and back again to marvel at the expanse of his tanned, sleekly muscled chest.

As he stirred to move back toward the bed, the muscles rippled and flexed down the length of his lean, tanned body, stirring Thalia to a maddening desire. She could not stop a blush from coloring her cheeks when she allowed herself, finally, to look at that part of him that was so fully aroused.

Seductively, Thalia beckoned a hand to Ian. He came to the bed and moved over her, straddling her with his knees. He closed his eyes and held his head back and groaned when Thalia leaned up on an elbow, her fingers circling his hardness, her mouth on him, making him feel as though he might explode from the intensity of the pleasure. His heart pounded. His loins felt as though they were on fire as her lips and tongue continued to send shock waves of desire through him.

And then he felt too close to the edge. He opened his eyes and guided Thalia back down on the bed, his heart thudding against his ribs as he gazed down at this woman he could now call his wife. His blood ran hot through his veins as he took in the sight of her slim and sinuous body—her perfect breasts, her slim, exquisite waist, and her slender legs. Everything about her was invitingly round. Her body seemed translucent today—gleaming.

"Never have I seen you as beautiful," Ian finally said. His heart seemed to be melting as he looked at her passion-moist lips, and again at her exquisitely soft and creamy flesh. His hands began to tease and stroke the supple lines of her body, his gaze burning upon her bare skin. "Thalia, I am so lucky to have you. Never could I have found anyone as beautiful. As wonderful."

Thalia squirmed with pleasure as Ian's hands found all of her delicate pleasure points, caressing and arousing her with the skilled tips of his fingers. Her hands rediscovered the contours of his face, then she placed a finger at his lips and moaned sensually when he sucked her finger within his mouth and his tongue flicked against it.

"You are driving me wild," she breathed, as Ian stroked the satiny line of her inner thighs, then centered on her throbbing, swelling love bud.

She closed her eyes, reveling in the feathery kisses he was spreading from her face, to her breasts, and then downward across her stomach.

As he continued to make his way down her body, her ragged breathing became slower. She gasped with ecstasy when his tongue took over where his fingers had been, bringing her closer to that brink of joyful bliss that she so vividly remembered from the other times while with him.

She gasped with ecstasy, and desire raged and washed over her when she felt the sweet wetness of his tongue as his hands spread her thighs apart, giving him access to her throbbing center. She felt her entire body heating up, all senses yearning for that magical moment of divine wonder.

And then Ian moved over her. He surged into her with one great burst of hip movement, a sensation of hot relief mingled with a passion shooting through him which drew his lips apart in a gasp.

Beginning his determined thrusts within her, his mouth sought her lips again. He kissed her hard, consuming and devouring her. Thalia returned the kiss with ardor, her fingers twining through his hair to bring his mouth harder into hers. Her whole universe seemed to start spinning around, so close to going over the edge into ecstasy. The spinning sensation rose up and flooded her whole body so quickly, it was like a great burst of light within her brain, overpoweringly sweet and wonderful.

Ian clutched Thalia to him, surges of warmth flooding through his body. Each thrust brought him closer to the ecstasy he desired, Thalia's hips responding to him as she thrust her pelvis toward him. He moved within her slowly, then powerfully.

A great gush of feeling overcame him. Brokenly, between gasps, he whispered her name as stabs of exquisite agony wracked his body.

And then they lay still, clinging, Ian's face buried in Thalia's breasts. Gently she stroked his head. "I love you so," she whispered, her whole body still tingling from the shared ecstasy.

Ian's hands swept down her body and up again, then he rolled away from her and sat on the edge of the bed. He reached for the champagne bottle and popped its cork. His whole body seemingly one continued pulsebeat, he poured a glass and handed it to Thalia.

Thalia moved to a sitting position, resting her back on the headboard of the massive bed. She took the glass and waited for Ian to scoot up next to her. Her eyes twinkling, her face flushed, her long, drifting hair resting across her breasts, she giggled when Ian moved beside her and clinked her glass with his.

"It's time for a toast," he said huskily, his eyes searching hers. "You first. What do you toast, my love?"

Thalia became thoughtful, then she smiled slowly over the rim of her glass as she placed it to her lips. "To a future of many more magical moments like this," she said, her mouth barely brushing the glass. "And now your turn, my darling."

Ian went thoughtful, yet he was heating up inside again as he watched her tongue running slowly over the rim of the glass as she waited for him to make the toast. His eyes became glazed over as his loins twitched, seeing her so damn seductive at this moment that it took all the willpower he could muster up not to throw the damn glass aside and grab her up into his arms and make love to her again.

He cleared his throat nervously as he forced his eyes away from her. He sighed, then smiled as he clanked his glass to hers again. "To a future of my keeping hold of my wits while around you," he said, his voice deep and husky. "You drive me to madness, darling. To madness!"

"I hope that I shall keep the ability to do so even when I am old and gray," Thalia murmured, as she tipped the glass to her lips and sipped the champagne as she watched in amusement as Ian drank his in one swallow.

Thalia set her glass back on the table and stretched out on the bed, seductively snaking her body toward Ian's. "Ian, I still want to play," she said, her lower lip curved into a pouting gesture. Running a fingernail up his thigh, she blushed when she saw that she was causing him to become highly aroused again, even though she had most surely intended that.

"You want to play, do you?" Ian said, his pulse racing. He set his glass down, then picked up the bottle of champagne and quickly straddled her, his knees locking her in place between his legs. His eyes gleamed into hers as he slowly tipped the bottle down close to one of her breasts.

"What . . . are you doing . . . ?" Thalia gasped, watching the golden champagne pouring slowly from the bottle, dripping onto a nipple which quickly hardened beneath the effervescent, bubbling liquid.

"You said that you wanted to play," Ian teased, now trailing the liquid over to her other breast, also wetting its nipple. "Darling, I know the most wonderful game of all."

Shivers of delight raced up and down Thalia's spine, the champagne cold and wonderful on her heated flesh. "And what is the name of this game?" she asked, sucking in a wild breath when Ian continued pouring the champagne on her, now trailing it across her stomach, and to the patch of hair between her thighs.

Thalia emitted a soft shriek when the champagne fizzed on her swollen center. Then she sighed and shook all over with desire when Ian set the bottle aside and, with his tongue, began tracing the trail left by the champagne. She curled her fingers through his hair and made the journey with him, urging his mouth closer to the most vulnerable of her pleasure points. She breathed hard. She closed her eyes.

Then she welcomed him back inside her. Only half aware of making whimpering sounds, she raised her hips to meet his steady thrusts, everything within her seeming to be whirling.

But too soon it was over again, and they lay side by side listening to the sounds of the ship and the ocean. The timbers creaked, the sea was calm, the waves slapping only lightly against the hull of the ship.

Ian broke the silence. "Never have you tasted so good," he teased, turning to face Thalia. He cupped her face within his hands and drew her lips to his. "We will have to try that again, luv."

Thalia shivered with ecstasy and molded herself into the hard, muscled contours of his body. "I have never felt so at peace," she whispered, then a frown shadowed her face. "I feel so guilty because of it."

Ian leaned away from her and gave her a stern look. "Don't," he said thickly. "Never feel guilty about finally finding some semblance of peace and happiness in your life."

"But my sister," Thalia said somberly.

"You have done the best you could for your sister," Ian said. "No one could do more. So, damn it, Thalia, stop feeling guilty. It was not meant for you to carry the burden of your family on your shoulders. Your mother and father would never have wanted this. Just relax, now, and take life as it comes to you, with all the happiness that it offers."

He lifted her chin so that their eyes met and held. "Take what happiness I offer you." He smiled. "And, darling, let's never have any more secrets from each other. Ours will be a free marriage, as well as a passionate one."

Thalia drifted into his arms to snuggle there contentedly. "You make me so happy," she sighed. "And, yes, let's always be truthful. I am sorry that I was forced to lie so often to you after we met. Never shall I lie to you again."

It came to her suddenly that this was the time for the truth she had planned to share with Ian as soon as she had the chance to tell him. A truth about Paul. She leaned away from him and looked up at him. Her lips parted with the confession, but was stopped when a knock on the door interrupted.

"Sir, I am leaving food at your door now," a cabin boy said from behind the closed door. "Good day, sir. You and your bride enjoy the meal."

Ian lifted Thalia away from him and reached for his discarded breeches on the floor. "Cover yourself with the comforter long enough for me to open the door and get the food," he said, his voice lighthearted, content.

Thalia drew the comforter up to her chin and waited patiently. Ian went to the door and opened it cautiously. After looking down both avenues of the corridor and seeing no one, he gathered up the silver-domed tray quickly and kicked the door closed behind him.

Succulent aromas wafted across the room, making Thalia's stomach growl. She looked hungrily at the tray as Ian placed it on the nightstand beside the bed, lifting its cover and laying it aside. Her mouth watering, she sorted through the food with her eyes, seeing so much that tempted her.

"The chef has prepared us a feast you will never forget," Ian said. He went to the sideboard and took plates and silverware from it, taking these back with him to the bed. "Now, luv, what will you choose first? There is turtle meat, fish, pork, chicken, duck or pigeon. The meats have been roasted, chopped into chunks, and marinated in spiced wine, then combined with cabbage, anchovies, pickled herring, mangoes, palm hearts, onions, olives, grapes and any other pickled vegetables the chef managed to bring aboard the ship to supply his kitchen with.''

Ian gave Thalia a dish and silverware. ''Dig in,'' he said, chuckling. ''You look ravenous. So am I.''

He leaned down closer to her face and kissed her brow. ''I always am after making love,'' he said softly. ''Luv, you may be responsible for your husband getting fat and lazy.''

Thalia patted his cheek. ''Never,'' she said, looking him up and down, at his solid physique. ''But if you do, I shall love you even then.'' Her eyes danced as she stared into his. ''That is, as long as you will allow me to be just as fat and lazy as you.''

''Heaven forbid!'' Ian said, moving quickly back to his feet. He took her plate and started scooping food onto it, then handed it back to her. He studied her, recalling that she had been ready to say something to him that seemed important before the cabin boy had knocked on the door.

''Why are you scrutinizing me so?'' Thalia asked, pausing with a fork full of marinated, roasted duck halfway between her mouth and plate.

''A while ago you seemed ready to tell me something,'' Ian said, pouring champagne into their glasses. ''What was it? Was it part of the mood of the moment that brought something else to mind that we had not spoken of yet?''

''Well, sort of,'' Thalia said, lowering her fork back to her plate. Her eyes wavered as she looked up at Ian. ''Ian, it's about Paul Hathaway. Something I failed to tell you earlier.''

A shadow seemed to flicker across Ian's face. He

picked up a glass and began turning its tall stem around between his fingers, staring down into the translucence of the champagne. "And that is?" he mumbled, unable to stop the unsteady beat of his heart, fearing what she may have kept from him. It surely could not be something good, for everything that had to do with Paul Hathaway had been unpleasant.

"Ian, you know that I said that Paul never took advantage of me sexually," Thalia said. She moved her plate of food aside and knelt to face Ian, splaying her fingers against his muscled chest.

Ian looked down at her, something akin to pain suddenly in the depths of his eyes. "Are you about to tell me that he did, eventually, force you to join him in his bed?" he said, his voice thin and drawn.

Thalia was taken aback by this, having never meant to give Ian even one moment's cause to worry. "Lord, no," she blurted out, flipping her hair back from her shoulders as she looked desperately up at Ian. "Ian, it is just the opposite. It was just as I told Daisy—Paul never touched me in that way. He never desired me. He couldn't."

Ian's eyebrows quirked and he looked down at Thalia, puzzled. "What do you mean, he couldn't?" he said incredulously. "My God, woman, what man could look at you and not desire you?"

"A man who is impotent," Thalia said, swallowing hard. "Ian, Paul was impotent. We never shared anything but hatred, he and I."

"Impotent?" Ian said, the word brushing across his lips in a gasp.

Then he set his glass down and rose to his feet, laughing so hard that Thalia gaped openly after him for a moment before joining in the laughter.

"Impotent?" Ian repeated, throwing his hands in the air as he continued to laugh until tears sprang from his eyes. "God is in his heaven, all right. He sent forth a punishment to that demon that was worse than death." He turned and faced Thalia, sobering. "If Paul did not have the ability to make love to you, my darling—oh, but what a fierce punishment it must have been for the man."

He went to Thalia and surrounded her with his hard, strong arms, and pressed her against him. "Thank God he was impotent," he said, thickly. "Thank God—for, Thalia, who is to say what further hell he would have put you through were he not?"

The stark truth of what Ian was saying made Thalia cling with a fierceness to her husband, glad to be imprisoned against him, feeling safe, feeling wanted, feeling—oh, so desired. . . .

CHAPTER THIRTY

SEVERAL MONTHS LATER
GLOUCESTERSHIRE, ENGLAND

AS THE CARRIAGE ROLLED ALONG THE WINDING
road toward Slad, Thalia clung to Ian's arm. Looking from the window at her right side, she was lost
deep in reverie, yet not so much that she could not
admire the countryside. Gloucestershire. Here
Thalia could feel God's presence where He had
fashioned the Cotswolds—gentle little promi-
nences mostly, hardly worthy to be called hills, but
worthy of every superlative for beauty.

Scattered through them, hidden in their folds
beside meadow, woodland, and stream, lay pretty
villages. When Thalia had taken long strolls as a
child, the miles had felt shorter and the paths less
steep, for she had been walking in the most
beautiful part of the countryside. In the Cotswolds,
she had wandered through the bluebells of May,
the purple clover and yellow vetch of summer, and

the gold of autumn leaves and grain stubble.

It was early morning now, the mist lifting reluctantly from the valleys, where, laced by dark foliage, mottled fields blanketed the rolling hills. Thalia's heart warmed with memories of the nights she had fled to be alone. As the mist had risen from the meadows and the full moon was able to silver everything it touched, the whole country seemed awash in sterling, breathtaking and quite magical. She had seen silver barns, silver lanes, silver air, and silver sky.

Thalia was brought back to the present and her pulse raced as the clip-clop of the carriage horse echoed hauntingly down the moist cobblestones as it entered the small village of Slad, where dew-laden flowers and picket fences bordered the quiet streets.

She scarcely breathed as her gaze absorbed everything that was still so very familiar to her. Aged church towers and spires, enduring monuments of faith, rose from the tiny village—a shadowed little place tucked away in a narrow valley. Homes and shops seemed to be yawning at this hour of the day when the sun was just touching their windows with a rebirth of golden light.

She leaned closer to the carriage window and suddenly pointed to a church spire. "Oh, Ian, look," she said, emitting a low sigh. He moved closer to her and leaned his head so that he could see what she was pointing at. "See the clock? Several years ago it stopped running for several months. But then it was fixed."

She looked over at Ian as the carriage rumbled on past the church. "Ian, I liked it better when it didn't work," she said softly. "Why did they give us time again?"

Ian chuckled. He took Thalia's hand and held it tightly. "I think I understand your feelings," he said. "Timelessness seems so right for the Cotswolds. England, itself, seems timeless."

"I knew you would understand," Thalia said, leaning to kiss his cheek. She again watched from the window, her heart racing. Soon. She would be at her mother and father's cottage soon.

"You said that your Uncle Jeremy moved into your parents' cottage after they died?" Ian asked, following her anxious gaze as the carriage began to pass the smaller, considerably poorer cottages on the other side of the village. "You said that he is widowed and that he, alone, is taking care of Viada?"

"Yes, widowed, he alone takes care of Viada," Thalia said forlornly. She swallowed hard, not wanting to cry, memories pressing in on her like a heavy weight on her heart. "And, yes, he makes residence in my childhood home." She shifted nervously on the seat. "You see, until then he made his home wherever he found a resting spot for the night. His occupation is not the sort that made him rich."

"You said that his occupation is—" Ian began, but stopped short when Thalia looked suddenly from the window and emitted a loud shriek of horror.

"Oh, no!" she cried, flinging the door open, bolting from the carriage as it came to a stop. "It can't be! Oh, Lord, where is Viada? Where is Uncle Jeremy?"

Ian jumped from the carriage and went to Thalia. He grabbed her by the waist and swung her around to face him. "You can't go in there," he said, frowning down at her. "Those walls that are still standing have surely been weakened by the fire."

Tears streamed down Thalia's cheeks. She implored Ian with her eyes. "Oh, Ian, everything that was precious to my parents and to me was in that house," she cried. "And now it is all gone. Nothing could have survived in that fire." Fear gripped her. "Perhaps even Viada died there. Or—or my wonderfully sweet uncle!"

Ian drew her close and hugged her to him. "We'll investigate and see how this happened and where the survivors are," Ian comforted her. "I will not believe that your sister died in the fire. Nor your uncle. As you see, some of the walls are still standing. That means that the fire must not have been all that fierce and consuming. Whoever was in there surely had time to get out."

Thalia paled and felt as if someone had knocked the wind from her when a terrible thought came to her. "My Lord, Ian," she gasped, looking quickly up at him. "This must be the work of Paul Hathaway! Most surely he gave the orders to have it burned! The man who followed his instructions must have arrived on a ship just before we did. Oh, God, Ian, Paul accomplished what he had threatened so many times!"

She jerked away from Ian and began running toward the house again. "I've got to see!" she cried. "I've got to search for my sister!"

"Thalia!" Ian shouted, running after her. "Stop!

Don't go in there!"

Ian's orders fell on deaf ears. Thalia entered the charred remains, trudging through the debris, oblivious of the ash that began clinging to her clothes and getting into her shoes. Crumbling walls rose above her on all sides, and the aroma of burned wood stung her nose and made her eyes water.

She bent over and began smoothing the ashes aside, tears now flooding her eyes. "Viada," she cried. "Oh, Viada."

Ian's shadow loomed over Thalia. He reached for her and took her gently by a wrist and drew her up before him. "You must leave with me now," he said firmly. "We'll seek answers elsewhere. Don't put yourself through this." He glanced up at the leaning wall. "Damn it, Thalia, it's not safe in here."

A loud voice broke through the silence. "Thalia, is that you?"

Thalia spun around, wiping her eyes to clear her vision, streaking ash across her face as she did so. Her heart warmed when she recognized Richard Hutton, the kindest of neighbors through the years of her childhood.

"Mr. Hutton?" she said, breaking away from Ian. She went to the man and looked up at him with desperate eyes. "Mr. Hutton, tell me how this happened. Where is my sister? Where is my uncle?"

Bald, short, and portly, Mr. Hutton heaved a heavy sigh, then looked over Thalia's shoulder at the remains of the cottage. "Rest easy, Thalia," he said, frowning. "Your sister and uncle are alive.

405

And all I can tell you about the fire is that it seemed to start when sparks jumped from the fireplace onto clothes drying in front of it." He gazed back down at Thalia. "Now as for where your uncle and sister have relocated, I can't tell you, but your uncle is still quite busy with his occupation. I'm sure if you wander up and down the streets of Slad long enough, you'll find him."

"Thank God they are all right," Thalia said, every bone within her seeming to relax with the news. "Thank you, sir. Thank you."

Mr. Hutton eyed Ian speculatively. "I see you've returned with a young man," he said. "Don't tell me that my little Thalia is a grown lady and married."

Thalia wiped her eyes again, laughing softly as she gazed rapturously at Ian. She introduced them and then Mr. Hutton left them alone, Thalia looking wistfully at the remains again.

"I wish that I could at least have found my mother's Bible, or perhaps her sewing basket that had always been brimming full of lovely different colors of threads," she said, her voice breaking. "If only I could have something to remember her by. Or just the past. Just anything would have been a treasure."

Her shoulders slumped. "Ian, I was right before when I said that nothing lasts forever," she murmured. "Even a beloved house, the shelter and refuge of one's childhood. One expects it to give way to time and the elements, but not a ghastly fire. It seems so unfair, Ian."

"But your mind should be at rest about what was

troubling you," Ian tried to reassure her. "Your sister and uncle are alive. And the fire was not started on Paul's instructions."

"I must find my uncle and sister," Thalia said, spinning around to walk toward the carriage. Then the shadow of one of the remaining walls fell across her path, making her gasp and turn to stare at it. "I wonder . . .?"

Lifting her skirt, Thalia ran back into the rubble again, toward the wall. Ian shook his head, this time not interfering. She seemed driven to find something of her past to cling to.

But what? What on earth could she expect to find? It was obvious that everything burnable had fed the flames.

Not dissuaded by the charred remains that lay around her, soiling her dress too much ever to be wearable again, Thalia bent to her knees beside the wall. Her heart raced as her eyes searched for the small hole that she and her sister had found in the crumbling plaster all those many years ago when they had been playing dolls on the floor beside this wall in their bedroom. When they discovered that they could squeeze things through the hole, they had decided to use it to hide young girls' secrets, knowing very well that no one would ever discover them.

What they decided to hide there were notes to each other, not read, just teasingly thrust through the hole so that the other would be filled with wonder over the secret shared only on paper. It had begun a game that had lasted through many years. One by one tightly folded pieces of paper had been placed through the wall of crumbling plaster. One by one secrets had been stored—preserved.

Thalia's fingers began digging at the plaster that had been weakened by the fire. Her breath was stolen when, after only a moment of scraping and digging, the morning light threw a sort of golden glow through the hole that she had opened with her eager fingers, revealing a handful of paper squares untouched by the flames or the heat of the fire.

Overcome with emotion, her hands trembling, Thalia reached for the long-hidden notes and gingerly gathered them up from the inner wall. Weak with overwhelming memories of times long past with her sister, she sat down in the loose ashes and lay the notes on her lap. One by one she opened them; the ink was only faintly visible, time having all but faded the childhood scribblings.

She lay hers aside and read Viada's, discovering her sister's true love for her—and oh, so many other sisterly affections that touched Thalia's heart with a slow, agonizing ache of missing her sister so much.

She read on, discovering that her sister, at age eight, had fallen in love with a choir boy, the same handsome lad that Thalia had watched at sixteen with what she felt was a keen passion.

Only recently had she discovered what true passion was. . . .

"Thalia, whatever are you doing?" Ian said suddenly from behind her. "What are you reading? And, Lord, will you look at your dress?" He placed a hand to her shoulder. "I think it's time we left, darling, before you decide never to say good-bye to your past."

Thalia looked quickly up at Ian, her ash-darkened face streaked with a fresh torrent of tears. She thrust the notes up at him. "I shall never have to say good-bye to my past," she murmured. "For, Ian, so much of it is here in these notes."

She rose to her feet, wincing as she tried to brush the skirt of her dress free of the clinging ashes, then shrugged, not truly caring. Her discovery was making up for much of her unsettled feelings. She felt as though Viada was there, now, looking over her shoulder, giggling, ready to thrust another note through the hole in the wall.

"My God, these are notes written by you and Viada," Ian said, quickly reading one and then another. "How did you find them? Why weren't they burned with the rest of the fire?"

Thalia took Ian's arm and hurried him toward the carriage. "I shall tell you everything, Ian," she said, glancing down at the notes in his hand. "But as I am telling you, we must start searching for Uncle Jeremy. Now that I've read these notes, I am so anxious to see Viada and share them with her."

They boarded the carriage after she told the driver to start going down the streets slowly. As she chattered like a magpie to Ian about the origin of the notes and where she and Viada had hidden them, she watched each house as the carriage passed it, looking intently up at their chimneys.

And then she saw him—her Uncle Jeremy. She leaned her head from the carriage window and shouted for the driver to stop. Ian followed her out, looking up at a dusky sort of fellow standing beside the chimney on the steep roof of a house, a long handled brush with round bristles in his hand. The man was black from head to toe, even blacker, it seemed, than the remains of Thalia's parents' house.

"Uncle Jeremy!" Thalia shouted, waving frantically. She ran up to the house and looked anxiously up at her uncle as he began descending a ladder, glancing down at her through eyes that peered through the mask of soot.

When he finally reached the ground, Thalia flung herself into his arms, not caring about the soot that covered him from his head to his toes. Just being able to hug her uncle again, to take from him the comforts that only uncles knew how to give, made all the soot in the world worth it.

"How'd you get back to Slad?" Jeremy asked, staring at Ian over Thalia's shoulder. "This man. Who is he?"

Wiping her nose with the back of her hand, Thalia spun away from her uncle and reached for Ian, who came and took her hand. "This is my husband, Ian Lavery," she said proudly. "Ian, this is my uncle, Jeremy Drake."

Then she turned serious eyes to her uncle. "Where is Viada?" she asked, her voice quivering. "We went by the cottage. We saw its ruins. Where are you and Viada making residence now? I am so anxious to see my sister. She is all right, isn't she?"

Her uncle patted her shoulder. "Viada is fine," he reassured, smiling down at Thalia. "Honey, she is more than fine. She's been adopted."

Thalia blanched and took a shaky step backward. "Adopted?" she gasped. "What do you mean, adopted? She was to wait for me to come and get her. I was going to take her home with me and Ian. We would never have to be separated again!" A sudden rage entered her eyes. "Uncle Jeremy, how could you have let this happen? Why did you? Why?"

"I didn't think you'd ever be back," Jeremy said, his voice weak. "I let her go because I thought it was best for her. It wasn't right her livin' without a mama's warmth and instruction. When I was approached by this family to adopt her, I let her go."

"Uncle Jeremy, I said that I would be back," Thalia said, a sob escaping from deeply inside her. "I promised Viada! I promised! Now she is gone. Where? I will go and get her. She's my sister. I want to look after her. It's only right that we are together!"

"You can't be," Jeremy said, lowering his eyes humbly, then looking up at Thalia with a deep apology in their depths. "You see, Viada was adopted legally. She now legally belongs to that family. She is their daughter."

"Well, I'll see about that," Thalia said, firming her chin. "Where is she, Uncle? I must go to her. Now!"

"You can't," Jeremy said thickly.

"I can and I will," Thalia argued.

"Thalia, Viada now lives in America," her uncle blurted out. "A very rich family from San Francisco loves her now as though she were their true child. They took her to their home and they are giving her an education she would have never had, had she remained here." He cleared his throat.

411

"Or had she lived with you." He looked at Ian. "Or had she lived with you and your husband."

He placed his hands on Thalia's shoulders. "Let it be, Thalia," he advised seriously. "Viada will have opportunities that most don't."

Thalia's head was spinning from these truths. She was torn with feelings for her uncle and so filled with grief for not being able to see her sister.

Yet, was not her sister safe? Perhaps happier than she could have been out in the wilds of Australia?

Schooling. Breeding. The best of everything?

Yes, Thalia did see that what her uncle had done was right. He, just as Thalia did, had only wanted what was best for sweet, innocent Viada.

Sobbing, Thalia moved into her uncle's arms. "I'm sorry I shouted at you," she said. "I'm so very sorry."

Jeremy stroked her long hair. "You're getting your uncle's filth all over you," he said, chuckling. "Yet I think you had a good measure of it on you from going through the remains of our cottage. Isn't that right?"

"Yes, I could not keep myself from going through my childhood home just once again," she murmured. Then her eyes brightened. She turned from her uncle and grabbed Ian by the hand. "Oh, Ian, show him the notes. He will so enjoy them!"

Ian reached for them in his pocket and gave them to Jeremy. He enjoyed watching Thalia and her uncle share, for what might be the last time, bits and pieces of their past.

Stepping out on the terrace of Cliff Lodge, which overlooked the sea, Thalia and Ian stood side by side, freshly bathed and quiet, both reflecting on the day's activities. The mist was streaming in from the sea in gauzy wisps and tatters. Far below, the sea hurled itself in an unending assault on the shore. Except for the surf's low thunder and the keen of the wind, there was no sound, and they stood there in solitude.

"Ian, you are so generous," Thalia said, breaking the silence. "My uncle has always been as poor as a churchmouse, and you have suddenly given him riches almost beyond his comprehension."

"Riches?" Ian scoffed. "Darling, a few gold coins is not riches."

"To my uncle—and to me—they are riches," Thalia said softly, hugging Ian to her side.

"One thing is for damn sure, he won't ever have to clean another chimney again for as long as he lives," Ian said, inhaling a determined breath.

"Maybe not," Thalia said. "But I doubt if he will be able to stay away. The chimneys are his homes. I imagine he'll be back doing his daily sweeping even before we board the ship to return to Adelaide."

Ian looked down at Thalia incredulously, but said nothing, for something deep within him had told him the same thing about Jeremy. He did seem to be a creature of habit and one who would not want to sit idly by while others did work that he was the best at doing himself.

"Ian, I am sad over not being able to see Viada, but happy that she is in good hands," Thalia murmured. "All along, while I fretted over her welfare, she was safe with her new family." She paused, then looked broodingly up at Ian. "Darling, I doubt if I shall ever see my sister again, for legal adoptions are tied up in all sorts of secret paper work. All I know is that she has been taken to San Francisco. Is San Francisco a large place?''

A chill coursed through Thalia when Ian gave her a frown instead of an answer. That was answer enough. She now understood that she, indeed, might never see her sister again. But that Viada was alive and well cared for seemed enough for now. Things could have been so different. Things could have ended in tragedy for both of them. Instead they had both found their own little peaceful corner in the world!

She looked up at the gulls, which were refusing to breast the wind, then leaned into Ian's embrace as he led her back inside the hotel room and closed the terrace door behind them.

''Tomorrow we head back to sea for Adelaide,'' he said huskily, his fingers at the buttons of her dress, slowly loosening them. ''But tonight we are alone. Tonight is ours, Thalia. Totally ours.''

Thalia drifted toward him and he kissed her with a lazy warmth that left her weak. He lifted her into his arms and carried her to the bed. Her gasp became a long, soft whimper as he lowered her dress from her shoulders, his fingers finding her breasts . . .

CHAPTER THIRTY-ONE

SEVERAL MONTHS LATER
AUSTRALIA

EIGHT MONTHS PREGNANT, THALIA WAS WADDLING around the kitchen in her new home. She placed a hand to her throat, feeling it constrict as the familiar urge to retch plagued her again. The long voyage from England had been one of pure misery, for she had spent more time with her head hanging over the rail than she had alone with Ian in their cabin. Only a few weeks out to sea, she had realized that she was pregnant. She was glad to finally get her feet on solid ground, yet her stomach was still queasy—and not only in the mornings.

She leaned her back against the kitchen table and bowed her head into her hands, paling as she fought back the nausea that was gripping her. She was determined that she would not retch this time. Each time she did, it felt as though her stomach was ripping apart.

"You are no better this morning, are you?" Ava asked, coming into the kitchen with an armload of soiled breakfast dishes. She placed them beside the basin of sudsy water and turned to Thalia, wringing her apron nervously between her fingers. "What can I do, Thalia? Perhaps I could help you back to bed?"

Thalia swallowed hard, the nausea thankfully passing. She looked at Ava, seeing her concern. "I'm fine," she murmured, smiling reassuringly. "And I'm not going to bed. I'm sick to death of being in bed half of each day. I want to enjoy my new house to the fullest."

Sweeping her hands over her flushed cheeks, she went to the window and gazed from it. "I can hardly believe that we're here," she said pensively. "All those long months on the ship I almost forgot about Hawke and Ian's friends getting the house ready for our return. And how wonderfully they made everything. The house so beautiful and close to the Murray River, the sheep fenced in as far as the eye can see, the flowers planted just for my pleasure. They thought of everything, Ava. Everything."

Ava moved to her side. "I planted the flowers for you," she said proudly. "You are the kind of lady who deserves flowers. I wanted to surprise you."

Thalia took Ava's hands and squeezed them affectionately. "I should have known that you were the one who planted the flowers and hung lacy curtains at all of my windows. You made my homecoming so very, very special."

"I'm glad," Ava said, bowing her head and

blushing bashfully.

Thalia rested her hands on her large abdomen, laughing to herself when she felt the baby kick at her hand. "Ava, if you don't mind, please do the dishes while I go and gather the eggs," she said. "I need a breath of fresh air. I'm so weary of this nausea and lightheadedness that persist in accompanying my pregnancy."

Ava hurried after Thalia, following her to the back door. "I think you need to return to bed," she fussed. "You can get as much fresh air as you need by opening your bedroom windows."

Inhaling a deep breath of air, Thalia opened the door and stepped out on the wide porch. "Ava, I have one full month left of my pregnancy and I will not spend that time in bed," she said stubbornly. "The doctor says that what I am experiencing can't harm the child. So I am the only one who is uncomfortable, and I am tired of it!"

"Thalia," Ava said, almost begging. But she sighed and said no more when Thalia lifted the egg basket and left the porch, marching determinedly toward the barn.

Ava shook her head, then shrugged and went back into the kitchen and began doing dishes, humming a merry tune, content to finally have a home—to finally have someone who truly cared about her. Those long months while Thalia had been gone had been the longest of her life.

But now Thalia was there!

Everything seemed so perfect!

Thalia was breathless when she finally reached the barn. Though it was mid-morning and the sun was bright, the barn was dark and cold as Thalia moved stealthily into it. It was large and cavernous, with a loft that was piled high with hay. Below the loft, horse stalls filled one side of the barn, while the other contained roosting bins for the hens. She reached for a lantern and lit it, carrying it and her basket farther into the barn, where the squawking of hens revealed that some were still laying their morning supply of eggs.

Fear gripped Thalia's heart when suddenly, out of the corner of her eye, she saw movement and then a man standing in the shadows. She turned to face the man, her heart pounding.

"Who is there?" she asked, her mouth dry. "What are you doing here?"

The man did not stir a muscle. Thalia could make out no more than his outline against the wall behind him. Slowly she lifted her lantern, then sighed with relief and lowered it again.

"Why, Kenneth, it's only you," she said, her voice sounding strangled with relief. "What are you doing hiding like that? You gave me quite a fright."

Kenneth Ozier stepped stiffly from the shadows. Thalia's eyes searched his face, and she saw that he was not smiling. His boyishness seemed to have turned into something sinister. There was something evil in his eyes!

Then her gaze shifted downward and she felt a sudden iciness soar through her veins when she saw her lantern reflected in the barrel of a pistol that he held aimed at her.

"Kenneth, what are you doing with that gun?"

Thalia asked, her voice quivering. She took a step backward. "Keep away from me, Kenneth. What has gotten into you? Why are you doing this? I thought you were a friend. Ian took you in. He gave you employment."

"Ian didn't know that I like bushranging better," Kenneth said, his lips lifting into a crooked smile. "I guess it slipped my mind to tell him that I was a bushranger before I was his errand boy." He took a step closer. "Surprised? Huh? That I'm not the gentle young man you thought I was?"

"You were a bushranger?" Thalia gasped.

"Yeah, and one of the best," Kenneth bragged.

"I can't believe this," Thalia exclaimed. "How could Ian not have known this?"

"Because Ian saw me as only a simple, mindless boy," Kenneth spat angrily. "Several months ago, Ian had great fun taunting and insulting me in front of everyone at Joe's Pub. I always remember insults. Now Ian's going to pay for his!"

"All along you have been kind and gentle only to wait until the opportune moment to get some sort of dark revenge for being insulted?" Thalia asked, amazed that she had any courage left to question him, the fear for her baby and herself almost overwhelming her.

"Not only because of that," Kenneth said, inching closer toward her. "I made a bargain with Paul Hathaway and I always keep my word."

"Paul Hathaway?" Thalia gasped, dropping her egg basket. "What are you talking about? What did Paul have to do with you?"

"He paid me well to stalk and kill you," Kenneth

419

said, chuckling beneath his breath. "So here I am. I got paid well to do a service, so don't you think it's about time that I do it? Your damn trip to England slowed my plans down. I can't wait no longer."

"Kenneth, no . . ." Thalia said, clammy with fear. She placed a hand on her abdomen. "Think of my child, Kenneth, if not of me. Oh, Lord, Kenneth, let my child live!"

A voice spoke up from the dark shadows. "Drop your gun, Kenneth. Now. I won't mind shootin' a bastard like you in the back."

Thalia turned with a start when a tall, dark stranger with green eyes stepped into view. Renewed fear dizzied her. She swayed, then steadied herself, her hands resting on her stomach in an effort to protect her unborn child.

Recognizing the voice without having to turn around to see the man it belonged to, Kenneth's spine stiffened. "Ridge Wagner," he said. "I wondered what rock you'd been hiding under, and here you are, interfering in my affairs again. I warned you, Ridge—don't get in my way."

"Kenneth, I had forgotten that you even existed until a few days ago when I was pondering an offer Paul Hathaway made me just prior to his death," Ridge said emotionlessly. "I refused the offer. But it came to me suddenly that he probably made the same offer to someone else just as greedy as me—and who did I come up with in my mind, but you."

"You were a fool to refuse Paul anything," Kenneth grumbled, his back stiff. "My pockets are lined with gold coins because of him. Yours could've been."

"At the expense of this lovely lady?" Ridge said, glancing at Thalia. "Ian's wife?"

"I didn't see you blink your eyes once when you helped raid those wagon trains," Kenneth accused him. "More than one woman lost her life during those raids, and I'm sure some of the slugs dug out of 'em had your name on them."

"Yeah, I'm sure of it too, and I'm not proud," Ridge grumbled. "Like I'm not proud to claim that I became a bushranger and rode side by side with the likes of you and that bastard Hathaway."

"But you did," Kenneth drawled. "And now what've you done? Traced me here to kill me to stop me from honestly earning the wages Paul paid me? Ridge, you're loonier than I thought if you think I'll allow it."

"And how did you plan to escape from Ian's wrath after you killed his wife?" Ridge spat. "You're a fool. The gunblast alone would've drawn Ian to the barn."

"I didn't plan to shoot 'er," Kenneth boasted, chuckling. "I planned to choke her with a thin piece of wire."

Thalia was looking from man to man, speechless and cold all over with revulsion and fear. She did not dare move. Any distraction might give Kenneth the advantage.

She gazed at Ridge, understanding now who he was. He was Honora's lost love—he was a friend of Ian's! Lover or friend, he had chosen the wrong side of the law. Surely Ian did not know. . . .

"Kenneth, your mouth has always been too big for your own good," Ridge said, steadying his aim at Kenneth's back. "Drop your pistol and turn around, or by God, I'll be forced to silence you forever. Damn it, Kenneth, if I have to, I'll shoot you in the back."

Thalia screamed when Kenneth spun around quickly on a heel and discharged his pistol at Ridge at the exact moment Ridge discharged his at Kenneth. Smoke and the stench of gunpowder filled the air. When the smoke cleared Thalia looked down at two bodies on the floor. One man was dead, the other only barely alive.

Wild-eyed, his revolver drawn, Ian rushed into the barn. "Thalia!" he shouted, heaving a deep sigh when she suddenly flung herself into his arms. He looked down at her and saw that she was not harmed—shaken terribly, but alive and well.

Then he became shaken himself when he looked down and saw two men lying in pools of blood, and recognized them both. He paled and broke away from Thalia. He flipped his Colt into its holster and knelt down beside Ridge. His gaze went to Ridge's blood-soaked shirt, then to his ashen face, his eyes hazed over with pain.

"Ridge—my God!" Ian said, his voice breaking. He lifted Ridge's head up from the floor and pushed some straw beneath it to pillow it. "Oh, God, Ridge, how did this happen? Why?"

Inhaling a deep, shaky breath, Thalia knelt down beside Ian. "Darling, he saved my life," she murmured. She glanced over at Kenneth's lifeless body, then back at Ridge. "If he hadn't come when

422

he did, Kenneth would have killed me."

Ian looked quickly over at her. "Kenneth was going to kill you?" he gasped. "Why? He was our friend."

Thalia's eyes lowered. "I think not, Ian," she murmured. "He never was a true friend."

Ridge reached a hand to Ian's arm and gripped it firmly. "There's so much to tell you," he said, coughing and gasping for breath. "But, mate, I don't have time." His body convulsed and he groaned as fresh pain shot through him. He latched on harder to Ian's arm. "Ian, you were the best friend I ever had and I let you down. I apologize, mate. For everything."

Ian leaned closer to Ridge. "Whatever you are talking about, I do forgive you," he said thickly. He could see and feel Ridge slipping away from him. "Damn it, you bloody bloke, hang on. You can't die!"

Ridge coughed, blood now curling from his nostrils and the corners of his mouth. "Do me a favor, mate?" he asked raspily.

"Anything," Ian agreed. "Anything. Just name it."

"Tell Honora that I never quit loving her," Ridge said, his voice fading. "Tell her, Ian. Will . . . you do that for me, Ian? Will you?"

Ian didn't have the opportunity to assure Ridge that the message would be delivered. Ridge gasped, his body stiffened, and his green eyes became locked in a death stare. . . .

Choking on a sob, Ian closed Ridge's eyes and lifted his locked fingers from his arm, grasping his friend's hand a moment longer while some warmth still lasted.

"Oh, Ian," Thalia sobbed. "It's so sad."

"Aye," Ian said, finally relinquishing Ridge's hand. He placed an arm around Thalia's waist and helped her up. "I doubt if I'll ever understand what happened here—what Ridge didn't get to tell me."

"Darling, I think I know."

"You do? How?"

"While Ridge and Kenneth were arguing before the shootout, Ridge disclosed many things—in particular that he had ridden as a bushranger."

Ian swayed as the truth struck him like a shot. "Surely you heard wrong," he gasped. "Not Ridge—"

"Yes, Ridge," Thalia murmured. "And the worst of it is that he rode with Paul Hathaway."

"No," Ian groaned, weaving his fingers frustratingly through his hair.

"Also, Ian, he had been approached by Paul Hathaway to kill me. He refused. But Kenneth took the assignment. All along, when he was pretending to be a friend, Kenneth was awaiting what he felt was the opportune moment to kill me."

Ian's gaze locked on Kenneth. "Damn him all to hell," Ian growled. "All along he had planned to kill you. Why didn't I notice that his behavior wasn't normal?"

"Because he was always so kind and cooperative," Thalia murmured. "Ian, he had all of us fooled. He also rode with Paul Hathaway's gang.

He agreed to the assignment to kill me not only for the money, but also because he wanted to get even with you for having embarrassed him one day in Joe's Pub."

Ian's eyes narrowed, now vividly recalling that day. "My teasing was all done in innocence," he rumbled. "But all along, he was planning some sort of twisted vengeance? He was even a member of Paul's gang?" He shook his head, sighing. "Well, it's over now."

"Yes, thank God, it's over," Thalia said, exhaling a quavering breath.

Ian gazed down at her, apology in his eyes. "It is, isn't it?" he asked softly. "You are going to be all right, aren't you? You're so pale."

Thalia handed him the lantern and clutched at her stomach as sudden sharp pains grabbed at her insides. "No, Ian, I'm not all right," she said, her voice thin. "Oh, Lord, all of this commotion and fright has brought on my labor pains!"

Ian blanched. "But, Thalia, you have another full month to go," he said anxiously.

"I don't believe so, darling," Thalia said, gasping as the pains came again sharply. "You'd best help me to bed. Then send someone for the doctor."

Ian placed a comforting arm around Thalia's waist and helped her walk slowly toward the house. "Walk easy, darling," he encouraged. "Just . . . walk . . . easy."

"Oh, Ian, I'm suddenly so afraid," Thalia cried. "What if it is too soon for our child? Oh, Ian, what if it is too soon?"

"Damn that Paul Hathaway," Ian mumbled. "He

may have his revenge after all. If anything happen
to our child . . ."

Thalia emitted a soft cry when the pain grippe
her again.

Sunshine was streaming through lace-dresse
windows. It was normally a time for Thalia t
awaken slowly and plan her day. But this was n
normal day. She had been in labor for hours, th
night seeming endless as pains wracked her body

Doc Raley stood at one side of her bed, Ava o
the other, Ian at the foot of it. The doctor motione
Ian aside and felt just inside the birth canal, finall
feeling the baby.

"Push, Thalia," he said, positioning his hands o
the baby's head. "One more push and we'll have u
a baby."

Weak, so tired and weary, Thalia bit her lower li
as a fresh pain assailed her. She pushed with all o
her might and could not believe it when she finall
heard a shout of joy from Ian, and soon after tha
the first cries of their child.

"My baby," she said, licking her parched lips
She held her arms out to the doctor. "Please let m
see my baby."

Doc Raley cleansed the baby, wrapped it in
soft blanket, then lay it in Thalia's arms. He wipe
his brow with the back of his sleeve. "It's been
long night," he said. "I think I need a cup o
coffee."

He left the room, but Ian and Ava remained
hovering over Thalia and smiling.

"Darling, do you see?" Thalia said, pulling bac

he corner of her blanket. "I have given you a son."

Tears streamed from Ian's eyes as he knelt down eside the bed. He reached his large hand to his on and touched the soft cheek. "Our son," he said n wonder. He laughed, his eyes dancing. "I think ve have Paul Hathaway to thank after all."

"Why, Ian?" Thalia asked, contentment swelling vithin her.

"Because of him we will have a son to enjoy for ne more month than we expected," Ian said, huckling. "Now wouldn't you say that is quite a wist of fate?"

"Yes," Thalia said, smiling up at him. "A wonder-ul twist of fate."

"Now we must name our son," Ian said, moothing his thumb over his son's brow.

"Ian, my father would have been so proud to ave a grandson," Thalia said softly. "Even proud-r if that grandson was named after him. Could we, an? Could we name him Charles Edward?"

"That's a mighty fine name, if you ask me," Ian aid, winking down at her. "Lord, am I glad that ou didn't want to make him a junior. One Ian avery in this family is enough."

"Well, perhaps not," Thalia said. "I want to ame our next son Ian. Please tell me that I can?"

Ian groaned, then leaned over Thalia and kissed er softly on the lips. "Darling, whatever you want o name our next ten kids will suit me just fine," he aid hoarsely.

Thalia's eyes widened. "Our . . . next ten . . . ?" he gasped, then laughed with him as he looked lown at her, his eyes dancing.

Ava approached the bed. "Can I hold Charles Edward?" she murmured. "Or do you think he's too tiny?"

Ian rose from the bed. He scooped his son up from Thalia's arms and placed him gingerly in Ava's. Never had Thalia seen Ava look so radiant. She choked back a sob, so moved was she by the scene.

CHAPTER THIRTY-TWO

TWO YEARS LATER
THE TERRITORY OF WASHINGTON—SEATTLE
CHRISTMAS EVE

SPELLBOUND, THRILLED FINALLY TO BE IN AMERICA, Thalia sat beside Ian in a sleigh pulled by a team of Belgian horses, sharing a fur lap blanket with her husband. The sleigh glided smoothly over the snow-packed street, as flakes still fluttered slowly from the sky. Thalia marveled at the spectacular scene. Beribboned greens wreathed and outlined the shops and buildings, the face of Seattle suggesting a deep and gentle peace.

"And what do you think of America so far?" Ian's mother asked.

Thalia's eyes were drawn across the sleigh where Donna sat opposite her, two-year-old Charles Edward snuggled on her lap beneath another blanket. Donna's new husband, Bryant, sat at her side, looking stately and handsome in a top hat and fur-lined coat, a diamond stickpin sparkling in the folds of his ascot.

"It is so very exciting," Thalia said. She strained suddenly to continue sitting erect when the sleigh began traveling up a steep street. She grabbed Ian's hand for support. "But is all of America—so so hilly?"

"No, not quite," Donna said, laughing softly.

As the sleigh leveled off again onto a straight, flat street, Thalia heaved a sigh. "Well, I truly don't mind the angle of the streets," she said. "Anything is better than being on the ocean for so many months to reach America." She gave Ian a glance and laughed nervously. "Perhaps I won't return to Australia at all. I'll keep my feet on solid ground right here in America."

"And I think I can find the perfect house for you," Bryant chimed in.

Donna patted his arm, interrupting him. "Now, darling, Thalia was only joking. She loves her home in Australia."

"Yes, I do," Thalia said, squeezing Ian's knee beneath the blanket. "It's home and I miss it terribly."

Ian smiled down at her. "There for a minute I thought I had lost you to America," he chuckled.

"Never," Thalia murmured.

"However, perhaps you can leave Charles Edward here with his granma," Donna said, turning her grandson to face her, his tiny face looking up at her beneath a red knit hat. His mittened hand touched her cheek. "Would you want to stay with granma, Charles Edward?" she asked, looking adoringly down at him. "Would you?"

Charles Edward nodded, his dark eyes innocently wide.

Donna laughed and drew him into her arms. She hugged him tightly. "Yes, I'm sure you would," she whispered. "And after only one night away from mama and papa, you'd quickly change your mind."

"Well, we're here," Bryant said as the driver of the sleigh guided it up a circular drive toward a house built into the side of a hill overlooking a lake. "We've only been living here for a month now."

Donna looked proudly at her husband. "Yes, Bryant thinks this is a perfect house for us—until he finds another that suits his fancy better," she said. "Perhaps I'd be better off if I didn't unpack my china the next time we move."

"Why, I think this house is absolutely beautiful," Thalia sighed as the sleigh stopped before the porch. The lawn was a tundra of drifts, and the boughs of the pine and cedar trees were weighted down with the snow. "It has the look of a cottage in the English countryside."

Thalia leaned a bit forward and gasped slightly when she spied something red peeking out through the folds of the snow. "My word," she said. "Is that roses? Are they still in bloom?"

"Roses bloom the year round in Seattle," Ian said, stepping from the sleigh. He placed his hand to Thalia's waist and helped her down, then gathered Charles Edward in his arms. "The climate is only one of the many reasons people are lured to settle here. It is excellent for those who do not like extreme heat or cold. And this much snow is rare."

He placed an arm around Thalia's waist as he led

431

her up the steps to the porch, following Donna and Bryant. When they entered the house, the sight inside stole Thalia's breath away. As she lifted her white fur hat from her head and her cape from around her shoulders, revealing a red velveteen dress hugging her curves, its bodice low, she looked around her in awe.

"Such a beautiful house," she sighed. His coat, gloves, and hat off, Charles Edward went to Thalia and took her hand. His gaze followed his mother's around the spacious room. "Charles Edward, isn't it all just too lovely?"

It was a quiet, darkened house, softly lit by the gentle flickering of candles. Natural greens had been plucked from the trees in the forest nearby and these garlands had been wrapped gracefully around the banister of a large staircase and around the picture frames. Wreaths of fir and laurel adorned the doors and walls. Sweet-smelling pinecones filled baskets and bowls everywhere.

Her wrap removed, Donna stood between Ian and Thalia, her arms around their waists. "So many people do not adorn their homes as I do because they fear that decking the halls might trivialize the true meaning of Christmas," she quietly explained. "I feel the greens fill the home with a festive spirit, and I am grateful for the perfume the decor brings to my house."

She stepped away from Ian and Thalia and took Charles Edward's hand. "Come," she said, smiling from one to the other. "Come into my dining room. I have something special to show my grandson."

Thalia lay her cape and hat on a chair and

followed alongside Ian into the dining room. Her eyes widened when she caught sight of something so marvelous she could not believe it was real.

"Oh, Charles Edward, do you see that?" Thalia asked in a sigh, bending to one knee beside her son. She took his hand. "Darling, do you see? I think we've just stepped between the pages of a magical storybook, don't you?"

A statuesque tree stood at the far side of the room at a window that overlooked the lake, its boughs heavy with myriad precious things. Amid many tapered candles were hung intricate paper cutouts, cookies, pieces of taffy, and tiny toys. There were also gilded ornaments, and strings of popcorn and cranberries. At the tree's peak floated a delicate angel.

"It's beautiful, Mother," Ian said, stepping to Donna's side and kissing her. "Thank you for making our homecoming so special. Especially for Thalia. I doubt that, as a child, she ever had anything as magical as that tree."

"That is only a small portion of the surprise that I have for Thalia," Donna whispered, her eyes mischievously brilliant. "Haven't you noticed that Bryant isn't here? He's gone to fetch the surprise. She should be arriving at any moment now."

"She?" Ian said, quirking an eyebrow. "Mother, whatever do you mean? What are you up to?"

The sound of someone knocking on the front door reverberated into the dining room and Ian's words faded. He eyed his mother quizzically, and then Thalia, whose trance had been broken also by the knocking.

Leaving Charles Edward to continue admiring

the tree, Thalia went to Ian's side and locked an arm through his. "Seems you have a caller, Donna," she murmured. "Should we retire to our rooms to give you privacy?"

Donna gathered the skirt of her blue silk dress up into her arms and began walking from the room. "Heavens, no," she said from across her shoulder. "It's probably only a neighbor. Everyone here, it seems, exchanges food for Christmas. It's a very popular thing to do in Seattle. People bake breads, cookies, candies, and chutneys and bring them for gifts. Perhaps today I shall receive something sweet to share with you all."

Donna stopped and turned to face Thalia. She reached out a hand to her. "Come, my dear," she encouraged softly. "Come to the door with me."

"Oh, but I shall be interfering," Thalia said, smoothing her hands down the front of her velvet dress. "Please do go on and greet your neighbor without me." Her hand went to her hair that was hanging loosely over her shoulders. She laughed nervously. "I must look a fright. I haven't brushed my hair since I removed my hat."

Donna went to Thalia and took her hand. "I insist," she said. She looked over at Ian. "Son, bring Charles Edward."

Ian grabbed up his son and laughingly placed him on his shoulders. "Come on, Charles Edward, let's see what my mother has up her sleeve."

The persistent knocking echoed through the house. Donna rushed Thalia to the door, but even before she opened it, tears welled up in her eyes as she gave Thalia an emotional glance. Then she jerked the door open widely.

Dizziness overcame Thalia when she discovered someone so precious to her standing in the snow on the porch beside Bryant.

Viada! Three years older, yet with the same baby face and sweet smile!

Viada recognized Thalia at that same moment. They both emitted loud squeals of delight and flew into each other's arms, crying.

Ian questioned Donna with his eyes.

"Viada," Donna murmured, wiping tears from her eyes. "Thalia's sister."

"How on earth did you manage this, Mother?" Ian asked, his heart warmed by the happiness his wife must be feeling at this moment. She had gone through hell and back fighting for her sister's welfare. And here Viada was—safe and sound and as pretty as a picture because she was a spitting image of Thalia!

Bryant locked an arm around Donna's waist, and she leaned into his embrace. "My darling here is not only a successful businessman but has proven to be quite a sleuth, as well," she said proudly. "He traveled to San Francisco and found Viada. He talked her adopted parents into letting her come and meet with her sister. He booked all of their passages to Seattle."

Ian looked past Thalia and Viada and saw a middle-aged couple step down from a sleigh and walk toward the house.

"And so we shall all celebrate so much good fortune this Christmas, my son," Donna said, choking back tears of happiness.

Thalia held Viada at arm's length, then turned and smiled at Ian, radiant with joy.

Thalia awakened from a sound, contented sleep to see the sun pouring through the bedroom window at her side. Yawning, she reached beside her for Ian, then leaned up on an elbow when she discovered that he had already left the bed, and apparently the room.

Again yawning, still filled with the delicious emotions of the previous day when she had finally been reunited with her sister, she rose from the bed and walked barefoot over plush, warm carpet to the window. She blinked her eyes, trying to believe what she was seeing. The snow was all melted—there was no sign of it anywhere!

Then she recalled having heard it raining through the night. The rain had washed the snow away.

"Merry Christmas, luv."

Ian's voice behind Thalia drew her around. Her silk gown clung to her as she ran to him. She started to pounce into his arms, then noticed that he was holding something behind him.

"You've brought me a gift?" she asked, her eyes bright.

"I guess you'd call it that," Ian said cheerfully.

"Let me see," Thalia said, yanking at his arm.

Ian pulled a bouquet of red roses around for her to see. Small drops of rain clung to their folds like sparkling tears.

Thalia took the roses and held them to her nose, inhaling the sweet fragrance. "Darling, thank you so much," she sighed. She gazed in rapture up at

Ian. "They are so lovely."

"Lovely, aye," Ian said, circling his arms around her waist. "But no lovelier than you, my wife."

"Oh, Ian," Thalia said, forcing back a sob. "Everything is so perfect now—oh, so perfect."

Ian swept the roses from Thalia's hands and laid them aside on a table. His muscled arms lifted her and carried her to the bed. He knelt down over her. "Roses after rain," he whispered, showering kisses across her face. "For me they will always be a symbol of our love—a love that is no longer filled with pain."

Thalia melted into Ian's embrace, and he awakened desire in her again, as though it were the first time.

Dear Reader:

I hope you have enjoyed reading *ROSES AFTER RAIN*. My next *LEISURE* book, *TOUCH THE WILD WIND*, will be published in February 1991. It is a stirring, passionate tale of Australia. Following that, in August, will be *SAVAGE PERSUASION*, a continuation of my "Savage Series", in which it is my endeavor to write about every major Indian tribe in America. *SAVAGE PERSUASION* will feature the proud Cherokee.

I love to hear from my readers. For my newsletter and an autographed bookmark, please send an SASE to:

CASSIE EDWARDS
Box 60
Mattoon, Il. 61938

My Warmest Regards,

Cassie Edwards

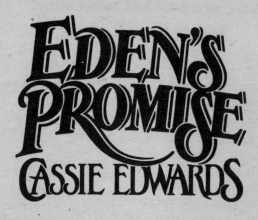

FOREVER GOLD

Catherine Hart's books are "Beautiful! Gorgeous! Magnificent!"

— *Romantic Times*

FOREVER GOLD. From the moment Blake Montgomery held up the westward-bound stagecoach carrying lovely Megan Coulston to her adoring fiance, she hated everything about the virile outlaw. How dare he drag her off to an isolated mountain cabin and hold her for ransom? How dare he kidnap her heart, when all he could offer were forbidden moments of burning, trembling ecstasy?

_____2600-7 $4.50 US/$5.50 CAN

Leona Karr

Colorado's Romance Writer of the Year!

FORBIDDEN TREASURE. Beautiful and unconsciously alluring, young Alysha had resigned herself to the dreary life of a seamstress. Then a carriage accident left her stranded at a lavish French castle, and Alysha was lured into a world of seduction and danger by darkly handsome Raoul de Lamareau, master of the chateau.

_____2707-0 $3.95US/$4.95CAN

A WANTED MAN.
AN INNOCENT WOMAN.
A WANTON LOVE!

Renegade Heart
Madeline Baker

When beautiful Rachel Halloran took Logan Tyree into her home, he was unconscious. A renegade Indian with a bullet wound in his side and a price on his head, he needed her help. But to Rachel he was nothing but trouble, a man whose dark sensuality made her long for forbidden pleasures; to her father he was the answer to a prayer, a gunslinger whose legendary skill could rid the ranch of a powerful enemy.

But Logan Tyree would answer to no man — and to no woman. If John Halloran wanted his services, he would have to pay dearly for them. And if Rachel wanted his loving, she would have to give up her innocence, her reputation, her very heart and soul.

_____2744-5 $4.50